TIE ME down

Special Edition

Melanie Harlow

USA TODAY BESTSELLING AUTHOR

*For Corinne Michaels,
extraordinary storyteller and friend.*

I'll be the one that stays 'till the end
    And I'll be the one that needs you again
    And I'll be the one that proposes in a garden of
roses
    And truly loves you long after our curtain closes
    But will you still love me when nobody wants me
around?
    When I turn 81 and forget things, will you still be
proud?

REX ORANGE COUNTY, "HAPPINESS"

FIFTEEN YEARS AGO

BECKETT

"Who wants to go first?" Cole asked.

All of us stared at the empty tackle box on my family's kitchen table. Griffin had brought it over, and I'd taken out all the trays so it could serve a different function.

Time capsule.

Since we were kids, my three best friends—Cole Mitchell, Griffin Dempsey, and Enzo Moretti—and I had planned on burying a time capsule the summer after we graduated from high school. We'd heard about time capsules years ago, in fifth grade social studies class, and all four of us agreed then and there that we were going to do it.

After some discussion, we'd agreed that it made the most sense to bury it somewhere on my family's farm. We figured anyone else's family might move someday, but Weaver Ranch had been in my family for over a hundred years and it would be in my family for generations to come.

I was going to make sure of it.

My plan was to major in finance, get an MBA, and secure

one of those Wall Street jobs where you could make millions if you had the brains, the guts, and the work ethic.

I had all three, and I'd use them to help my family.

"I'll go," said Griffin, placing his beat-up backpack on the table and reaching inside it. He pulled out his graduation tassels, a photograph of him standing between his dad and grandfather in front of the open hood of an old truck they were restoring, and a folded sheet of paper.

"What's that?" Moretti asked, pointing at the paper.

"It's a copy of the letter from the Marine Corps telling me when and where to report to boot camp."

We nodded and watched Griffin put those three items in the box. He was heading out in three weeks for Parris Island, the first of us to leave Bellamy Creek and our tight foursome. In August I was leaving for Harvard, where I had a full academic scholarship, and Cole was headed to a local college, where he planned to study law enforcement. Moretti was already working full-time for his family's construction business, as he had since he was fourteen.

The last thing Griffin pulled from the backpack was a dirty, scuffed-up baseball. "From the day I hit the game-winning home run against Mason City High to clinch the title," he said reverently. "I signed it, in case you guys put a baseball in too. That way we'll know whose is whose."

We all nodded. Baseball was sacred to us—the only thing more sacred was our friendship.

Griffin placed the ball in the box as if it were made of glass.

"Okay, who's next?" I asked.

"I'll go." Moretti placed a brown paper bag on the table. From it, he pulled out a newspaper clipping from the Bellamy Creek Gazette about his record streak of stolen bases and a takeout menu from DiFiore's, his favorite restaurant, which was owned by his cousins. Then he took out one of his senior portraits and added it to the box. Not a small one, either—a five-by-seven.

"Really, Moretti?" Griffin gestured to the photo. "A big picture of *yourself*?"

"Hey, I happen to think I look good in this shot. What if I go bald or something? I'll want to look back and remember when I had amazing hair. And cheekbones." He placed the picture in the box.

Laughing, I shook my head. It was typical Moretti. He was vain and egotistical, but you couldn't ask for a more loyal friend. I'd miss him. I'd miss them all.

"And I also have a picture of *us*, so piss off." He took out a snapshot of the four of us after one of our last games, four cocky eighteen-year-olds in ball caps and dirty uniforms, grinning at the camera. He added it to the box and looked across the table. "Cole? Want to go next?"

"Okay." Cole opened up a large Ziplock bag and took out a folded sheet of paper. "Our baseball team roster and season record," he said, placing it in the box. "And I have the ball from the no-hitter I pitched this year. I signed and dated it."

"Such a good fucking game," Griffin said, clapping Cole's back. "That's the best I've ever seen you pitch. Man, I'm gonna miss those games."

"Me too," I said, hating the hollowed-out feeling in my gut. "Think we'll ever play together again?"

"Hell yes." Moretti guffawed. "We'll be like those old dudes who come out on Thursday nights every summer with their beer bellies and rickety old knees."

We all laughed too, unable to imagine ourselves with paunchy guts and stiff joints.

The last thing Cole placed in the box was a photo of all of us with our dates the night of our senior prom. Cole had taken his girlfriend, Trisha; Griffin had taken a girl he'd been dating on and off since Christmas; Moretti had taken his flavor of the month; and I'd taken a friend, since the girl I *wish* I could have asked—Maddie Blake—was off limits.

"Your turn, Weaver." Cole looked at me. "Let's see what you got."

From a plastic grocery sack, I pulled out a copy of my acceptance letter from Harvard, my treasured Mickey Cochrane baseball card, and two photographs. The first was of the four of us taken in our caps and gowns right after the graduation ceremony, and the second was a shot of Maddie and me taken a minute later. I had an arm around her shoulders, and she had an arm around my waist, her cheek nearly resting on my chest.

I'd hardly been able to breathe.

"What's that second picture?" Cole asked, because I'd tried to hide the photo of Maddie and me behind the first one.

"It's nothing." I picked up the box top and tried to put it on, but Moretti—whose reflexes were quick—reached into the box and grabbed the photos, shuffling them so the pic of Maddie and me was on top.

He grinned. "Aha. *Now* I get it."

"Fuck off." I grabbed the pictures from his hands and put them face down in the box.

"Whose picture was it?" Cole asked.

"The girl of his dreams," Moretti said. "But Weaver, you do realize that actually telling her you like her would be a better idea than putting her picture in a tackle box you're going to bury in the dirt?"

My jaw clenched. "I can't do that, okay?"

"You could," he insisted. "You just won't."

It was easy for Moretti to say. He was never tongue-tied around girls and could charm anyone he met. Even teachers and moms adored him. They liked me too, for different reasons—I was polite, quiet, and responsible. But I had to think before I spoke to a girl, and sometimes I thought so long, I missed the chance to say what I wanted to.

Especially to Maddie.

Cole closed the box and secured the latch. "Should we bury it?"

"Yeah. Let's do it," Griffin said. "I gotta be home for dinner at six."

We went out the kitchen's wooden screen door, which squeaked open and slapped shut like it always did, a familiar sound I never thought I'd miss later in life, or even think about once I was gone.

I was wrong about that.

I was wrong about a lot of things.

We trooped into the yard and looked around at the big red barn, the paddocks, the chicken coop, the vegetable garden, the pastures beyond. It was my favorite time of day on the ranch—the sun was just starting to set, dusting everything with gold. Somewhere out in the fields my dad was still working, and I felt a little guilty that I'd knocked off early today.

"What's a good spot?" asked Moretti.

"What about over there near the tree?" I suggested, gesturing toward an old maple between the horse paddock and barn. From its thick, sturdy branches hung a swing my sisters and I had played on as kids, but that wasn't my favorite memory of it. Not anymore.

"Sure," Cole said. "It just has to be somewhere that won't get too dug up."

"The tree roots might be an issue." Griffin lifted his cap off and replaced it.

"We'll go halfway between the tree and the barn. Let me go get a shovel." Leaving them there, I went into the shed and grabbed the shovel.

A few minutes later, I'd dug a big enough hole and Griffin knelt down to place the tackle box inside it. We all shoved dirt back into the hole and I patted it down with the shovel.

"Think we should mark the spot?" Cole asked.

"Nah, we'll remember where it is," said Moretti.

"When are we gonna dig it up?" Griffin wondered. "Like, twenty years from now?"

I shrugged. "Sure."

We all stared at the fresh dirt, trying to imagine life twenty years in the future. It wasn't easy.

"What do you think we'll be like then?" Cole asked.

Moretti laughed. "You'll be a cop. Married with two kids, a picket fence, and a dog. Maybe a receding hairline."

Cole laughed and gave him a shove. "Fuck off."

"I'll probably look exactly like my dad." Moretti didn't sound too happy about it. "Complete with all the gray hair my wife and eight kids are gonna give me."

"You're going to have *eight kids*?" I asked him.

He shrugged. "I'm a Moretti. We don't do anything small."

"I wonder if I'll still be in the Marines," Griffin said, looking into the distance, "or back here working with my dad at the garage."

"I bet you come back," Moretti said. "I'll still be here, hopefully running Moretti & Sons. If I'm not the boss by the time I'm thirty-eight, someone punch me in the face."

Cole looked at me. "What about you, Beckett? Think you'll come back here after college?"

"Nah, Beck's not coming back here," Moretti scoffed. "He'll be too busy making his millions on Wall Street."

Laughing, I shrugged. "I don't know yet."

We were all silent for a moment, the weight of separation and an unknown future suddenly pressing heavily on us. We'd been best friends—brothers, really—for so many years, it had never truly hit us that the day would come when things would change, and we'd go our separate ways . . . maybe forever.

"Let's make a pact." Moretti sounded serious, more serious than I'd ever heard him. "That no matter where we end up in life, twenty summers from now we come back to this spot and dig up our time capsule together."

"Deal." Cole put his fist out, like we did before games.

"Deal." Griffin touched his knuckles to Cole's.

"Deal." Moretti added his fist.

"Deal." I added mine.

A couple minutes later, we walked back toward the house, and I stopped off in the shed to put the shovel away. Closing the door, I hurried to catch up with them, throwing one final glance over my shoulder toward the maple tree.

I wondered if when I stood there twenty years later and we unearthed the box, I'd still be thinking about the same girl, or if she'd be a distant memory. Maybe I'd laugh at how big my crush had felt at eighteen. Maybe I'd have already had sex with like *five* girls or something—right now I was the only virgin left among us. But that didn't bother me.

Much.

I wondered if I'd be happy. If I'd be rich. If I'd have a good job. For a second, I even wondered if the four of us would still be best friends.

Then I caught myself—of course we would.

They say friends are the family you choose, and the four of us had chosen each other a long time ago.

Some things never change.

CHAPTER 1
BECKETT

"I'M GOING TO CHICAGO TODAY," my father announced at the breakfast table. "I need the box with the handles."

I picked up my coffee mug and studied my dad for a moment. He was still wearing his pajamas, and his white hair was sticking out in several directions.

"You mean the suitcase?" I asked.

"Yes. That's it." He nodded in satisfaction and began buttering his toast. "I need the suitcase. Do you know where it is?"

"Probably in the attic. But why are you going to Chicago?"

"That's where the game is tonight."

"What game?"

He looked at me like I was nuts. "The baseball game. It says so right there on the schedule."

I glanced at the fridge, where a Detroit Tigers schedule was held in place by a magnet that said I Love My Uncle, a gift from my seven-year-old niece, Daisy.

"Do you have tickets for the game?" I asked, even though I knew damn well he didn't.

"Tickets!" he scoffed. "Players don't need tickets. And I'm the best chance they've got to beat the Sox."

"Right." I regarded my eighty-one-year-old dad for a long moment, torn between wanting to chuckle at the vision of him in a Detroit Tigers uniform—strutting out to the plate, adjusting his cap and giving the pitcher his most cantankerous old-man stare—and wanting to yell at him to stop with the goddamn nonsense, he wasn't a Major League Baseball player and he never had been.

He was a retired farmer with bad hips, arthritic hands, and a slow-as-molasses-in-January geriatric shuffle. It would take him a fucking month to get around the bases.

But rather than point this out, I took a sip of coffee instead.

Usually when confronted with his *moderate cognitive decline*, as the doctor called it—although how anyone could refer to his wild imaginings as *moderate* was beyond me—I tried to use reason and logic with him. Keep him grounded in reality. But nothing made my father more belligerent than being told what he believed wasn't real, and I was trying to have more patience with him.

"I'll find the suitcase for you," I said.

"Good. I'll pack after breakfast," he went on. "I don't want to miss the train. Can you give me a ride to the station?"

I took another sip and a deep breath. "Sure, Dad."

"Thanks." He dug into his breakfast again.

Not particularly hungry, I glanced out the large window next to the table that overlooked the ranch. It was a gorgeous June morning—the blue sky was cloudless, the sun was out, and the ground was dry for once. I'd been up since five, had watched the sun rise over my first cup of coffee, then gone out to do the morning chores before coming back inside to wake up my father and get his breakfast—a complete reversal of parent-child roles that never failed to make my head spin.

But rather than dwell on that, I went over the day's work in my head. As the owner and sole full-time employee at

Weaver Ranch, my to-do list was endless. I had a couple part-time hands, but most days, keeping this place running was a one-man show starring yours truly.

My days were long, dirty, sweaty, demanding, and occasionally made me question my sanity. In addition to all the physical labor, I also made all the executive decisions that kept us in business and paid all the bills that kept the lights on. But after years spent in high-rise Manhattan office buildings feeling penned in by cubicles and choked by greed and neckties, I could say with certainty that I wouldn't trade this life for any other.

Now, were there things about it I'd change?

Hard yes.

Starting with the man seated across from me, who was prattling on about how someone must have taken his baseball uniform, because he'd looked for it this morning and it wasn't where it was supposed to be.

"I'll find it for you," I told him. "Or maybe Amy can help you. She should be here any minute."

"Amy?" My dad brightened at the mention of my oldest sister.

"Yes. She's coming over to spend the day with you."

"Amy Maureen. April nineteenth, nineteen seventy-nine."

"That's right." Listing the full names and birthdates of his kids was something he liked to do to prove he was still with it. "How about Mallory?" I prompted, naming the middle sibling.

"Mallory Grace. January twentieth, nineteen eighty-two."

"And me?"

"Beckett Eugene. October second, nineteen eighty-seven."

As always, I cringed a little at my middle name. "Right. And who won—"

"The Twins," he said, a smug look on his face, because he'd anticipated my next question. "The Minnesota Twins won the World Series that year over the St. Louis Cardinals, in seven games."

I grinned. His long-term memory, especially for baseball stats, was still pretty sharp. "That's good, Dad."

"You were just a baby," he recalled, his blue-gray eyes alive with the memory. "You were just a baby when I watched that game." He looked over his shoulder toward the center of our house. "But where's that room I was in?"

"That was the old house. We built a new one, remember?" After I'd moved back to Bellamy Creek four years ago, I'd had the clapboard farmhouse my great-grandparents had built on the property torn down in favor of a big, rambling timber frame structure.

"Oh." My father scratched his head and continued staring into the two-story great room, with its massive stone fireplace and oversized dark leather furniture, its thick rugs and blankets in earth tones that mimicked the views outside, and the huge windows overlooking a deep front lawn. "Well, if I had a map, I could find my way home."

Sadness squeezed my heart. He was always talking about maps, and I knew it was because he felt lost, but no map was going to take him where he wanted to go. "You ready to get in the shower?" I asked, changing the subject.

"I took one already."

"No, you didn't. Come on, finish your breakfast and then I'll help you. I told Amy you'd be all dressed and ready to go into town when she got here." I knew that would get him going. My dad loved getting out of the house—actually, what he really loved was wandering off on his own, although we knew better than to take our eyes off him now. "She said she'll take you for a haircut."

His chin jutted. "I could take myself for a haircut if you hadn't stolen my truck."

"I didn't steal your truck, Dad." I got up from the table and carried my coffee cup and empty plate to the sink.

"Well, then, you stole my keys," he said, following me to the kitchen. "I haven't been able to find them for a week."

In reality, I'd taken his car keys away from him about six months ago, and his beat-up old truck was still in the garage. "You don't need keys. Amy's going to drive."

"Amy!" he shouted. "She can't drive. She's just a kid."

I rinsed his plate and coffee cup before taking him by the shoulders and steering him out of the kitchen. "Come on. Shower."

We headed for the master suite, which was off the far side of the great room. When the house had been completed, my father had offered to let me have the spacious first-floor bed and bathroom, but he was already struggling a little with his hips, and I knew it wouldn't be long before stairs were too difficult. And I didn't really need all that space. I wasn't even sure why I'd let Enzo, whose company had done the work, talk me into the large walk-in closet or the soaking tub.

After helping my dad choose clothing for the day, I laid it out on the bed and instructed him to get in the shower. "I'm going to knock on the door in five minutes, and then it will be time to get out."

"Okay." He nodded and ambled off to the bathroom.

Thankfully, I didn't have to help him bathe or dress yet, and he could still handle his own personal hygiene. But I knew the day would come when I'd be responsible for those things too.

When I got back to the kitchen, Amy was coming in through the mudroom, keys in one hand and a travel mug in the other. Like me, she had our dad's slate blue eyes and sandy brown hair that would brighten to blond every summer. Hers was pulled back into a ponytail. "Morning," she said.

"Morning. You're here early."

"Yeah, I woke up before my alarm and decided to get on

the road." She shrugged. "It's summer. The kids can get their own breakfasts."

"I appreciate the help," I said, leaning back against the counter. "He refuses to go back to the day program at the senior center, but I can't keep running back in here to check on him. And I worry about him trying to use the oven again."

She nodded solemnly. "Think it's finally time we talk about assisted living?"

"No." My answer was still firm. "Not yet. I just need some help during the day while I work. And it's not even really hard stuff—just keeping him occupied and fed. Making sure he takes a nap. Getting him to his appointments. I put another ad in the Bellamy Creek Gazette, but no one has called yet. I feel like word's gotten out that he fires everyone."

She sighed and took a sip of her coffee. "How's his morning going?"

"Not bad." Shaking my head, I smiled. "He's a little concerned about finding his suitcase so he can pack up and get to Chicago on time. I mean, how are the Tigers gonna beat the Sox without him?"

She laughed. "I have no idea."

"He thinks I stole his uniform."

"You bastard."

"And his truck."

"*Rude.*" She was joking, but her eyes were sad.

I felt it too, but if we didn't sometimes laugh with each other about our dad's behavior, we'd have drowned in sorrow.

"He did cheer up when I told him you'd be taking him to town for a haircut," I told her. "He's probably thinking he can give you the slip and get to the train station."

"He'll forget about the train once he's in the salon chair. He *loves* the girl that cuts his hair—he goes on forever, telling her all about his baseball career." She shook her head. "You have to wonder where he gets that stuff. All those stats he rattles off, the crazy stories. Where's it coming from? His high school days?"

"Probably some of it—he was a great fucking player, and he could have played college baseball if he'd been able to go away to school. He had the talent as well as the brains."

"Yeah," my sister said, misty-eyed.

Our father had been the only son in his family, and by the time he'd graduated from high school, his dad had died, and his mother and sisters needed him to stay home and run the farm.

Once, as a kid, I'd asked him if he'd been mad about that —I certainly would have been—but he'd shrugged and said no, he'd always known where he was needed most and what would matter in the end.

I never forgot that.

"However," I went on, "he's also getting his high school career mixed up with some of the best moments in MLB history. Do you know how many times I've heard him describe the Willie Mays over-the-shoulder catch from the 1954 World Series like he made it?"

She grinned. "Game one? Top of the eighth? Deep fly ball to center field?"

Exhaling, I shook my head. "I gave up arguing with him on that one."

"Why do you argue with him at all?" She turned to the sink, rinsed out her mug, and set it upside down on a paper towel to dry. "You know it's pointless."

"Because half the time, I feel like he *knows* what he's saying is ridiculous, and he's just doing it to get under my skin."

"Why would he do that, Beckett?" she asked, pulling the dishwasher open and loading our breakfast dishes.

"To get back at me for stealing his truck or his keys or his freedom. Or whatever else he thinks I've robbed him of." I rubbed my face with both hands. "I'm just trying to help him hang on to reality. But it's slippery."

"I get it." My sister's voice was soft as she closed the dishwasher and faced me. "And I'm sorry you're dealing with this on your own every day. I wish I could be here more."

"It's okay. You and Mallory did more than your fair share around here while I was young."

My mother had left when I was still in diapers, and my sisters had practically raised me while our dad worked his fingers to the bone to convert the struggling dairy farm his grandparents had started into a small cattle ranch.

Being a rancher hadn't always been my career plan, but after earning my MBA at Yale, I'd spent five years working for a hedge fund on Wall Street, where I made a fuck ton of money before I realized I hated what I was doing. Then just as I was questioning everything, my father developed health problems and contemplated selling the ranch—it was like a punch in the gut from the universe.

I knew where I was needed most, and what would matter in the end.

"Well, someone had to keep you out of trouble," Amy teased. "Make sure you learned your ABCs and ate your spinach."

"Spinach." I made a face.

"Come on, you needed it. You were such a scrawny kid, now look at those Popeye biceps!" She came over and squeezed my upper arm. "They're practically busting out of your sleeves!"

"Knock it off." I pushed her hand away and checked my phone. "I gotta get Dad out of the shower or he'll be in there forever."

"He likes the shower that much?"

"No, he just forgets he soaped up already and does everything all over again," I said, heading out of the kitchen. "He can remember every detail of that damn Willie Mays catch from 1954, but he can't remember if he washed his armpits five minutes ago."

She laughed. "You're a good man, Beckett Weaver."

After rapping my knuckles on my dad's bathroom door a few times and hearing the water go off, I headed back through the kitchen into the mudroom.

"He's getting dressed now," I told my sister. "His haircut is at eleven, he'll need lunch right after that, and then a nap around one."

She tightened her ponytail. "We'll probably have lunch in town. Can I bring you anything?"

"Nah." I sat down on the mudroom bench and tugged on my boots.

"I'm good here until about two. Does that give you enough time?"

"Yeah. Maddie Blake is supposed to arrive around three, and I'll need to clean up first."

"Oooh." Her tone took on a mischievous lilt. "Maddie Blake."

I looked up from lacing my boots. "What's that supposed to mean?"

She shrugged, all big eyes and innocence. "Nothing at all. I mean, so what if the girl you had a giant crush on in high school is moving in with you? Happens all the time."

"Jesus Christ, Amy. We were just friends. She lived across the street. We did homework together. She had a boyfriend." As I ticked off the list of reasons why Maddie Blake and I had never gotten together, my tone grew more defensive. "Now she's a single mom who just went through a divorce."

"Relax," she said soothingly. "I'm not *accusing* you of anything. I'm just saying it was obvious you liked her."

"And she's not *moving in with me*." I stood up, glad for my six-foot-four inches of height and broad chest. "She and her son are staying here temporarily while she fixes up her mother's old house and gets it ready for sale."

Amy wrinkled her nose. "Good luck getting much for that place. The roof looks like it's about to cave in."

"Exactly why I told her she should stay here. Moretti's gonna meet us over there later today and give us an estimate on what it'll take to renovate."

"*Us?*" Her eyes twinkled again.

"Her."

"You said *us*."

I stared her down. "I meant *her*."

My sister's mouth tipped up on one side. "You still have a cru-ush," she sing-songed.

Rolling my eyes, I grabbed my hat from the rack and clapped it on my head.

"If she's still cute, you should take her out on a date while she's here." My sister followed me as I went outside.

"Why?"

"Because it's something that adult humans do for fun."

I kept walking. "I don't have time for fun."

"You know, just because you traded your suit and tie for jeans and boots doesn't make you any less of a workaholic!" she shouted as I headed for the barn. "You need a personal life, Beckett! You need some excitement!"

"I've got excitement." Deflecting from the topic of my personal life, I turned around and walked backward a few steps, arms wide. "Hell, my dad plays centerfield for the Tigers, and just yesterday, he told me if I have a good season, he can probably get me on the team!"

"A good season at what," she teased, "old man baseball?"

I stopped moving and pointed a finger at her. "Hey, you're

talking to the biggest hitter on the Bellamy Creek Bulldogs, the *four-time* champions of the Allegan County Senior Men's Baseball League. A little respect, please!"

Laughing, she put her hand on her chest and bowed down.

As she fucking should.

Grinning, I turned around and resumed striding toward the barn. It *was* kind of funny that my three best friends and I had ended up playing those Thursday night games we used to make fun of, complete with stiff knees and aching shoulders. Luckily, we were all in good shape—no beer bellies yet—although there was no denying we'd aged a bit.

But Griffin was still a force at first base, Cole remained our star pitcher, Moretti was still the fastest runner, and I was still good behind the plate and reliably hit the most home runs each season. We weren't eighteen anymore, but we felt like it again when we were on the field. And best of all, our friendship was still solid.

In the barn I saddled up my horse, Pudge—named for legendary Detroit Tigers catcher Ivan "Pudge" Rodriguez—and rode out to rotate our herd of Highland Cattle from one paddock to another, which had to be done almost every single day from late spring through December.

I worked alone all morning, which was fine. Ranching was solitary work most of the time, at least for a guy like me with a small operation. I was quiet by nature, so I never minded the long stretches of time to myself, but it did give me a lot of time to think.

Usually I thought about my dad—worrying about his mental decline, wondering how long it would be before his physical health began to deteriorate as well, berating myself for being hard on him when maybe my sister and the doctors were right and there was nothing I could do to slow the progress of his dementia.

But today it wasn't my father that occupied my thoughts. It was a beautiful brown-haired girl from my past.

A girl with bottle green eyes and a wide, full mouth she always covered up when she laughed, because she thought it was too big for her face.

A girl who was faster and better at math than I was and loved to tease me about it—when she wasn't helping me understand a problem I couldn't figure out.

A girl I'd kissed once under the maple tree, but dreamed of kissing a thousand times.

I wondered if Maddie remembered that day. We were seniors, and it was springtime. The prom was only a few weeks away, and we were at my house studying for our AP calculus exam on a Sunday afternoon. She'd seemed unusually quiet and withdrawn—normally she chirped like a sparrow, filling up all the silence I left. But today she wasn't talking, and every time I looked at her she was chewing her full bottom lip, concentrating hard on the tip of her pencil on the paper. Eventually, I heard her sniffling, and I looked over, shocked to see tears dripping from her cheeks.

I'd known Maddie since we were in first grade, and I'd never seen her cry.

"Come on," I said, putting my pencil down. "Let's take a break."

She nodded and stood up, following me out the back door and into the late afternoon sun. I knew she liked our horses, so I'd headed for the barn, thinking it might cheer her up to be around them. But before we reached the barn doors, she broke away from me and ran over to a thick old maple tree, propped her forearms against its rough brown bark and sobbed.

Stunned, I watched her for a moment, feeling useless and awkward. Once I reached out to pat her back, then changed my mind and shoved my hand in my pocket again.

"I'm sorry," she wept. "You must think I'm crazy."

There were words on the tip of my eighteen-year-old tongue—words like *actually, I think I'm in love with you*—but they were stuck. I wasn't even sure what love was, but every time she was near, I felt dizzy and out of breath, kinda sick to my stomach but also like I could lift a tractor off someone or maybe scale a twenty-foot wall. I mean, was that love? Or was it a chemical imbalance?

I stuck to safer topics.

"Are you worried about the calc test?"

"No. I mean, yes—I am, but that's not why I'm upset right now. It's my m-mother," she said, her breath hitching.

"Oh."

"She's j-just so h-hard on me."

It was true. High standards were one thing, but Mrs. Blake's expectations for Maddie were insane. Anything less than an A was garbage. There was no such thing as second best. Mistakes weren't allowed. Maddie had gotten a C on the first calculus quiz of the year and hadn't been allowed out of the house for a week. I'd gotten a D, and when my dad had seen how upset with myself I was, he'd shrugged and told me not to worry about it—learning from mistakes was part of life.

"She doesn't love me." Maddie turned to face me, her green eyes shining with tears.

"I'm sure she does." I rubbed the back of my neck to keep myself from touching her. "She's your mother."

Maddie shook her head violently. "Mothers don't always love their children."

I wanted to argue, but how could I? My own mother had abandoned her husband and three children and never looked back. Did you do that if you loved them? No one had ever explained it to me—my mother was not a subject we discussed in our house, nor did we talk about our feelings. But at least I had my sisters around. Maddie was an only child, and had never known her dad.

She was calmer now, speaking quietly. "I know it's just the way she is, and most days, I can take it. I'm used to it. But sometimes I just feel so alone."

"What about Jason?" I asked, unable to disguise the bitterness in my voice. Her dickhead boyfriend was known for three things—his family's money, his drinking, and the way he constantly cheated on the girls he dated.

"Jason doesn't love me either," she said morosely.

"So why are you with him?"

She looked me right in the eye and lifted her shoulders. The breeze ruffled her hair. "I don't know."

Tell her to dump him, I thought to myself. *Tell her she can do so much better. Tell her she's the first thing you think of every single morning, and the last thing you think of at night, and you'd be good to her. You'd be so damn good to her.*

But I choked on the risk of rejection.

And the moment passed me by.

Lowering her chin, she looked at the ground beneath our feet. "Jason told me last night he doesn't even want to go to the prom. He just wants to go to the afterparty so he can sit around and get drunk. And I know it's stupid, but I was really looking forward to dancing at my prom, you know?"

"I'll dance with you," I blurted. It was the best I could do.

"Huh?" She looked up at me.

"I'll dance with you." My heart was like a thousand horses' hooves thundering across a field. "At the prom."

She smiled, tilting her head. "What about *your* date?"

"I don't have one yet."

"Why not?" she asked, her tone slightly scolding. "What are you waiting for?"

What do you think? I wanted to shout at her.

But instead, I did something crazy—I took her face in my hands and crushed my mouth to hers.

A tiny squeak of surprise came from the back of her throat,

but she didn't push me away. Two seconds later, I came to my senses and stepped back.

Both of us were breathing hard.

Her eyes were huge.

My hands were shaking.

"You should—you should ask Katie Keaton to prom," Maddie said in a strange, high-pitched voice. "She has a crush on you."

I swallowed hard. "I'll think about it."

"Good." She turned back toward the tree and braced one hand on it, placing the other over her stomach. Her shoulders rose and fell with quick breaths.

Fuck, fuck, fuck, I thought, hanging my head. I'd kissed someone else's girlfriend. I was no better than goddamn Jason. And I'd probably wrecked my friendship with Maddie too. I wouldn't have blamed her for leaving right that second.

But she didn't.

She moved around the tree and spotted the old swing hanging from a branch above. Lowering herself onto the wooden seat, she wrapped her fingers around the ropes. Then she leaned back and peeked at me. "Give me a push?"

I stared at her, and everything I saw—the slightly pink nose, the wide eyes, the dappled sunlight on her soft brown hair—made me weak in the knees. But if she wanted to pretend nothing had happened, I was good with that.

From behind her, I grabbed the ropes, took a few steps back, then let go. When she swung back toward me, I put my hands on her back and gently pushed, again, and again, and again. Eventually we went back inside the house to finish studying.

We never talked about the kiss again.

Three weeks later, I beat the shit out of Jason at the prom afterparty. I did it because he'd gotten too drunk, fooled around with another girl, and a tearful Maddie had asked me for a ride home. As we were walking out, he came after me, calling me an asshole and accusing me of trying to steal his girlfriend.

To this day, my friends claim it's the maddest they've ever seen me. It might be the maddest I've ever been. Not because he called me a name, but because he had Maddie and he didn't deserve her. And in my eyes, the only thing worse than a man who mistreated an animal was a man who mistreated a woman.

I've never been sorry.

But that was fifteen years ago. I'd grown up a lot since then.

And I'd worked on Wall Street long enough to know that plenty of liars, cheats, and scumbags had riches they didn't deserve and got away with being assholes on a daily basis. You couldn't beat up everybody.

At quarter after one, I made my way from the barn back toward the house. On the way, I glanced over to where that maple tree still stood. Even the swing was still there, moving slightly in the breeze, its ropes frayed by weather and time.

The sight of it made me smile. I could practically see teenage me going in for that kiss like it was do or die—which was exactly how it felt.

But life had led us in different directions. Maybe I'd always have a soft spot for Maddie Blake, but the past was past.

All I wanted to do now was help a friend.

CHAPTER 2

MADDIE

"ARE WE THERE YET?"

I glanced in the rearview mirror at Elliott, buckled up in the back seat. As usual, he had a unicorn barrette clipped to one side of his head, its rainbow-colored strands of faux hair nestled within his adorable blond curls. His big brown eyes met mine in the mirror, and I could see in them all the impatience and misery of an energetic six-year-old on a five-hour drive.

"Not yet, buddy. One more hour."

"But I'm hungry," he whined.

"I packed snacks for you."

"I ate them all."

"Even the cupcake?"

"I ate that *first*."

Laughing, I spotted a sign for a gas station travel center. "You're lucky I need to use the bathroom, kiddo. We'll get off at the next exit."

In the mirror, I caught the little smile on his lips before he went back to whatever game he was playing on his tablet.

"When we get there, can we still go to the diner where you

used to work?" he asked. "The place where you can sit at the counter?"

"We sure can," I said, picturing the round chrome-and-red vinyl stools that used to line the old-fashioned counter where I'd spent four summers serving shakes, sundaes, burgers, and fries to tourists and locals alike. "They used to have the best chocolate milkshakes ever."

"Do they have strawberry milkshakes?" asked Elliott, who never chose something brown—or any other color, for that matter—when there was something pink to be had.

"They did back then. I bet they still do." I exited the freeway and spotted the travel center over to the right. "I know this is a long drive. But you'll like where we're going. I'll show you all the places I used to play when I was a kid, I'll take you to the beach, and we're going to stay on a real farm."

"Beckett's farm?"

"Yes." I'd told Elliott all about Beckett Weaver—how we'd grown up across the road from each other, what good friends we'd been, how he'd generously invited us to stay with him.

"Tell me again the animals he has."

"Well, he definitely has cows and horses. But I think he also has chickens. And maybe a dog."

"Any pigs?" he asked hopefully, since he imagined them to be his favorite color, even though I'd told him that most real-life pigs aren't the bubble-gum hue they appear to be in cartoons.

"We'll find out."

"Can I *pet* the animals?"

"Sure. I bet he'll let you feed them too." I put the car in park and looked back at him. "There are *lots* of chores on a farm, and I told him we planned on helping out."

He grinned and kicked his (pink) cowboy-booted feet. He'd asked for some cowboy boots when I told him we'd be staying on a farm for a few weeks. We'd gone shopping, and he'd fallen in love with the pink pair in the girls' section of the store, rather than the black and brown pairs set out for boys. I let him choose the ones he really wanted, thrilled with the smile they put on his face.

Seeing it again now, I breathed a sigh of relief. He would be okay. We would be okay.

The last couple years had been rough.

My asshole ex, Sam, an orthopedic surgeon with a thriving practice and a roving eye, had humiliated me yet again with another public affair. Fed up with trying to take the high road and keep the marriage together for Elliott's sake, I'd worked up my nerve and finally filed for divorce.

After a paltry attempt to talk me out of it—not because he loved me, but because divorce "looked bad"—Sam agreed to let me stay in the house and give me primary custody of Elliott, which was all I wanted. In exchange, I'd taken the lump sum his lawyers had offered instead of monthly spousal support and put every last dime into an educational trust for Elliott.

I didn't want Sam's money. And I didn't need it. Maybe I hadn't finished medical school, but I was a pediatric nurse practitioner with a job I loved and a salary that was more than enough to support me and my son.

What I wanted was a fresh start . . . but I also needed a little closure.

I was heading up to my hometown of Bellamy Creek for the first time in over a decade in order to sell my childhood home. My mother had left it to me in her will seven years ago, but the shock of her death had hit me hard, and I'd been unprepared to deal with it right away.

Lucky for me, tourism was big business in the picturesque lakeside town, and rental properties were always in high demand. I'd hired the first property manager to answer my ad, grateful when he promised to get the whole place cleaned out and rented quickly. But he'd turned out to be lazy and dishonest, skimming from the rent and letting the property fall into disrepair. Last year, I'd gotten a phone call from the county about the home's dilapidated condition and overgrown yard.

I'd fired the manager right away, but I'd been right in the middle of my divorce and hadn't had the time or emotional energy to travel up to Michigan and deal with it.

I was in a much better place now, and I was actually looking forward to showing Elliott where I'd grown up.

Plus, I'd get to spend time with Beckett.

Just thinking about seeing him again made my stomach flip-flop and my lips curve into a smile.

Sam certainly hadn't cared that I was taking Elliott away for a couple weeks. He was free to see his son whenever he wanted to, but he canceled their planned visits about half the time.

Not that I was surprised, I thought, as I took Elliott's hand and led him into the travel center. Sam had been growing distant ever since it was obvious that Elliott wasn't a "typical" boy—at least in Sam's mind—meaning one who wanted to wear jeans and play with trucks all the time. He liked jeans and trucks just fine, but he also liked dresses and Barbie dolls, and I wasn't going to tell him that was wrong. Because it wasn't.

We are who we are, and we deserve to be loved for it.

"Use the bathroom," I instructed Elliott, who was still standing by the sinks when I came out of a stall, admiring his shimmery unicorn barrette in the mirror.

"I don't have to go."

"We're not leaving until you do, so best get to it." I

scrubbed my hands and gave him a matter-of-fact look in the mirror.

He sighed and rolled his eyes but went into a stall.

A moment later, the woman a few sinks down spoke up. "You know, he should be using the men's room," she said coldly.

I glanced her way. She was older—maybe in her late sixties—with unnaturally yellow hair and beady, judgmental eyes. "He's only six," I told her.

"He's a *boy*." She set her mouth in a prim line. "He should use the *boys'* bathroom."

"I see," I said, drying my hands with scratchy brown paper towels. I knew what her issue was with my son, and it wasn't just about the bathroom.

"If you don't start treating him like a boy now, it will be too late. You're confusing him." She crossed her arms over her chest and sniffed. "It's terrible parenting."

Steaming mad, I tossed the paper towel into the trash, willing myself not to blow up—to instead set a good example for my child, who'd come out of the stall and was washing his hands next to me. "Come on, Elliott. Let's go get a snack before we hit the road again."

"Where's his father?" the woman demanded. "Does he know you dress his son like a girl?"

Elliott glanced down at his pink T-shirt and frowned, and my fury reached the boiling point.

I grabbed Elliott's hand and turned on her. "Currently his father is too busy buttering the biscuit of his latest girlfriend to care about raising his son, so it's up to me to teach the important life lessons—and one of them is that it's pointless to engage with rude, narrow-minded people who never learned to treat others with decency and respect. So *thank you* for this educational opportunity."

While her pruney mouth hung open in surprise, I pushed open the door and sailed through it, Elliott right beside me. I was still fuming as we waited in line to pay for our snacks.

Elliott looked up at me. "Boys can wear pink, right?"

"Of course they can." I squeezed his hand. "You remember what Pinkalicious said in the book, right? Pink is for everybody."

"Why did that lady say those things?"

My heart threatened to break. "Because some people haven't learned to appreciate all the different things that make human beings special and wonderful. They think there's only one way to be."

"But why?"

Because they're assholes, I thought. "Because they weren't taught love and acceptance."

Elliott touched his unicorn barrette. "Did that lady make you mad?"

"Unkind people always make me mad." I stopped and took a deep breath. "But I probably shouldn't have said those things. That wasn't kind either."

"Why did you say Daddy was buttering a biscuit?"

"Uh, never mind." Thankfully, it was our turn at the cashier, and I nudged him forward. "Come on, put your snacks up there. I'm anxious to get back on the road."

"To see your old house?"

"Mostly to see my old friend," I said with a smile. "I've really missed him."

As I turned onto the familiar sun-baked dirt road I'd grown up on, it struck me how little it had changed.

The same split-rail fence bordering Weaver Ranch on the right, the same small, ramshackle houses on the left. I slowed the car and rolled down the windows, breathing in deeply. The smell was familiar too—hay, manure, fields of corn and sugar beets. Even the sound of tires spitting gravel took me back. It was like time had stopped.

With one big exception.

"Wow. Who lives there?" Elliott asked.

"That must be the new house Beckett built," I said as the home came fully into view. It was stunning—a rugged structure of timber and stone and glass that would have looked just as natural against the craggy peaks of Montana as it did in the gently rolling hills of west Michigan. I slowed to a stop in front of the driveway. "It's beautiful, isn't it?"

"Is that where we get to stay?"

"It sure is." I smiled, proud of Beckett, and happy for him.

Not that I'd ever doubted he'd succeed at anything he set his mind to. Beckett was one of the smartest guys I'd ever known—and the best *kind* of smart guy, the kind who never had to put anyone else down to prove how good he was at something. And he was good at a lot of things. School, sports, being a friend . . . kissing.

Heat crept into my cheeks. I wondered if Beckett ever thought about the one and only time things had gotten romantic between us. We'd never talked about it, not even when I went to see him in Manhattan seven years ago, right after I discovered Sam was cheating on me for the first time.

I was hurt, angry, scared—and six months pregnant with Elliott. Desperate for a friend, I'd turned to the one person I knew I could trust not to judge me for jumping into a marriage with someone I hardly knew. Beckett understood how the sudden death of my mom the year before had affected me, how scared and lost I'd felt.

All my life, my purpose had been to live up to her expectations—then she was gone, and I'd felt completely unmoored. I'd dropped out of medical school at Northwestern and taken a job as a barista, which was how I met

Sam, who came into the coffee shop where I worked every morning.

Sam quickly swept me off my feet, offering comfort and stability at a time when I was lonely and lost. He said he was crazy about me and promised me a good life if I'd move back to his hometown outside Cincinnati, where he was about to start working at his father's practice. He said he wanted a family, and I'd pictured being surrounded by children, cousins, aunts, uncles, grandparents—all the things I'd grown up longing for. So I'd eloped to Vegas with him and moved to Ohio, but my dreams were quickly shattered.

When I showed up at Beckett's door, pregnant and miserable, he let me cry on his big, broad shoulder and assured me I didn't have to stay married to Sam to have a good life. But he understood why I was willing to forgive my husband and try again—I wanted our child to grow up with two parents. Neither Beckett nor I had been so lucky.

I remembered the way he'd slept on the floor while I was there, giving me the sofa bed in his tiny Manhattan studio. Beckett had always been a gentleman.

And after I finally left Sam for good, he'd been my first call.

"Hey, stranger," I'd said, choking back tears.

"Maddie?"

"How are you, Beckett?"

"Fine. It's really good to hear from you. How are you doing?"

"I'm good—better than I've been in a long time." I paused and took a breath. "I left Sam."

"Left him? Like, divorced him?"

"Yes."

A pause. "It's about fucking time."

"I know," I said, laughing a little in spite of everything.

"Are you really okay, Maddie?"

"Yes, I'm really okay. And listen, I'm sorry it's been so long since we've talked."

"You don't owe me an apology."

"Let me say this, okay? I feel sick about not keeping in better touch."

"I understood why you couldn't," he said quietly.

"I know you did. But I should have realized sooner that Sam didn't have the right to tell me who I could or couldn't be friends with." I sighed. "I wasted a lot of time trying to win someone's approval who was never going to be satisfied. Story of my life, right?"

He didn't reply right away. "Where are you now?"

"I'm still in Cincinnati, but I'm actually heading up your way as soon as Elliott—my son—is out of school."

"You're moving back to Bellamy Creek?"

"No, it's just a visit. I've got two weeks' vacation at work and thought it would be nice for Elliott to see where I grew up. But my main goal is to get my mother's house fixed up to be sold."

"That could be a big job. The house is in pretty rough shape."

I frowned. "Yeah, the property manager I used turned out to be worthless. It's been vacant for nearly a year now, so I'm sure it needs some TLC."

"Uh, it probably needs more than that."

My stomach turned over. "Is it that bad?"

"I don't mean to scare you," he said quickly. "Maybe it's just the exterior that needs work. With a fresh coat of paint and some landscaping, it might be perfectly fine." His tone wasn't convincing.

"Do you know anyone who might be able to do the work?"

"Yes. Enzo Moretti—you remember Enzo, he graduated with us—is a contractor and does a lot of home renovations. I'm sure he'd be willing to come take a look and give you an estimate on the cost to get it ready to sell. Want me to ask him?"

"That would be perfect," I said, relieved. "Thank you so much."

"No problem."

"I can't wait to see you. How's your family?"

"Pretty good. I'm the best uncle ever."

I laughed. "Of course you are. How's your dad?"

"Physically, he's in good shape. Mentally, he's got some issues."

"Oh, no. Like Alzheimer's?"

"That hasn't been confirmed yet, but it's pretty likely."

"I'm sorry. Does he live with you?"

"Yes." He exhaled. "Some days are better than others. I built a bigger house for us, so at least we have more space."

"Do you have help?"

"My sisters each try to come one day a week. I really need to hire somebody, but for now, it's just me." He chuckled. "I don't get out much."

"Well, maybe we can sit at your kitchen table and do some math problems for old times' sake."

His deep, resonant laughter made my insides warm. "Or we could just have a beer and some conversation."

"That sounds good too." I promised to get in touch in a few weeks, and we hung up. That night, I slept better than I had in weeks.

Something about Beckett's voice was so reassuring. Maybe it took me back to a simpler time. Maybe it reminded me that no matter what, someone was always in my corner. Maybe it was just a deep, masculine sound, and some primitive part of my brain was wired to feel safe and protected when I heard it.

Two days later, he called me back.

"Hey, I hope you don't mind, but I took a closer look at the house. It's in no condition for you to stay there, Maddie."

"Really?" My heart plummeted. "Shit. I guess I'll have to rent a room or cottage somewhere."

"You could try, but everything is pretty booked up around here already. The tourist season is even busier than it was when we were kids."

I groaned and put a palm to my forehead. "Serves me right for putting this off so long. I guess I'll have to stay outside town."

"Or you could stay here," he offered.

"Beckett, that's so sweet. But we couldn't do that."

"Why not? We have plenty of room. You and Elliott can each have your own bedrooms upstairs, and they share a full bath."

"Are you sure it wouldn't be an imposition on you and your dad?"

"My dad would love having someone to talk to besides me. He's mad at me all the time anyway." Then he laughed. "You'd be an entirely new audience for all his baseball stories. And you'd be right across the street from your mom's house."

I chewed my lip. "Gah, I'm tempted."

"Then do it."

"Only if you promise to put us to work while we're there."

He laughed. "Deal. Chores are never-ending on a ranch."

I smiled. "Elliott is going to be so excited. He loves animals."

"Plenty of those around here. I can't wait to meet him."

Elliott's voice broke through the memory. "*Mommy!*" he hollered from the back seat, as if he'd said it a hundred times and I hadn't answered. "Are you even listening?"

"Sorry." Guilty, I glanced over my shoulder at him. "I was daydreaming. What did you say?"

"Are we going to go in?"

"Not yet." Focusing on the road again, I took my foot off the brake and kept driving. "I want to see my old house first.

We're early anyway. I told Beckett we'd be here at three, and it's just after one."

"You said we could get a milkshake."

"We can," I told him, turning left into my old driveway. "I just want to—"

But I couldn't finish my sentence. My mother's house, the one I'd grown up in, was in shambles.

Actually, shambles might have been too quaint a word.

The roof sagged. The porch drooped. The white paint had flaked and peeled so much the home appeared gray. On the second story, one of my old bedroom windows had been replaced with cardboard. The grass and shrubs were so overgrown, there were weeds shooting up through the porch floorboards. A squawking crow flew out of the chimney. The whole scene looked like something out of a horror movie.

Although if the place was haunted, it would not be by my mother, who'd been a housekeeper and kept the place immaculate. She wouldn't even be caught dead here—literally.

"What *is* that place, Momma?"

"That's—that's my old house."

"You *lived* there?"

"It didn't look like this back then." I put the car in park, turned off the engine, and got out.

Tears sprang to my eyes, which surprised me. It wasn't like I had a ton of happy memories here. Mostly when I thought about this house, I heard my mother's voice saying things like, "Do you know how hard I've worked so you can go to college? Do you have any idea the opportunities you have that I didn't? Do you think anyone is going to hand you things in life, Maddie? You have to work for them. You have to be better than everyone else. You have to be laser-focused on the future all the time, or you'll end up dependent on a man—and you can never, ever trust a man to take care of you the way you'll take care of yourself. Men always break their promises."

Congratulations, Mom. You were right about that.

Squaring my shoulders, I went to let Elliott out of the car. "Come on, honey."

He hopped out of the car and took my hand, and together we made our way up the cement walk, where dandelions and prickly weeds grew up through the cracks. I was a little nervous about stepping onto the porch, but upon closer inspection it did appear the boards would hold us. From my purse, I dug out the key the property manager had sent me, cursing his name under my breath.

Pushing the front door open, we stepped into the house.

"Ew. It stinks in here." Elliott held his nose. "Can I wait outside?"

"Stay on the porch," I said. "I'll be out in one minute."

After checking out the kitchen, which I immediately regretted, I went upstairs to peek at my old bedroom—in addition to the missing window, the closet door was off the hinges, and there was a seriously creepy fist-sized hole in one wall. The other bedroom was in slightly better shape, but the bathroom, with its rusty sink and stained toilet made me wonder if I should just burn the place to the ground and walk away.

Outside, I took Elliott's hand. "Come on. Let's go see if Beckett's home. And if he's not, we'll head into town for lunch."

I drove back to Beckett's, turning into the driveway beneath a huge arch that said WEAVER RANCH overhead. After parking in front of the three-car garage, we followed a stone walkway that led to the home's front entrance. It was lined with cheerful yellow daffodils and vibrant green hostas, and on either side of the wide wooden front door was a potted bleeding heart. I pointed at the welcome mat. "Can you read that?"

Elliott looked at it. "Love grows here."

"Good job." Smiling, I knocked three times.

When no one answered, I pulled out my phone and texted Beckett. **Hey! I'm at your front door. We're a little early, sorry. Traffic wasn't as bad as I thought it would be on a Friday morning.**

When he didn't answer my text, I knocked again. A dog began barking inside.

Elliott looked up at me and whispered, "I hear a dog."

"Me too. But maybe no one is—"

Just then, the thick front door was pulled open, and Beckett's father appeared, a black and white Border Collie at his heels. Mr. Weaver had aged considerably since the last time I'd seen him—so much that it shocked me. His hair was completely white and sticking up a little on one side, like he'd been lying down. It also seemed like he'd shriveled a little bit —I remembered him as big and burly—but I recognized his blue eyes.

"Mr. Weaver?" I said, smiling. "Hi. It's Maddie Blake."

He looked confused. "Mallory?"

For a moment, I felt confused too—then I thought maybe he was mistaking me for Beckett's sister Mallory, who also had dark hair.

"No, *Maddie*." I glanced over my shoulder. "Maddie Blake? I used to live across the road. I was a friend of Beckett's?"

Something flickered, and I thought it might be recognition. "Are you here to take me to the train station?"

I blinked. "No, I—uh, I'm here with my son Elliott, and—"

"Can *he* take me to the train station?" Mr. Weaver asked hopefully.

Elliott started to giggle.

"What? No." Flustered, I elbowed my kid, trying to get him to stop laughing. "Maybe we'll just come back later when—"

"Dad!" boomed a deep voice from inside. "What are you doing at the door?"

Mr. Weaver turned toward the voice, pushing the door open wider. That's when I saw Beckett coming down the stairs.

In nothing but a towel.

My jaw dropped. I couldn't help it.

Beckett had always been attractive, with an athlete's build and a boyishly handsome face, but time had been *incredibly* good to him.

His jaw had grown more chiseled, his cheekbones more defined. My eyes wandered hungrily over his bare skin. His shoulders were wide, his biceps bulged, and his chest and abs were an anatomical study in muscle definition. His hair appeared darker than it used to be, and the skin on his face and forearms was slightly more golden thanks to all the time he spent in the sun, but his eyes were the same soft blue I remembered. When they caught mine, I found it a little hard to breathe.

But then, I'd always found it a little hard to breathe around Beckett. I was just good at hiding it.

Hitting the foot of the stairs, he stopped and stared. "Maddie," he said. "You're here."

"Hi." My skin felt sweaty beneath my jeans and T-shirt. "I'm sorry to just show up this way. We went to the house, and it's such a mess, I—"

"No, it's okay. Give me one minute." He pulled the towel a little tighter around his hips. "Dad, can you please show Maddie in? I'm going to get dressed, and I'll be right down."

"Sure," Mr. Weaver said, looking happy to have company. The dog wagged its tail excitedly.

Beckett turned for the stairs, which he went up two at a time.

I couldn't take my eyes off him. He had a beautiful, muscular back, and that towel could not hide his fantastic ass. At the top of the stairs, he turned and glanced down—and *one hundred percent* caught me gawking at his butt.

Embarrassed, I turned my attention to Elliott, who'd dropped to his knees to hug the Border Collie, and Mr. Weaver, who was closing the front door.

"What was your name again?" he asked me.

No joke, I had to think about it.

"Uh, Maddie. Maddie Blake."

He brightened. "There's a family who lives across the road named Blake. A lady and her daughter. I told my son he should marry that girl, but he claims she doesn't live there anymore. Any idea where she went?"

I had to smile. "I think she moved away."

"But she's just a girl," he said, growing distressed. "Maybe she's lost."

"Actually, I think she's okay," I said gently. "I think she's all grown up now, and even though she's made some mistakes, she's right where she needs to be."

Mr. Weaver studied me for a moment. "You know what? You almost look like that girl."

I laughed, glancing up the stairs again. "Sometimes I still feel like her."

CHAPTER 3
BECKETT

FUCK. She was *here*.

I'd just gotten out of the shower when I heard the dog barking. I rarely closed my bedroom door these days, in case my dad needed something and called out, and as soon as I poked my head into the hallway, I'd seen my father pull open the front door. Heard him talking.

So far, he hadn't made a habit of conversing with people who weren't there, so maybe that's why I went rushing down the stairs with nothing on. I really didn't expect to see anyone. Mostly I was worried he'd escape the house.

Instead, there were Maddie and her son standing on my front porch.

My heart thudded hard and fast. She was just as beautiful as she'd ever been, maybe more so. Torn between wanting to wrap my arms around her and feeling like I might die of embarrassment, I'd chosen dignity and kept my distance. If the crimson color in her cheeks was any indication, she felt just as awkward about the towel situation as I did.

Praying my dad could handle playing host for a couple minutes, I'd run back up the stairs to put clothes on, but right before entering my room, I'd been unable to resist glancing down at her again—and noticed she was looking up at me.

And there was something about her stare that made my body temperature rise.

But then she'd turned away, and I was left wondering if I'd imagined it. After all, Maddie had never looked at me as anything other than a friend our entire lives. If she felt an attraction to me, wouldn't she have shown it by now?

Inside my room, I threw on jeans and a clean navy blue T-shirt, ran a comb through my hair, and put on my watch. Then I raced out of my room and back down the stairs, hoping my father hadn't had time to say anything too outrageous or offensive to Maddie and her son.

To my relief, they were seated in the great room conversing amiably. My dad was on the couch across from Maddie, and Elliott was playing with DiMaggio, our Border Collie, on the floor in front of the fireplace.

"Your home is so beautiful, Mr. Weaver," Maddie was saying. "You must love it."

"Yes." My dad nodded in agreement. "If I had a map, I could find it."

"Hey," I said, entering the room. "Sorry about that."

Smiling, Maddie rose to her feet and moved toward me. "That's okay. Now that you're not all wet, can I give you a hug?"

"Of course." I scooped her small frame into my arms and held her against my chest, refraining from resting my lips on her hair like I wanted to. "It's great to see you."

"You too. And you smell good," she said, rising up on her toes to sniff my neck.

"You caught me at the right time. Usually I smell like sweat and the barn."

Laughing, she released me and stepped back. "I kind of like the smell of a barn. Is that weird?"

"Definitely." I glanced over at her son. "Want to introduce me?"

Her eyes lit up and she nodded. "Elliott, come here please. This is my friend Beckett."

The skinny, golden-haired boy popped to his feet and came over. Right away I noticed the pink cowboy boots, princess T-shirt, and barrette in his hair.

"Hi there." I held out my hand. "I like your boots."

"Thank you," Elliott said, putting his small hand inside mine. For a little kid, he had a nice firm handshake. "I just got them."

"They'll come in handy around here, that's for sure."

"He can't wait to visit the barn," Maddie said, running her hand over her son's curls. At first glance, he didn't appear to resemble his mother much, but when he smiled, I saw her full mouth and the tiny cleft in her chin.

"We can visit the barn any time you want," I told him.

"Now?" Elliott asked hopefully.

"Sure, if it's okay with your mom."

"It's fine. I suppose lunch can wait a little, as long as you're not starving." Maddie sighed, closing her eyes a second. "And I've already seen the house. I'm not all that anxious to see it again."

"Don't worry," I said. "Moretti is going to meet us over there later this afternoon. I just need to call him when we're ready."

"Can DiMaggio come to the barn too?" Elliott asked.

"Sure," I said, happy to hear that Elliott had been given the dog's correct name. Half the time, my father referred to him as Ruth, our previous dog, who'd been gone for a dozen years. "Dad, you want to come out to the barn with us for a few minutes?"

"Is it time to do the milking?"

"We don't have dairy cows anymore, Dad."

"Of course we do. I just milked them this morning." He rose to his feet. "Let me get my boots on."

"They're in the mudroom," I told him. "Come on, I'll help you."

Maddie gave me a sympathetic look as we made our way through the kitchen to the mudroom. "I see what you mean."

"Just wait," I said quietly. "Has he told any baseball stories yet?"

"No, but he *did* ask me to take him to the train station. Is that related somehow?"

"That's how he's going to get to the game," I explained with exaggerated patience.

"Does Bellamy Creek even have a train station anymore?"

"Nope. It had an old, abandoned depot, which was moved in like 1980 or something, and it's now part of the Historic Village. But he doesn't believe that. So I took him there one time, trying to prove it, and he sat in that fucking museum depot for an hour, baffled that not a single train came by."

"Did he believe you then?"

I shook my head. "Nope. He said I must have taken him to the wrong place."

She laughed sympathetically. "You're very patient."

"I try," I said. "Some days it's easier than others."

We reached the mudroom, and I dropped to my knees to help my dad get his boots on. A moment later, we were outside in the sunshine, heading toward the red barn. Elliott scampered ahead with DiMaggio, and my dad shuffled slowly but steadily in front of Maddie and me.

"I'll apologize now for anything he might say that's off-putting," I told her. "He doesn't mean to be rude, but when he gets angry or frustrated, he has no filter. And he'll probably forget your name every day."

"That's okay. I had a talk with Elliott about it. We'll be fine." She glanced at me. "I want to be helpful to you while we're here, Beckett. If that means keeping an eye on your dad, or even just keeping him company, I'm happy to do that."

"He'll probably try to get rid of you. He's fired three perfectly good caretakers," I said grumpily. "Or driven them to quit."

"I can handle it," she assured me.

"You're also going to be pretty busy with the house."

She groaned. "Don't remind me. I'm half hoping Enzo tells me it will be cheaper to tear it down and sell the land."

"He might, but I doubt it. He likes a challenge."

We watched as Elliott spotted some goats in a paddock on the far side of the barn. He stopped and turned back to us. "Can I go over there?"

"Sure," I called. "The goats are friendly. But they're escape artists, so don't open the gate, okay?"

"Okay!" Elliott ran right up to the fence, and sure enough, a few goats came over to him right away. He looked back at us delightedly and began petting their heads, talking to them.

"He looks so happy." Maddie's voice caught with emotion. "I tried to keep him shielded from as much divorce bullshit as I could, but every night I go to sleep hoping I didn't fuck up my kid."

"Isn't that what parenthood is?"

She laughed ruefully. "Sometimes it feels that way. But I want to do better than just keep him fed and clothed and breathing, you know? I want him to grow up confident and joyful and unafraid to be who he is. I want him to know kindness and acceptance, and show it to others. I want him to know unconditional love," she said fiercely, "the kind I never had."

I glanced at her, fighting the urge to take her hand. I shoved mine in my pockets instead.

"Oh, look at them." Maddie laughed softly. "How cute."

We stopped walking and watched as my dad reached the fence and stood beside Elliott, telling him random facts about the farm and about goats. Elliott stood on the lowest rung of the metal fence and listened with rapt attention, shyly stroking the goats' heads and necks, doing his best to hug them.

"Is that okay?" Maddie asked. "Can he pet them?"

"It's fine. He seems like a sweet kid."

"He is, thank you."

"I take it he likes pink."

"He *loves* pink," she confirmed. "Definitely his favorite color. And he's never met a unicorn he didn't adore."

"He'd get along great with my niece Daisy. She's seven."

She smiled up at me. "Maybe we can get them together while we're here."

"Sure. You're here for two weeks, right?"

"That's definitely the longest I could stay. But I've got two weeks off from work, yes."

I forced myself to stop staring at her mouth and studied the muddy toes of my boots. Standing so close to her was making my heart beat faster, and I realized that even though fifteen years had gone by, I still felt something for her.

It was too bad things couldn't be different for us.

But that was impossible. I had my dad to take care of for the rest of his life, and she had her son to raise. If ever we'd had a chance, we'd missed it.

"You like your job?"

"I really do. It's a smaller pediatric practice, but I know all the families so well. Most days, it doesn't even feel like work."

"That's great."

She nodded. "I don't have a fancy office with M.D. on my nameplate, but I love what I do. It took me a while to see that *that's* what matters, you know?"

"I know exactly."

"Hey, want to come eat lunch at the diner?" Maddie elbowed me. "My treat. I promised Elliott a milkshake."

"Sure, sounds good. Let me call Enzo real quick," I said, pulling my phone from my pocket. "The sooner we know what we're dealing with over there, the better."

"Perfect."

I tapped Moretti's name in my contacts, put the phone to my ear, and waited for him to pick up. That's when I noticed that Maddie was staring at the maple tree.

"The swing is still there," she said.

I looked at it for the second time today and saw myself going in for that kiss again. "Yeah."

She smiled and laughed softly. "Some things never change."

Enzo said he would meet us at four, which gave us just enough time to peek in the barn and introduce Elliott to the horses before heading into town.

My dad had already eaten lunch, of course, but since he didn't remember doing it, he was more than happy to come along and eat again. He hadn't gotten much of a nap in, but he didn't seem cranky. In fact, he appeared to be enjoying Elliott and Maddie's company a lot. With any luck, he'd tire out early this evening, and I'd have a few hours of peace before going to bed.

Elliott got a kick out of sitting on the stools at the counter, and my dad had a ball telling stories about coming to the diner when he was young. It was where they hung out after baseball games, he said, and when we were done eating, he took Elliott by the hand and led him over to the wall by the door where faded black-and-white high school team photos were hung.

Pointing his knobby finger at one of them, he said, "Right there. That's me."

Elliott looked back and forth between the strapping seventeen-year-old in the photo, wearing a baseball uniform and cap, and the stooped old man next to him. "That's you?"

"Of course it is." My father stood a little taller. "Can't you tell?"

"Absolutely," Maddie said, moving closer to study the photo. "It looks just like you." Then she smiled at me over her shoulder, making my blood rush a little quicker. "And just like *you*."

"Beckett's photo is over here." My dad turned to the opposite wall and pointed to a color photo. "See? There he is."

"Oh my goodness, look at that!" Maddie squealed, rushing over to it. "I recognize almost everybody. There's Enzo Moretti and Griffin Dempsey and Cole Mitchell." She glanced back at me. "Are you still close friends with them?"

I nodded. "And we still play baseball together."

Her grin widened. "Wow, some things *really* never change." Then she turned to the photo again. "Look, Elliott. That's when Beckett and I were such good friends. I used to go to baseball games and watch him hit lots of home runs."

"Can you still hit home runs?" Elliott asked me.

"Occasionally," I said, laughing.

"Can you show me how to do it?"

"We can do a little batting practice while you're here, sure. You like baseball?"

"Yes," he said as we headed out onto the sidewalk. "I play tee ball."

"That's a good place to start," I said. "I played tee ball too when I was a kid."

"But I want to hit a home run *without* the tee," he told me, his face concerned. "Can you teach me how?"

"I can definitely try."

"Good, because I think my dad would like that better. And maybe if I could hit a home run without the tee, he'd come to my games."

I managed a tight-lipped smile at Elliott, but my hands curled into fists at my sides.

Maddie put a hand on my back.

At home again, I sent my father into his room to rest and helped Maddie and Elliott take their bags upstairs.

I had two guest rooms, one on either side of a full bath. My room, which had its own full bath attached, was across the hall.

Elliott raced up ahead of us and checked out both rooms. "Can I have the one with the bunk beds?" he asked hopefully.

"Sure," Maddie said.

He grabbed his pink duffel bag from Maddie's hands and disappeared into the room we called the "bunk room" for its two sets of stacked beds. My nieces and nephews slept there sometimes if they stayed over.

"I thought you might like this one," I said, leading Maddie into the other room. It held a queen-sized bed covered with a floral comforter and brightly colored throw pillows, all of which my sister Amy had picked out. I set her bag down next to the dresser. "There are clean towels in the bathroom, but let me know if you need anything else."

"This is perfect, Beckett," said Maddie. Walking over to the window, she pushed the curtains aside and looked out. "God, I forgot how beautiful it is here. Or maybe I never appreciated it."

"Yeah, sometimes that's how it goes." I liked the way the

sun coming in the window gave her dark hair warm streaks of reddish gold.

"Mom, guess what! I can see the goats from my window!" Elliott cried from the next room.

Maddie laughed. "That's great, buddy."

I checked my phone. "We've got about fifteen minutes before we have to meet Enzo. I'll let you get settled."

"Beckett, wait."

Before I could leave the room, she came toward me, arms outstretched. Next thing I knew, they were looped around my neck, and her body was pressed flush against mine, chest to chest.

"Thank you," she said. "This means so much to me."

"It's no big deal." My voice cracked as I said it, and I swallowed, praying I wouldn't start to get hard with her body so close to mine. I knew she'd feel it.

"It is." She clung tighter. "I like to think I'm a strong person, that my experiences have taught me resilience. But right now, I feel taken care of, and that's nice too. So thank you."

"You're welcome," I said, trying to keep my thoughts clean and my hands in an appropriate place on her back. Meanwhile, my caveman brain wondered if I'd have time to lock myself in the bathroom and jerk off before we went across the street.

"You've always been so supportive of me." She let go of my neck, sliding her palms down my arms and taking my hands in hers. "And while I'm here, I promise to do everything I can to make your life easier."

"Maddie, you don't owe me anything. That's not how friendship works."

She shook her head. "God, Beckett, can't you ever just be an asshole about something?"

"Put me in a room with your ex," I told her, "and you'll have your answer."

Just before four o'clock, Maddie, Elliott, my father, and I drove down the road to her old house in my truck. Elliott wasn't too keen to go inside, so he and my dad sat on the porch steps to wait—but not before I double-checked the splintering old boards would actually hold them.

After walking through the house, I tried to sound encouraging when Maddie asked what I thought, but deep down I wasn't sure the place was worth saving, unless it really meant something to Maddie.

Back outside, we circled the house, surveying the overgrown weeds and tangled brush. "I can help you with the landscaping," I said. "I don't think that would take more than a few days to get under control. But let's get Enzo's opinion on the structural issues."

When Enzo pulled up a couple minutes later, there was someone in the passenger seat.

"Who's that with him?" Maddie asked, shading her eyes with one hand.

I squinted at his SUV. "Oh, it's Bianca. His wife."

"Enzo got *married*?" She sounded shocked, and I didn't blame her. Enzo had been a notorious ladies' man back in our high school days. "I can't believe you didn't say anything!"

"It was just a few months ago. Come on, I'll introduce you."

Enzo and Bianca got out of the car, but while he stood back, studying the house with a critical eye from the gravel driveway, she came bounding straight for us. "Hi, guys!"

Maddie held out her hand to the petite redhead. "Hi! I'm Maddie. It's so nice to meet you!"

Bianca smiled and shook it. "It's nice to meet you too— I've heard so much about you."

Glancing at me, Maddie laughed nervously. "Good things, I hope."

"All good things." Bianca grinned and looked back at her husband. "Honey, what are you doing? Come and say hi."

"I'm coming." He strolled up the walk and smiled at Maddie with his usual easy charm. "Hey, Maddie. Nice to see you again."

"You too. Congratulations on your marriage." She looked back and forth from husband to wife, clasping her hands beneath her chin. "I just heard the news. That's wonderful."

Bianca laughed and hooked her arm through Moretti's. "It's wonderful *now*. Took a while."

Maddie looked a little confused, and the rest of us laughed.

"I'll explain later," I said. "For now, why don't you take them through the house?"

"Okay." Maddie exhaled, wrinkling her nose. "Prepare yourselves. It isn't pretty."

"Pretty can come later," said Bianca confidently. "I'm actually an interior designer and I'd be glad to help you get the place into shape. Enzo and I love this kind of thing."

"You have no idea how glad I am to hear that," Maddie said. "I have zero experience, a limited budget, and I'm somewhat strapped for time."

"Don't worry." Bianca sounded sure of herself, even as she eyeballed the sagging porch. "We can help."

After being introduced to Elliott and saying hello to my dad, Moretti and Bianca followed Maddie through the house. I tagged along too, curious about their opinions.

Bianca chirped a mile a minute about what could be done with the interior—"I'm totally seeing a modern Victorian hideaway"—but Moretti was mostly quiet. He knocked on some walls, peeled off some wallpaper, peered into closets, opened kitchen cabinets, scrutinized ceilings, and examined wires and pipes.

Outside again, he walked around the house, studying the roof and the foundation. Then he stood in the driveway again, regarding it from fifty feet.

"Well?" Maddie said anxiously. "What's the verdict?"

"I've seen worse."

Bianca rolled her eyes. "Babe, be a little more specific please."

"It can be renovated," he said, walking toward us again. "But it won't be all that fast. I can give you the best possible deal on materials, and Bianca is great at making the best use of space and getting a high-end look for less, but the labor could get costly, and I'm not sure when I can spare the guys. You said you're strapped for time?"

"I've got two weeks. I have to get back for work and Elliott has summer camp."

Moretti shook his head. "It will definitely not be done in two weeks, but I don't think you need to be here on a daily basis as the work is being done. If you trusted me or Beckett to make decisions—"

"I would," Maddie said quickly.

"And Bianca to get it decorated," he went on.

"One hundred percent." Maddie smiled at Bianca. "I loved all your ideas."

"Then I think it would be a good investment," Moretti concluded. "But let me get back to you with a more specific timeline, some drawings, and an estimate. I'm just going to take a few measurements."

"Okay," Maddie said. "Thank you so much."

"So what else will you do while you're here?" Bianca asked as Moretti headed inside again, this time with his tape measure and a notebook.

"Show Elliott around my old stomping grounds, take him to the beach, that kind of thing." Maddie smiled at me. "And hopefully be a help to Beckett on the ranch. We're so grateful to be staying there."

"Isn't it a beautiful home?" Bianca gushed. "I just love it. Sometimes big houses lose that homey, cozy feeling, you know? But not that one."

"Not at all. It's very warm and inviting. Two things this place is *not*." Laughing, she jerked her thumb at her old house.

"Yet." Bianca smiled reassuringly. "But don't you worry. We'll turn it into a little country oasis with just the right balance of vintage charm and modern convenience. And with a location like this, just ten minutes from town and the beach? It'll be snapped up in a heartbeat."

Maddie's expression was dubious. "If you say so."

"I do." Bianca remained confident. "You know what? Let's have a drink while you're here. You need to meet Blair, who's married to Griffin. Oh, and do you know Griffin's sister, Cheyenne? She's getting married next weekend to the fourth musketeer, Cole Mitchell, so she might be a little busy, but we—"

"Oh my goodness!" Maddie's jaw dropped. "Griffin is married too? And his sister Cheyenne is marrying Cole?" She looked over at me accusingly and slapped my arm. "Beckett Weaver! Why didn't you tell me any of this before?"

"I don't know." I shrugged. "You just got here."

"I've been here for *hours*." She exchanged a look with Bianca, who sighed in agreement.

"Men do not understand the important things. Here, take this." Bianca reached into her purse and pulled out a business card, handing it to Maddie. "And call me. I think the girls might get together tomorrow night."

"Great. Thank you so much," Maddie said, tucking Bianca's card in her pocket.

Moretti came out of the house and down the steps toward us. "Okay. I have what I need." He squinted at the overgrown bushes and weed-ridden lawn surrounding the place. "You'll probably want to hire some landscapers."

"Beckett said he could help me with that."

Moretti smirked at me. "I'm sure he did. I'll be in touch over the weekend."

"Sounds good. Thanks so much."

"Hey, what are you guys up to tonight?" he asked. "We're heading into town for drinks with Griffin and Blair later. Want to meet us?"

"Nah, I can't." I glanced at my dad, who was making his way toward us from the porch steps.

"Beckett, go ahead," urged Maddie. "I'll be home with Elliott anyway. I can keep an eye on things."

"Maybe another time." I was actually looking forward to having a couple beers with Maddie after my dad went to bed. Catching up for real, with no distractions.

"Suit yourself. Ready to go?" Moretti asked his wife.

"Yes." Bianca took his hand and gave Maddie a smile. "Don't forget to call me."

"I won't."

"Bye, Elliott! Nice meeting you! Bye, Mr. Weaver," Bianca called, giving them a wave. Moretti waved too, and they began walking down the gravel driveway.

"Hey, wait a minute!" my dad yelled as they reached their SUV. "You guys going by the train station? I could use a lift."

Maddie and I exchanged a look, and she smiled sadly, gently touching her heart, like it was bruised.

Mine too, I thought. *Mine too.*

CHAPTER 4
MADDIE

WHEN WE GOT HOME, Elliott went out to the barn with Beckett and I went up to my room to unpack, since I hadn't had time to do it before.

I put underwear, socks, shorts, jeans, T-shirts, a bathing suit and my pajamas into the dresser drawers and hung a few nicer items in the closet. Not that I'd brought anything too fancy—a couple sundresses and a white blouse. Beneath them I placed a pair of flats, some flip-flops, and a pair of wedge sandals. Back in Ohio, I had a closet full of designer clothes and shoes I rarely wore, a bathroom vanity lined with expensive perfumes, a jewelry box that glittered with pricey gifts from Sam that never made up for his lack of real affection and further revealed how little he cared to know me.

I was a jeans and sneakers girl. I didn't need the fancy shit. What I'd wanted was something worth more than money.

A knock on the closed bedroom door startled me. "Come in," I called.

The door opened and Beckett appeared. "Hi. Sorry to bother you."

"You never bother me." I stuck my hands in my back pockets. "What's up?"

"Just wondering if chicken is okay for dinner. That's what I was planning to make."

"Of course." I moved toward him. "Let me help. In fact, why don't you let me make dinner?"

"Because you're a guest."

"I'm not a *guest* guest." I swatted playfully at his firm chest. "I'm an old friend staying with you, and I'd love to make dinner tonight."

"Okay," he said with a shrug. "I'm sure whatever you make will be better than what I'd do anyway."

"What were you going to do?"

"Uh, something with chicken. And maybe some noodles."

I laughed. "Let me take a look in your pantry and see what I can come up with."

His eyes dropped to my mouth. "I think there might be some more asparagus in the garden."

"Oooh!" I rubbed my palms together, excited by the thought of cooking with ingredients freshly pulled from the ground. "Come on, let's go out to the garden and see. And let's bring Elliott. Maybe he'll eat asparagus if he picks it!"

After poking around in Beckett's fridge and pantry, I decided to make chicken paprikash, one of the few dishes I'd learned to make from my mother, who was of Hungarian descent. Despite the complicated relationship she and I had, I always enjoyed cooking with her. And making a recipe she'd learned to make as a girl somehow made me feel connected to extended family, even though I'd never known any.

In the garden, Elliott helped pick asparagus and radishes.

He was delighted by the color of the radishes and gave them an honest try, but wasn't crazy about the taste. The asparagus, we tossed in a little olive oil, sprinkled with some salt and pepper, then put them in the oven to roast.

Once the food was on the table, we sat down to eat, Beckett across from his father, me right next to Beckett, and Elliott across from me. I was so used to meals with just the two of us, this felt like a special occasion.

"This looks incredible, Maddie," said Beckett. "Much better than anything I can make."

"That's true," said his dad.

I laughed. "Thank you. I really love cooking and rarely get to cook for more than two. A six-year-old doesn't have a very adventurous palate, so I make a lot of comfort foods."

As we ate, we chatted more about the house and what might be done to fix it up.

"Bianca is so nice," I said. "I'm glad she came with Enzo today."

"She is nice," he agreed, "and she's perfect for him. But the funny thing is, they couldn't stand each other for the longest time."

I listened with wide eyes to the story of how they fell in love only after they'd already gotten married. "Are you serious? They hated each other and got married just to fool his family so he could inherit the construction business?"

"I'm sure they would tell the story differently, but yes, it was *that* ridiculous and we all thought they were crazy." Beckett shook his head. "But somehow it worked out."

"Seems like it." I took a bite of my chicken. "And Griffin is married too?"

"He got married last December."

"Anyone I know?"

"Nope, she's from Nashville. She runs a bakery in Bellamy Creek—it's really good. She makes amazing apple pie."

"Is it as good as Betty Frankel's?" I joked. Bellamy Creek's claim to fame—at least according to a highway billboard outside town—was that it boasted the best apple pie in the Midwest since 1957.

"Actually, it is. Betty Frankel is gone now, but Blair Dempsey is keeping the legacy alive. Her place is right on Main Street."

"I'll definitely check it out." I took a sip from the beer Beckett had brought me. "And Cole's getting married too, huh? Next weekend?"

"Yes, next Saturday night." He grimaced. "I have to give the toast."

"You don't want to?" I asked in surprise.

"It's not that I don't want to. I just don't love public speaking. And talking about sentimental things is not my strong suit."

"Well, Cole must trust you to do it right or else he wouldn't have asked you."

"He didn't have a choice. Back in high school, believe it or not, we drew names of who'd give the toast at each other's weddings," he said wryly. "And I picked Cole."

I laughed. "You guys are so funny. And I have one hundred percent faith in you. You'll find the right words."

"I hope so. Right now, all I have are crumpled up pieces of paper with terrible baseball metaphors. And they deserve better. His fiancée is Griffin's sister, Cheyenne—she's a kindergarten teacher at the elementary school." He paused, and spoke quieter. "I don't know if you heard, but Cole lost his first wife, Trisha, to a blood clot when she had their daughter, Mariah. She's nine now."

"Oh, how awful." My heart ached for the teenage sweethearts I remembered from high school. "So Cole's been a single dad all this time?"

Beckett nodded. "He and Mariah lived with his mom until recently. They just bought a big old house by the creek earlier this year. Their wedding is going to be in their backyard."

I sighed. "I love that. I'm happy for him."

"Me too." He took a drink and set the bottle down again. "Cheyenne had always been crazy about him. Finally, he noticed. The rest of us saw it a long time ago."

"Sometimes it takes people a while to see what's right in front of them," I said.

Beckett looked at me for a moment and picked up his beer.

After dinner, Beckett went to help his father get ready for bed. After sticking Elliott in the shower, I did the dishes and cleaned up. By the time Beckett returned to the kitchen, I was wiping down the stone counters.

"You didn't have to do all that," he said. "You're a—"

"Hush, cowboy." I gave him the stink eye and put up my dukes. "Don't make me get feisty with you."

Laughing, he held up his palms in surrender. "Where's Elliott?"

"I put him in the shower and said he could have some iPad time if he was quick about it."

"Want another beer?" he asked, going to the fridge and grabbing one for himself.

I hesitated, wiping my hands on a dishtowel.

"Come on, it's Friday night," he cajoled, popping off the cap.

As he took a sip from his beer, I found myself staring at his mouth, thinking about that kiss again, wondering how a moment from so long ago could seem so vivid.

Flustered, I averted my eyes. "Okay. But let me get Elliott in bed and take a quick shower."

"No rush."

Upstairs, I checked on Elliott—he was already in his unicorn pajamas, playing a game on his iPad in one of the top bunks—and jumped in the shower.

After drying off with a thick, fluffy towel, I put on denim shorts and a plain white tank, throwing a soft blue cardigan over my shoulders. Deciding against blow-drying my hair since it would take too much time, I combed it out and left it damp and hanging around my shoulders. It's not like this was a date.

Even though I shaved my legs. And rubbed lotion into my skin. And took my birth control pill three hours ahead of schedule.

But I couldn't help it. How long had it been since I'd wanted to feel pretty for someone? I was considering putting on a little makeup when I caught my reflection in the mirror.

Stop it, I scolded myself. *You are going downstairs to have a beer and catch up a little. Just because you always had a secret crush on him doesn't mean you need to gloss up your lips and lashes at this late date. Those butterflies in your stomach are ridiculous.*

Still, I gave myself a little spritz of perfume before switching off the bathroom light and heading into Elliott's room. "Hey, you. Time for bed."

"Five more minutes?" he pleaded, as always.

"Nope. It's been a long day. And people wake up early on a farm. I heard you tell Beckett you were going to help with the morning chores." From his small suitcase I pulled his unicorn nightlight and plugged it into an outlet by the bed.

"He said I can feed the goats," Elliott said excitedly.

"Well, then, you better get to sleep. If you miss the wakeup call, someone else will do it."

Elliott handed me his iPad without further argument.

"Did you brush your teeth already?"

"Yes."

"Are you lying to me?"

"No. Smell my breath." He leaned over the bunk's rail and blew air on me.

"Good enough." I took his charger from his backpack and plugged the iPad in. "I love you, and I'll see you in the morning."

"I love you too." He blew me a kiss. "Night."

"Night." I blew one back.

Leaving his bedroom door cracked open, I headed toward the stairs in my bare feet, but curiosity got the better of me when I passed Beckett's open bedroom door.

Pushing the door open all the way, I stepped inside and glanced around. With the hall light on behind me, I took in the king-sized bed—made, but with rumpled covers, as if it had been done quickly, or maybe in the dark—the dresser and mirror, the nightstand and lamp.

On the dresser were a few framed photographs, and I couldn't resist taking a closer look. I tiptoed deeper into the room and picked one up. It was a family shot taken at our high school graduation. Beckett stood with his father on one side and his two sisters on the other. Everyone was smiling broadly, and the deep blue of our graduation robes brought out the color of Beckett's eyes. Suddenly I remembered taking the photo, using a camera that belonged to one of his sisters. I'd also posed for a picture with Beckett that day. Later, he'd given me a copy of it, and I'd kept it on a bulletin board in my freshman dorm room. It had gotten lost in one move or another—I wondered if Beckett still had a copy.

Replacing that frame on the dresser, I picked up another one. This photo was of Beckett and an adorable little dark-haired girl about four years old who was riding on his back, her arms around his neck in a death grip. She had her cheek pressed against his, and both of them were grinning. I figured it must be one of his nieces, maybe even the one who liked unicorns.

The last picture was of Beckett, Enzo, Griffin, and Cole,

wearing huge grins, ball caps, and dirty baseball shirts that said Bellamy Creek Bulldogs on the front. It looked fairly recent. Smiling, I set it down. There was something so comforting about knowing their friendship had endured. It spoke volumes about their character.

With one last glance at that big bed—did he always sleep alone? I experienced a sharp-edged stab of jealousy for any woman who'd spent the night with him—I snuck out of the room and hurried down the stairs in my bare feet. Beckett was sitting in the middle of one couch looking at his phone, but he got up when he saw me.

"Have a seat," he said, keeping his voice low. The sun had gone down and only one lamp was on, making the room cozy and intimate despite its size. "I'll grab you a beer."

"I can get it." I went into the kitchen, where I pulled a beer from the fridge. After tossing the cap in the trash, I went back out to the great room. Briefly I wondered if I should choose the couch opposite him, but since we had to stay a little quiet so we wouldn't wake anyone, I decided to join him. I sank into the corner, tucking my feet beneath me.

"Cheers," I said, holding up my beer.

Beckett lifted his eyes from my legs and touched his bottle to mine. "Cheers."

We both took a sip. The windows were open, letting in the sounds of an evening out in the country—no traffic, no sirens, no next-door neighbors blaring music on their patios—just the chirping of crickets and the buzzing of June bugs. A soft, warm breeze brought the scent of the fields. I took a deep breath and let it out.

"Elliott in bed?" Beckett asked quietly.

"Yes, and he wants to get up in time to help feed the goats in the morning, so I told him to go right to sleep."

Beckett chuckled. "Sounds good, but that's gonna be early."

"How early?"

"Usually just after five."

My eyes widened. "Here I thought school mornings were bad."

"Eh, you get used to it. And I'll tell you what, I'd rather wake up at five and head outside than get in a car and go to an office."

I nodded, taking another sip. "Tell me about how you decided to leave New York."

Keeping his voice low, he told me about how he was making more money than he'd ever thought possible, but never felt like he fit in there. He hated corporate culture, and he loathed the avarice it fed on. While guys he'd hired on with bought luxury apartments, boats, and Porsches, he'd just kept investing his money, sending it home, or saving it.

"I stayed in that same shitty studio apartment you saw when you came to New York," he told me.

"It wasn't shitty, it was just small. But I was grateful to have a place to stay and a shoulder to cry on. And for the record, you could have shared the bed with me. You did not have to sleep on the floor."

He chuckled. "Yes, I did."

"Beckett, I told you then and I'll say it again now—I trust you. I will always trust you."

He didn't say anything for a moment, then he tipped up his beer, finishing it off. "I'm gonna have one more. You?"

I held up my bottle, which was still half-full. "I'm good."

When he got back, he sat slightly farther away from me on the couch, and I tried not to be disappointed. "So what made you finally move back here?"

"My dad, actually."

As I finished my beer, I listened to him tell me about his dad's declining health and how he realized it wasn't enough to send checks home anymore.

"My sisters told me he was thinking of selling the ranch because he just couldn't run it alone," he said. "That's when it hit me—I was in the wrong place. New York was never going to feel like home. I gave my notice and moved back here within a month."

"No regrets?"

He seemed to think about that carefully. "I look back sometimes. But not at New York—or that life—with any regret."

"What do you look back on and regret?"

He glanced at my legs again. "Nothing. Can I get you another beer now?"

I looked at the empty bottle in my hand. "Sure, why not? But cut me off after this. Three is my limit, even on a Friday night."

He set his bottle on the coffee table and left the room. When he returned, he handed me a beer and sat a little closer this time. He smelled *so good*. My pulse picked up, and I tried to ignore it by taking a drink.

What on earth was wrong with all the single women around here? Why weren't they beating down the door, wearing perfume and their nice underwear beneath their short skirts, bringing him casseroles and apple pies? Would it be weird to come right out and ask why he was still single? After two beers, I felt brave enough to do it.

"So I'm curious," I said, tucking a strand of damp hair behind my ear. "All your friends are getting married. Have you ever thought about it?"

He shrugged. "Not really."

"How come?"

"At this point, I've got all I can handle running the ranch and looking after my dad. Dating someone would be tough." He thought for a moment before going on. "And I've . . . struggled with serious relationships."

"How come?"

He hesitated. "I just didn't find having a girlfriend an easy thing to balance with my goals. Other things were more important to me. And she never liked hearing that."

"So there was *someone*." I tipped my head and smiled, even though jealousy flared in my gut. "Who was she?"

He exhaled and took a drink. "Her name was Caroline."

"What was she like?"

"Smart. Driven. Successful."

I hated her a little. "What did she do?"

"She was a producer at NBC."

"Beautiful?"

He jerked one broad shoulder. "Yeah. She was beautiful."

"What did she look like?"

"She was tall and blond."

Of course she was, dammit. I took a drink of my beer to wash down the resentment. Not that I'd expect him to date a hideous gremlin, but did he have to describe the exact opposite of me? "Why'd you break up?"

"Which time?"

I smiled. "The last time."

"I announced I was moving back here."

"She didn't want to come with you?"

"I didn't ask her."

"Oh." I felt better. Bitchier, but better. "Why not?"

He didn't answer right away, just studied the bottle in his hands. "Things with us were always temporary. She wouldn't have stayed to the end."

"How do you know?"

"Because no one ever does."

My gut instinct was to argue with him—to take the side of soulmates and true love. But all I could think of was my own failed marriage. And my mother's warnings. And even Beckett's mom abandoning her family. I wanted to believe in happily ever after, but what evidence did I really have that it existed? That it wasn't just blind luck for a fortunate few?

"But Caroline and I fought a lot even before that," Beckett

went on. "She was always on me about being so closed-off. She claimed she could never tell how I felt. And she said I never prioritized her or us over work." He shrugged. "Which was true. I didn't."

"Beckett," I scolded lightly.

"What? Should I have lied? Pretended to feel something I didn't?" he asked, a little testy. "This is why I don't do relationships. I don't want to have to explain my feelings constantly. And I don't want to lie."

"No. I didn't mean that." I sighed, shaking my head. "It's good that you're honest. Sam told me a bunch of bullshit about how much he valued family to get me to marry him and move to Ohio. Turns out, his job was always more important. Also, his gym membership, his hair, and his extracurricular love life."

Beckett's jaw clenched, and he tipped up his beer.

"But I'm finally rid of him, and I made myself a solemn promise—no more jerks." I paused. "Even though that seems to be the only type of guy I ever attract."

Beckett opened his mouth, and then closed it. Took another drink.

"What? Say it."

"It's nothing."

I gave him a flat look. "Beckett. We've known each other too long for that."

"I was just thinking that's the only type of guy you ever *chose*."

My shoulders drooped. "You're right. My track record sucks."

Beckett exhaled, pinching the bridge of his nose. "Fuck, Maddie. I'm sorry. I shouldn't have said that."

"It's fine. It's the truth."

He paused. "Can I ask you something?"

"Go ahead."

He looked at me intently. "Why *did* you always choose

jerks? You could have had anybody."

Heat rushed my face, and I looked at my lap. "I don't know about that."

"I do."

Swallowing hard, I met his eyes again. They were so blue and soft and curious. I wanted to spill my guts to him, tell him all the things I wouldn't let myself say back then.

But I couldn't. Even after all this time, I just couldn't.

"I don't know why I chose jerks," I lied. "I guess I was just young and stupid."

"You were never stupid, Maddie. You were the smartest person I knew. That's why I always wondered."

His deep, quiet voice made the butterflies in my stomach whirl and flip and crash into one another. *Go home, butterflies,* I thought. *You're drunk.*

I picked at the label on my beer bottle. "You know, you asked me that question once before."

"I did?"

"Yes. It was before prom, and you asked me why I was with Jason. We were here studying, but I was upset, so we went outside." I glanced at him. "You remember?"

He swallowed. "Yes."

"You kissed me that day," I blurted.

His eyes held mine, but he said nothing.

"We never talked about it."

"What was there to talk about? You had a boyfriend. I shouldn't have done it."

"Maybe not, but I was glad you did."

He stared at me like he didn't believe it. "Why?"

"Because it made me feel good." I managed a smile, although my throat had grown tight. "Even if you only did it because you felt sorry for me."

"You think I did it because I felt *sorry* for you?"

"Well . . . yes." I felt confused. "Wasn't that the reason?"

"Uh, no. That was not the reason." He laughed a little and shook his head.

"How was I supposed to know the reason? You never said anything!"

"I think I was hoping that kiss would have a different effect on you," he said wryly.

"Like what?"

"Like maybe you'd realize that your boyfriend was a fucking asshole and you'd go to the prom with me instead."

I stared at him. "Beckett. You didn't ask me."

"I couldn't—you had a boyfriend." Shaking his head, he took another drink. "Anyway, it doesn't matter now."

"I guess not." But somehow it felt like it did. I picked at the label on the bottle again. "Who did you end up asking?"

"Uh . . ." He had to think. "Katie Keaton. Because you told me to."

"I did?"

He nodded. "I'm pretty sure it was your idea."

"Did you have fun?"

"Yeah. She wasn't too thrilled when I said I was leaving to take you home. But it was okay."

I remembered how Beckett had walked me to the door—I'd been a sobbing mess—and made sure I got in okay, never once laying a finger on me. Not even a hug. "Well, good. I'm glad one of us had a nice romantic night."

"I didn't say it was romantic."

"You mean you didn't get lucky?"

He made a noise at the back of his throat. "I didn't get *that* kind of lucky until college. I was the only one of my friends who waited that long."

"I love that. It shows that it really meant something to you."

That made him laugh.

"It wasn't meaningful?"

"It was too fast to be meaningful. She was more experienced, and I had no idea what I was doing."

"Come on, it couldn't have been that bad."

"Oh. It was," he assured me. "It was so bad, she felt sorry for me and offered to give me a few tips on what girls liked."

My jaw dropped. "Seriously?"

"Yeah. It was quite an education."

I tried to imagine what he might have learned and immediately pictured his head between my thighs, right here on the couch. Heat swept across my chest and back, and desire fluttered at my core. Hot and woozy, I had to set my beer bottle down and take off my cardigan.

Beckett watched me set my sweater aside. "What about you?"

"What about me?" I picked up my beer again and took a sip, desperate for something to cool me off.

"Who was your first?"

I winced, unhappy with the memory. "Jason. He was always pressuring me, and one day I just gave in. It wasn't romantic. Or good."

"That makes me want to kick his ass all over again."

I smiled at him. "If I could go back, I'd do it all differently."

"Would you?"

"Yeah." I finished my beer and studied the bottle in my hands. "I slept with Jason because I was looking for something that felt like love. I didn't have the real thing."

"You could have," he said quietly.

My breath caught, and I looked over at him. "What?"

"Nothing." His cheeks colored, and he stood up. "It's late. I should—"

Just then, a door opened and Mr. Weaver appeared in his pajamas. "Have either of you seen Cynthia Mae?"

CHAPTER 5
BECKETT

"SHE'S NOT HERE, DAD," I said firmly, surprised at how even my voice sounded. My insides felt like I was on a runaway horse.

"But I was with her this afternoon. Now I can't find her."

I tossed back the rest of my beer and set the bottle down on the coffee table. "Come on, it's late. Back to bed."

"But did she call?" he persisted as I walked toward him.

"Not today," I said truthfully.

Actually, the fucking truth was that she hadn't called in thirty-two years.

"Shouldn't we at least check that answering machine thing?" he asked.

"I already checked it." Placing my hands on my dad's shoulders, I turned him toward his bedroom. "No messages."

I didn't even look at Maddie as I steered my father through the bedroom door. But I felt her eyes on me.

DiMaggio, curled up in his dog bed in the corner of the room, picked up his head when we entered. "Go back to sleep, boy," I told him.

I sent my dad into the bathroom to guard against a night-time accident, and while I waited for him, I berated myself for all the shit I'd just said to Maddie. What the hell was the point in dredging up the way I felt about her back then? Or asking her why she liked jerks? Was I trying to punish her? What was I expecting her to say about it *now*?

Maybe it was the alcohol. Talking about my feelings was *not* something I normally did—it was something I avoided. But Maddie was so easy to talk to, and even though I'd never admit it, life here could get lonely.

Anyway, I wasn't sure what the fuck was going on with me tonight, but as soon as I got my dad settled, I needed to say goodnight and get the hell upstairs before I said something I'd seriously regret in the morning.

Or worse, put my hands on her.

I suppressed a groan, thinking of her bare legs, the scent of her perfume, the way she'd peeled that sweater off her shoulders. One glimpse of her cleavage in that little white tank top and I'd nearly lost my mind and said *don't stop there.*

Christ, I was a dick. All she wanted was for me to be a friend to her. Not another asshole who wanted to get her clothes off. For fuck's sake, she'd just gotten divorced. Her child was upstairs. She was here because she *trusted* me.

My dad came out of the bathroom and I put him back to bed, glad when he didn't fight me. "See you in the morning," I said, pulling the bedroom door shut behind me.

Maddie wasn't on the couch anymore, and I thought maybe she'd already gone upstairs. But I found her in the kitchen, standing at the sink rinsing out our empty beer bottles.

"Got a returnables bin?" she asked.

"In the garage. I'll take care of it. You can go up to bed." I took the empty bottles from her and ducked through the mudroom into the garage, dropping each bottle into the bin with a clank. But when I went back into the kitchen, she was still standing there, leaning back against the sink, her hands draped over the edge of the counter.

"Is your dad okay?" she asked.

"He's fine. He sometimes has trouble sleeping."

"Who's Cynthia Mae?" Her voice was quiet. "Was that your mom?"

"Yeah."

"Does he—does he do that often? Ask where she is?"

"Lately he does."

"And she's been gone for how long?"

"Thirty-two years."

Her mouth turned down. "That's tough."

Leaning back against the counter, I folded my arms over my chest. "The weird thing is, he *never* talked about her when I was growing up. So to hear her name now is sort of jarring."

She came over and stood next to me, so we were hip to hip. "Do you remember her?"

"No." I hesitated. "Sometimes I think I do, but I was so young it's not likely. I've only seen pictures."

"Why'd she leave?"

"I don't know for sure. It wasn't something we ever talked about." I paused. "She wasn't from here—she worked for an out-of-state developer that was putting up condos on the beach. Maybe she thought life on a ranch would be something different than it was. Something easier."

"That could be true."

"Or maybe she just up and changed her mind about having a family. Maybe she fell for someone else and ran off with him." I shrugged. "Who knows?"

She rubbed my back. "I'm sorry."

"It's fine. It was a long time ago. And she's just *one* of the things from his long-term memory butting into his short-term memory. It's like he's trying to fill the gaps in his mind, and the past is the only material he's got."

"Sometimes the past is so real though, don't you think? I mean, just being back here is making me feel seventeen again.

The memories are so vivid. The emotions so close to the surface."

Fucking tell me about it.

She looked up at me, her hand still on my shoulder blade. "He's lucky to have you."

Since I was about to lose my mind and kiss her, I decided it was time to say goodnight. "Well, it's late. I'm going to turn in."

"Same," she said, stifling a yawn.

"Go on upstairs. I'll turn off all the lights and make sure the house is locked up." I kept my arms crossed over my chest, fists clenched beneath my biceps, praying she wouldn't hug me.

"Okay. Goodnight, Beckett."

"Night." I held my breath until I heard her footsteps on the stairs, and then exhaled.

Jesus. The next two weeks were going to be torture. How was it possible that fifteen years had gone by, and I still struggled to breathe normally when she was in the room?

After making sure all the doors were locked, I turned off the kitchen lights and went into the great room. The lamp was still on, and I noticed that Maddie's light blue sweater was still on the couch. I picked it up.

It was light and soft, and for a moment, I just stood there with it in my hands. Then I lifted it to my face, inhaling deeply. The smell of her perfume sent heat radiating up my spine.

A noise from the direction of the stairs made me turn, and my adrenaline spiked. Fuck—was she there? Had she seen me sniffing her clothing like a creep?

My heart hammered as my eyes frantically searched the dark, but I was alone. Breathing a sigh of relief, I draped the sweater over the arm of the couch, turned off the lamp, and made my way upstairs in the dark.

Maddie's door was shut, and the light was off.

Thank God.

Inside my bedroom, I got ready for bed and slipped between the sheets. Normally I had no trouble falling asleep, but tonight, I lay on my back for a while, staring at the ceiling.

If I was another kind of guy—a guy like Moretti maybe, or even Griffin—I might have worked up the confidence to kiss her tonight. Flirt with her. Touch her. Maybe even invite her up to my room.

But that wasn't me.

I'd never been a player or a ladies' man. I never chased anyone. I liked sex as much as anybody, but I had no problem saying no to it, especially if I suspected the encounter would come with expectations. As Caroline had been fond of pointing out, I was a shit boyfriend.

You never put me first.

You're distant and detached.

You give nothing emotionally.

But I couldn't offer what I didn't feel.

Would it be different with Maddie?

I had no idea, but God, I wanted her.

I thought about her soft skin and the scent of her sweater and the way those full lips might feel moving across my chest. I thought about my hands in her hair, my tongue in her mouth, easing my thick, hard cock inside her body. I imagined the way she'd move, the sound of her breath, the way those green eyes would pop if I said all the filthy things I was thinking. Or just did them.

Groaning inwardly, I got up and made sure my door was closed all the way. Then I got back in bed, tossed the covers aside, and slipped my hand into my boxer briefs. Fisted my cock. Stroked once. Twice. Three times.

Pictured her on the couch. Her shoulders. Her hands wrapped around the beer bottle. Her bare legs. If we'd been alone in the house tonight, I'd have taken off those little shorts. Buried my face between her thighs. Fucked her with my tongue.

Then I'd have picked her up and carried her to the stairs. Maybe we wouldn't even have made it to the bedroom. Maybe I'd have taken her right there on the steps—her back against the wall, her legs wrapped around me, my cock driving inside her over and over again.

And she wanted it. She wanted me.

As I worked my hand up and down my hot, hard flesh, I imagined words dripping from her lips into the darkness.

Yes. Now. Harder.

Fuck me. Don't stop.

Never knew it could be like this . . .

Your cock is so deep, you feel so good . . .

You're gonna make me come—so close, so close, so close—

Pulsing heat erupted inside me, releasing the tension in short, rhythmic bursts of slick heat all over my fist and stomach. Struggling to stay silent, I clenched my jaw and fucked my hand, wishing it was her, angry that it wasn't and probably never would be. Why did I have to want her so badly?

Afterward, I lay back, breathing hard, heart pounding. A moment later, I got up and went to the bathroom.

As I cleaned up, the anger faded and I couldn't help feeling a little guilty about what I'd done. She was always my favorite fantasy, but it did seem wrong to get myself off to her while she was in my house. But I supposed it was a better idea than risking our friendship by making an impulsive move I'd regret.

Returning to the bedroom, I pulled my door open partially, listened for a moment, and heard nothing. Across the hall, Maddie's door was shut, and I stood there for a few seconds, staring at it.

Did she ever touch herself at night? Who did she think about? Was it ever me?

If I'd knocked softly on her bedroom door tonight instead

of taking matters into my own hands, would she have welcomed me in or turned me away?

Maybe it was better not to know.

The following morning, I was a little groggy as I got dressed. When I left my room, Maddie's door was still closed, and so was Elliott's. It was barely five-thirty, and I didn't want to wake them, so I kept my footsteps quiet on the stairs. It was possible Elliott had decided the early wakeup was too brutal and chosen to sleep in instead—I didn't blame him. At his age, I hadn't liked getting up before sunrise either.

That's why I was shocked to see both Maddie and Elliott already awake and dressed and waiting for me in the kitchen.

"Good morning," Maddie said softly, flashing me a smile that made my chest tighten. She was seated at the kitchen island with a cup of coffee in her hands, and she wore a green top that matched her eyes. "Can I get you a cup of coffee? I made a whole pot."

"Good morning. I can get it, thanks." With the image of fucking her on the stairs in my head, I went to the cupboard and took down a mug. After filling it, I took a deep breath and turned around. "You two are up early."

"Elliott was so excited, he couldn't sleep." Maddie laughed, leaning over to ruffle his curls. "He came into my room before four and asked if it was time to get up yet. I had to put him back to bed."

Elliott grinned sheepishly and took a sip of his orange juice.

I laughed too. "Not even I get out there that early."

"What time does your dad wake up?" Maddie asked.

"I usually get him up once I'm in from the morning

chores. But he sometimes wanders out sooner, which is fine as long as he doesn't try to use the stove. The last time he did that, he forgot he'd put eggs in the pan." I shook my head. "It wasn't good."

"Have you thought about those safety guards? Although he's handy, so he'd probably figure out how to remove them." She pressed her lips together. "It's hard, isn't it? He's an adult, but you have to worry about him like you would a child. Yet you can't treat him that way, because he's still got enough cognitive function that it's probably incredibly frustrating and annoying for him."

"Yep." I took another sip of hot coffee, not that the caffeine was going to help calm my racing heart. "That's it exactly."

Her eyebrows knit together. "Why don't you take Elliott out to help you with the chores and I'll stay here and get breakfast going? That way if he wakes up and wanders out, I'll be here to make sure he's okay."

"That would be great, but I don't want you to feel like you have to babysit him." I hesitated. "Chances are, he'll have forgotten your name and what you're doing here. He might get ornery with you."

She waved a hand in the air. "Listen, I'm probably useless at farm work, but I know how to cook and how to talk to people."

"Okay. We'll give it a try. If he gives you any trouble, just pour him some coffee and a bowl of Cap'n Crunch."

"Cap'n Crunch?" Her head fell back as she laughed.

"Yes. He loves it. I don't let him have it that often, because it's just a bowl full of sugar, but it distracts him in a pinch."

"Got it. But I think we'll be fine."

A few minutes later, Elliott and I headed out. He wore the pink boots again today, with blue jeans and a gray hoodie. The unicorn barrette I'd noticed yesterday was fastened in his hair again. I wondered if kids ever made fun of him for liking "girly" things like unicorns and the color pink.

Yesterday Maddie had mentioned wanting him to grow up unafraid to be himself—did that mean he'd already been subjected to mean comments or name-calling? I glanced at the little guy walking next to me, so excited to help out and spend time caring for the animals, and felt a wave of protectiveness.

"Come on," I said, nudging his shoulder. "We can start by feeding the goats."

After the morning chores were finished, we went back inside the house, where the aroma of sautéed onions made my mouth water.

In the kitchen, Maddie was pulling a big iron skillet full of eggs from the oven. My father sat at the table in his pajamas and robe, his hair messy. But he appeared to be enjoying his cup of coffee and I saw no sign of Cap'n Crunch.

"Wow," I said, as Maddie set the skillet on top of the stove. "What's that?"

"Nothing fancy," Maddie said. "Baked eggs with greens and caramelized onions. You guys were quick out there."

"It was quick because Elliott was so helpful." I smiled at her son. "He's really good with the animals."

"The goats are my favorite," said Elliott, who'd left his dirty boots in the mudroom next to mine and stood beaming in his socks. He hugged himself. "They're so cuddly."

"Go upstairs real quick and wash your face and hands," said Maddie as she sprinkled parmesan cheese over the eggs, "and you can tell me all about it."

I scrubbed my hands at the sink and poured another cup of coffee before sitting across from my father. The table was set for four, complete with actual napkins, not just paper towels. A plate stacked with toast and a bowl full of green apple slices was out, as well as a pitcher of orange juice. "Morning, Dad."

"Morning." He glanced over at Maddie in the kitchen and spoke conspiratorially. "That lady was here when I woke up."

"That's Maddie Blake, remember? She arrived yesterday. She's going to stay with us a couple weeks."

"She seems nice," he said. "And she reminds me of someone."

"Oh yeah?" I lifted my cup. "Who?"

"I'm not sure. Maybe it'll come to me." He shrugged. "She said she'd take me to town today."

"What do you need in town?"

"To get a haircut," he said, as Maddie set a trivet on the table and the iron skillet on top of it.

Rather than remind him he'd just gotten a haircut yesterday, I chose to move on, recalling how his doctor had told me that trying to set the record straight all the time only led to anger and frustration for both of us. "This looks incredible, Maddie. Thanks for making breakfast. We don't normally eat so well in the morning, do we, Dad?"

But my dad was studying Elliott, who'd sat down in the chair next to him. "Who are you?"

"I'm Elliott," he said, reaching for a piece of toast.

I spoke loudly and clearly. "Elliott is Maddie's son."

"Oh." He studied Elliott for a moment. "Are you staying here too?"

"Yes," Elliott replied.

"Well, good. That's good." My dad nodded in satisfaction. "You'll like it here. Sometimes they don't let you out when you ask, but mostly the people are nice."

"Thanks," I said drily, taking another sip of coffee. Maddie laughed softly beside me, placing a hand on my knee. She only left it there a second, but my body reacted as if she'd unzipped my jeans beneath the table.

"I told your father I'd take him into town later," she said, serving Elliott some eggs.

"See?" my dad said, pointing at her as if I'd accused him of lying about her offer.

"That's fine, as long as it's not too much trouble." I shifted in my chair, trying to adjust the crotch of my jeans, which had grown hot and tight.

She smiled as she handed Dad the spatula. "It's not."

"Beckett said he'd take me for a ride in a four-by-four," Elliott said excitedly. "He has to go check on the fences and he said I can come and maybe even drive."

"If it's okay with your mom," I said quickly.

"It's fine." Maddie placed some apples on Elliott's plate. "But you have to finish your whole breakfast."

"And he said he can teach me how to hit home runs today!"

Laughing, Maddie sat down and picked up her fork. "That's a lot in one day."

"I've got some help this afternoon, so I should be able to finish up what I need to by about three," I explained, serving myself some eggs. "And then I thought I'd take Elliott over to the ball field for a little batting practice."

"That sounds great. He'll love it."

"Dad, you can come too, if you'd like," I offered. "We can go after your nap."

"Okay." Then he leaned toward Elliott. "That's another thing. They make you take naps here."

"I hate naps," said Elliott.

Maddie gave her son a piercing look. "That's enough. Eat."

Throughout the meal, Elliott jabbered away about feeding the animals and gathering eggs, my father interrupted with stories about baseball, and Maddie listened intently to them both. She also repeated her name for my dad at least three times but never with a trace of impatience.

As for me, I mostly stayed silent. I was often quiet in a crowd, not because I was bored or inattentive, but because I never felt the need to hear myself talk, and I learned a lot about other people by observing them. For instance, I could tell Maddie was a loving, playful mom who always maintained her sense of humor while still being firm about the rules. I could tell that she'd raised a polite, sensitive, inquisitive child. I could tell that my dad felt comfortable with them and wanted to impress them too. He trotted out his Willie Mays catch as well as the time he'd hit a grand slam to win the state tournament his senior year of high school. (At least that one was true.)

"That reminds me," Dad went on, looking at Maddie. "You think you can give me a ride to the train station today?"

"I think maybe we can fit that in," she said companionably. "But I'll definitely need you to show me around town first. It's been a long time since I went shopping in Bellamy Creek. I won't know where anything is."

My dad looked pleased. "I can do that. I've lived here all my life. I won't even need a map."

"Great! After I get these breakfast dishes done, we'll head out."

"I'll go get dressed," he said, pushing back from the table.

"You want help, Dad?" I asked.

He gave me a look like I was nuts, even though I laid out his clothes every single day. "No! And you better hurry up, or you'll miss the bus."

I watched him head for his room and shook my head. Any other day, I might have tried to give him a reality check. Demanded to know if he looked at me and saw a schoolboy or a full-grown man. Today I was able to take a breath and smile. "He'll probably come out in his pajamas. I'll check on him in a minute."

"Can I be excused?" asked Elliott. "I finished."

Maddie examined his plate. "Yes, you may. But please take your dish carefully over to the sink and put it on the counter. Then go upstairs and brush your teeth."

He gave her an exasperated look but dutifully slid off the chair and went to the sink, carrying the plate with both hands.

"Thanks for offering to stay with my dad today," I said when we were alone. "I can't tell you how helpful it is that I won't have to be worried about him all afternoon."

"I'm so glad," she said, laying her fork and knife on her empty plate and rising to her feet. "I don't mind at all, and I'd much rather spend the day window-shopping downtown than yanking weeds at my mother's place."

"But we should get on that," I told her, stacking some dishes and following her into the kitchen. "Maybe tomorrow."

She nodded, placing her dish in the sink and then standing still for a moment, looking out the window above it.

I went back to the dining table, grabbing the skillet, the toast plate, and the empty fruit bowl. When I returned, she was still standing there.

"You okay?" I asked, setting everything down on the counter.

"I'm fine." She cleared her throat and turned around, her smile sheepish. "This is going to sound so dumb, but I really enjoyed this morning."

"What about it?"

"Everything. Waking up early. Seeing Elliott so excited. Cooking breakfast. Sitting around a table and taking the time to talk and listen while we ate. Enjoying each other's company without rushing off somewhere. It felt like . . ." She struggled for the words and tossed her hands up. "Like how I always imagined having a family would be."

"Oh."

"Growing up, it was just my mother and me at meal-times," she went on, "and mostly all she did was criticize or warn me what would happen if I let up on myself. I can't tell you how many times I wished for a dad who'd make bad jokes or a brother who'd kick me under the table."

"Or a sister. Sisters kick too," I told her.

She laughed. "A sister would have been great. I'd have liked *any* siblings. I wanted more kids too, but Sam didn't."

"I'm sorry."

Her shoulders rose. "Maybe I'm just meant to have Elliott, and I'm fine with that. I love being his mom and I get to take care of kids at work too. But I still wanted—this," she finished, gesturing to the room around us. "Sam rarely ate breakfast with us. He was out of the house every morning before Elliott and I were even awake because he liked getting a workout in before going to the office. And he came home too late every night to have dinner with Elliott and me. It got lonely."

I thought about the meals my dad and sisters and I had while I was growing up, seated around the old kitchen table, dogs underfoot, my sisters both jabbering at once, and my father trying to hear Ernie Harwell calling the Tigers game on the scratchy AM radio he refused to get rid of because he said it brought his team luck. Those dinners were noisy and not terribly delicious and usually followed by an argument about whose turn it was to do the dishes, but they were never lonely.

How could her ex not have appreciated what he had?

"Anyway." Maddie stood taller and brightened up. "My point wasn't to get mopey, it was to thank you for inviting me here. I'm so glad I came."

"You'll always be welcome."

She smiled. "Thanks."

On my way out to the barn, I tried to think of *one thing* that would be better than seeing that smile at the breakfast table every morning.

Nothing came to mind.

Not one fucking thing.

CHAPTER 6
MADDIE

"THAT'S THE BELLAMY CREEK GARAGE," Mr. Weaver told me, pointing across the street to the old firehouse that had been repurposed into an auto repair shop decades ago by Griffin Dempsey's family. "Frank Griffin owns it."

I was fairly certain Griffin's father was gone now, but I nodded and smiled. "I should take my car in for a tune-up. I noticed it was making a funny noise on the way here."

"You should," he said. "You won't get better service anywhere else."

"Thanks for the tip."

Mr. Weaver moved slowly, but it was a gorgeous day, and I had no problem at all with his leisurely pace as we strolled up and down Bellamy Creek's Main Street, ducking in and out of stores. Some had been there forever and some were brand new to me, but every shopkeeper we saw greeted Mr. Weaver fondly and introduced themselves to me—some of them even remembered me or mentioned knowing my mom. While Mr. Weaver didn't seem to recognize anyone, he'd always shake their hands and nod hello.

Out on the street, he was playing the role of tour guide and seemed to enjoy every minute of it.

"See that building there?" He pointed at the old Main Street Theater. "That's where I took my first date."

"Really?" I linked my arm with his. "Tell me about it."

"Her name was Evie Clemson, and I took her to see *Vertigo*. She looked just like Kim Novak."

"A beauty, huh?"

He nodded. "Prettiest girl in our class."

"Did you have a nice time?"

"Yes," he said, "although after the show, we went to the diner and I accidentally dumped a chocolate malt in her lap."

"Oh, no," I said, laughing. "Did you have to take her home early?"

He shook his head. "Not that I recall. We were having too much fun. She was a good sport." Suddenly he stopped, scratching his head. "I must have gotten turned around. The shoe store should be right there. And next to it the five-and-dime."

I glanced at the storefront he was looking at and saw a striped awning that read Bellamy Creek Boulangerie in elegant script. "Oh, how cute," I said. "It looks like a little Parisian pâtisserie."

"Oh, wait a minute," he said. "I think this is the place with the apple pie."

I recalled Beckett telling me about Blair Dempsey's bakery last night and figured this must be the place. "Should we go in? Maybe we can bring home a pie for dessert."

Mr. Weaver liked that idea and moved ahead to open the door for me. Inside, the décor was bright and charming and French-inspired—small round café tables, tiny white octagonal floor tiles, huge display cases showing off dozens of pastries, quiches, and breads. I'd never been to Paris, but I felt like I'd stepped off the Champs-Elysées rather than Main Street. I breathed in deeply—the aroma made my mouth water and my stomach growl.

"We should have breakfast," Mr. Weaver said, moving toward the display case full of croissants and scones.

"Well, we had breakfast, but how about lunch?" I glanced around, spying an empty table near the front window. "We can sit right over there."

"Okay." He began to study the offerings closely, leaning forward, his nose practically against the glass.

"Hi, Mr. Weaver!" called a woman from behind the counter. Her honey-blond hair was pulled back into a pony-tail, and she wore a bandana like a headband, the knot at the top of her head. She was strikingly beautiful, with big eyes, thick lashes, and a friendly smile. "How are you?"

"Good." He looked up and struggled to place her.

"Blair Dempsey," she said, placing a hand on her chest. "Griffin's wife." Then she looked at me, her smile widening. "And you must be Maddie."

"Yes," I said, surprised that she knew my name.

"Griff and I saw Bianca and Enzo last night," she explained. "They talked about seeing the house with you."

"Oh." I returned her smile. "It's so nice to meet you."

"Can I have the strata?" Mr. Weaver asked.

"You sure can," Blair replied. "I used eggs from your chickens to make it this morning. Maddie, would you like to try some?"

"Yes, please. It looks delicious."

"Go ahead and take a seat. I'll bring it over to you."

"Should I pay for it now or afterward?"

She waved a hand. "It's on me. I never charge the Weavers because Beckett is always giving me eggs or veggies from the farm for free. Or handing out steaks to his friends."

I laughed. "That sounds like a nice arrangement."

"It is."

Mr. Weaver and I sat down at the table by the window, and a moment later, Blair came by with two plates of strata and two settings of silverware wrapped in napkins and tied with twine. "Here you go," she said, setting them down. "Bon appétit."

"Thank you," I said, untying the twine.

Blair smiled. "Hey, any chance you could meet up later? Bianca, Cheyenne, and I are going to grab a glass of wine after dinner. Just the girls."

"I wish I could. But my son is in town with me, and I wouldn't feel right about leaving him."

"Well, give it some thought. I bet Beckett and Mr. Weaver would love to have a guys' night. They can watch the baseball game. Nothing they like more than baseball." She patted his shoulder. "Right, Mr. Weaver?"

He nodded. "Did I ever tell you about the catch I made over my shoulder in center field?"

"I'm not sure," she said, glancing toward the counter. "But I've got a customer, so I'll remind you to tell me about it next time." She winked at me. "If you can come tonight, grab my number from Beckett. I'm pretty sure he has it."

"I've actually got Bianca's card," I said.

"Perfect." She beamed. "Hope you can make it. Good to see you, Mr. Weaver."

He waved goodbye, barely looking up from his plate. I didn't blame him—the strata was delectable.

Before we left, I complimented Blair on the meal and asked if we could get an apple pie to take home.

"Of course." She boxed it up, tying it with twine, and shook her head when I took out my wallet. "Nope. On the house."

Sticking a twenty-dollar bill in her employee tip jar, I met her murderous stare with a triumphant smile. "Thanks again for lunch. Hopefully I'll see you soon."

Mr. Weaver and I walked back to the car, which was parked along a side street. On the driver's side, I unlocked the doors and placed the pie on the floor in the back seat, while he stood at the passenger side, looking around.

"Was there anything else you wanted to do downtown?" I asked.

"I don't think so," he said. "But I could have sworn the train station was right around here somewhere."

"I think it moved," I told him honestly.

"I think you're right." He looked despondent. "Maybe I could take a bus to the game. Or you could give me a ride."

"Tell you what," I said, since I'd learned quickly that distracting him was the best way to deal with this situation. "Let's head back to the house and see what Beckett thinks."

"Good idea. Beckett's smart about some things." He paused. "Not everything. But some things."

When Beckett heard about Blair inviting me to join the girls for a glass of wine, he encouraged me to go.

"Why not? It would be fun," he said as we walked from the car to the baseball field later that afternoon. He carried a duffel bag full of equipment—balls, a couple gloves, a batter's helmet.

"What about Elliott?" I looked at my son, who was scampering ahead, carrying a bat, wearing a Bellamy Creek Bulldogs cap. He'd been grinning ear to ear since the moment Beckett had put it on his head.

"He'll be fine. We'll have a guys' night. We'll watch the game."

I laughed. "I don't want you to think I expect you to babysit my kid. You had him all afternoon. Did he slow you down?"

"Not a bit. And it was a huge relief knowing you were with my dad today." Beckett spoke quietly so his father, walking slightly ahead of us, wouldn't hear. "I never worried about him once, and I was able to get much more done in half a day than I often can in a full day because I didn't have to keep coming inside to check on him. Elliott is an excellent listener and a fast learner."

"Well, I'm glad. And your father was no trouble at all. We actually had a nice time."

"Did he try to escape?"

"Nope. He was my tour guide. He gets bonus points for knowing what stood where fifty years ago, and for all the cool historical stories. For instance, did you know that the building where DiFiore's Italian restaurant is now used to be the stagecoach stop for Bellamy Creek?"

"I did not," he said.

"Or that Blair's bakery used to be a five-and-dime?"

"Didn't know that either."

"Did you know he took his first date to see *Vertigo* at the Main Street Theater, and she looked *just* like Kim Novak?"

He snorted. "Of course she did. And he made a great over-the-shoulder catch in 1954."

"And afterward, he took her to the diner for a chocolate malt, and he was so nervous he spilled his all over her."

That made him laugh. "Poor Dad."

"He made me fall a little in love with Bellamy Creek again. There's so much history here, and everyone was so sweet and friendly. It made me sad I've stayed away so long." I elbowed him playfully. "You should ask him about his stories sometime."

"The only ones he ever tells me are about baseball—and half of those aren't even his."

"Well, maybe you could ask him more specific questions. Or next time you take him downtown, let him play tour guide for you."

"He probably prefers you," he said, nudging my side. It was the kind of affectionate touch that might have been flirting, except that Beckett never flirted with me.

Or did he?

He was so hard to read. Every time I thought maybe he was looking at me a little differently, a little hungrily, the moment would evaporate, and I was left doubting it happened at all.

Like last night.

I'd realized when I got up to my bedroom that I'd left my sweater on the couch, and I'd silently tiptoed back down the steps to grab it.

Just as I reached the bottom of the stairs, I saw him standing next to the couch with his face buried in blue cashmere.

I'd stopped and stared, blinking at him in the low light. He held the sweater to his face for a moment, and I saw his shoulders rise, as if he were inhaling deeply.

A noise escaped me—a quick, high-pitched gasp.

Desperate to escape unseen, I darted back up the stairs two at a time, then slipped into my room and carefully shut the door so it made no sound.

After snapping off the light, I sank down on the edge of the bed and placed a hand over my thundering heart. It was so loud that I *thought* I heard Beckett come up the stairs a moment later, but I wasn't sure.

That was the thing—I couldn't be sure about *any* of it. I spent the entire night tossing and turning, and by morning I'd been convinced the whole episode was in my mind. After all, I'd definitely been tipsy after those beers. And this morning at breakfast, he'd been business as usual. No lingering looks, no flirty comments, and certainly no touching. Beckett was a man who always kept his hands to himself.

For the first time in my life, I sort of wished he wasn't.

We spent a solid hour at the ball field, and I took pictures and video of Beckett teaching Elliott how to grip the bat, keep his eye on the ball, and step into his swing. He also taught him some base-running tips, such as taking a couple shuffle steps before pivoting and running from first to second as quickly as possible. Of course, Elliott missed ninety-nine percent of the balls Beckett patiently "pitched" at him, and he wasn't a terribly quick or coordinated athlete, but he was having the time of his life out there on the field.

Mr. Weaver served as catcher for a while, throwing balls back to Beckett with a surprisingly good arm, and then joined me on one of the dugout benches in the shade.

"What do you think?" I asked him. "Is he destined for a career in the Majors?"

Beckett's dad scratched his head and answered diplomatically, "I'm not sure."

Laughing, I snapped another shot of Beckett helping Elliott choke up on the bat and widen his stance. Miraculously, he hit the very next ball Beckett lobbed at him from about fifteen feet away. Stunned, Elliott stood still for a moment, watching the ball.

Beckett, who could easily have grabbed the ball out of the air, "missed" it in dramatic fashion, jumping for it and falling to the ground with an empty glove.

Elliott started to crack up.

Next to me, Mr. Weaver got to his feet. "Run!" he hollered through his hands.

Elliott took off for first base, both hands on his helmet because it was too big for him. While Beckett chased the ball, fumbling and dropping it several times, Elliott rounded first and headed for second.

"Keep going!" shouted Mr. Weaver, shuffling as fast as he could over to stand along the third baseline.

Beckett pretended he was going to throw the ball to third,

cocking his arm way back—then stopped. "What? No third baseman! Then I'll have to tag you, runner!"

Elliott, who was rounding third, looked at Mr. Weaver, who was waving him home. The smile on his face nearly blinded me.

"Go! Go! Go!" I cheered, clapping my hands.

Beckett was making a beeline for home plate, yet somehow managed to look like he was struggling hard to beat Elliott there.

"Slide!" Mr. Weaver yelled.

I winced as Elliott, who'd never slid into a base in his life, dove headfirst toward the plate, arms outstretched—more of a belly flop than a slide. The helmet bounced off.

"Nooooo!" Beckett reached home plate and tagged Elliott's back with the ball a full second too late.

"Safe!" Mr. Weaver spread his arms, palms down. "Home run!"

I snapped a quick picture. "Great job, Elliott!"

He got to his feet, sweaty and dirty, but glowing with pride. "Thanks."

I went jogging out to the plate. "Did you hurt yourself?"

"Nah," he said, but he rubbed one knee and then both elbows.

"That was awesome." Beckett clapped him on the back. "You did a great job running the bases and looking to the coach for the sign to keep going."

"Did you like the slide?" Elliott asked, looking up hopefully.

"I loved it," Beckett replied, scooping up the batter's helmet. "I'd say you won the game for your team and deserve an ice cream cone."

"That sounds good to me too." I smiled gratefully at Beckett.

He shrugged, like it was no big deal, although the color in

his cheeks deepened slightly. Was he flushed from exertion? The sun?

Or was there something heating up between us?

"You're sure it's okay if I go?" I asked, lingering in the kitchen with my keys in my hands. Earlier I'd texted Bianca that I could make it to girls' night, and she'd replied with a bunch of happy emojis and said they were meeting at seven o'clock at a wine bar called The Avignon.

"I'm positive." Beckett snipped the twine on the bakery box containing the apple pie and opened it up. "I mean, I think you're crazy for choosing wine and fancy French cheese over beer and good old American apple pie, but that's just me."

I laughed, watching him lift the pie from the box and set it on the counter. "It does look good. Maybe I'll have a piece when I get home."

"If there's any left."

"You three are going to eat that *whole pie*?"

"We might." He took plates down from the cupboard. "I could probably eat half of it by myself. I'm a big guy."

"A gentleman would at least save me a small piece," I teased.

He glanced at me over one broad shoulder. "Then I guess you'll just have to wait and see if I'm in the mood to be a gentleman tonight."

My stomach flipped. For a second, I felt flustered and tongue-tied—which was silly. For God's sake, he was just talking about saving me some apple pie . . . right?

"Uh, I told Elliott he could stay up until I got home, but

that he should take a shower and put his pajamas on at eight, eight-thirty at the latest."

"Got it."

"And he can have a piece of pie and maybe a snack, but no pop."

"Okay."

"But he probably shouldn't have too much to drink after eight, or else he might have an accident."

"Understood."

I glanced down at my jeans and plain white T-shirt, which I'd dressed up with my wedge sandals and some delicate gold jewelry. "Am I dressed okay?"

"You look great."

"You didn't even look at me."

"I didn't have to."

I smiled, feeling heat in my cheeks. "Thanks. I'm sure I'll be back by nine, but feel free to call me if you need me to come home sooner."

Finally, he turned around, his expression a little exasperated. "Maddie. Go. I can handle things here. Elliott's a breeze. He's helpful, polite, and unlike some other people living here, I bet he doesn't argue when you tell him Ronald Reagan isn't the U.S. President."

I laughed again. "Okay, I'm going. Have fun."

The drive to The Avignon took about ten minutes, during which I obsessed over what Beckett had said to me.

I guess you'll just have to wait and see if I'm in the mood to be a gentleman tonight.

It was hard not to wonder if the boundary between us was shifting.

Or what would happen if one of us crossed it.

The moment I stepped through The Avignon's glass door, I heard my name.

"Maddie! Over here!"

I looked in the direction of the voice and spotted Bianca waving at me. She was seated with Blair and another woman who had a sandy blond ponytail at a high-top table near the bar. When I reached them, I immediately recognized the woman with sandy hair as Cheyenne Dempsey, Griffin's younger sister.

"Hey," I said, smiling at all of them as I slid onto the fourth stool at the table. "It's so good to see you. Thank you so much for inviting me out tonight."

"Of course," said Bianca, who was perched on the stool to my right. "We're glad you could make it."

"Gosh, you haven't changed a bit." Cheyenne smiled at me from across the table, and I remembered what a bubbly, friendly girl she'd been. "You look exactly the same as you did in high school."

"Well, thanks, but I've got some crow's feet and stretch marks that say otherwise," I said, setting my phone on the table and my purse at my feet.

"I love your braids," said Blair, seated to my left.

"Thanks." I laughed nervously, touching the end of one. "I'm teaching Elliott, my son. He loves to do my hair."

"That's so cute," Cheyenne said. "There was a boy in my class last year—I'm a kindergarten teacher—whose favorite thing to do at free time or during recess was style the girls' hair." She laughed. "He was running his own little salon in the corner of the playground!"

I smiled. "That's adorable."

"I thought so—his dad did not." Cheyenne wrinkled her nose. "He's one of those super macho guys who thinks we need to dress boys in pants and girls in dresses. Boys play with trucks and girls play with dolls. Boys are loud, and girls are quiet."

"That poor kid," said Bianca with a frown. "Some people don't deserve to be parents."

"My ex was kind of like that," I admitted. "Elliott isn't a stereotypical boy either. He loves pink and unicorns and occasionally likes to wear dresses. He likes dolls and tea parties and princesses. But he also likes sports and dinosaurs and jeans."

"But there's nothing wrong with that," said Bianca fiercely.

"No, there isn't," I agreed. "And Sam, Elliott's father, might have been able to handle the unicorns and tea parties, but sometimes Elliott would fill out video game profiles on his iPad as a girl. Like it would ask for his gender, and he'd put girl."

"Why are they even asking that?" Blair shook her head.

I shrugged. "Probably for marketing purposes. But Sam freaked out about it. He said to Elliott, 'You know you're a boy. Don't lie.' As if it was a matter of dishonesty."

"What a dick," said Bianca, her blue eyes narrowing behind her glasses. "Sorry if that's offensive."

I shook my head. "It's the truth."

"So does Elliott *want* to be a girl?" Cheyenne asked curiously. "Or does he feel like he *is* one?"

"Not necessarily," I said. "I've asked him that. He said he likes being a boy, but he likes doing some things that girls get to do—like wear pink or have tea parties. He told me he put *girl* on that video game profile just for fun. I mean, the kid is six. I think it's too soon to box him into anything in terms of his identity. I just want him to feel free to be exactly who he is."

"That's the kind of mom I want to be too," said Bianca.

Then I laughed, a little embarrassed that I'd gotten so worked up. We hadn't even ordered wine yet. "Sorry, ladies. I get emotional about this—not just because of Elliott, but because I was raised by an overbearing mother who pushed me hard to be something *she* wanted me to be."

"What was that?" Blair wondered.

"A doctor, because they make a lot of money, and she never wanted me to be dependent on a man, since—her words here—men always break their promises." I sighed. "I never knew my dad, and she refused to even name him. My guess is that he was married and lied about it, but that's just a guess."

"That would definitely explain her opinion about men," said Cheyenne.

"You didn't want to be a doctor?" asked Bianca.

"I never felt free to consider what I wanted or didn't want. Not until my mother died." I paused. "Which actually led to a complete existential crisis that ended up with me quitting med school in my second year and running off to marry a guy who proved my mother right, but that's another matter entirely." I waved a hand in the air. "And I hope it doesn't sound like Elliott isn't a happy kid. He's actually really comfortable with who he is and loves himself almost as much as he loves Beckett's goats."

"Oh my God, those goats are so cute, aren't they?" Bianca grinned. "I'm more of a city girl, but even I think they're adorable."

The server came by and took our order, and a few minutes later we each had a glass of wine and a plate of cheese and charcuterie to share.

"So I want to hear about you guys," I said, after a sip of a cool Michigan white from Cloverleigh Farms. "I've known your men pretty much all my life, so it's really fun for me to hear your stories."

For the next hour, I heard all about how Blair met Griffin when her car broke down on Main Street, and she was stranded in Bellamy Creek just long enough to steal the gruff mechanic's heart. All three of them spoke in rapturous voices about Blair and Griffin's beautiful December wedding—a snowstorm had prevented many guests from attending, including Blair's family in Tennessee, but the smaller affair turned out to be more intimate and romantic than planned.

"It was perfect," Blair sighed. "I wish I could do it all over again."

"Then there was *my* wedding," said Bianca, making them all laugh.

"Beck was telling me a little about it last night," I said. "Definitely not a conventional love story, but still incredibly romantic."

"It was." Cheyenne reached over and patted Bianca's hand. "I don't care what you say, B, everyone in that courtroom could see you two were meant for each other."

"Anyway," Bianca said, blushing a little, "we did things a bit out of order, but it worked for us. I'm not sure we'd ever have ended up together any other way."

"And Cheyenne is up next!" Blair clapped her hands.

Cheyenne squeezed her eyes shut and groaned. "God, as much as I want to marry that man, I'm so nervous that I'm forgetting something. Planning a wedding in three months is not easy."

"We have been over this a thousand times." Blair spoke soothingly to her friend. "Everything is in place. It's going to be perfect."

"Everything is in place," Cheyenne repeated like a mantra, her eyes still closed. "It's going to be perfect." Then she opened them and looked at me. "Oh Maddie, you have to come!"

I smiled at her, imagining what a beautiful bride she'd make. It was also a pleasure to feel so included in their tight little group. "It's next weekend?"

"Two weeks from tonight." She giggled. "And Beckett needs a date."

I laughed nervously. "Well, I'd love to come, although I'm not sure I'd be Beckett's first choice for a date."

"Why not?" Blair asked, as Bianca and Cheyenne exchanged an *oh brother* look. "From what I hear, Beckett's always been crazy about you."

"I don't think that's true." I picked up my wine glass, which was already empty and tipped it up, hoping for a few drops.

"Um, yeah. It is." Bianca laughed, tucking her red hair behind her ears. "It's common knowledge among the guys that Beckett has been pining for you since high school. We've all heard the prom story."

"He kicked that guy's ass," said Cheyenne.

"Hard," added Blair.

My cheeks were growing warm. "That's because Beckett is a good guy. He did it to defend me."

"Beckett is a good guy," allowed Bianca, "but he did it because he *liked* you."

"Anyone else for round two?" I asked, looking around for our server.

"Definitely." Blair waved him down. "And then we're going to talk more about this Beckett thing."

"There's no thing," I insisted, fiddling with the end of one braid again. "There's never been a thing."

"Why not?" Blair pressed.

"Because we've always been just friends."

"You've never been attracted to him?"

I bit my lip, then decided to admit the truth. "I've *always* been attracted to him."

"So then why—"

"It's hard to explain," I went on. "All I can say is that I never let myself admit it."

"Enzo said you dated a lot of jerks back then." Bianca looked like she felt bad for saying it. "Was he wrong? Like, were they actually misunderstood bad boys with hearts of gold?"

"Um, no." I cringed, a twisted smile on my lips. "They were actually jerks. I've got a knack for picking them."

The server approached, and Blair put her hands up. "Okay, hold—let's come right back to this Beckett thing."

"There's no thing," I repeated weakly.

Bianca pushed her glasses up her nose. "Maddie, I saw you guys together yesterday, and the first thing I said to Enzo when we got in the car was, 'Beckett is still nuts about her.' And he said, 'Yep.'" She laughed. "It's the way he looks at you, Maddie. You can just tell."

Her words had my heart stumbling over its next few beats.

Was she right?

CHAPTER 7

MADDIE

WE EACH ORDERED ANOTHER ROUND, and while we were waiting for it, I quickly used the bathroom. Back at the table, I picked up my second glass of wine and took a sip.

"Okay," said Blair. "Let's keep talking. I'm super curious why you think Beckett has never been interested in you, yet his three best friends—who've known him since childhood—all think otherwise."

"Because he never said anything about it."

Bianca kept pushing. "Okay, but guys don't always use their words. You're saying he's never given you the *slightest* indication he had feelings for you?"

I hesitated, dropping my eyes to the table.

"He has!" Cheyenne's eyes popped. "Tell us!"

"This is *so* dumb, you guys," I said, my face growing hot. "It was *so* long ago. It meant nothing."

"We will be the judges of that," Blair said.

Bianca patted my hand. "We're very good at judging things."

"Okay." I took a breath. "A million years ago, when we

were seniors in high school, Beckett kissed me. Like, out of nowhere, grabbed me and kissed me."

Cheyenne gasped. "Really?"

"Yes." For a moment, I was standing underneath that maple tree again, shocked to feel Beckett's warm, firm lips on mine. Chills swept down my arms.

"What kind of kiss?" asked Blair. "Like a sweet, friendly kiss?"

"No." I shivered with delight. "Like a rough, hard, knock-the-breath-right-out-of-you kiss."

"Was this before or after the prom thing?" Bianca asked.

"It was a couple weeks before. We were studying for a math test at his house, but I was upset and couldn't concentrate, so we took a study break and went outside."

"Upset about what?" asked Cheyenne, leaning forward.

"The AP calc exam, my overbearing mother, my asshole boyfriend . . . all of it was caving in on me. I felt like I was drowning. I remember we were standing under this big tree, and I was crying, then suddenly he just grabbed me and kissed me. But it was over really fast, and we never talked about it again."

"Why not?" Blair asked with wide eyes.

"I think we were both kind of in shock—we didn't know how to handle it. It was so out of character for him, and I had a boyfriend at the time." I lifted my shoulders. "I always thought he did it because he felt sorry for me."

"I bet there was more to it." Cheyenne spoke confidently. "I bet he'd been holding back that kiss for a *long time*."

"Maybe . . ." I played with the end of one braid again, thinking about our conversation on the couch last night. "He holds back a lot. Even now. Like, he'll say something or do something that could be interpreted as suggestive, but then the next minute, he's back to being all friend-zone again. And I wonder if I imagined it."

"What kind of thing do you mean?" Bianca asked.

I hesitated, but ultimately gave in to the need for confidantes. It felt good to talk about my feelings, and even though I didn't know these women well, somehow they inspired my trust. Maybe it was that they knew and loved Beckett.

"Last night," I said. "I saw something." After another sip of wine, I told them about coming downstairs to see Beckett holding my sweater to his face.

"Oh." Cheyenne touched her heart. "That's so sweet."

"The guy is seriously into you, Maddie." Blair shook her head. "You don't smell someone's clothes unless you want to be close to them."

"What did you do?" Bianca asked.

"I panicked and ran away." I laughed at the memory. "You should have seen me trying to scramble up the stairs as fast as I could without making any noise. And by the time I was back in my bedroom, I wasn't sure I'd seen anything at all."

"I think you know what you saw." Bianca's tone was confident. "You just don't know what to do about it."

"Can you blame me?" Sighing, I picked up my wine and stared into it. "I mean, it's *Beckett*. You guys know what he's like."

Bianca sighed. "He's that strong, silent type. Like an Old Hollywood cowboy."

"And I like that about him—it's hot," I admitted. "I like that he projects strength and masculinity without being a toxic, arrogant dickhead. But it's hard to know what he's thinking."

"And I feel like he's *always* thinking," said Blair. "He's definitely ruled by his brain, not his—his—" Suddenly she looked like a demure Southern belle, like if she'd had a handheld fan, she might have hidden behind it.

"Hormones?" offered Cheyenne.

"Good grief, you guys." Bianca's expression was pained. "Can we not say *dick*?"

I laughed. "He *is* ruled by his brain. But also his moral code, this really strongly-ingrained sense of right and wrong. Look at how he gave up his lucrative Wall Street job to come home and save the family farm. Look how he takes care of his dad, day and night. Look how he offered Elliott and me a place to stay because he didn't want us staying at my mother's shitty old house."

"Even good guys have urges," Cheyenne pointed out.

"But even if he had an *urge* around me," I said, getting hot and bothered by the thought, "I get the feeling he thinks acting on it would be wrong."

"Why would he think that?" Blair wondered.

I ticked off the reasons. "Because I'm his friend. Because I just got out of a terrible marriage. Because I'm a guest at his house."

All of us were quiet a moment, and then Blair started to laugh. "I was a guest at Griffin's house too. And he tried to be all chivalrous and well-behaved about it. He lasted one night."

"But Griffin and Beckett are different," Cheyenne said. "Griff always had that *fuck-it*, impulsive side to him. Beckett doesn't."

"Nope. He's got no fuck-it side at all, at least not that he shows me." I sighed, shaking my head. "But maybe I should be glad about that."

"Why?" Bianca asked. "You're two consenting adults. Can't you just have some fun?"

"What if we cross the line just for fun and it's a mistake?" I fretted. "Our friendship, which we're just getting back, could suffer. It could even be ruined."

"That's definitely a risk," Blair agreed, and the others murmured in grudging agreement.

"But you guys, I can't stop thinking about him." I closed my eyes, my voice taking on a desperate tone. "And not just because he's gorgeous and has that insane body. He's so sweet with his dad, and we've got history, and you should have seen him with Elliott this afternoon." I told them about batting practice. "Watching a man—a real man—interact with Elliott that way, teaching him something, being so patient and understanding and encouraging, it just . . ." I shivered. "It just did something to me."

"I bet I know where," joked Bianca.

I laughed, but it turned into a moan. "I'm just so scared to make a mistake. I do *not* make good decisions where men are concerned."

The girls were silent as they pondered the situation.

"But this isn't some asshole from your past." Blair sat up taller. "This is Beckett. We *know* him. I vote you kiss him and see what happens."

"I'll second that." Cheyenne swirled her red wine in her glass. "And I think *you* have to take the initiative. Guys like Beckett sometimes need a push to act on their physical impulses—permission to go all alpha male on you. Cole was the same way."

"He was?"

She nodded. "I pretty much had to seduce him."

"How'd you do it?"

"With an accidental sext."

I laughed, but the thought of trying to seduce Beckett— over text or in person—raveled my stomach into knots. What if he turned me down? "No way. I couldn't."

"Offer to marry him if he'll get you pregnant," said Bianca, her eyes dancing.

I burst out laughing. "There will be no sexting and definitely no getting married or pregnant. Honestly, I'd be happy to spend one night with him. I just don't want the price to be too high."

Bianca reached over and covered my hand with hers. "We're only teasing you. I love that you and Beckett value each other's friendship so much—that you have this history of being there for each other. You're right not to throw that away just to scratch an itch."

"Well, *he's* always been there for *me*," I said guiltily. "It seems like I've always been the needy one."

"Did you not just tell us tonight how you spent the day with his dad?" Cheyenne asked. "I'd bet you a million bucks that's the nicest thing anyone could do for Beckett these days. Even better than a blow job."

"I'm not sure about *that*," said Bianca under her breath.

"Okay, maybe not a blowie," Cheyenne admitted. "But just about anything else."

"Thanks, you guys." I smiled at all of them. "I'm really glad I came tonight. I needed this."

A few minutes after nine, I texted Beckett. **Hey, I'm going to be a little later than I thought! Sorry. Having too much fun. We're paying the bill now.**

Beckett: No rush.

Me: How are things going?

Beckett: All good.

"See? This. This is what he gives me." Laughing, I flashed my screen around the table. "Two-word answers."

"At least you get two," sighed Blair. "Griff is all about the grunty one-word answers. Sometimes all I get is one *letter*."

We settled the bill, hugged goodbye, and I used the bathroom one more time before hitting the road for home. On the drive back, it struck me that I'd had a more enjoyable evening with Bianca, Cheyenne, and Blair than I'd had with any of my friends back home recently. Since the divorce, many of them had pulled away from me, not that I'd been very close to anyone to begin with.

But finding new friends was difficult as an adult, although Bianca, Blair, and Cheyenne made it seem easy. And everyone had been so kind in town today. What had made Bellamy Creek feel so small and stifling when I was younger—the way everyone knew everyone else and was interested in their business—now felt kind of nice. People genuinely cared.

At nine-thirty, I entered Beckett's house through the front door and pushed it shut behind me. I could hear the television on in the great room—sounded like a baseball game—and headed in that direction.

When I got there, I burst out laughing.

Beckett was playing Elliott's favorite game—unicorn ring toss. This involved wearing a headband with a unicorn horn on it and letting Elliott toss pink satin pillow rings at your head, attempting to score.

Elliott, whose curls were damp, was wearing his pajamas. "Hi, Mom!"

Beckett, standing opposite him about six feet away, turned and looked at me. "Hey. How was your girls' night?"

"Great," I said, covering my mouth with one hand and wrapping the other arm around my stomach. "How was everything here?"

"Excellent," Beckett replied as Elliott tossed a ring that hit Beckett's head but missed the horn. "I'm really good at unicorn ring toss. But I'm not that good at being the unicorn."

"He's too tall," complained Elliott.

"How about this?" Beckett dropped to his knees. "Now try."

Elliott narrowed his eyes like he was concentrating hard and tossed the ring—it caught the horn this time. He pumped his fists in the air. "Yes!"

"Good job," I said, moving farther into the room. Mr. Weaver was dozing on one couch, DiMaggio next to him. I sat down on the other and pulled a pillow onto my lap.

Beckett got to his feet. "All right, I think this unicorn should retire now."

"Elliott, put the game away, okay?" I made eye contact with my son and made sure he knew not to argue. "And thank you for getting ready for bed like I asked."

"Beckett said he'd only play the game if I put my pajamas on at eight o'clock," Elliott said with a shrug. "So I did."

I looked at Beckett. "Smart."

He tapped his temple, grabbed his beer off the coffee table, and took a quick drink. "Can I get you anything?"

"No, thanks. I'm going to put Elliott to bed in a sec. How's the ball game?"

"Good." Beckett looked at the TV. "Tigers are up by two. Dad was a little miffed by a call in the third inning, and he was pretty sure he saw Cynthia Mae in the stands at one point, but overall, he's had a good night."

"I'm glad." But instead of looking at the screen, I watched Beckett help Elliott put the game away. He wore a dark gray T-shirt that hugged his arms and chest. His jeans were faded and frayed at the hems. His hair was slightly mussed from the headband, and I wanted to smooth it with my fingers.

When the game was back in the box, he picked up his beer bottle again. As he tipped it back, I watched the muscles in his throat move and imagined pressing my lips to the skin just beneath his sharply angled jaw. My stomach tightened, and I crossed my legs tighter, gripping the pillow hard. There were so many places on his body I wanted to touch. Places I'd glimpsed yesterday when he'd come to the door in a towel—abs and chest and shoulders—but also places I'd never seen.

The backs of his muscular thighs.

That round, firm ass.

Those V lines—surely he had those V lines.

Without thinking, I brought my fingertips to my mouth. Of course, that was the exact moment he chose to look over at me, and there I was groping a pillow and fondling my bottom lip.

Embarrassed, I jumped off the couch, tossing the pillow aside. "Come on, Elliott. Time for bed."

"Five more minutes?" he asked, clasping his hands under his chin.

I shook my head. "Nope. This is late enough, and you were up very early. I can't even believe you're still awake."

"We go to bed early around here, champ," said Beckett. "Those goats will be looking for you come five-thirty."

"Okay." Easy as that, he hurried for the stairs with his quirky little walk.

I gave Beckett a grateful look. "Thanks for the assist."

"No problem. I need to get Dad to bed now anyway. He's been asleep for almost an hour." He glanced behind me, toward the kitchen, and spoke a little quieter. "I saved you a piece of pie."

I laughed, raising my eyebrows. "So you *did* decide to be a gentleman."

He shrugged. "Old habits die hard."

"Well, thank you. I think I'm too full to enjoy it tonight, but I'll try some tomorrow."

"Okay." He reached for the remote and switched off the television. "Time for bed, Dad."

Mr. Weaver's eyes flew open. "Is it over?"

"Yep," he lied.

"Did we win?"

"Yep."

"Good."

Beckett helped his father to his feet and herded him and DiMaggio toward the bedroom. "Night," he called to me over one shoulder.

"Night," I said softly, disappointed the evening couldn't end another way.

Which was ridiculous, really, I thought as I went up the

stairs. Despite what the girls had said tonight, what could come of things getting hot and heavy with Beckett anyway, other than a very awkward scene at the breakfast table tomorrow morning? Would the orgasm be worth it?

Wait, I told myself as my core muscles clenched at the thought of Beckett in that towel, and I grabbed the handrail. *Don't answer that.*

"Did you have a fun time tonight?" I asked Elliott, tucking him in tight.

"Yes. Can we call Dad tomorrow? I want to tell him about my home run."

"Sure." I kissed my fingers and touched his cheek. "Night, buddy. I love you."

"Night, Mom. I love you too."

I was just leaving his room when I decided that I wanted to try Blair's apple pie after all. Granted, it was a distant second to tracing Beckett's V lines with my tongue, but good pie was good pie.

After ditching my sandals in my closet, I tiptoed back down the stairs and into the darkened kitchen. Finding the pie in the fridge, I pulled it from the box and sliced myself a small piece. In the pantry, I hunted for some tea, happy to discover a box of lemon chamomile. I filled the kettle and turned on the burner beneath it, then selected a mug from the cupboard that said Cloverleigh Farms on it.

While I was waiting for the water to boil, I heard a deep voice behind me.

"Changed your mind?"

I whirled around with my hand over my heart. "Oh! You scared me."

"Sorry." Beckett's smile was amused.

"I decided I wasn't too full for pie."

"Good decision."

"Want some?"

"Nah." He ducked into the garage and tossed his empty beer bottle into the bin. "But I'll join you. If you want company."

"Sure." Behind me, the kettle began to whistle, and I quickly pulled it off the heat. "How about some tea?" I asked, pouring hot water over the teabag.

"No, thanks." He grabbed another beer from the fridge and took a seat at the island, which had four counter stools.

I carried my tea mug and pie plate to the island, sitting next to him. "Elliott had such a great day. Thanks for everything."

"My pleasure. My dad had a great day too. He asked if the strata lady was going to be here again tomorrow."

I laughed. "The strata lady? Is that my name now?"

"Unless he's thinking of Blair. But I'm pretty sure it's you."

"We had a nice time. I'd be glad to take him downtown again." I tasted the pie and moaned quietly. "Oh my God, I see what you mean. This is every bit as good as Betty Frankel's."

"I agree." He tipped up his beer.

"I had so much fun tonight. Girl talk is good therapy."

He cocked his head. "You needed therapy?"

I laughed. "Doesn't everyone?"

"I wouldn't know. I've never been." He tipped up his beer. "It sounds like torture to me."

"Really? I love my therapist. She's helped me so much."

"With what?" he asked, then he looked contrite. "Sorry, is this private? You don't have to tell me."

"No, it's okay. I don't mind talking about it. In fact, I think saying things out loud helps me work through them. It's keeping things bottled up that's harmful."

He took another drink. "What things did you keep bottled up?"

I looked at my plate and pushed some apple filling around. "Where my mother was concerned, a lot of anger and resentment. But my therapist helped me reframe some of my mother's behaviors."

"How so?"

"Well, for example, in my mother's eyes, pushing me so hard to be financially secure was a way to show me she loved me. She wanted me to have an easier life than she'd had. She didn't want me to struggle." I sighed. "But that's not what I wanted from my mom—I wanted to hear that she loved me and would have been proud of me no matter what. I had to forgive her for that."

Beckett nodded. "And have you?"

"Yes," I said carefully, "but it's sort of an ongoing thing. I'm hoping that selling the house gives me a sense of closure. I'm still working to let go of a lot of guilt and fear she instilled."

"Fear of what?"

"Failing to live up to people's expectations. Letting people down. Making the wrong choices. I mean, let's face it, I've made some doozies."

He shrugged. "Everyone makes mistakes."

"Right, but . . ." I took a breath and admitted something I'd only ever said in therapy. "One of the things my mother used to say to me over and over was that I wasn't capable of making good decisions. That she knew better than I did what was best. You hear that enough times, you start to believe it. You don't trust yourself. I mean, when I look back, sometimes I'm shocked I had the nerve to quit medical school."

"But you did it," Beckett said firmly. "And it was the right decision."

"But then I married Sam."

"And now you have Elliott."

I sat up taller and smiled. "Yes. Now I have Elliott. Being his mom has been the best thing that ever happened to me. And I'm very proud that I went back and got my nursing certificate and a job, even though Sam didn't want me to work."

"See? You know what's best for you."

My spirits lifted, and I dug into my pie again. "Well, I'm a work in progress. But I'm okay with that."

Beckett took another drink. "Think you'll stay in Ohio?"

"Yes." Setting my fork down, I picked up my tea. "Not because I love it so much, but it's the only home Elliott has ever known. There's been enough disruption in his life without uprooting him without good reason. And Sam isn't the *best* father in the world, to say the least, but even an okay dad is better than no dad at all. I don't want Elliott to grow up without one."

"Family is important. I missed mine a lot when I was gone. My friends too. Even this town."

I nodded. "I get it. When I was younger, I couldn't wait to leave Bellamy Creek, but as an adult—especially a mom—I can see all the benefits of growing up here. It's such a safe, close-knit place. Everyone is so friendly. People I haven't seen in fifteen years hugged me today and remembered my name! It made me feel so good."

He smiled. "I'm glad."

"Speaking of friends, it was so fun tonight to hear the stories of how everyone met and fell in love. I was dying laughing at the image of Blair getting out of her car in that white dress, and then fainting on the sidewalk."

Beckett shook his head. "I wasn't there, but I have always been able to picture it perfectly."

"Cheyenne invited me to the wedding." I swirled the last bit of tea around in my mug.

"That would be fun."

"Are you a groomsman?"

He nodded.

"Think I could tag along? Unless you have a date," I went on quickly.

"Just my dad, if he's having a good day. He's my usual plus-one at these things."

"Well, I'd love to attend, although I'd have to figure out what to do with Elliott." I finished my tea and set down the mug. "Maybe one of the girls knows a sitter."

"I could ask my sister Mallory to come over with my niece."

"Really?" I straightened up. "Oh my gosh, that would be perfect!"

"She'll be here tomorrow. I'll ask her then."

"Thanks." Smiling, I rose to my feet, and carried my plate and mug over to the sink.

Beckett got up too, heading for the garage door, and a moment later I heard the clink of his bottle when he placed it in the bin. Returning to the kitchen, he said, "We can get going on the yard cleanup tomorrow."

"Okay." I rinsed my plate and mug and put them in the dishwasher. "But if you're too busy, I understand."

"I'm not. I want to help you."

Closing the dishwasher, I turned to face him. "Thank you. And thanks for listening tonight."

"What are friends for?"

Our eyes were locked, and the room suddenly felt thick with tension. I thought of Blair's advice—*I vote you kiss him and see what happens*—and licked my lips.

Beckett's jaw ticked. His eyes were on my mouth.

If I took a step toward him, would he meet me halfway?

But I remained still, and Beckett stayed where he was, his arms folded over his chest.

Unsettled, I looked at the clock and saw it was ten-thirty. "Well, it's getting late. I guess I'll turn in."

Beckett cleared his throat. "Me too. I'll get the lights and lock the doors."

"I'll wait for you."

He looked at me a moment, and I thought he was going to insist I go up to bed, but he didn't. Once the back door was locked, he turned off all the kitchen lights, and I followed him into the great room.

I waited at the bottom of the stairs while he locked the front door and switched off the one lamp he'd left on. As he moved toward me, I started up the steps. He followed behind me.

My pulse was racing for no good reason. All I was going to do was say goodnight at the top of the stairs. Maybe give him a hug.

I wasn't going to kiss him.

I wasn't going to touch him.

I wasn't going to suggest it might be fun to play naughty naked unicorn toss in my bed.

My feet took each step slowly, but I swear to God I was sweating by the time I reached the top. The upstairs hall was dark and silent. I paused outside my bedroom door.

When Beckett reached the landing, he headed for his bedroom. "Night."

I opened my mouth to say goodnight—I swear I did.

But that's not what came out.

"I need to tell you something," I blurted.

He turned and faced me.

"I want to answer your question." My heart raced, and my fingers locked over my stomach.

"What question?"

"You asked me—last night—why I always chose jerks."

"You said you didn't know."

"I lied. I do know."

He was silent a moment. "So tell me."

I took a step toward him. "I chose jerks because they didn't ask anything of me. They didn't *expect* anything of me. They didn't even want much from me—just skin."

Beckett took a deep breath, his chest expanding.

"That's why I couldn't be with you," I whispered.

"Because you think I would have expected perfection?"

"Because you would have deserved it."

He exhaled and shook his head. "You're wrong."

"I'm sorry. This is stupid." I squeezed my eyes shut a moment. "I don't even know why I'm telling you this right now. It's not like I can go back and do things differently. I guess I just wish I would have been brave enough to tell you the truth back then."

"What's the truth?"

"That I wish I could have been yours. I know you would have been good to me."

He said nothing for ten full seconds, during which my heart banged painfully against my ribs and I regretted *everything*.

"Listen, forget I said anything," I said quickly. "I don't know what Blair puts in that apple pie, but—"

"I have something to tell you too."

I swallowed. "You do?"

"Yeah. Several things, actually." He moved closer to me, so close I could feel his breath on my lips. "First, I'm glad you finally answered my question. It's been bothering me for fifteen years. Second, you're right. I would have been good to you. And third, no—we can't go back and do things differently. The past is past."

"Yes. Well, goodnight." Tears of mortification burning my eyes, I spun away from him, but he grabbed my arm.

"But there's one more thing."

"What?" I whispered.

"I sleep with my bedroom door open. But I want you to

think hard before you take advantage of that. Because I'm not eighteen anymore, and I'm no longer in the mood to be a gentleman."

Then he let go of my arm and disappeared across the hall.

With my legs trembling, I slipped into my room, shut the door and leaned back against it, fanning my face.

Holy. Shit.

He'd left it up to me.

But his invitation was clear. I hadn't imagined it.

And before I thought about it too hard and blew my chance to be with him, I raced into the bathroom, pulled my braids out, and brushed my teeth. Back in my bedroom, I whipped off my clothes and pulled on the pineapple-print tank and matching shorts I'd brought to sleep in. Not exactly my sexiest lingerie, but in my defense, seduction hadn't been on my to-do list when I'd packed my bags.

Then I took a deep breath, opened my door, and snuck across the hall.

CHAPTER 8
BECKETT

FINALLY, I fucking said it.

And it felt damn good.

If she stayed in her own room tonight, fine, but at least I wouldn't wake up tomorrow regretting that I'd kept silent.

Could make for some awkward conversation over break-fast, but fuck it—I'd been honest. I'd told her the truth. She knew how I felt and what I wanted. After all this time, there was some relief in that.

Was it possible I'd gone too far?

Hell yes.

Maybe she was across the hall right now thinking I was just another jerk who wanted skin. Maybe she'd never trust me again. Maybe she'd even pack her bags tomorrow and leave.

But at least I'd taken the risk instead of choking on it.

Slipping into bed, I lay on my back, hands behind my head. My heart felt like a bowling ball, knocking around hard and heavy inside my chest.

For a few tense minutes, I heard nothing.

And then.

Footsteps in the hall.

The quiet closing of my bedroom door.

A longed-for whisper in the dark. "Beckett?"

I sat up. "Come here."

She rushed onto the bed, our mouths colliding. My hands in her hair. Her arms around my neck. My tongue in her mouth. Her back against the mattress.

I lifted myself off her only for the fraction of a second it took to lose my boxer briefs. She whipped off the top she wore. I yanked her shorts down her legs and tossed them aside. Then I stretched out above her again, my body on fire, my mouth ravaging hers, my mind exploding with one word —*finally, finally, finally.*

We moved like a time bomb was ticking. Already her hands were wrapped around my cock, her grasp tight as she worked them up and down. My hips moved instinctively, thrusting my thick, hard flesh through her fists, my self-control pushed dangerously close to its limit.

"I want you inside me." Her breath was hot against my lips. "Right now. It's safe—I'm on the pill."

But it wasn't just being safe I was concerned about. I wanted to take my time. I'd been fantasizing about this forever.

Not yet, I thought, as she rubbed the tip of my cock between her legs.

Slow down, I told myself, as I pushed inside her.

You're being a fucking dick, I moaned in my head, while my body began to move over hers.

But I couldn't stop. She was so beautiful, she was right here, she was everything I'd ever dreamed of. And she wanted me—I could taste it on her tongue, hear it in her breath, feel it in the way she rocked her hips beneath me and the way her nails clawed my back.

Desperate to make it good for her but too carried away to take my foot off the gas, I buried myself as deep as I could and rubbed the base of my cock against her clit. She moaned and moved her hands down over my ass, gripping me tight.

Our skin grew slick with sweat. Our kisses more ravenous. Our sounds louder and more desperate.

I moved faster. Harder. Deeper.

My headboard knocked against the wall in loud, rhythmic thumps that seemed to shake the foundation of the house.

I didn't care.

All that mattered was my name on her lips and her heels on my thighs and her nails on my back and my cock inside her and hearing her say *right there, don't stop* and her body hot and wet and tight and pulsing around me. As soon as she cried out in release, I reached the breaking point and careened right past it, pouring myself into her with thrust after powerful thrust. She was *mine, mine, mine* in that moment, and nothing could take her away from me. It was the most intense and gratifying orgasm I'd ever experienced, and I knew it was because I'd been waiting for it for so long.

I was trying to catch my breath when I heard a noise downstairs. "Oh, fuck."

"What?" she said, still panting.

"Stay here."

Reluctantly I lifted myself off her, felt around the ground for my underwear and tugged them on. Then I grabbed a pair of sweatpants from a drawer and shoved one leg in, hopping in the dark as I tried to get them all the way on and open the door at the same time.

"Beckett, what's wrong?"

"I'll be right back." Tugging the pants over my hips, I tied the drawstring as I hurried into the hall and went down the stairs two at a time. I strode into the kitchen, where the lights were on and my father was pulling pots and pans out of the cupboard. I squinted at him. "Dad, what are you doing?"

"I'm making breakfast." He set a large iron skillet on the granite counter with a loud *clank* and tightened the belt on his robe. "I heard noises upstairs, but you didn't come down, so I thought I'd just get breakfast going."

"It's not morning yet."

"Do we have any eggs?" He scratched his head. "Maybe strata lady can bring us some. Is she coming back?"

I pinched the bridge of my nose and willed myself to be patient. "We can have eggs tomorrow for breakfast, Dad. But it's only midnight. It's not time to wake up yet."

"Everything okay?" Maddie entered the kitchen in her pajamas, which I hadn't noticed before had pineapples all over them.

"Oh, good, you're here," my dad said, looking pleased.

"I'm here." She smiled at him, looking so sexy and adorable with her messy hair and puffy lips and pineapple pajamas, I wanted to throw her on the kitchen island and have my way with her all over again.

Jesus Christ, I hadn't even tasted her. What the fuck was the matter with me?

"Everything's fine," I told her. "Dad heard a noise and thought it was morning."

"It sounded like banging," my father said.

Maddie and I exchanged a look, and she covered her mouth with one hand.

"It's late, Dad. Come on, let's get you back to bed."

"But what about the eggs?" he said as I led him from the room.

"We'll have eggs tomorrow." Over my shoulder I mouthed *I'll be right back* at Maddie, and she nodded.

After making sure Dad didn't need to use the bathroom, I hung up his robe, got him back into bed, and said goodnight. "I'll be in to wake you when it's time for breakfast just like always, okay?"

"I don't see why I can't get up and make breakfast when I want to," he said, sounding like a stubborn child and a cranky old man all at once. "If you're not going to let me live in my real house, you could at least let me eat when I'm hungry."

"This is your real house, Dad." I spoke quietly but firmly.

"Bullshit," he said cantankerously. "You think I don't know what you're trying to do?"

I exhaled. Counted to three. "And what's that?"

He thought for a moment. "Steal my money."

"What would you do with money, Dad?" I asked testily. I should have been falling asleep with Maddie's head on my chest right now, or trying to coax her into round two so I could make up for being a two-pump chump the first time.

Another pause. "I would get a new uniform."

"A new uniform?"

"Yeah. That's why they don't let me play. Someone took my uniform, and I don't have the money to buy a new one." He pointed at me. "You're trying to keep me from playing."

In the back of my mind, I wondered if this was some kind of latent pushback against setting aside his college baseball dreams to stay here. For that reason, I didn't have the heart to argue.

I softened my tone. "Right now, I'm just trying to get you to go to sleep, okay? We'll discuss this tomorrow. Goodnight."

He harrumphed, and I left his room, closing the door behind me.

In the kitchen, Maddie had put the pots and pans away. "Did we wake him up?" she asked, closing the drawer beneath the stove.

"Probably."

"I knew I was too loud." Guilt flickered across her face.

"It wasn't just you. Pretty sure I made a decent amount of noise too. Not to mention the bed knocking against the wall."

She nodded, eyes wide. "I'm surprised we didn't wake Elliott."

"Are you positive we didn't?"

"Yes. I checked on him before I came down."

"Good."

We stood there a moment longer, our eyes locked, her arms crossed over her chest, mine hanging limp at my sides, when all I really wanted to do was hold her. But did she want that?

Maybe what happened tonight was going to be like that kiss beneath the maple tree, where we were going to pretend like it didn't happen and go on with our regularly scheduled lives.

Or maybe it hadn't been good for her. For fuck's sake, I'd gone at her like a greyhound out of the gate.

Not my finest performance.

"You look very serious," she said. "And I don't want to be that girl who needs to ask what a guy is thinking after sex, but I'm really wondering what you're thinking."

"For one thing, I'm thinking I should apologize."

She looked surprised. "For what?"

"For my, uh, speed and general lack of finesse." I grimaced. "It was not supposed to be over so quickly. Or end with me jumping out of bed to prevent my dad from burning the house down."

"It's probably a good thing it was over quickly, or else we'd be calling the fire department right now." Her lush mouth curved into a shy smile. "And it wasn't *too* quick. As a matter of fact, I sort of liked the pace. I didn't have time to be nervous."

"Nervous?" I stared at her. "What would you be nervous about?"

"Come on, you know me." She moved closer, poking at my bare chest. "I get nervous about things."

I wrapped my arms around her waist. "You had *nothing* to be nervous about. I was the one who boasted last night that I'd learned how to please a woman. And then when I had the chance to prove it, I forgot everything. It was freshman year all over again."

She laughed. "It wasn't, I promise. You pleased me quite beautifully. In fact, I don't think I've ever been quite so pleased before in such a short amount of time."

I groaned. "That's not *exactly* the record I'd like to hold with you. I kept telling myself to calm down, but I couldn't. I was a fucking bull in a china shop, smashing everything."

"Listen, there's something to be said for a woman being so irresistible to a man it renders him unable to control himself— provided she's *invited* the bull into the china shop, of course. Which I had. It was me that snuck into your bedroom, remember?"

Was she kidding? I'd never forget that as long as I lived. "I remember."

"Good." She sighed, focusing on her fingertips, which brushed softly over my chest. "Beckett?"

"Hm?"

"We didn't ruin our friendship, did we?"

"Doesn't feel like it."

"But what if—"

"Hey." I shook her gently. "Let's not invent things to worry about."

"I'm not inventing them," she insisted, meeting my eyes. "It's a real thing that happens. Two people are friends and then they have sex, and everything gets weird. Don't you remember that scene from *When Harry Met Sally*?"

"No."

"Well, I do." She shuddered. "It's a woman's worst nightmare."

"Why?"

"Because she's feeling all warm and cozy and happy, and he's just like 'Get me the fuck out of here.' But he's not *saying* that." She tapped her knuckles on my sternum. "That's you.

You're so quiet and thinky all the time. You don't volunteer what's on your mind."

I had to laugh. "Thinky?"

"Yes! But I need the talky. Or I'll fill in the blanks with bad stuff. I've got this voice in my head that loves to do that."

I shook my head and tightened my arms around her. "Maddie. Do I seem like I want to get the fuck out of here?"

"No," she admitted.

"Would it help if I told you that I've wanted you like that since we were seventeen?"

"Really?"

"Or that keeping my hands off you last night took every ounce of my self-control?"

Her eyes widened, like she was a little bit scandalized. "You hid it well."

"Thank you. But you can stop worrying." I kissed her forehead. "We did not ruin our friendship."

She smiled. "And it won't be weird tomorrow?"

"It won't be weird tomorrow."

Her body relaxed and she pressed her cheek to my chest. "Good. Because I like having you in my life."

I held her for a moment, resting my lips on her hair, gently caressing her back, feeling warm and protective and wishing there was some way—any way—to keep her in my arms until the sun came up.

But I knew that was impossible.

Eventually she sighed and said, "I guess we should go get some sleep, huh?"

"Probably."

Neither of us moved for another thirty seconds, and then she started to laugh. "Come on, or we'll be standing here all night."

After turning out the lights, we walked up the stairs hand in hand, and whispered goodnight in the hallway between our bedroom doors.

It felt all wrong as I watched her disappear into the darkness of the guest room and close the door behind her. But what could I do? The divide that separated us was bigger than just a hallway.

Back in my own bedroom, I left the door ajar and got back into bed alone.

CHAPTER 9
MADDIE

I SHUT the door as softly as I could and crawled back into bed, pulling the covers up to my shoulders and curling into a ball, as if the memory of Beckett's body on mine was something that might escape if I didn't hold onto it tight enough.

I never wanted to forget this feeling. Not for one moment.

Closing my eyes, I let the scene play out again to the soundtrack of my beating heart.

The hallway carpet beneath my bare toes. Pushing open his door. Whispering his name—a question. His silhouette in the dark. His deep, quiet voice giving me the answer.

Come here.

I'd run toward the bed like a runaway train, crashing into his hard, warm body so violently it had knocked the breath out of me.

My stomach muscles tightened as I recalled our impatient hands tearing at clothes, our eager tongues desperate to taste, our feverish pent-up desire demanding we race to the finish line without stopping—as if we were scared the chance might be taken away from us at any second.

Rolling onto my back, I put my hands over my belly, breathing in deeply. How long had it been since a man had touched me that way? Kissed me that way? Ravaged me that way—like he had to have me or he'd lose his mind, but also like he actually cared about what *I* was feeling?

It might have been over fast, but I was used to fast. What I *wasn't* used to was feeling like what I needed mattered.

My husband had not been faithful. But because of the way I was wired, I couldn't stop trying to please him. This meant disconnecting my hurt feelings, numbing myself to the psychological pain of feeling like I wasn't enough. But that emotional detachment spilled over—in the end, I couldn't feel a fucking thing during sex, and I stopped pretending I could. When Sam stopped bothering with me, I didn't blame him. And I no longer cared. At that point, I associated sex with insecurity—and who needs more of that?

But *Beckett*—sighing softly, I curled up on my side again.

It wasn't just that he had the strongest, hottest body of any man I'd ever been with and knew how to use it. It was knowing that I meant something to him. It was giving into something that had been there all along. It was sharing myself with him in a way I'd only fantasized about, and discovering the real thing was even better.

It was allowing myself to *feel*.

I wasn't an idiot. I knew Beckett wasn't in love with me. I knew he was probably lonely here with only his dad for company. I knew whatever this thing was between us was temporary fun.

But standing there in that kitchen with his big, strong arms around me, feeling warm and safe and protected and wanted, like everything was going to be okay . . . that was a *good* feeling. I wished it didn't have to end.

Out of nowhere, an unwelcome voice from the past spoke up, tarnishing my glow.

You can't rely on a man, Magdalene. You can't expect someone else to take care of you.

I frowned into the dark. *I'm not expecting anything,* I argued back. *I just had a nice time with him.*

But the voice wouldn't let up.

Just make sure you keep your head on your shoulders and not in the clouds. You have a child to think about now. You can't afford any irresponsible mistakes.

I grabbed my pillow and put it over my head, attempting to drown out the noise.

I wasn't being irresponsible, I was being human. I'd just wanted to feel close to him tonight. It's not like we were hurting anyone.

Just be careful. Don't get so caught up in fuzzy feelings, you forget what's fantasy and what's reality. You've always struggled to tell the difference. That's why you get hurt.

I rolled to my other side, jerking the covers over my shoulders, annoyed that my mother still reigned over some part of my subconscious. That her warnings should still have sway. I wasn't an anxious kid anymore—I was a grown-ass woman. Like Beckett said, I knew what was best for me.

Not that I wasn't going to be careful, because I was.

But I was going to enjoy this too.

CHAPTER 10
BECKETT

I OVERSLEPT—I'D been dreaming about her—and it was close to six by the time I opened my eyes and checked the time.

"Fuck," I muttered, tossing the covers aside. But as I rolled out of bed, I couldn't help grinning. I felt like a guy who'd been buying lottery tickets all his life and finally hit the jackpot.

I threw on some clothes and hurried downstairs, noticing that Maddie's bedroom door was ajar. My heart tripped faster at the thought of seeing her.

She was in the kitchen, pouring a cup of coffee. I stopped short at the sight of her back, remembering the way she'd arched it for me. The scent of her neck. The curve of her hip under my palm. The crotch of my jeans grew tighter.

She turned around and smiled, making my heart lurch. "Good morning," she said.

"Morning." Once I managed to get my legs working again, I went right for the coffee pot. "How'd you sleep?"

"Good." She held her mug with both hands. "You?"

"Good. Too good." I poured myself half a cup, which was all I had time for. "Elliott awake yet?"

"Yes. He's getting dressed."

"Okay." I took a quick sip. "I'm gonna get started because I'm behind and we've got church at nine, but send him out to the barn as soon as he's ready."

"You go to church?" she asked, her voice rising steeply.

I cocked a brow. "You sound surprised. Should I be offended?"

"No," she said, laughing a little. "I just don't remember you attending church back in high school."

"I think I skipped out a lot back then. My dad and sisters always went." I took two more swallows of hot coffee and set down the cup. "I'm not particularly religious, but Dad likes to go, and it's an outing I can handle—I like the ones that have a definite start and end time."

She nodded. "I get it. We'll go with you."

"You don't have to," I said, heading for the mudroom.

"I want to." She followed me and stood in the doorway while I put my boots on. "If that's okay."

"Of course it's okay. After that, I've got some work to do around here, but Mallory is coming to spend the afternoon with Dad, so we can get started with the yard cleanup at your mom's."

"That sounds great. I'll get breakfast going and send Elliott out to help you as soon as he comes down. Do you like oatmeal?"

Backing up toward the door, I grinned at her. "This morning, I like everything."

What Maddie called oatmeal turned out to be a mouthwatering concoction with apples and raspberries and pecans baked in the oven and drizzled with maple syrup.

"Elliott, that's enough with the syrup." Maddie's voice was stern.

Her son giggled and continued to drown his breakfast. "But I like maple syrup. It's one of the four main food groups."

I smiled at him over the top of my coffee mug. "My nieces and nephews love *Elf*."

"So does Elliott," Maddie said, shaking her head as her son licked his fingers. "They played it at a theater near us around the holidays, and I took him to see it. For weeks he begged to put syrup on his pasta."

"We should go to the movies," my dad announced.

Maddie smiled across the table at him. "Yesterday, we poked our heads into the theater on Main Street, remember? You told me the story about seeing *Vertigo* there. You said your date looked just like Kim Novak."

"She did." He looked smug. "She was the prettiest girl at school. Her name was Evie Clemson and she wore a red sweater."

I stared at him. It was amazing to me the way his memory worked. He could tell you what his date was wearing to the movies in 1958 but in an hour, he wouldn't be able to tell you he'd had oatmeal for breakfast.

"I wonder what happened to her," Maddie said.

"She went away to college." My dad looked thoughtful as he ate a bite of his breakfast. "I don't know what happened to her after that. She never came back. But she used to come to all my baseball games."

"Speaking of games, when is *your* next baseball game?" Maddie asked me. "I hope I can catch one while I'm here."

"The first one is next Thursday night."

Her face lit up. "Oh good, I'll still be here!"

"Can we play baseball again today?" asked Elliott.

"Probably not today, buddy," I told him. "Too much work to do."

"Okay." Elliott looked sad, and I remembered what it was like to be his age, waiting for my dad to be done with work so we could play ball.

"Maybe we can fit in some batting practice before dinner," I said. "But that means I'll definitely need your help today with some chores."

He sat taller in his chair. "I can help with chores."

We finished breakfast quickly and left the dishes in the sink, hurrying to our rooms to change so we'd get out the door on time for the nine o'clock service. At eight-thirty, I was waiting for everyone in the mudroom when Maddie came around the corner.

"Listen, if you don't have time for baseball today, it's okay," she said, slipping an earring through her earlobe. "I know how busy you are."

"I'd love to play ball with Elliott again." I was having a hard time keeping my eyes where they belonged. She'd put on a flowered sundress that showed off her narrow waist and scooped at the neck.

"You're staring at my cleavage." She put a hand over her chest and whispered, "Is this dress too low-cut for church?"

"No." I met her eyes. "You look beautiful, and it's fine for church. I'm just an asshole."

"You're not. And if we weren't going to church, I'd love your eyes on me that way. It's been a long time since someone has looked at me like . . ." Her expressive mouth curled into a smile. "Like a bull in a china shop who wants to smash everything."

I groaned. "Please tell me I will get a chance to make up for that."

But before she could answer, Elliott came racing into the mudroom, dropping to the floor to tug on his pink boots. He'd changed from the denim shorts and T-shirt he'd had on earlier into a bubble-gum pink dress with a purple-sequined heart on the front. The unicorn barrette was stuck on one side of his head.

"No, Elliott, those boots are dirty," Maddie admonished. "Can you please go back up to your room and get your clean sneakers?"

"No." He stood up and looked down at his feet. "These are my favorite shoes."

Maddie appealed to me. "Beckett, tell him that church is not the place for dirty boots."

But Elliott was staring up at me so earnestly, and he was so proud of those boots, I didn't have the heart. The poor kid was probably going to have to deal with a lot of people staring at him for wearing a dress—he could at least walk in there with the added confidence his boots gave him.

"Tell you what," I said. "Let me grab a rag and wipe them off a little. Then they'll be in perfect shape for church. Go on into the garage." I opened the door, and Elliott scooted through it.

"Thank you," Maddie said, shooting me a grateful smile. "Should I go check on your dad?"

"Maybe. Just knock loud on the bedroom door. He's probably brushing his teeth for the fifth time. But we need to get going or we'll end up parked a mile away from church, and he's a slow walker."

"I'll get him." But as she turned to walk away, I couldn't resist grabbing her by the arm and yanking her right back to me, kissing her hard.

She laughed. "Beckett, we're going to be late."

"The minister will understand when he sees you in that dress." I pressed my lips to her collarbone. "But my mind is wandering into territory that is not appropriate for church, so I'm going to go clean some boots now."

Laughing, she playfully pushed me away. "Go. I'll see you in a minute."

We managed to leave on time, but still ended up parking several blocks away. Maddie and Elliott walked hand in hand up the street ahead of my father and me.

As we made our way toward the church, my father tugged my sleeve. "Hey."

"What is it?"

"I think that's the little girl from across the street. She came home." He pointed at Elliott.

"No, Dad, that's Maddie's son, Elliott."

"I mean the one in the pink dress."

"Yes, I know. That's Elliott."

He stopped walking. "The baseball kid?"

"Yes."

"Why's he wearing that dress?"

"He likes it."

"For a disguise?"

"No, he just likes wearing dresses sometimes. It's not a big deal." I nudged him forward. "Come on. Keep walking."

He started moving again. "I never knew any boy that wore a dress."

"Well, things have changed."

"But when?" he asked, genuinely perplexed. "When do all these things change? I don't understand."

I put a hand on his shoulder, wishing I could explain it to him. "Over time, I guess. But it doesn't really matter exactly when. What matters is that he's the same kid. He just likes blue jeans sometimes and pink dresses other times."

My father shuffled along the sidewalk as he thought that over. As we reached the church steps, he shrugged and said, "Okay."

"*Maddie* was the little girl across the street," I said as we began to climb the steps. "She's all grown up now."

He stopped and looked at me. "You found her?"

"Yes," I said, to save time.

"So are you gonna marry her now?"

I glanced up to where she and Elliott were waiting for us in front of the open double doors. "No, Dad. We're not getting married. We're just friends."

He started to laugh as he climbed the steps again. "This is one of those things you're not so smart about."

I stood there for a second looking after him, wondering if *he* was totally confused or I was.

As we walked up the center aisle of the sanctuary, I noticed a lot of people looking at us, but in all fairness, Maddie and Elliott were new faces in a small town, and my father and I usually came to church alone. Everyone looked curious, but most people smiled, and only a few whispered behind their hands.

"Is this okay?" Maddie asked softly, gesturing to a pew on the right about halfway up.

"Sure," I said.

Elliott slid in first, followed by Maddie, and then me and my dad. As soon as we were settled, Maddie leaned toward me and whispered, "There are like a thousand eyes on me. I can feel them."

"Relax. It's only because they're trying to figure out who you are. And lots of them are probably trying to place you."

"What if it's because of this scandalous dress?" She flattened a hand over her sternum. "Are they clutching their pearls?"

"Only *my* eyes are on you because of the scandalous dress," I said quietly. "So could you move your hand please? It's blocking my view. And I need something good to look at if the sermon's boring."

Her mouth fell open. "I've never seen this side of you, Beckett Weaver."

"Better get used to it."

She stifled a giggle as we rose to our feet. "Yes, sir."

Around one o'clock that afternoon, I was standing at the kitchen counter scarfing down a turkey sandwich and wondering how I could get Maddie alone tonight when I heard the front door slam. A moment later, my niece Daisy came racing into the kitchen out of breath. "Uncle Beckett! I lost another tooth!"

"Did you? Let me see."

She flashed me a jack-o-lantern grin.

"You sure did. Did the tooth fairy come?"

"No, because I just pulled it out on the way here. See?" She dug the tooth from her shorts pocket and proudly showed it off.

"Don't lose that, Daisy," said Mallory, entering the kitchen. "Hey, Beck."

"Hey." I took another bite of my sandwich. "You want a little bag for that tooth, Daisy?"

"Good idea." Mallory set her purse down on the island. "I'll get it."

"I was hoping you'd come with your mom today," I said to my niece. "There's someone I want you to meet."

"Who?" Her big blue eyes lit up.

I wolfed down the last of my sandwich. "My friend's son Elliott."

Her shoulders sagged a little, her pert nose wrinkling. "Oh. A boy."

Laughing, I went over and tugged one of her pigtails. "Listen, someday you're going to love boys."

"Not today," she muttered with an eye roll.

"Who's Elliott?" my sister asked, pulling a small plastic sandwich bag from a drawer. "Here, Daisy, give me that tooth."

"Maddie Blake's son. She's in town dealing with the sale of her mother's old house, and she brought him along." I tried to make it sound casual so she wouldn't get ideas, but her eyes immediately sparkled. "They're staying here."

"Ooh. Maddie Blake," she said dramatically, zipping up the baggie and clutching it to her chest. "I can practically hear your teenage heart beating from across the room."

I scowled. "You're as bad as Amy."

"We had eyes, Beckett," she said, smiling as she tucked the bag into her purse. "We could see the way you looked at her."

"Like how?" Daisy asked.

"Like this." Mallory adopted an exaggeratedly dreamy expression and sighed heavily. "He was in *looooove* with her."

"Will you stop dogging me?" I got my sister in a headlock and rubbed her scalp with my knuckles.

"Ow! No, I can't. I'm your sister." She wriggled out of my grip. "Where's Dad?"

"Taking his nap. When he wakes up, snack as usual, and then the afternoon pills. After that you can do whatever."

"Got it."

"I'll be with Maddie over at her old house, working outside. But Elliott can stay here and play with Daisy. I think they'll get along great. He's six."

"Sounds good," Mallory said. "It's a gorgeous day, they can play outside."

"But I brought my Barbies." Daisy was clearly annoyed that she'd have to forego Barbies to play with a boy. "I was going to set up their jacuzzi on the deck like last time."

"Actually, Daisy, I think Elliott would love to do that," I

told her. "He also has a unicorn game he can show you, and if you'll let him, he'd probably braid your hair."

Daisy's brows went up. "Really?"

"Really?" echoed my sister, a quizzical look on her face.

"Yeah." I gestured for them to follow me. "Come on. I'll introduce you."

As expected, Elliott and Daisy hit it off immediately. Within minutes of meeting each other, they were giggling away on the deck, unpacking Daisy's Barbie case and filling the Barbie jacuzzi with water from the hose. Although he'd changed out of his dress and back into shorts and a T-shirt, he still wore the pink boots and unicorn barrette in his hair, and I could see Daisy trying to puzzle out how this boy could be so different from her older brother and every other boy she knew.

"He's adorable," said Mallory quietly as the three of us watched them. "And I love the pink boots."

"Thanks. Daisy is so sweet—this is perfect." Maddie smiled at her. "You're sure it's okay to leave him here?"

"Of course." My sister shooed us away. "Go. Take as long as you need. Caden, my son, has baseball all day and my husband is with him. We don't have to be back at any particular time. I can make supper too."

"Thanks," I said. "We'll probably be a few hours, but if you need anything or have a question, just call."

Outside, Maddie and I loaded up my truck with landscaping equipment, gardening tools, and yard waste bags, and headed out. I tried and failed to keep my eyes from her butt in the short denim cut-offs she wore, her breasts in the tiny yellow tank top, her bare legs, the back of her neck, her hair in a high ponytail I wanted to wrap around my fist. Every single inch of her turned me on.

But I didn't want her to know what I was thinking—her comment about the jerks who only wanted skin from her was still in my head—so I kept my hands to myself.

We drove over to her mom's, and for the next few hours, we worked alongside each other under the sun, weeding, mowing, trimming, and cleaning up years' worth of neglect.

We poured sweat. We slapped at bugs. Maddie reapplied sunscreen to her face and shoulders three times. I took off my shirt.

"I should have worn a hat," she said. "My face is going to be pink."

"I can go get you one."

"No, that's okay. But you should let me put some sunscreen on your back," she said, coming over to where I was crouched down, digging out some stubborn, overgrown shrubs in front of the porch.

"My skin is used to it."

"Beckett! You should take better care of—oh, my." She put a hand on my shoulder blade. "Are those marks from *me*?"

"What marks?"

"These scratches." Her fingertips brushed over my skin. "It looks like you were clawed by a lioness."

I grinned at her over my shoulder. "Good."

A car pulled into the driveway, and I stood up. "Moretti's here. He texted me earlier he might come by."

"Oh my God! Put your shirt on," she whispered frantically.

"Why?" I laughed. "So he doesn't feel bad about himself?"

Flustered, she gestured at my upper body. "So he doesn't see those marks! Oh God, they're on your chest too."

"He's not going to see the marks," I said under my breath as Moretti got out of his SUV. "Guys don't notice that stuff."

"But Bianca's with him," she said as Bianca got out of the passenger side. "And women do."

I glanced around for my sweaty T-shirt but didn't see it anywhere, and ten seconds later they were approaching us.

"Hey guys. How's it going?" Moretti called. "Looks like you're making some progress."

"It's going," I said. "Slowly but surely."

"I think it looks much better already." Bianca smiled brightly. "You guys are working hard out here in this heat. We should have brought you some cold drinks."

We moved into the shade of a birch tree and made small talk for a couple minutes, and then Moretti spoke seriously. "So listen, it's going to be a little bit before I can get a crew over here. This is a really busy time for us."

"I understand," said Maddie, looking a little crestfallen.

"You can always look around for another company." He shrugged. "There's some other guys who do good work around here."

"He doesn't really think that," Bianca said, shaking her head.

Maddie tried to smile. "I'd rather have your company do it. So are you thinking late summer?"

"Probably. But there's another option." Moretti exchanged a look with his wife. "Bianca and I have been talking about it since we left here."

"What is it?" Maddie asked.

"We'll buy it from you," Bianca said eagerly. "We'll give you a fair price for the condition it's in now and pay cash up front. We've been thinking about taking on more rental properties, and both of us think this one will be popular, given its size and location. It's not right on the water or anything, but it's not far from the public beach."

"Really?" Maddie brightened considerably. "You'd be interested in buying it?"

"Sure," Moretti said. "That way, you'd get the money right

away and you wouldn't have to worry about the timeline or the work being done."

"Wow. That would be amazing." Maddie smiled at them both. "Where do I sign?"

Moretti laughed. "I haven't even mentioned a price yet. Don't you want to negotiate?"

"Should I?" Maddie looked worried. "I mean, I trust you."

He looked at me. "This is not a businessperson."

I shook my head. "Nope."

"Well, now you guys are making me nervous." Maddie twisted her hands together. "Would there be a reason not to sell it to you?"

"Only if you were thinking you'd get more money out of it once the renovations were complete," Moretti said. "And you would, of course, but this would save you the cost and trouble of doing the work."

"Right." She nodded, her brow furrowed.

Remembering what she'd told me last night about doubting her ability to make the right choices for herself, I touched her shoulder. "We're just teasing you," I said quietly.

Our eyes locked, and I knew she understood.

"Okay," she said with a nod. "My gut instinct is that this is the best way to go."

"Great. Let me write up the offer, and you can take a look at it," Moretti said. "I'm still working on the numbers, but I think somewhere around eighty-five to ninety thousand is about right, given its square footage, the size of the lot, the location, and its condition."

"Sounds good to me," Maddie said more confidently.

Moretti laughed again. "I wish all deals could go down this easily."

I laughed too, but I realized when she sold the house, it might mean goodbye forever. What reason would she have to come back to Bellamy Creek? Would she come just to see me?

Don't be selfish, I told myself as the three of them continued to chat about the renovations. *This isn't about you.*

It was good she was leaving, in fact. I didn't have any room in my life for a relationship, long-distance or otherwise. She'd sell the house and go home, and we'd stay friends. That's what I wanted. That's how it would be.

Easy. Uncomplicated. Best for everyone.

But my chest had started to ache.

"Honestly, this is such a relief," Maddie said, glancing at the house. "I should have dealt with this place years ago, but couldn't quite bring myself to do it."

"I get it," Bianca said. "Childhood homes always come with some heavy emotional baggage. It can be hard to let go."

"I will gladly say goodbye to the heavy emotional baggage accompanying this house," Maddie said, pretending to brush dirt from her hands. Then she glanced at me. "My good memories in Bellamy Creek are safe and sound."

"I'll get paperwork over to you this week." Moretti glanced at me. "Feel free to keep working here, though. I love free labor. Would you mind taking out that dead tree over there? Looks like it'll be a pain in the ass."

"Fuck off," I told him with a grin. "If this place is yours now, I'm out."

He laughed. "I don't blame you. Coming to practice this week?"

Bianca tugged Maddie's hand. "Hey, come inside with me for a moment. I want to tell you about an idea I had for the kitchen."

I watched her follow Bianca up the steps, admiring her curvy body and kicking myself again for being so fast last night.

Moretti's laughter yanked me from my thoughts.

"Sorry, what did you ask me?" I frowned. "Something about practice?"

"Dude." He glanced over his shoulder at the house, into

which Maddie and Bianca had just disappeared. "You're still a mess over her. It's like senior year all over again."

I swallowed hard, unable to deny it.

"Did something happen?" he asked.

I rubbed the back of my grimy, sweaty neck. "Uh, yeah."

"Does that mean those marks are from her?" He gestured at my chest. "Or did a rosebush attack you?"

"Those are from her."

"Damn." Moretti looked amused and impressed, crossing his arms over his chest. "So it finally happened. How was it?"

Cringing slightly, I shook my head. "Don't ask."

His jaw dropped. "It wasn't good? After you waited all that time?"

"It was amazing. It was just . . ." I grimaced. "Over really fast."

Moretti's head fell back as he laughed. "So go slower next time."

"I don't know if there'll be a next time."

"Why not?"

"Because it's really hard with her son and my dad in the house. Last night we managed to wake up my father, who started taking out pots and pans in the kitchen at midnight because he heard noises upstairs and thought it was morning." I shook my head. "Our timing is shit."

"I don't know." Moretti shrugged. "Who's to say there's ever a perfect time?"

"I keep thinking I'm an idiot for waiting so long."

"You think you'd have lasted longer when you were eighteen?" He shook his head. "I assure you, that would not have been the case."

"Yeah, maybe not." I wiped sweat from my forehead with my arm. "It just sucks that we can't be alone. And once the house is sold, I doubt she'll be back."

"Let me ask you something. Who's with your dad and Elliott right now?"

"My sister Mallory."

"So what the fuck are you doing yanking weeds, asshole?" Moretti asked. "You finally got the girl. Grab her and get out of here."

I looked at the house again. "Yeah. Maybe I will."

CHAPTER 11
MADDIE

THE MOMENT the door was shut, Bianca spun around and said breathlessly, "Oh my God, I saw the scratches on his back, tell me everything right now."

I laughed and shook my head. "I *told* him to put his shirt back on."

"I'm glad he didn't! Now you have to tell me how it happened. Did you make the first move?"

I hesitated. "Yes and no."

"Go on." Bianca gestured frantically with both hands.

"After I got home last night, we sat at the kitchen table and talked for a while."

"About how you wanted to jump his bones?"

I laughed. "No. Mostly it was stuff about my mom, just baggage I've had to work through. But he listened like he really cared."

"Because he *does*, Maddie."

"He has this way of making me feel so good about myself," I gushed. "I always feel so safe with him—safe enough to admit that I'd always had feelings for him, and I was sorry I'd never told him."

Her jaw dropped. "So did you kiss him?"

"Not right then." I felt the blush creeping into my cheeks and the sly smile overtaking my lips. "But later I snuck across the hall into his bedroom."

She squealed and jumped up and down. "You didn't!"

"I did. Because right before we went to bed, he said two things that pushed me over the edge."

"What did he say?"

"He said he slept with his door open, but that I should think hard before I did anything about it, because he was no longer in the mood to be a gentleman."

Bianca fell back against the front door and fanned her face. "Dead. *Dead*."

"I about died too. Then I raced into my room and put on the stupid pineapple pajamas I'd packed, and tiptoed across the hall."

She laughed. "Pineapple pajamas?"

"They were all I had," I said with a helpless shrug. "I didn't exactly pack for a hot time."

"I bet it was hot anyway, by the looks of those scratches."

I nodded, my stomach cartwheeling at the memory. "It was hot. It was *everything*. But . . ."

"But what?"

"It wasn't enough," I admitted. "I want more."

"So get yourself some more." She laughed. "I'm sure *he's* willing."

"It's hard for us though—his dad and my son are always around." I told her what happened with Mr. Weaver last night.

"Oh no," she said, dissolving into giggles. "That's so awful. I'm sorry, I don't mean to laugh."

"Go ahead and laugh—we did. His poor dad didn't realize what he'd heard. And at least we didn't wake Elliott." I shuddered. "That would have been worse. I feel guilty just thinking about it."

"Stop it. So you have to sneak around a little, big deal."

She flipped a wrist. "I think that adds to the fun. And you *deserve* some fun, Maddie. So does Beckett. You've both been through a lot, you genuinely care for each other, and there's no harm in what you're doing. You have nothing to feel guilty about."

"Thanks. I do feel relieved that it wasn't awkward between us this morning. I don't think we ruined our friendship."

"It's really too bad you don't live closer," she said with a sigh. "I could see you two being really good together."

"I don't know about that." I chewed my bottom lip. "He flat out told me he doesn't do serious relationships."

"Why not?"

"He says he's not good at them."

Bianca screwed up her face. "Has he ever tried? Enzo said he hasn't dated anyone seriously in the last few years."

"He had a girlfriend in New York," I said hesitantly. "But he said he always put work first, and she didn't like that. I mean, who would?"

"But that was then, this is now."

"I still think work comes first for him—actually I think his dad comes first now," I said. "But after his dad, it's the ranch."

"Yeah. A long-distance relationship would be tough for him." She thought for a moment and smiled devilishly. "Maybe you should move back."

A loud knock on the door made us jump.

"What's going on in there?" Enzo's voice boomed.

"Don't tell Enzo I said anything," I whispered.

"I won't. Pinkie swear." She held out her pinkie to me and I hooked mine through it and squeezed.

When she pulled the door open, both Enzo and Beckett stood on the porch looking at us suspiciously. "You've been in here for ten minutes," Enzo said. "How long does it take to tell her about a new kitchen layout?"

"Ten minutes," said Bianca smoothly, heading onto the porch. "But we're done. Come on, let's go to the grocery store. I need a few things to make dinner. Hey, what are you guys doing later? I'm cooking tonight. Want to come over?"

"Thanks, but I can't. I'm not sure how long my sister can stay," said Beckett as we made our way down the porch steps. "She's with my dad this afternoon."

"And I've got Elliott," I said. "But I appreciate the invitation."

"Well, listen, if your sister can stay a while longer, Beckett, feel free to come over around six. Doesn't have to be a late night." Bianca hooked her arm through her husband's. "Grilled peaches with burrata, arugula and pesto. Summer squash lasagna . . ."

Beckett groaned. "You're killing me."

"She kills me every day," Enzo said.

I laughed and waved goodbye as he opened the passenger door for his wife, then got in on the driver's side. "They seem so happy together," I said, watching them drive away.

"Yeah." But Beckett's eyes were on me. "You ready to get out of here?"

"Definitely."

We cleaned up and loaded the truck, then jumped into the cab. Beckett started the engine and rolled down the windows to combat the stuffy heat, but didn't shift gears.

"What's wrong?" I asked, glancing over at him.

"I don't want to go home."

"Where do you want to go?" I looked down at my filthy clothes, my dirty hands. "I need a shower before going anywhere in public. Or a jump in the lake."

He looked over at me. "Want to go swimming?"

"Now?"

"Yeah."

"Sure." I checked the time on the truck's dash. "But it's already four. Do we have time for the beach?"

"Nope." He threw the truck into reverse and backed up.

"Where are we going? Beckett!" I laughed, grabbing the dash as he careened out of the driveway and took off down the road, tires spitting gravel. "I don't even have a bathing suit."

"You don't need one."

We passed the turn-off to the lake, and I glanced over at him. "Are you kidnapping me?"

His lips tipped up. "Yes."

I gave up trying to figure out our destination, closing my eyes a moment and letting the hot, gusty wind blow the straggling hair from my ponytail off my face. It felt so good to *not* be the adult in charge. I surrendered to the feeling, my heels on the dash, a smile on my face.

When the truck slowed, I opened my eyes and sat up taller.

"What's this?" I asked when he turned off the road into a driveway blocked by a metal gate and a sign that said PRIVATE PROPERTY.

Beckett didn't answer. He jumped out, opened the gate, and a minute later, it was closed again behind us and we were bumping along down a dirt path that wound through the trees and curved along the hills.

"I hate when you don't answer my questions!" I slapped playfully at his arm.

He laughed as we pulled into a clearing. "I know."

"Oh my goodness. This is so beautiful!" Ahead, I saw a massive pond, sunlight shimmering on its surface. A wooden dock jutted into the water on one end, a rowboat tied to it. Surrounding it was a thick forest of trees with silvery green leaves fluttering in the breeze. "Is this property yours?"

"Yeah. It borders the north end of the ranch. I bought it when I moved back and put the pond in a couple years ago."

Squealing with excitement, I clapped my hands. "It's so beautiful. Can we swim in it?"

"Sure. Come on, I'll race ya."

Before I could say another word, he'd jumped out, slammed the truck door, and taken off running toward the water.

I hopped out too, following as fast as I could, but Beckett was much faster than me. By the time I covered the distance between the truck and the dock—only about fifty yards or so —he'd already ditched his boots, socks, and jeans. I was still trying to get my sneakers and socks off when he dove into the water in just his boxer briefs, scaring a family of ducks who took off the moment his body hit the surface.

"No fair!" I shouted when he appeared again, shaking water droplets from his hair.

He rubbed his eyes and laughed. "Totally fair."

While he watched, I wiggled out of my shorts and tank, tugged my ponytail holder from my hair, and jumped in wearing my bra and panties.

The water was cool and felt delicious on my hot, sunburned skin. When I surfaced, Beckett was treading water next to me. "It's about eight feet here," he said.

"Definitely over my head."

"That's why I mentioned it." He looked concerned as he reached out one hand. "You okay?"

"I'm fine. This feels so good." I let my fingers touch his as I floated on my back. The sky was cloudless and blue, so bright I closed my eyes. "Do you come here a lot?"

"Not really. Sometimes to fish."

I snapped my head up. "Wait. There's fish in here?"

His blue eyes glittered in the sunlight. "Yeah. You don't like fish?"

I made a face. "I like them just fine in aquariums. I don't like *swimming* with them."

He laughed. "They won't bother you. Believe me, they're moving in the other direction right now."

"Good." I splashed him gently. "But if I get attacked by

some sort of sea monster, it's your fault."

"The only monster who might attack you is me," he said with a grin. "But if you'd rather go for a ride in the boat than swim, we can do that."

"I'll go for a boat ride." I swam over to the ladder and climbed up, Beckett watching me from the water. Suddenly I was conscious of my utilitarian beige underwear. "You know, if I'd have known this visit was going to involve you seeing my skivvies, I'd have packed differently."

He came up behind me, and my eyes drifted over his impressive physique. His dark blue boxer briefs hung low on his hips, exposing those V lines I'd imagined last night. Instinctively, I reached out and traced one side with my finger, from where it started to where it disappeared beneath the waistband. Beneath the material, his cock moved as my hand got closer.

I pulled it back.

"Why stop there?" he asked.

I met his eyes. "You want me to keep going?"

"Is that a serious question?"

"Yes." I laughed and looked around. "We're standing out here on a dock in the middle of the day."

"It's my dock."

"But can anyone see us?"

"No one can see us." He reached for me, pulling my body against his, wet skin to wet skin. His thickening erection pressed against my stomach. "What kind of cowboy kidnaps a girl and takes her to a public place?"

"Can you even call yourself a real cowboy?" I teased, wrapping my arms around his neck. "Where's your horse? Shouldn't you be trying to ride me off into the sunset or something?"

He put his lips to my ear. "I'll ride you any way you want."

I shivered, even though I was hot all over. "Right here,

right now?" I asked, moving one hand between us, slipping it inside his waistband this time. Curling it around his thick, hard flesh, I recalled the way it felt inside me and my insides quickened.

Instead of answering, he put his mouth on my throat and undid my bra. A second later his hands were on my ass, hauling us both to our knees.

He put my back on the warm wooden dock and stretched out beside me, his fingers easing beneath the edge of my underwear. Using his thumb against my clit, he rubbed soft circles that had me moaning and rocking my hips beneath his hand. With his tongue teasing mine, he worked two fingers inside me, groaning as he plunged them in deep.

I moved my hand up and down his length, anxious to feel him moving inside me, desperate to feel irresistible once more, longing for that deep sensual connection I'd felt with him last night.

"Beckett," I said, bucking up beneath his hand. "Now."

He groaned. "But this time I wanted to—"

"No!" I grabbed his head, forcing him to look at me. "I just want you inside me again. Don't make me wait."

He hesitated, and I was afraid I'd have to beg. I stared into his blue eyes and knew I wasn't above it.

But then he was tearing my wet panties off and shoving his briefs from his legs. He moved over me and I opened my thighs to cradle his hips. As he eased inside me, he pinned my wrists to the wood above my head, and I looked up at him, every inch of me alive and on fire. Every beat of my heart reminding me that I could still feel. Every gasp and sigh and growl and moan an affirmation that drowned out every other voice in my head.

We moved in perfect sync, as if we'd always been this way together, and maybe we had in our dreams. "I used to imagine this," I said breathlessly, as my body stretched to take him in, "what it would be like with you."

"And?" he managed, moving slow and deep.

"It's better," I whispered, my eyes moving over his broad chest and wide shoulders and gorgeous mouth and back to those faded blue eyes that made me feel so safe. "It's so much better."

And then we were lost to it—the sun beating down on our skin, the water lapping beneath the dock, the scent of sweat and sunscreen and sex all around us. He drove into me with abandon, and I cried out as the orgasm broke open inside me, my eyes closing, my body contracting around his. He came right after me, his body going plank stiff as his cock throbbed, his grip tightening on my wrists.

In complete contrast to how I'd learned to disconnect from my body during sex, I reveled in every sensation, I relished being in my skin, I held still so I could feel every rhythmic little pulse of him inside me. I never wanted it to end.

My God, I thought, barely able to breathe. *Was this how it was always supposed to be?*

"I was going to build a house on this property. That's why I bought it."

Beckett's voice was low and quiet as he brushed his fingertips over my bare back. I was lying on my stomach on the dock, arms crossed beneath my temple, eyes on him. He lay on his side next to me, head propped on his hand. The sunlight was warm on my skin.

"Why didn't you do it?" I asked.

"Wasn't much point. I could already tell that my dad wouldn't be able to live alone much longer. So I rebuilt the old house for us instead."

"Well, it's really beautiful."

"Thanks."

"And big."

"Yeah."

I hesitated before asking my next question, but decided to go for it. "Do you see yourself having a family there one day?"

Beckett's hand stilled on my lower back. "Probably not."

"How come?"

"It just doesn't seem like it's in the cards for me, with my dad and all. But I like being an uncle," he said, moving his hand up and down my spine again. "All of the fun, none of the hard stuff. I get to send them home when I'm done playing with them."

I smiled. "Fair enough."

"I do wish they lived closer. I like having kids around." He was silent for a moment. "I've been thinking of selling this land to Griffin."

"Really?"

"Yeah, he and Blair want a bigger place—they're just living over the garage right now, in Griffin's apartment. But they want more space. They want a family."

"Ah."

"I guess at one point, Griff's dad was gonna buy this land and build here once he retired. But he had a heart attack and died before it could happen."

"That's too bad."

"Yeah. Griffin doesn't want that to happen to him, where he works his ass off and saves all his life, and then his body gives out before he can slow down. But land around here isn't cheap, and banks can be assholes. He's struggled to get business loans in the past, and a lot of property goes to developers."

"So you're going to help him out?" I asked, rolling to my side. "Give him a deal?"

"Yes. He's like a brother to me. And it's not as if I need all this property. I like the idea of Griffin and Blair building a place here, having a bunch of little Dempsey monsters running around just like we used to."

I smiled. "I think it's a great idea. Have you told him yet?"

"No. It's been in the back of my mind for a while, but I haven't said anything. I'll probably wait until after Cole's wedding." He rolled onto his back and tucked his hands beneath his head, closing his eyes to the sun. "It's hard to believe all three of my best friends will be married soon."

"Is it weird for you?"

"Nah. Whatever makes them happy."

I scooted a little closer to him and put my head on his chest. His skin was warm and dry. "You deserve to be happy too, you know."

He chuckled. "I am."

"You are?"

"Yes. It doesn't look the same for everybody."

I sighed. "You're right. God knows I've never been as unhappy as I was when I was married."

"Marriage is tough," he said. "I mean, I hope it works out for my friends and my sisters, but it's a lot to ask of someone, you know?"

"What is?"

He didn't answer right away. "To stay forever."

Immediately I thought of what he'd said the other night— that no one stayed until the end. "You don't think it's possible to love someone forever?" I asked, drawing small circles on his chest with one fingertip.

He thought for a few seconds. "I think maybe it's possible, for some people, but I think it's too much to *expect*. It's all so unpredictable. You never know what the future will bring. And I think it's a mistake to make promises you're not sure you can keep."

"Or promises you *know* you can't keep," I added, thinking of my ex.

"Exactly. Although there is one promise I want to make to you."

I picked my head up and looked at him. "What's that?"

"The next time we're alone, I promise to take my time. For fuck's sake, there are so many things I want to do to you, and I keep going off like a rocket."

"I feel like that's partly my fault," I said, laughing a little.

"Me too." He growled menacingly, then flipped me over so I was on my back and he was above me. "All those things you say to rush me, and the way you use your hands—next time I kidnap you, I might have to tie you down." He wound my hair around his fist, pulling gently. "I'm good with a rope, you know."

My stomach tightened. "I bet you are, cowboy."

He lowered his lips to mine and kissed me hungrily. When I slid my palm down his abs and rubbed his thickening cock, he groaned. "You're doing it again."

"Doing what?"

"Making me want things I can't have. We have to get going."

I smiled. "You're right. We've been gone longer than we said. Your sister is probably wondering what happened to us."

"She probably guessed what happened to us," he said, letting go of my hair and getting to his feet. He reached down to help me up. "My sisters have been ruthless, teasing me about you."

I let him pull me to my feet and tried to fasten my bra, which still hung on my shoulders. "They have? Why?"

"Here. Let me." He turned me around and hooked it for me. "Because they *claim* they saw the way I looked at you back in high school."

I laughed, grabbing my shorts from the dock and stepping into them. "Awww. You were a perfect gentleman back then."

"You didn't know what I was thinking," he said, pulling on his jeans.

"That's probably a good thing." I reached for my tank and tugged it over my head. "In my mind, you were always a safe place."

"I still want to be that for you."

He sounded so serious, I turned to face him. "You are, Beckett."

"I mean it." He reached out and pulled me against his warm, bare chest. "Even though we can't have the kind of future my friends have, I'll always be your safe place. That's a promise I can keep."

Pressing my cheek against his skin, I looped my arms around his taut waist. "Thank you."

We stood that way for a moment, embracing in the late afternoon sun, and even though I knew better, I sort of wished it could last forever.

Not only that, but I looked over at the trees and imagined a house in the clearing—with a wide front porch and a hammock on one end and a garden on the side and flowers blooming in window boxes and Elliott racing down to swim in the pond with friends so close they were more like cousins and Beckett and I following behind, hand in hand.

Are you crazy? shouted the voice in my head. *You've been here one fucking weekend. You just heard him say he doesn't want that kind of future. You chased a fantasy once before and look where it got you.*

I squeezed my eyes shut, blocking out the view and the voice all at once.

I didn't need the past intruding on this warm, lovely present. So what if it was temporary? It was enough.

It had to be.

CHAPTER 12

BECKETT

"HOW'D IT GO?" Mallory was sprinkling salt over a baking tray full of fresh-cut sweet potato fries as Maddie and I came in from the mudroom.

"Good." I went over to the fridge and grabbed two cold bottles of water. "We worked for several sweltering hours before Moretti showed up and offered to buy the place. He timed it just right."

My sister laughed. "Seriously?"

"Yeah. Pretty sure he was in his car across the street watching with binoculars while we busted our asses in the front yard." I handed one bottle to Maddie and uncapped the other. "Where's Dad?"

"On the deck with the kids and the dog. Sitting in the shade with his puzzle book while they play Barbies." She swapped the salt for pepper.

"They're still at it, huh?" Maddie asked.

"Yes. They've been playing and chatting nonstop," said Mallory. "You'd never guess they just met today."

Maddie laughed. "Elliott is in heaven, I'm sure. Have they been playing Barbies the whole time?"

"Mostly, although they took a brief break to play salon, and he braided her hair. Elliott is so talented!"

"He loves brushing and braiding hair," Maddie said. "And putting on makeup too."

"They get along so well," Mallory said, sticking the tray in the oven and setting a timer. "We're going to have to tear them apart when it's time to go."

"She's welcome to stay over," I said, after chugging half the bottle of water.

"Thanks, but she's got camp in the morning." Mallory turned around and seemed to really see us for the first time. Her expression was puzzled. "Did you guys go swimming or something?"

Maddie touched her damp, matted hair. "Um . . ."

"After we cleaned up, we drove over to the pond to cool off," I said. "It was hot."

"I bet it was." Leaning back against the counter, Mallory didn't bother to disguise her smile. "Did you swim in your clothes?"

"Yes."

"Guess they dried fast."

I frowned at my sister, warning her to behave. "What's for dinner? I take it you're staying."

"Yes. Feel like grilling some burgers? Maybe some hot dogs for the kids?"

"Sure. Let me just grab a quick shower."

"Can I help you with anything, Mallory?" Maddie asked, snapping a ponytail holder around her soggy hair.

She shook her head. "Nope, I'm good. It's nothing fancy. Just burgers and fries."

"I'll get cleaned up too and then I'll put together a salad. I can also set the table. Maybe we can eat out on the patio?"

"Perfect."

Maddie smiled. "I'll be right down."

"No rush." Mallory glanced pointedly at both of us. "Have a nice shower."

I gave her the finger as we left the kitchen.

"She knows," Maddie whispered as we went upstairs.

"She knows."

"Is it okay?" We reached the top and she turned to face me, a worried look on her face.

"Of course it's okay. I might be her younger brother, but I'm a grown man, and this is my fucking house." I wrapped my arms around her waist and kissed her lips. "I do what I want in it. So any time you want to sneak across this hall, my door is open."

She smiled up at me. "Good to know."

After dinner, I tossed some easy pitches at Elliott and Daisy, who took turns batting and fielding the few hits they managed. Maddie played catcher while my sister and dad sat on lawn chairs and cheered everyone on.

When the light faded into dusk, we sat on the deck and watched the sun set as Daisy and Elliott ran around with some sparklers I'd found in the garage. DiMaggio played at their heels, excited to have two young, energetic kids around. I nursed a beer, happier and more relaxed than I'd been in a long time.

I glanced over at Maddie, who sat next to me sipping from a glass of white wine. Her skin glowed in the warm amber light. When she smiled, her eyes crinkled slightly at the corners. When she laughed, she still covered her mouth like she used to when she was young. But her lips were perfect— so full and soft and tempting.

She looked over and caught me staring. "Are you looking at my sunburned face?"

I smiled and rubbed the back of my neck. "No."

"Is your neck still bothering you?"

"It's just a little stiff."

"Here, let me." She got out of her chair, set her wine glass on the table, and stood behind me. "You did all that work for me today. I owe you."

"You don't," I said, but then I groaned with pleasure as her fingers began kneading my sore muscles. "But it does feel good."

My sister laughed. "In other words, he doesn't want you to feel obligated, but he also doesn't want you to stop."

Maddie laughed and worked at a kink with her thumb. "What's going on here? You've got a giant knot."

I couldn't even talk, her hands felt so fucking good on me.

"So Cole's wedding is coming up," Mallory said. "Beck, have you written your speech yet?"

"Could you not call it a speech? It's just a toast."

She laughed. "What's the difference?"

"A speech goes on for like ten minutes. I'm going to talk for ten seconds."

"Beckett Weaver, you better do right by your friend," Mallory chided. "Are you going to Cole's wedding, Maddie?"

"I'd like to," she replied hesitantly. "It sort of depends."

"Are you busy next Saturday night, Mal?" I asked. "I meant to ask you."

"I'm not, in fact. And I'd be glad to come down and stay with Dad and Elliott. I'll bring Daisy, and we can stay over, since it's a Saturday night. She doesn't have camp on Sundays."

"That would be amazing," Maddie said. "I know Elliott would love that too. Thank you so much."

"My pleasure. I'll just bunk in with the kids."

"I might need to ask your advice about where to buy a

dress," said Maddie. "I didn't really pack anything appropriate for a wedding."

"I'm sure whatever you packed is fine," I told her, wincing as she increased the pressure.

Maddie laughed. "Spoken like a true man."

"Ignore him," Mallory said. "If you want something dressy, like cocktail dressy, your best bet is probably Main Street Bridal."

"Beck, do you think the wedding is cocktail dressy? Or more like snappy casual?"

"I have no idea what either of those things mean," I told her. "I'm wearing a suit. It's blue."

Mallory laughed. "Are you friendly with Cheyenne, Maddie? Maybe check in with her."

"Yes, and I will. I need to let her know I'm coming anyway. Oh, and I need to get them a wedding gift."

"Who's getting married again?" Mr. Weaver asked.

"Cole and Cheyenne," I answered. "The invitation is on the fridge. You're invited too if you'd like to go for a little bit."

"Cole Mitchell?"

"Yes."

"Is he old enough to get married?"

I glanced at my father. "He's thirty-three, Dad. Same as me."

He tilted his head. "Can that be right?"

Mallory leaned over and patted his arm. "I still picture those guys as kids sometimes too. Seems like we just watched them graduate from high school, doesn't it?"

"Hey, speaking of graduation," Maddie said. "Do you by any chance still have that photo of us that was taken after the ceremony? I used to have a copy of it, but it got lost along the way."

"I don't think so," I said quickly. Of course, I knew exactly where my copy of that photo was—buried in a shoebox between the barn and the maple tree where I first kissed her.

"Oh, I remember taking that picture," said Mallory. "It was so cute. You sure you don't have it somewhere, Beck?"

"I'm sure."

Maddie sighed. "It *was* a cute picture. I wish I still had it."

"Neither of you has changed a bit since then," Mallory said. "And I think it's great that you're in touch again. You were such good friends."

Maddie laughed, moving her hands to my shoulders. "The crazy thing is, it almost feels like we never lost touch."

"Some friendships are just like that," said Mallory. "You can go a long time without seeing each other and when you're together again, it's like no time has passed."

As Maddie continued to rub one shoulder and then the other, I watched Daisy and Elliott laugh joyously as they twirled on the grass, waving their sparklers in the air against a pink and orange sky. The scent of the lilac bushes bordering the deck mingled with the earthy smell of the barn on the breeze. Everything was bathed in the perfect, hazy golden light of the magic hour as the sun slipped toward the horizon.

I didn't often wish for the impossible, but in that moment I found myself longing to pull Maddie onto my lap and stop time forever.

I didn't want Daisy to age. I didn't want my dad's mind to deteriorate. I didn't want Maddie to leave again. I didn't even want the sun to go down.

I just wanted *now*, forever.

Later, I walked my sister and niece out to the car while Maddie and Elliott tried to FaceTime her ex. I thought it was better I wasn't in the house when that happened anyway. I didn't really want to hear his voice, or worse, see his face.

"Thanks for helping out today," I said to my sister.

"No problem," she said, opening the back passenger door of her minivan for Daisy. "Hug Uncle Beckett goodbye," she told her daughter.

My niece clung to my legs a moment, and I rubbed her back. "See ya, kiddo. Thanks for coming to hang out."

She looked up at me. "Can I play with Elliott again?"

"Definitely. Did you have fun?"

"Yes." She tilted her head. "You're sure he's a boy?"

I laughed and tweaked one of her braids. "I'm sure."

She hopped in the car, and Mallory shut the door. "I wish I could help you out more than once a week. Amy said you put another ad in the paper?"

"Yeah. Hopefully I'll get some replies soon." I glanced toward the house. "I need to find someone like Maddie. She hung out with him all day yesterday. They made breakfast together, she took him into town for lunch, he gave her a tour . . . then we all went over to the ball field and played around a little. Dad even got out on the field. He loved it."

Mallory laughed as she walked around to the driver's side. "I asked him what he did yesterday, and he said, 'Not much.'"

I shook my head, following her. "Figures. His short-term memory is pretty much shot. Ask him what his date wore to the movies in 1958, though, and he can tell you."

"Poor Dad." She opened the car door. "And poor you. Too bad Maddie's not moving back for good, huh?"

I gave her a look. "Stop."

"Come on, Beck. There's *something* between you." She patted my chest. "Relax, I think it's nice. It's healthy. What's not healthy is being cooped up in here with Dad day in, day out."

"It is nice to have her here," I admitted quietly. "And getting to know her son."

She grinned. "Such a cool kid."

"But she lives in Ohio, Mal. End of story."

"Boo. That ending stinks."

"Maybe around three next Saturday if that works?" I asked, anxious to move on from the topic of Maddie and me. "I think I have to be at Cole's by three-thirty."

"Of course. Don't worry about a thing." She rose on tiptoe and ruffled my hair. "Just get all dressed up and show Maddie a good time. Make it the prom night you never had."

I frowned. "How did you know I wanted to take Maddie to the prom?"

"Please." She rolled her eyes. "Everyone in the house knew. Even Dad."

"He did?"

"Yeah. After you left to go get your date, he wondered aloud why you hadn't asked Maddie. And then—I'll never forget this—he said, 'I bet he marries that girl.'"

Laughing, I shook my head. "He needs to get over that. We're not getting married."

She gave me a hug. "Hang in there. I'll see you in a week. And don't hesitate to call me if you need a break sooner. You don't have to be Superman, doing all the things."

I flexed my biceps. "But I make such a good Superman. Don't I, Daisy?"

She giggled from the back seat. "Yes!"

Mallory laughed too as she slid behind the wheel. "Even Superman had a Lois Lane. Don't forget that."

Inside, I let the dog out one last time, got my dad into bed, and finished loading the dishwasher. I was almost finished when Maddie entered the kitchen.

"Hey," I said. "Did you make your call?"

"Yes." She frowned, leaning on the island and crossing her arms. "Sam gave Elliott about five minutes before saying he had to go because he had plans. And he was totally distracted the entire time. I think his girlfriend was there."

"I'm sorry."

"It's okay." She closed her eyes and took a breath. "I don't even bother getting my hopes up anymore with him."

"How's Elliott?"

"He's okay. He's in the shower right now, and then I told him he could have some extra iPad time before bed."

"Sounds good." I loaded the last few pieces of silverware and put in the soap. "Daisy is very excited to come back and play with him."

She laughed gently. "He won't stop talking about her either. I'm so happy she was here today, even if she wasn't as excited about his home run story as he'd have liked."

"What about his dad?" I shut the dishwasher and started it.

"He said something like, 'That's great, bud, but you have to learn to do that when it *counts.*'"

I turned around to see her scowling and didn't blame her. "I'm sorry."

"I am too, for Elliott." She shook it off. "Anyway, I just wanted to come down and say goodnight."

"Oh. Okay."

She walked toward me, twisting her hands together. "It's not that I don't want to come to your room tonight. I just don't think I should. Elliott is feeling sad about the phone call, and if he wandered into my room and I wasn't there, he'd be scared."

"You don't owe me an explanation, Maddie. It's okay." But my heart had sunk to my heels.

She put her arms around my waist and smiled up at me. "I'll be thinking about you. And I'll see you bright and early."

"I'll be thinking about you too." I slipped an arm around her waist and kissed her quickly, before my body could get too excited. "Goodnight."

"Night."

I watched her leave the room with half a hard-on and a heavy heart but told myself it was probably for the best.

As it turned out, however, I saw her long before bright and early.

But first, I heard the click of the door as it shut.

Felt the shift of the mattress as she climbed onto it.

Smelled her perfume.

Rolling onto my side, I stared at her in the dark, wondering if this was a dream.

She peeled off her shirt and tossed it aside. "I couldn't stay away."

I reached for her, turning her body beneath mine, pinning her wrists to the mattress and kissing her savagely, possessively, like she might try to escape. "Good."

"Do you think we can be quieter this time?" she whispered.

"I don't know," I told her, keeping my voice low as I moved my mouth down her throat and chest, inhaling her scent. "We can try."

She laughed softly, but it turned into a sweet little moan as I stroked her nipple with my tongue. I moved my hand to the other breast, kneading it gently before teasing its stiff upturned peak with my fingers. She cradled my head in her hands and arched her back as I licked and sucked and traced circles. "You're not helping," she whimpered. "That feels so good."

"I'm just getting started." Moving lower, I kissed my way down her stomach before sliding her underwear off her legs. I pushed her knees apart and pressed my lips to one soft inner thigh, then the other. "And I plan to be here for a while."

"No, no," she whispered frantically, trying unsuccessfully to grab me by the arms and yank me up. "What are you doing?"

"I'm keeping a promise." I put my tongue between her legs and stroked her, soft and slow, again and again, up, down, side to side.

"We don't . . . we don't have time . . . for that particular promise." But her grip on my biceps loosened.

"This is my bed, in my room, at my house," I reminded her, licking her like ice cream off a spoon. "What I say goes."

"But—but we have to hurry . . ." Her voice trailed off as I slid one finger inside her, then another. She was warm and soft and wet, and my cock bulged with need.

But I would not be rushed this time.

"There will be no hurrying tonight," I whispered as she fell back on the mattress. I eased my fingers deeper. "Scream into a pillow if you have to, but I'm about to fuck you with my tongue, and I'm not going to stop until you come."

"Oh God," she moaned quietly. "I'm in so much trouble."

But she gave herself up to it with delightful surrender, her hands clutching at the sheets, her hips flexing, her breathing quick and desperate as I devoured her like a man starved.

I couldn't get enough of her taste, the way she moved, those helpless little sounds she was making. Beneath my tongue, her clit grew swollen and firm. Her body began to tighten around my fingers. A moment later, she grabbed a pillow and smashed it over her face, attempting to muffle her cries as the orgasm moved through her.

The tremors had barely subsided when she threw the pillow aside and reached beneath my arms again. I went eagerly this time, crushing my mouth to hers, putting her taste on her tongue. She reached between us and sheathed my cock with her hand, working her palm up and down my thick, hard length.

I groaned, thrusting into her fist until I couldn't take it anymore. Positioning myself between her thighs, I pushed inside her, choking back the deep, loud moan threatening to erupt from my chest.

She wrapped her legs around me, threading her fingers into my hair. "God, this feeling. I can't describe it." She pulled my head down so her lips touched mine, whispering softly. "But I need it. I need *you*."

Hearing her say she needed me while my cock was buried inside her was nearly enough to make me lose control, but I held onto it—barely—gliding into her body with long, slow strokes, a little deeper every time. Her hands moved down my back and over my ass, pulling me closer, urging me to go faster. I felt the edges of my strength fraying like a rope.

"I love you inside me," she whispered in my ear. "I had to have it tonight."

Groaning aloud, I reached beneath her and dragged her sideways on the bed so the headboard wouldn't bang against the wall, knowing I was nearly at the breaking point. How many times had I fantasized about her this way—her dark hair spilling onto my pillow, her legs open for me, her breath heavy with desire, her voice soft and desperate as she spoke my name in the dark, told me she needed me, whispered she loved me inside her?

"Come again for me," I growled, moving harder and faster, keeping my body tight to hers.

"I will," she panted, moving her hips in sync with mine. "For you. For you."

I don't know what it was about hearing her repeat those two words, but suddenly I was exploding inside her, pouring myself into her with every throb, and I didn't stop until my body gave out and my world went dark.

Collapsing, I rolled to my side so as not to crush her, holding her close. Resting my lips on her warm forehead, I took a second to catch my breath.

"Were we quiet?" she whispered.

"Quieter than last night at least."

"That's not saying much." She giggled softly. "I almost died when your dad was like, 'It sounded like banging.'"

A laugh rumbled low in my chest. "Me too."

We stayed like that for a few minutes, our breathing in sync, the house quiet, her leg slung over my hip. Drowsy and relaxed, I was almost asleep when she wriggled from my arms. "I'll be right back, okay?"

"Okay." I released her, turning onto my back as she slipped from the bed into my bathroom. Putting my hands behind my head, I closed my eyes and breathed in—the scent of her lingered on the sheets. I hoped she'd stay a little longer.

I'd never been big on cuddling—another complaint of Caroline's.

You never just want to hold me.

You pull away when I try to hold you.

You only want to be close to me during sex.

Usually when she hurled these accusations at me, I told her that I just wasn't a physically affectionate person—it had nothing to do with her. I hadn't grown up in an environment where physical affection was abundant, so I'd never internalized a need for it.

My dad wasn't demonstrative that way, and my sisters were more likely to poke and slap at me than embrace me. I knew they cared, but without a mother around to communicate in a language of hugs and kisses when I was a child, I'd never learned to express myself that way. Nor had I ever craved it.

Until now.

The bathroom door opened and Maddie appeared, her naked skin glowing faintly in the dark. She moved silently toward the bed and stood at the foot. "Hey."

I propped myself up on my elbows. "Hey."

"I should probably go back to my own bed . . . but I don't want to."

"Then don't."

"What if Elliott wakes up?"

"You don't have to sleep here the whole night. Just stay for a little bit." I reached for her.

She took my hand and allowed me to tug her back into bed. "Okay, but don't let me fall asleep."

"I won't." I pulled the covers to our waists and wrapped her in my arms. "Everything okay?"

"Yes." She hesitated. "I took my pill earlier, in case you're concerned. I never forget."

"I trust you."

"I only stayed on it because it helps regulate my cycle."

I wasn't sure how to reply. "Okay."

"I didn't want you to think I run around sleeping with people. I don't."

"I didn't think that."

"You're the first since my divorce."

"You're the first in a long time for me too."

She hugged me tighter and sighed. "My sunburn is awful. I'm going to look ridiculous in the morning. Like a lobster. You won't think I'm pretty anymore."

I chuckled. "I'll always think you're pretty. Does it hurt?"

"Right now, nothing hurts."

Smiling, I pressed my lips to her hair.

A few minutes later, I could tell she'd fallen asleep. Her

breathing was deep and regular, her body was soft and relaxed. I allowed myself a little time to just enjoy the feel of her sleeping in my arms, knowing that she trusted me in all things. But when I caught myself dozing, I squeezed her gently. "Hey."

"Hm?"

"Not that I wouldn't keep you right here all night, but I'm so comfortable, I'm worried I'll fall asleep too."

"Mmm." She nestled even closer. "I'm comfortable too. As hard as your body is, it's surprisingly warm and cozy. I could get used to this."

My heart stumbled a little.

"But I should go." She sighed, planted a kiss on my chest, and sat up. "I'll see you in the morning."

"Okay." I watched her fumble around in the dark, tugging up her underwear and slipping her shirt over her head. Then she knelt on the bed again and kissed me quickly.

"Goodnight," she whispered.

"Night."

A moment later, I was alone again.

But the scent of her lingered, along with the memory of her body next to mine.

And her words.

I could get used to this.

Had she meant it?

For a few minutes, I let myself picture what it might be like—Maddie and Elliott living here with my father and me. Breakfast together every morning. Dinner together every evening. Elliott could attend Bellamy Creek Elementary, just like we had. Maddie could find a nursing job with a pediatrics practice in town. We'd be like a family.

Just as quickly as the fantasy entered my mind, reality came along to shatter it.

Was I insane?

It had been two fucking days.

We'd known each other forever, sure. We'd had some good sex. And being open about my attraction to her was like a deep breath of spring air after being cooped up all winter.

But Maddie wasn't going to leave her home and job in Ohio for me—she wanted Elliott to have stability and familiarity. She wanted his father to play a role in his life. And she loved what she did and where she worked. She wasn't going to give all that up to move back to Bellamy Creek, even if her dickhead ex would allow it.

For what?

The charm of small-town life aside, I'd be taking care of my father well into the foreseeable future. I couldn't ask her to shoulder that burden with me. It wouldn't be fair.

She'd be welcome to visit me whenever she wanted, and my bedroom door would always be open.

Anything beyond that was impossible.

CHAPTER 13
MADDIE

ON TUESDAY AFTERNOON, I met Bianca and Blair at Main Street Bridal, where Cheyenne was having her final fitting. We sat on a pink velvet settee and sighed as we watched Cheyenne come out of the dressing room and make her way to the three-paneled mirror.

Her dress was white lace over champagne satin and fell to the floor in a simple A-line shape. The neckline had a deep V, as did the back, and the short flutter sleeves showed off her graceful arms. It was a formal gown but had a slightly Bohemian feel to it too.

She stepped onto the podium and smiled at us in the mirror. "Well? What do you think?"

"Oh, Chey," breathed Blair, putting a hand over her heart. "I'm going to cry."

"No crying." Cheyenne's smile grew even wider. "This is a happy occasion. I waited my whole life for it."

"These are tears of happiness, okay?" Blair dug a tissue from her purse. "Just let me."

"It's really beautiful, Cheyenne." Bianca stood and went over to admire the sleeves more closely. "The lace is exquisite."

"I agree," I said, catching her eye in the mirror and giving her a smile. "Stunning. The champagne color beneath is perfect with your hair."

"You don't think it's too fancy for a backyard wedding?"

"Not at all," I assured her. "It's just right."

"Cole is going to lose his mind." Blair dabbed at her eyes.

"You should see Mariah's dress. It's so pretty." Cheyenne laughed. "Hard to tell who's more excited about this wedding, her or me."

"Well, it's been a long time coming," said Bianca, clasping her hands beneath her chin. "And I cannot wait to watch you two say your vows."

The seamstress approached, fussed over Cheyenne for a moment and pronounced the gown a perfect fit.

"Thank you," said the bride-to-be, stepping off the podium. "Now let's look for you," she said to me, a gleam in her eye. "We need to find something that will bring Beckett to his knees."

Laughing, I rose to my feet. "I'm all for that."

The girls helped me find a few dresses to try on, and I ended up falling in love with a flowing maxi dress in a pretty shade of dusty blue that reminded me of Beckett's eyes, with a deep plunging V in the front and dramatic low back with crisscross straps. The skirt fell to the floor in soft, rippling folds, and I imagined how they might swish and swirl. Would Beckett ask me to dance?

"That's the one," Bianca said.

"I agree." Blair nodded. "It's perfect."

Even though it was slightly too long, the seamstress assured me she could hem it in time. She brought me a pair of strappy nude satin sandals in my size, and I took off my flats and slipped the heels on my bare feet.

"Much better," she said, kneeling down to pin the hem.

"You think it's okay?" I asked the girls, who stood behind me.

"I think it's gorgeous," Blair said confidently. "And you'll look divine next to Beckett. The guys are wearing navy suits, right?"

"Yes," answered Cheyenne with a smile. "My colors are navy, peach, and champagne. You'll fit right in."

"I will be in the background," I told her with a laugh. "But those colors sound so beautiful."

"I can't wait," she sighed.

"How many people are coming?" I asked.

"We invited about a hundred, and we have eighty-three who responded yes." She crossed her fingers. "Hopefully the weather cooperates. The reception is under a tent, but the ceremony will be out in the open, and I don't want anyone to melt in the heat. Or get rained on."

"It's going to be perfect," I said.

"At least you won't have a blizzard," added Blair. "I don't know what I was thinking, choosing December for a wedding in northern Michigan."

"You were thinking you didn't want to wait to marry the love of your life." Bianca nudged her friend's shoulder.

"You're right," Blair agreed. "I didn't."

I smiled, but inside I wondered what that was like—to be excited to marry someone because you loved them so much. Sam and I had eloped to Las Vegas, but I'd spent half my wedding night watching him play blackjack. I couldn't think of one romantic thing about it. Even his proposal had been lackluster.

Hey. I have to go to Vegas for a conference. What do you say you come along and we get married?

"How did Cole propose?" I asked Cheyenne.

She smiled dreamily. "On Valentine's Day. In *our* room at the Inn at Cloverleigh Farms, the one we'd stayed in for Blair and Griff's wedding. It's where we first got together."

I nodded and looked at Blair. "What about Griffin?"

"Believe it or not, with a billboard on the highway," she

said, shaking her head. "He is not one for grand gestures, but I have to hand it to him—it was pretty amazing. And I was totally shocked."

"Wow. That's so romantic."

"Oh, I can top that," said Bianca. "Let me tell you, nothing says *spend forever with me* like a used engagement ring that says 'Love Always, Ricky' when your future fiancé's name is Enzo."

I laughed. "I bet he made it up to you though."

She grinned. "He did—took him a little while, but he did."

"Okay. All set," said the seamstress, rising to her feet. "Just leave it in the fitting room, and I'll grab it. When you check out, make an appointment to pick it up next week, and bring the shoes back to try it on."

"Thank you, I will." As I stepped off the podium, I looked down at my bare toenails peeking out from the top strap. "Wish I had time for a pedicure."

"Ooh, you should come with us next Friday morning," Cheyenne said. "I could call and try to add you to our appointments."

I smiled at her. "Thanks, but I'll manage. I don't want to leave Elliott and take off for the salon. And I'm trying to keep Mr. Weaver out of trouble during the day so Beckett can work without worrying."

Cheyenne nodded. "I understand."

"Speaking of Beckett, I need to get home before he has to leave for baseball practice."

On my way to the fitting rooms, I passed a bride coming out to the mirrors. She wore a big white dress and a wide happy grin, her cheeks flushed with excitement. Behind her, a woman that might have been her mother carried the dress's long train. She was smiling too, her eyes misty.

I stood aside so they could get by me. "Gorgeous gown," I said.

"Thank you. It's my final fitting." The bride giggled nervously. "I can't believe it."

"You look beautiful," I told her. "Congratulations."

She thanked me again, and they disappeared into the salon. Pulling aside the velvet curtain of my fitting room, I took off the blue dress and hung it up. As I slipped my floral sundress back over my head, I wondered if I'd ever experience that kind of excitement—the kind that emanates from your heart and lights you up from the inside out and makes you feel like the luckiest, most beautiful girl in the world because someone loves you enough—you, just as you are—to promise you forever and mean it.

Had I forfeited my chance already?

Or was there still hope?

"Anyone have time for a quick drink at the pub?" Blair asked as we left the salon and stepped out onto the sidewalk. "We could sit at one of the outdoor tables."

"Me," said Bianca, clapping her hands. "It's Enzo's turn to make dinner. I've got an hour."

"I wish I could, but I have to get home," Cheyenne said, draping the heavy garment bag holding her dress over one arm.

"I should get back too," I said. "Beckett was trying to work, keep his dad occupied, and keep an eye on Elliott all at the same time when I left."

"How's everything going with you guys?" Bianca asked.

"Good." I could feel the heat creeping into my cheeks. "Really good."

"Wait, what did I miss?" Blair grabbed my arm. "Did something happen since I saw you Saturday night?"

"Um, yes." I exchanged a grin with Bianca.

"Does this mean there is now officially a *thing*?" Cheyenne squealed.

"I suppose," I said, laughing. "There's *something*, at least. I'm not sure how official it is."

Bianca let out a huge breath, as if she'd been holding it in for an hour. "God, it's been so hard keeping that in for two days!"

"I know you only have a minute, but give us the quick version," Blair begged. "Did you end up having to make the first move?"

"Sort of." I told them about Saturday night—our conversation in the hall, sneaking across to his bedroom, the scene in the kitchen afterward.

"Oh no," Cheyenne said, laughing a little. "Poor Mr. Weaver. And poor you. It must be tough to get alone time."

"It *is* tough," I said. "We managed to steal an hour or so on Sunday afternoon at this pond on his property—"

"Oh, I *love* that place," said Blair wistfully. "It's such a beautiful spot."

I smiled, remembering what Beckett had told me about offering to sell the land to Griffin. "I've snuck into his room the last couple nights, but I always have to sneak right back out. Elliott sometimes looks for me in the middle of the night. I don't want him to find an empty bed and get scared."

"You said his sister is watching Elliott the night of the wedding, right?" Bianca asked. "Maybe you two could spend the night away somewhere. Like at a hotel or something."

"I don't know if I'd feel right about that," I said hesitantly. "As much as I'd like to spend a whole night with Beckett, it would feel kind of irresponsible to abandon Elliott to do it. And I'm not sure Beckett would leave his dad overnight either. He has to help him get ready for bed and dressed in the morning and everything."

"Wow." Blair shook her head and sighed. "I can't imagine

what that must be like, to have to take care of your parent that way. If Griff and I ever have kids, I hope they're as good to us as Beckett is to his dad."

"But you guys will at least have each other," I said. "Mr. Weaver doesn't have anyone else."

"Has he ever told you what happened to his mom?" Cheyenne asked curiously. "Why she left?"

I shook my head. "Nope. And he claims it was so long ago that it doesn't matter, but I think deep down, it must."

"I agree," said Bianca. "I mean, maybe that's why Beckett has never had a serious relationship. Something like that can really mess with you."

"Maybe." I shrugged. "But you know how Beckett is. He'll never say that. What guy would?"

They all murmured in agreement and Cheyenne checked her phone. "It's almost five, you guys. I better go."

We said goodbye, and Blair and Bianca walked down the sidewalk toward the pub, while Cheyenne and I turned toward the public parking lot at the end of the block.

"That's so great about you and Beckett," she said. "Is there a chance you'll try to make it work long distance?"

"I'm not sure," I said honestly.

"Does Elliott ever spend weekends with his dad?"

"He's supposed to, but Sam cancels a lot."

She glanced at me. "That must be hard."

"Unfortunately, Elliott is learning that he cannot depend on his father to keep his word. But he sees a therapist every other week, so I'm hoping that helps him recognize it's not his fault." I laughed a little. "We both see a therapist, actually."

"Mariah sees a therapist too," Cheyenne confided. "In fact, so does Cole."

"Really?" We reached the lot, and I turned to face her.

"Yes. I don't think he talks about it much, so Beckett might not even know, but he started going last year, when we first got together."

I nodded, recalling what Beckett had told me about Cole losing his first wife. "Did he feel like he needed permission to date again or something?"

"Not so much that as he needed to deal with his fear of loss—of losing someone he loved. Things with us got serious quickly, and it scared him."

"Wow. So did therapy help?"

"Definitely." She smiled. "I doubt we'd be getting married next Saturday if he hadn't dealt with those demons. So I think you're doing the right thing in seeking therapy. And in sending Elliott."

"I told Beckett the other night I thought everyone needed therapy," I said, laughing. "He said it sounded horrible to him."

She sighed. "Yeah, Beckett is probably like Cole was. He thought men just have to tough it out. And maybe Beckett is telling you the truth when he says it doesn't matter about his mom leaving. He was just a baby, right? Does he even remember her?"

"No. He's only seen pictures." I paused. "But he said this one thing the other day, and I can't stop thinking about it."

"What did he say?"

"He was talking about marriage, and he said he thinks it's too much to ask of someone—to stay forever."

Her brows rose. "Really?"

"Yes." I bit my lip. "It made me feel sad, but I couldn't even argue with him."

"Why not?"

"Because what if it's true? What if he's right and *I want to be with you forever* is just something people say when what they really mean is *I want to be with you for now*?"

Cheyenne took a deep breath. "I wish I had the answer. I

think it's something you just feel in your gut. In your bones. In your heart."

I slapped my hands over my face and groaned. "God, I'm a terrible person. Here you are getting married next weekend and I'm droning on about doubt and fear. I'm so sorry, Cheyenne."

"Hey, it's okay." She reached out and rubbed my shoulder. "Experience has made you question whether real love exists, but give it time. If I've learned anything, it's that love cannot be rushed. You can wish on every star and birthday candle and fluffy dandelion head for twenty years, but you can't will it into being. It happens when it happens."

I smiled. "I'm really happy for you. And for Cole."

"Thanks." She returned the smile. "I'm so glad you'll be at the wedding. And you know what?"

"What?"

"Don't worry about what's down the road. If I could do anything differently, I'd go back and tell myself not to agonize so much. It took a lot of patience and strength to hold out for what I really wanted, but it was worth the wait. And I truly believe what's meant to be will be."

"You're right," I said, lifting my chin. "I'm going to stop worrying."

"Good. Love is sneaky, you know. It tends to hit you when you least expect it." Above us, thunder rolled softly in the distance. Cheyenne looked up and laughed. "Just like lightning."

I laughed too, giving her a quick hug. "We better go. I'll see you soon."

When I got home, I found Mr. Weaver and Elliott sitting at the kitchen table eating giant bowls of Cap'n Crunch.

"What's this?" I asked, setting down the bag with my new heels in it.

"We got hungry," Elliott said, lifting a heaping spoonful of cereal to his mouth. "Eugene said we could have a snack."

"Eugene?" I raised my eyebrows.

"He said to call him that," Elliott answered defensively.

"I did." Mr. Weaver took a bite of cereal. "Mr. Weaver made me sound like an old man. I don't want to be an old man."

I laughed, and he winked at me. It seemed like he was having a really good day today. It was definitely the sharpest he'd been since I'd arrived.

"Is it okay?" Elliott asked, dripping milk on the table.

"It's fine," I said, crossing my arms. "But what are we going to do about your dinner?"

"We can have it later. After our snack, Eugene is going to teach me to play gin rummy."

"That sounds like fun," I said. "While you're playing, I'll get dinner together and we can eat a little later tonight. Where's Beckett?"

"In the barn." Elliott tried to unhinge his jaw to fit the towering pile of Cap'n Crunch on his spoon in his mouth.

"Okay. I'm going to go out and let him know dinner will be a little later," I said, heading for the mudroom. "I'll be right back."

I went out the back door and headed across the yard for the barn. Darker clouds were rolling in from the west, and a cool breeze moved through the hot, humid air, ruffling my dress around my legs. Thunder continued to rumble every couple minutes, and the air smelled like a storm.

Stepping through the open double doors, I flapped at a fly that buzzed around my head and let my eyes adjust to the dim light.

Dust and chaff swam through the air like fish in an aquarium. Pudge, Beckett's horse, stuck his nose out of his stall, as if he was hoping for some attention. I rubbed his velvety nose before moving on, my flats shuffling over hay-strewn concrete. I reached the end of the barn without seeing Beckett and figured I must have missed him when I walked by the tack room. But when I backtracked and poked my head in, he wasn't there either. Thunder growled again overhead, a little louder now.

When I heard creaking boards above me, I looked up. "Beckett?" I called.

He didn't answer. I looked around and spotted a wooden ladder leading to the hay loft. I went over and climbed up, spotting him as soon as my head cleared the rectangular opening. It was a large rectangular space with hay bales piled along the perimeter and tossed haphazardly on the floor. It was slightly darker up here, although grayish light slanted in from windows at either end.

"Hey," I said, reaching the top.

"Hey." He glanced at me, making my breath hitch. His forehead was shiny, his jeans were a mess, and his T-shirt was stained with sweat. His boots were caked with mud, his hair looked like he'd tossed his hat somewhere and run his fingers through it, and if I got near enough, I knew he'd probably smell like a hard day's work.

Still, he was the hottest man I'd ever seen.

I moved closer. "Whatcha doin' up here all by your lonesome?"

"Seeing how badly the roof needs repairing. We don't use this space much for hay storage anymore since I put up the new sheds, so—" He laughed as I slipped my arms around his waist, pressing my chest to his. "You're not gonna want to get that close, Mad. I'm filthy. And I don't even want to think about what I must smell like."

"You smell like a man. Like a cowboy." I tipped my head

back and winked at him. "And cowboys happen to turn me on."

He groaned, and against my stomach, I felt his cock start to swell through his jeans. "Did you come up here to torture me?"

"Maybe." I moved one hand to his crotch and rubbed the thickening bulge, my insides igniting.

"What did I tell you about teasing me that way?" he growled, backing me toward the bales of hay lining one side of the loft.

"I forget," I said breathlessly, moving my hand up and down over thick denim. "Maybe you should remind me."

"Maybe I should do more than that." He gave me a gentle shove, and I toppled backward onto a pile of scratchy golden hay. Thunder boomed again. The shadows in the loft grew deeper. "Don't move," he said.

I stayed where I was, panting and anxious, while he looked around. Then he walked over to the opposite wall and grabbed a length of rope hanging on a nail. As he sauntered toward me again, he wound it through his big, strong hands.

"What's that for?" I asked, my voice a little shaky, more from excitement than fear. My heart raced as I looked up at him.

"That's to make sure you don't torture me while I have my way with you." Dropping to his knees, he worked fast, not only tying my crossed wrists together but securing them to a post just behind my head.

"What are you going to do to me?" I tugged against the restraints, but they were knotted tight.

He looked amused. "Told you I was good with a rope." He pushed my dress up to my waist and yanked my panties down. Then he tossed both legs over his shoulders and lowered his head between my thighs.

"Beckett!" I cried out as his tongue swept up my center. Rain began to drum against the roof. "We don't have time!"

"You're not the boss here." He drew circles around my clit, making my entire body tingle. "I am."

I moaned, relieved that for once I could be loud while he did this to me—he was so fucking *good* at it. "But what about—"

"They're fine."

"But it's raining—"

"So they won't leave the house."

"But I said I would—"

"Woman, do I need to tie up your jaw too?" Reaching beneath me, he pinched my ass—hard—before stroking me again with his tongue. "Now be quiet so I can make you come with my tongue before I do it with my cock."

"How am I—supposed to be quiet—during any of that?" I gasped for breath as he set my whole body on fire, every muscle in my body pulling tight. "You make me want to scream."

"Then scream," he said calmly. "I'll enjoy it."

In less than two minutes, the rain was pounding against the barn roof and I was crying out at the top of my lungs, yanking at the ropes around my wrists, bucking up beneath him, my legs locked tight around his head, his fingers digging into my thighs.

The moment the tremors subsided, he took off his belt, whipped off his shirt, and unzipped his jeans, shoving them down around his hips. Then he stroked his towering cock while I watched with wide, greedy eyes. "This is exactly what you wanted. Admit it. This is why you came up here in that dress you know I like. You did it on purpose."

"Yes," I said, desperate for him, pulling against the ropes even though I knew I couldn't escape and my wrists were rubbed raw. His eyes raked over my body—dress hitched to my waist, breasts straining against the bodice, bare thighs open to him. He was so gorgeous and sexy, his chest massive and slick with sweat, the muscles in his arms bulging, his cock big and hard, I writhed on the hay in front of him, unashamed to let him see how much I wanted him. Unafraid to say the words. "Beckett, I've never wanted anyone the way I want you."

"You have no idea what you do to me." His voice was raspy with desire, his blue eyes dark as storm clouds. "What you've always done to me."

"Show me," I pleaded. "Let me feel. You can punish me for it—you can tie me down, scold me, bruise me. But let me feel the way you want me. Let me feel like I'm yours."

With a deep groan rumbling in the back of his throat, he pushed inside me and began to move. Unlike the past two nights in his bed, it wasn't sweet or gentle—it was rough and sweaty and dirty. He fucked me like I asked him to, like he wanted to punish me. Like he wanted to leave marks on my body. Like he wasn't sure whether he'd hated me or loved me all these years.

But it ran deep, what he felt. It ran deep and hot and strong, uncontrollable as lightning, unstoppable as rain. The hay beneath me was firm, the loft floor solid, but I felt as if I were dangling off the edge of a cliff. I jerked my hands at the ropes that bound them, desperate to cling to him so he could pull me back to safety.

My helpless cries of pain and pleasure mingled with Beckett's labored breaths and anguished cursing through a clenched jaw. His hands gripped my thighs and yanked me toward him while his hips drove his cock into me in an unceasing, savage rhythm until we both groaned in agonized relief as the tension between us exploded. Everything around me turned to gold and nothing mattered except his body pulsing inside me and my wild, crazy heart and this fire burning between us that refused to die down.

As he untied the ropes and tenderly kissed the inside of each wrist, I realized I didn't even want it to.

But I wasn't sure I had a choice.

CHAPTER 14
BECKETT

I LOWERED her dress before getting to my feet and hitching up my jeans. "You okay?"

She propped herself up on her elbows. "I don't know. I might not be able to walk back to the house."

"Good." Smiling, I offered her a hand and helped her to her feet.

Running her hands up my abs and chest, she shook her head. "Your body is insane."

"My body needs a shower." I looked around for my shirt, spied her underwear, and scooped it up. "I think these belong to you."

"Thanks." She stepped into them while I grabbed my shirt, tugged it over my head, and slipped my belt through the loops. Rain thrummed loudly on the roof above us.

"Sounds bad out there," I said. "Do you want me to grab an umbrella for you?"

"No. I'll be okay."

"What about your dress?"

She cocked her head and poked her hands on her hips. "*Now* you're worried about my dress? After you threw me down in the hay and nearly ripped it off me?"

"Uh, yes?" I laughed. "Sorry, I don't know what the right answer to that question is."

"Are you sorry you were so rough with me?"

"Another hard question. This is a tough test."

Sighing, she went over to the ladder and started down. "Never mind. But if someone asks me why I have rope burns on my wrists, I'm telling them you tied me up in the barn and had your way with me. You only pretend to be a gentleman."

I came down after her, jumping from the third rung to the ground. "Are you implying I don't have nice manners?"

She crossed her arms over her chest. "I'm afraid so."

"Huh." I grabbed my hat off the peg it was resting on near the tack room door and placed it on my head. "Then I guess I'll have to prove you wrong."

"What do you mean?"

I strolled toward her, and she backed up.

"Beckett Weaver, you've got a wicked look in your eye. What are you—"

Moving too quick for her to get out of my way, I grabbed her by the waist and threw her over my shoulder.

She squealed and thumped on my back. "Beckett! Put me down!"

I headed out of the barn and into the pouring rain. "I'm saving you from the mud like a gentleman. It's a mess out here."

"You didn't even shut the barn doors!" she yelled.

"I'll go back out."

Laughing, she continued to squirm and struggle, but I had an arm locked tight around her thighs. There was no way she was getting away from me. With the rain soaking us both, I made my way across the yard and climbed the steps to the side porch, where I set her down.

"Oh my God, I'm drenched," she said, looking up and letting the rain pelt her face.

"But your feet are clean."

She looked down at her flats. "I guess they are. So thank you."

I tipped my dripping hat to her. "Ma'am."

She laughed and wound her arms around my neck. "I take back what I said. Your manners are fine."

Lowering my voice, I leaned closer to her, pressing her back against the house. "Does that mean I can have my way with you again later?"

Her eyes lit up, but her expression was coy. "We'll see about that."

The rain continued to pummel our skin, but I didn't care. Unable to resist those lips that had always tempted me so, I lowered my mouth to hers and kissed her deeply, my tongue stroking hers, my hands sliding up the back of her wet dress. She clung to me, her body pressed against mine, her mouth open. In my head, I heard her soft voice begging—*let me feel like I'm yours.*

There was nothing I wanted more. Nothing I'd ever wanted more.

Reluctantly, I tore my mouth from hers, and we stood for a moment, eyes locked, breathing hard. "Maddie," I said, my voice hoarse. I took her face in my hands. For a moment, we were eighteen again, standing under that maple tree, and there was something I had to tell her. Something that needed to be said.

"What?" she whispered.

But the words refused to come.

"Nothing." I kissed her forehead. "Go on in the house and get dry."

Then I turned and left the porch, heading back across the muddy yard toward the barn with long, angry strides.

The storm passed quickly, but our seven o'clock baseball practice was canceled since the field would be too soggy. Griffin, who served as unofficial team manager, texted the three of us with the news at six-thirty.

We could go to the gym instead, Cole suggested. **Get a workout in.**

Or we could skip working out and head to the pub. **Get a few beers in**, texted Moretti.

I vote beers, said Griffin. **Weaver can break the tie.**

I was up in my room, peeling off my wet, dirty clothes. My back was aching a little, so I didn't really feel like lifting. Downstairs, Maddie was making spaghetti and garlic bread, and the whole house smelled amazing. I kind of just wanted to stay at home. But I hadn't hung out with all three of my friends in a while, and Maddie would be here when I got back. Maybe I could have dinner here and then meet the guys afterward.

Beers, I texted. **I'll meet you at 7:30.**

After a quick shower, I threw on jeans and a T-shirt and went downstairs. My dad and Elliott were playing cards at the kitchen table, and Maddie was tossing pasta with tomato sauce at the stove. With Dad and Elliott distracted, I pressed up close behind her and wrapped my arms around her waist. She'd traded her wet dress for shorts, a tank top, and that soft blue sweater. I kissed the side of her neck and inhaled the scent of her skin.

"Beckett," she scolded in a whisper. "They'll see us."

"I don't care," I told her, but I let her go. "By the way, practice was canceled. But if it's okay with you, I'll meet the guys for a beer after dinner."

"Of course it's okay." She licked sauce off her finger and carried the pasta bowl over to the table. "We've got big plans here. Your dad and I are going to dig out some old photo albums—he wants to show me some of his baseball pictures

—and Elliott claims he's going to whoop my derrière in gin rummy."

"Whoop your *butt*," Elliott clarified.

She gave him a stern look as she set the bowl down. "We don't say *butt* at the table."

"Maybe *you* don't," he muttered, making my dad laugh.

Maddie sighed. "Clean up the cards and go wash your hands." She came back to the kitchen as the oven timer went off. "Beck, can you pull the bread out while I grab us some plates?"

"Sure. Thanks for making dinner." While no one was in the room, I pulled her into my arms and kissed her. "You spoil me."

She smiled, her cheeks going pink. "It's my pleasure."

"You don't really have to go back to Ohio, do you?"

She laughed. "I think my boss would appreciate it if I showed up for work when I'm supposed to."

"What if I tied you up and refused to let you go?"

Her eyes widened, her smile amused. "Where would you keep me?"

"Hmm." I buried my face in her neck. "The bedroom. No —the kitchen. I love when you cook. But the barn was fun too. I can't decide."

"Tied up in a barn." She laughed and playfully pushed me away. "You really know how to make a girl an offer she can't refuse."

The oven timer beeped again, and I switched it off before grabbing an oven mitt. "A cowboy doesn't *offer* to tie a girl up, Maddie. He just does it."

"Well, in that case," she said, swatting me on the butt, "I suppose I'll have to watch myself around you."

I glanced at her over my shoulder and felt the cracks in my heart widen. "Damn right."

By eight o'clock, the guys and I were seated at our favorite table at the back of the Bulldog Pub, working on our second beers. We'd already discussed the lineup for next Thursday's game, talked shit about the Mason City Mavericks—our first opponent of the season and chief rival in the Allegan County Senior Men's League—and argued about whether MLB superstars were worth their astronomical salaries.

Once baseball talk was exhausted, Moretti turned to Cole. "So you ready to get hitched?"

"I hope so," he said with a laugh, "since a hundred people are coming to watch it happen."

"You sure you don't want any kind of bachelor party?" Griffin asked.

"I'm positive." Cole shook his head. "Been there, done that. I'm happy with this right here."

"And we should be at your house by three-thirty that day, right?" I asked.

"Yeah. Ceremony is at five, but there are pictures before." Cole took a long drink from his beer. "There are pictures about fifty fucking times that day."

Griffin groaned. "I remember that. And then we got them back and Blair was like, 'Dammit, why aren't you smiling in any of these?'"

"I didn't mind the pictures," said Moretti.

I laughed. "Of course you didn't."

"Cheyenne says you're bringing Maddie Blake with you," Cole said to me. "That's cool."

Just hearing her name made heat rise in me. I nodded and tipped up my beer.

"Oh yeah, I heard she was staying with you." Griffin glanced sideways at me from my right. "How's that going?"

"Good." I tried to sound casual. "She just came to town to sell her mom's house. Actually, Moretti's going to buy it."

"Oh yeah?" Cole looked at Moretti.

He shrugged. "It needs some work, but I think it's a good buy for the location. It'll make a good rental property."

"She's really relieved that you offered," I told him. "This makes things a lot easier on her."

"She's got a son, right?" Cole asked.

I nodded. "Elliott. He's six. Such a great kid."

"I bet he loves being on the ranch." Cole tipped up his beer. "Mariah is always asking to come back and ride a horse again."

"Anytime," I told him. "She's always welcome."

"So is there anything going on between you and Maddie?" Griffin asked.

"Not really." I pretended to get interested in the game that was on the TV above the bar.

Cole laughed. "Is that a yes or a no?"

"I think it's a '*Yes, but I don't want to talk about it.*'" Griffin tipped his chair back on two legs. "Am I right?"

I shrugged. "It's complicated."

He balled up a soggy cocktail napkin and threw it at me.

"Fuck off." Laughing, I threw it back. "Look, we're having fun together. That's all I can say."

"Fun is good. How long is she in town?" Cole asked.

"She has to go back next weekend. Right after the wedding." I ignored the pang in my gut as I said it.

"What about after that?"

"We haven't really talked about it."

Moretti spoke up. "From what she's said to Bianca, she's pretty into you."

Across the table, I did my best impression of the Moretti smolder. "I mean, who wouldn't be?"

He laughed. "Dickhead."

"Didn't you put her photo in our time capsule?" Cole asked.

"Oh yeah," Griffin said slowly. "I forgot about that."

"I don't remember," I lied. "I might have."

"*I* remember," Moretti said. "You did. That's how fucking long you've been into her. So all I'm saying is, now that you guys finally managed to hook up and it's a good thing, why throw it away?"

"I'm not throwing anything away," I said irritably. "But I'm not really into the idea of a long-distance relationship. I can't see how it would work. End of discussion."

But on the drive home, I thought about what Moretti said. It's not like he was entirely wrong. I *had* been into Maddie forever, and it *was* a good thing between us. But I wasn't throwing it away—I was being realistic. I was being honest.

My friends couldn't understand. Their choices were different than mine because their options were different. None of them had to run a business and take care of an aging parent on their own. Sure, Cole had Mariah, but she was getting more independent every day, as opposed to my father, who was growing *less* independent.

Maybe someday circumstances would be different, but you couldn't make a promise to someone about *someday*. No one wanted to hear that. It wasn't fair. Especially to someone like Maddie, who gave so much of herself trying to please other people.

But as I pulled into my driveway, knowing she was inside the house had me excited to walk through the door.

Coming home to her just felt good.

"Hey. Did you have fun?" Maddie looked over at me from where she sat with my father on one couch, an old photo album on her lap. Elliott was playing with DiMaggio on the floor by the windows.

"It was okay. I'm tired." I rolled my shoulders again. "And I think I did something to my neck today."

"Want me to try to work out the knots?"

"Nah. I'll just take some ibuprofen before I go to bed."

"Come here." She stood up and held the album out to me. "You sit and turn the pages, and I'll rub your neck and shoulders while we look at the pictures."

I did as she asked, taking her place next to my dad and opening the album on my lap. It was probably the oldest one we had, the first few pages full of grainy old black and white shots with white borders from even before my dad's time.

"There's the old house," my father said as I studied a photo of my grandparents standing in front of the old farmhouse. "I don't exactly know what happened to it. But that's where I grew up."

It struck me how much my dad resembled *his* dad in his old age, and I knew that I was probably looking at my own future too. Would someone sit down and look at photos of me someday and wonder who I was and what my life was like?

I turned the pages as Maddie's fingers worked on my sore muscles. It was soothing and painful at the same time.

"That was my first dog, Cobb," my dad said, pointing a thick, knobby finger at a photo of himself around age eight with a German Shepherd. "All my dogs were named for baseball players."

The next page had lots of baseball photos of my dad, and he pointed to each uniform and told us which team he played for that year and sometimes included a highlight from that season.

As I turned the pages, the pictures went from black and white to faded color—birthdays and holidays and baseball games and summer afternoons on the farm. Some of them I'd never seen before, but when I asked about the people in them, my dad could tell me just about everyone's name and something about the occasion when the photo was taken. I tried to commit some of the details to memory, so that I'd be able to name the family members and tell the stories one day—although I wasn't sure who'd want to hear them. I just knew I didn't want them to be lost to time. Suddenly I was glad we were doing this now, before my father's memory failed him completely.

Then I turned another page, and there she was.

"Oh, *there's* Cynthia Mae," my dad said, as if he'd misplaced his wife the other day.

He tapped the photograph of a pretty woman with a scarf tied over her auburn curls, a baby in her arms. She sat on a couch, my father beside her, his arm around her shoulders. The smile on his face was one of love and pride. In his eyes was nothing but joy. "She's holding Amy in that picture. We'd just brought her home from the hospital."

"That's your mom, Beckett?" Maddie asked softly, leaning closer to the album, so close I could smell her perfume.

But my throat was so tight, I couldn't answer right away. And I couldn't take my eyes off my father's image. It was like looking in a mirror—the same eyes, the same coloring, the same wide shoulders and muscular arms. Even his hands looked like mine. The wide palms, which I knew must have been thick with calluses. The visible veins. The long fingers.

He must have thought he had everything good in front of him. He must have looked at his wife and baby daughter and felt like there was nothing he wouldn't do for them. He must have thought they were only at the beginning of what they'd build—a family, a home, a life together.

Even she looked happy to be in that moment, a brand new baby in her arms, a husband at her side. How had things gone so wrong?

I cleared my throat. "Yes."

"She's beautiful," Maddie said. "She looks like Mallory."

I turned the page. There were more pictures of my mother with my sisters as toddlers, and one of her holding an infant I assumed was me. But the light had gone out of her eyes. The smile was gone from her face. Had she already decided to leave? Was that the last time she'd held me? Had she known it then? How could you bring yourself to walk away from someone you loved the way a mother was supposed to love her child? Had she even said goodbye?

My dad said nothing else about her, and I was glad.

The album's next few pages had goofy pictures of my sisters dressed in fluorescent leg warmers and roller-skates, their hair teased and their eyeliner heavy. Maddie laughed at snapshots of me as a skinny, gap-toothed kid in baseball pants that were too short for me, and gasped when she saw a photo from what I guessed was eighth grade of me, Griffin, Cole, and Moretti sitting on a tractor out back.

"Oh, look at you guys," she said, almost like she was sad about it. "Just babies."

There were more baseball pictures, and some newspaper clippings too, from my high school years. "I didn't even realize you saved all this, Dad."

"Of course I did," he said. "You'll want to show your own kids someday."

I swallowed hard and turned the page, and there was the photo of my three best friends and me after graduation, the copy of which I'd put in the time capsule.

Maddie sighed. "So handsome."

"So young," I said, thinking about everything that had happened since then.

"I always felt like I had four sons," said my dad, pointing at them. "They were always running around here. And you." Suddenly he looked back at Maddie and smiled. "You were always at the kitchen table."

She laughed. "I was here a lot, wasn't I? But you know what? I loved it over here. It was always so homey and comfortable. My house was always so quiet and empty by comparison."

"I always told Beckett he should—"

"Okay, time for bed," I interrupted, because I had a feeling I knew how he was going to finish that sentence. I closed the album and stood up. "Ready, Dad?"

"I guess." He scratched his head and rose to his feet. "Time sure does fly, doesn't it?"

"Yes."

"But you know," he said, glancing at Maddie and then back at me. "Some things never change."

Later, when the house was dark and silent, Maddie crept across the hall into my room.

"Hey," she whispered, slipping into bed beside me.

"Hey." I wrapped her warm body in my arms and pulled her to my side.

"Were you sleeping?"

"Nah."

"I wasn't sure if I should come in here tonight."

"Why?"

"I don't know." She played with the hair on my chest. "You seemed a little tense earlier. Not just in a muscular way."

I was silent a moment. "Yeah. I guess I am."

"Want to talk about it?"

"Nothing to talk about, really."

She kissed my chest. "Liar. But if you don't want to talk, it's okay."

"You're actually going to let me get out of talking?"

"Yes. I am." She snuggled closer, wrapping her arm around my torso. "I'm growing more comfortable with your silences."

"Good."

She lasted exactly ten seconds. "But I am a good listener, just so you know."

"I know."

"Was it the old pictures?"

"I thought you were comfortable with my silences."

"I may have overestimated my comfort level."

Exhaling, I wondered if I could even articulate it. "I guess they made me a little sad."

"I could tell. Because of your mom?"

"Actually, it was mostly because of my dad. I guess it just hit me hard tonight how different his life has been from what he imagined for himself as a husband and father. And seeing those photos of him—he looks so much like me—it was just sort of a strange feeling."

"I get that." She picked her head up and looked down at me. "You *do* look like him in those photos. It struck me too."

I tucked her dark hair behind her ear, and she pressed her cheek into my palm. "I feel like I'm going to blink and be eighty-one, sitting there on the couch with white hair and arthritic hands, looking at photographs and wondering where my life went," I confessed.

"You'll know, Beckett. It will all be right in front of you." She got to her knees, sitting back on her heels and spreading her arms. "You'll have this incredible place that *you* built. You'll have this ranch that *you* kept alive. You'll have amazing family. You'll have three best friends—the same three best friends you've had since you were a kid—who would probably take a bullet for you. And you'd take one for them."

"I would," I said seriously.

"And you'll have me." She straddled me and reached for

my hands, lacing our fingers together. "You'll always have me."

I swallowed hard. "Maddie, I—"

"Shh," she said, leaning over to kiss my lips. "I'm not asking for any promises. I know you can't make them."

"I wish I could," I told her honestly.

"I just like being with you, Beckett." She moved her lips across my jaw, down my neck, over my chest. "You make me feel good. And tonight, all I want is to make *you* feel good."

"You already have."

She picked up her head and looked up at me. "Are you saying you don't want the blow job I was about to give you?"

My cock jumped. "Uh, no. I am not saying that."

"Good. Then just relax. Let me make it all better." She lowered her head again, but I put my hand beneath her chin.

"Wait." I reached over and snapped on the lamp on my nightstand. "I want to watch you."

She gave me a seductive smile that sent my blood rushing hot and hard straight to my cock before she yanked her pineapple shirt over her head. She tossed it aside and continued to kiss her way down my body, those soft, full lips like heaven on my skin. Tugging the waistband of my underwear down slightly, she ran her tongue along my abdomen, making my stomach muscles quiver and flex. After pulling them all the way off, she traced the V from my hips to the tip of my cock with her index fingers. Then she leaned down and retraced the path with her tongue, first on one side, then the other. I held my breath, waiting for the first stroke across the crown.

She laughed softly.

"Is something funny?" I asked, propping myself onto my elbows.

"I was just thinking about when we were teenagers." She looked up at me with mischief in her eyes. "Like, what if I'd done this back then? Dropped to my knees beneath the kitchen table? Put my mouth on you like this."

And there it was—the soft, velvety sweep of her tongue circling the tip of my cock.

I groaned as I watched her, my entire body shivering. "You don't want to know what would have happened."

"Tell me." She licked the length of my shaft, bottom to top.

"You'd have had a hot mouthful in about three seconds."

Her eyes flicked up to mine. "I used to have this one fantasy about you." She licked me again from root to tip.

"You did?"

"Yeah." She wrapped her fist around me and swirled her tongue across the crown.

"What did I do?"

She didn't answer right away. Instead, she took the tip of my cock between her lips and sucked gently, making my entire lower body tighten—abs, thighs, core.

"Instead of studying, you took me up to your room." She did it again, taking a little more of me into her mouth this time. "You kissed me like I wanted to be kissed. You undressed me."

"Yes," I whispered through clenched teeth as she took me a little deeper, sucked a little harder.

"And you held me like I wanted to be held."

"Yes." She took me to the back of her throat, and I couldn't help rocking my hips—slowly and gently, so I didn't lose control—my hands clenching the sheets.

After a moment, she pulled me from her mouth and slipped my swollen flesh through both fists. "You put your hands all over my body. You touched me everywhere. You let me touch you. You said you wanted me to be your first."

"Fuck." I was so hard, so desperate for her, I felt like the teenager she was describing. "I did want that."

"And I wanted you to be mine, but I was scared," she whispered, lowering her mouth to me again, licking me like candy. "Because you were so big. I thought you might hurt me."

She sucked again, taking me in deep, using her hands along the hot, slippery length of my erection. I fisted one hand in her hair and rolled my hips beneath her.

"But we couldn't stop ourselves. And it did hurt," she said, pausing for a breath. "But just for a minute. You were so gentle with me. You said you wanted to make me come."

"And did I?"

"Yes. I couldn't get enough. I still can't." She took me in deep again, and this time I couldn't hold back. With my hand clenched tight in her hair, I fucked her mouth hard and fast, nearly out of my mind with the need to release all the tension in my body. But before it happened, I pulled out and flipped her onto her back.

"Don't you want me to finish?" she asked breathlessly, wiping her mouth with her wrist.

"I need to be inside you." I licked my fingers and eased them between her legs, but she was already wet and swollen with desire, which pushed me closer to the edge. "Like I wanted to then."

She didn't argue, and seconds later I was plunging into her, and she was muffling her cries in my shoulder. I didn't last much longer than I would have at eighteen, but as the orgasm tore through me, I felt her body pulsing around mine and felt closer to her than I'd ever felt to anyone.

"Don't go back to your room tonight," I whispered, brushing her hair back from her face. "Stay here with me."

Her expression was torn. "I want to."

"Just this once," I said. "Stay until the sun comes up. I'll make sure you get back to your room early." I kissed her softly. "I promise."

"Okay," she whispered. "I'll stay."

A few minutes later, she was nestled along my side in the dark, my hands gently caressing her back.

"So was that true?" I asked. "That story you told—did you really have fantasies like that about me?"

"Yes," she said, laughing softly. "All the time. Didn't you ever have a fantasy about me?"

I kissed the top of her head. "They were all about you."

She snuggled closer, and we fell asleep.

In the morning, I got to see her in the first pale pink light of the day, and she'd never looked more beautiful. It felt so right to have her there with me—to kiss her goodnight and hold her in my arms as we drifted off and wake up to kiss her in the morning. I wished I didn't have to let her go.

But I woke her up as promised, and after slipping back into her pajamas, she went hurrying back across the hall to her own room.

We did that every night for the next week, and each morning she stayed a little longer in my bed, the light growing more golden on her skin.

Each time, it was harder to let her go.

CHAPTER 15

BECKETT

THE FOLLOWING Tuesday I was walking out of the barn to head in for dinner when motion caught my eye over by the maple tree. I glanced over and saw Maddie in the swing. She'd twisted the ropes over her head and was letting them unravel and spin her around.

Amused, I headed in her direction. "Doesn't that make you dizzy?"

She laughed and straightened herself out. "A little."

As I got close to her, déjà vu hit me hard—the dappled sunlight on her dark hair, the breeze rustling the maple leaves above our heads, the acceleration of my heart. "You know what this reminds me of?"

Her green eyes sparkled. "The day you kissed me?"

I nodded. "I thought I was going to die."

That made her laugh. "If you kissed me?"

"If I didn't."

Smiling softly, she tipped her head against one rope. "I'm sorry I didn't see things more clearly back then."

I shrugged. "We were young. I'm not sure I saw things clearly either. I just acted on impulse."

"But maybe if I hadn't been so scared, we could have . . . I don't know. Had more time together. Had more of a chance."

Her words made me sad, but they weren't wrong. No matter how good this felt with her, it wasn't like we really had a chance. It was too late.

"Want to give me a push?" she asked.

"Sure." Moving behind her, I grabbed the ropes, pulled her back toward me, and let her go. Each time she came back, I put my hands on her back and gave her a gentle push. Until one time, instead of pushing her, I caught her around the waist and held on.

She giggled. "Hey! The ride stopped. What happened?"

"I don't know. It was another impulse, I guess." Carefully, I lowered the swing until her sneakers were on the ground.

Rising to her feet, she turned to face me and wrapped her arms around my neck. "An impulse to kiss me again?"

"An impulse to catch hold of you," I told her, "and not let go."

"Don't." A whisper, soft but fierce. "Don't."

That night after practice, the guys and I hit the pub for a couple beers. Afterward, Moretti and I walked to the parking lot together.

"I've got a check for Maddie," he said. "We just need to set up a time for signing the paperwork."

"Sounds good."

"Maybe she could come by the office tomorrow?"

"Probably. Have Bianca text her." I chuckled. "She'll probably have my dad with her. He's like her shadow these days."

"Oh yeah? That must be helpful."

"It's beyond helpful. I don't know what I'm going to do when she leaves."

"So ask her to stay," he said easily.

I frowned. "I can't do that."

"Sure, you can."

"She's got a job in Ohio," I told him. "She's got a house. Elliott's dad is there. She's not going to move up here just to keep my dad out of trouble."

Moretti laughed. "You're right—she's not. She's going to do it for *you*, asshole."

"I don't want her to do it for me," I said, scowling at my feet as we walked.

"Why not?"

"Because then I'm under pressure."

"Pressure to . . ." he prompted.

"To be worth the upheaval to her life. To Elliott's life."

"You don't think you are?"

I didn't answer right away. "What if she moved back here and things fell apart?"

Moretti shrugged. "I guess you guys would have to decide if that's a risk worth taking."

"It's not. I can already tell you it's not."

"So you'd rather have her living five, six hours away? Getting together once a month or something? Probably less? Letting it die out that way? Because you know that's what would happen," he argued, "especially with how much you work and the time you spend taking care of your dad."

"At least she wouldn't end up hating me."

"Dude, that is a fucking lame-ass excuse for not even trying."

I struggled with a comeback, because I knew he was right. Instead, I made up a different lame-ass excuse. "She might not even want to try. I'd hate to put her on the spot."

Moretti stopped walking and faced me. "Listen. I've known you a long time, I've seen you two together, and I think you're wrong about this. If you want her in your life, tell her. If she says no, fuck it." He shrugged. "At least you tried. But you've spent a lot of years waiting for this. And I'll say to you what I said to Cole when he was first into Cheyenne—don't lie, don't say shit you don't mean, just tell her the truth."

"The truth, huh?"

"Yeah. Women love it when you get all honest and vulnerable and shit."

I grimaced. "Vulnerability doesn't sound like my thing."

He rolled his eyes. "It doesn't sound like *any* man's thing. But you have to do it." He pointed a finger at me. "And don't fuck this up, or you're going to be ninety years old wishing you hadn't chickened out at thirty-three, and I'll be there to say *I told you so.*"

Swallowing hard, I nodded. "I'll give it some thought."

That night I struggled to sleep, even with her right next to me. After gently waking her so she could tiptoe back to her own room, I gave up. Throwing on some clothes, I headed out by myself to do the chores a little earlier than usual.

While I worked, I thought of nothing but her.

How beautiful she was, inside and out. How seamlessly she fit into my life. How much joy she brought. Not just to me, but to my dad too.

Over the past week, she'd been endlessly patient with him, and beyond generous with her time. She and Elliott took him anywhere he wanted to go—downtown, the lighthouse, the library, the diner. She bought him an antique map of the area, and he spent hours studying it, pointing out things he remembered. They even went to the Bellamy Creek Historic

Village, toured the museum, bought candy in the old-fashioned General Store, and sat in the train station with him, eating peppermint sticks and waiting for a train that was never going to come.

I thought about Elliott too—about how lucky his father was to have a son so smart and funny and caring. So quick to help. Quick to laugh. Quick to learn. He treated the animals with sensitivity and kindness, and he was responsible and diligent in everything he did. I never had to ask him twice to complete a chore, and he never quit working until he'd done the job fully and correctly. When you told him he did a good job, his brown eyes lit up, and his grin was a mile wide.

It made me furious that Maddie's ex was such a dick he couldn't appreciate all the things that Elliott was because he was too busy focusing on what he wasn't. Or too wrapped up in himself. How was Elliott supposed to learn that a real man didn't neglect his children? Didn't put his own needs first? Didn't lie or cheat or take the easy way out?

I thought about the lessons I'd learned from my father.

A real man had honor and respect. He protected his family. He worked hard to provide for them. He knew who he was and what he stood for, and he wasn't afraid of anything . . . except maybe expressing his feelings.

But that was just it.

I knew who I was. I knew what I stood for.

But what I felt for Maddie fucking terrified me.

I was a numbers guy. I'd made a lot of money performing complex financial analysis and assessing risk. And I'd been good at it—the numbers told me when a high risk was worth taking, and when it wasn't likely to pay off. So it was hard, looking at the odds of something like forever, to believe that they were in my favor.

I mean, what the hell was love anyway?

Was it that wobbly-kneed feeling I got when she walked in a room? Was it that heart-pounding thing that happened when she kissed me? Was it that aching need to be inside her I experienced when her skin was next to mine? Was it the warm, possessive rush in my veins when I held her at night? Was it the million things I wanted to do for her, big and small? Was it all the promises I wished I could make for the future? All the things I wished I'd said in the past?

Or was that just a unique form of torture that would ease up when she was gone?

How could you ever know for sure?

When I came back in the house, Maddie was making breakfast in the kitchen.

The moment I saw her, my knees did the wobbly thing.

"Morning," she said as she stirred something in a big bowl. "You're up early today."

"Yeah." I tried to go to the coffeepot without touching her and couldn't. Catching her around the waist, I pressed my lips to her cheek. "I was grumpy after you left me. Couldn't sleep."

She set her whisk aside and hugged my arms. "Me neither."

I kissed her once more and went for the coffeepot. "Elliott still asleep?"

"Nope. He's getting dressed. He wouldn't skip out on morning time with the goats for anything. He's going to miss them like crazy when we leave."

"Any time he wants to come visit them, he's welcome," I said, trying not to think of the kitchen without her every morning.

"Okay." She smiled at me, and my heart stuttered. "I have to run by Moretti's office to sign some things this morning.

And I have to go into town to pick up my dress for the wedding this afternoon. I'll take your dad with me."

"He'll love that." I took a sip of coffee. "I actually had a few replies to my ad for a caretaker this week. I'll make some calls today."

"Oh, good." Her smile was relieved. "I'll feel so much better when I leave if I know you have help."

I took another quick gulp and set the cup down. "I'm gonna wake Dad and head back out. My guys will be here any minute and I need to check in with them before I ride out and rotate the herd."

"You don't want breakfast?" Her expression was dismayed. "I'm making waffles."

"Tempting, but I don't have time this morning. I've been a little lax about work the past week, and I have to knock off a little early today so I can pick up my suit from the dry cleaner."

"Let me do that for you," she said. "I'm going to town anyway."

"You don't have to run my errands. You do enough."

"Just text me a list—I'll do them. I'm also going to do some laundry. If you put your dirty clothes in the laundry room, I'll throw them in too."

I shook my head. "Maddie, you don't have to do my fucking laundry."

"It's selfish, I promise." She came over and wrapped her arms around my waist, tipping her head back to look up at me. "It makes me feel good to do things for you. And I'm leaving soon."

I kissed her, a little longer and deeper than I should have since Elliott could have walked into the kitchen at any moment, but my heart was doing that pounding thing, and it felt too good to stop.

When we heard quick little feet coming down the stairs, we pulled apart.

"Guess I'll go wake Dad," I said, adjusting the crotch of my jeans. "I hope he's not ornery this morning. I don't have time to fool around."

"Tell him strata lady is cooking breakfast," she said, laughing as she picked up her whisk again. "That'll perk him right up."

It was a long day out in the hot sun. Around three, I took a break for a cold drink but was disappointed to find the house empty and silent except for the sound of the dryer. On my way to the fridge, I saw a note on the counter.

Beautiful day, heading downtown and then to the beach. Wish you could be with us.

M

Maddie's handwriting was strangely familiar. Looking at it, I recalled the small senior picture she'd given me. I'd read the back of it so many times, I'd memorized it.

Beckett, thank you so much for all the times you were there for me. You are a great friend, and you have the best blue eyes ever. I will miss you so much, please keep in touch! Love, Maddie

I'd given her a picture too, standing right by her locker after school one day, and she'd eagerly flipped it over to see what I'd written on the back. It made me chuckle now, thinking how her mouth had dropped open in outrage.

"What? No fair! You can't give me a picture without writing on the back!"

"What am I supposed to write?"

"I don't know. How you feel."

How I felt? The back of that photo wasn't nearly big enough.

But I grabbed a pen from my backpack and pulled a

binder out to write on. She handed me the photo again and I turned it over, jotting down a few words.

Eagerly, she picked it up and read out loud. "Have a good summer. Beckett." Her nose wrinkled as she looked up at me. "Really? That's it?"

I laughed. "It's more than I wrote on anyone else's."

"But isn't there anything you'll, like, *remember* about me?"

Was she kidding? There wasn't anything I'd *forget*. "Sure."

"Like what? Write it down." She handed the photo over again, and I added something at the bottom.

Holding it up again by one corner, she read, "P.S. You always smell good." Then she laughed as she tucked it into a pocket in her backpack. "I'll take it. Thank you."

Setting the note back on the counter, I headed outside again, smiling at the memory. Imagining her at the beach— playing in the sand with Elliott, chatting with my dad under a big umbrella, diving into the waves. Wishing I was with them.

Missing her, as always.

Later that night, after Elliott and my dad were both in bed, I took her hand and tugged her toward the front door. "Come with me."

"Where are we going?" she asked as I led her outside.

"Not far."

"I don't even have shoes on."

"You're okay."

While she'd been upstairs with Elliott, I'd pulled my dad's old pickup out of the garage, spread out a few thick blankets over the empty bed, and tossed in a few pillows.

"What's this?" She laughed softly as we approached the rusty old truck in the driveway.

"It's a date." I lowered the tailgate and offered her a hand. "Hop in."

Smiling, Maddie took my hand and climbed into the cargo bed.

I got in after her and lay back on the pillows, one hand behind my head. "Now come here."

Her smile grew even wider as she snuggled up to my side, tucking herself beneath my arm. "Are we camping out tonight?"

"Not the whole night. I just thought it would be nice to get out of the house for a while. I feel bad I can't really take you anywhere."

"Don't. There's no place I need to go. I just want to be with you."

I kissed the top of her head. "I noticed how clear the sky was all day and figured it would be a nice night to look at the stars."

She shifted slightly so she could look up and murmured in appreciation. "Oh, it *is* a clear night. I forgot how much better you can see stars in the country. I've been in the city too long."

My eyes scanned the inky blank canvas studded with brilliant points of light. "I agree."

We lay there for a few minutes, looking up at the night sky, listening to the crickets and the occasional hoot of an owl. A soft breeze whistled through the trees, although the air was warm.

After a couple minutes, she cuddled up to my side again, placing one hand on my chest. "So is this the kind of date you'd have taken me on in high school?"

"Hmm. Good question." I thought for a moment. "I probably would have taken you for a drive in a truck—maybe even this one, since it's older than dirt—but I'm not sure about looking at the stars. I probably would have been more interested in looking at you without your clothes on."

"How about now?" Her hand drifted lower, sliding over my stomach and onto my crotch. Beneath my jeans, my cock began to swell.

"Some things never change."

Laughing gently, she started kissing my neck and continued to move her hand over the growing bulge in my pants until I groaned.

"Should we take this inside?" I asked.

She unbuttoned and unzipped my jeans. "Think anyone can see us out here?"

"Nope. Not that I'd care."

She sat up and grabbed another blanket, covering the lower halves of our bodies. Then she wriggled out of her shorts and swung a leg over me, straddling my hips. "I don't care either."

I slipped a hand between her legs, finding her warm and wet. Desire surged through me. "This might not even last long enough for anyone to see."

Smiling in the dark, she tugged down my jeans just enough to free my aching cock. I positioned myself between her thighs and stifled a loud moan as she slowly lowered herself onto me, inch by inch. "Fuck, that feels so good."

"Yes," she whispered, her eyes on mine. She braced her hands on my chest and began to move, rocking her hips in a slow, sinuous motion.

My hands stole beneath her shirt, gripping her waist. Already the tension in my body was mounting, heat gathering like a storm. She didn't rush, and I loved the way her eyes closed and her mouth fell open as she took what she wanted, using my thick, hard length for her own pleasure. I willed my body to be patient, pushing back against the urge to grab her by the hips and jerk her up and down on my cock, hard and fast.

But watching her ride me slowly and seductively was no less arousing, and within minutes I was dangerously close to climax. Cursing, I grasped her thighs and held her down. "Don't move."

She laughed lazily. "What's wrong?"

"You're too fucking hot. I'm about to lose control." My cock pulsed once inside her, making her gasp.

"I felt that," she whispered, starting to move again.

"You're going to feel a lot more if you don't slow down," I warned.

Falling forward, she braced her hands on my chest and rocked her hips faster and rougher, her breath coming in quick, hot bursts. "Do it. I want more. Let me have it."

I gave up trying to fight it and let her fuck me until I came, my hands on her ass, a low ragged growl escaping my throat. She cried out once as her body convulsed over mine, and I felt the spasms rippling through her.

She collapsed on top of me, breathing hard. "Oh God," she panted. "I can't believe I did that."

"Did what?" I struggled to catch my breath too.

"Had sex in a truck. And a hayloft."

"Don't forget the dock."

"Oh my God, the dock. What is even happening to me? I'm someone's mom."

"You're not *my* mom."

"I know, but . . ." She lifted her chest off me and looked down. "I've never done anything like this before."

"I haven't either."

"And I can't even imagine it with anyone else. You bring it out in me."

"Good." I couldn't help feeling possessive as I squeezed her ass. "I like that you're only this way with me. Let's keep it that way."

She lowered her lips to mine, and I felt her smile.

Upstairs, I coaxed her into my bedroom. "Come lie with me for a while."

"Let me get ready for bed, then I'll come back."

A few minutes later, she silently tiptoed into my room, peeled off her pajamas, and curled up alongside me in bed. I was nearly asleep when she picked up her head from my chest and looked at me. "Beckett."

"Hm."

"I have to tell you something, and I don't want you to be mad."

Opening my eyes, I gave her a funny look. "Okay."

"You promise?"

"I can't imagine there's anything you could tell me that would make me mad. Unless you've been faking your orgasms."

"I have not been faking my orgasms," she said dutifully.

"Then shoot."

She got to her knees and sat back on her heels. "Okay. First, let me say that I am not proud of myself."

"Maddie. Spit it out."

"Okay." Squeezing her eyes shut, she exhaled. "I Googled Caroline."

"Oh."

"And then I sort of cyber-stalked her."

"Why?"

She shrugged. "I don't know, because I was curious. Because I was jealous. Because it's something that women do to torture themselves—we look up a guy's ex and then obsess over all the ways she's better than we are."

I put a hand behind my head. "That's messed up."

"I know. But I did it today while your dad was taking his nap. And I hate myself for it."

"Maddie, she's not better than you in any way."

Her jaw fell open. "Beckett, I *saw* her. She's perfect. She looks like Nicole Kidman and Blake Lively had a baby."

I laughed. "That doesn't even make sense."

"You know what I mean. She's so tall and leggy. She looks amazing in everything. Her hair is that perfect shade of Daenerys Targaryen blond. Her blowout is always flawless. Her eyebrows are killer."

"Her eyebrows?"

"Yes." She covered her forehead with both hands. "I hate my eyebrows. I never hated them before, but I hate them now."

"Maddie, you're being ridiculous." I tugged her arms down. "You have nothing to be jealous about or torture yourself over. And if you're curious about something, you can ask me."

"I can?"

"Yes."

She bit her lip. "How long were you together?"

"Two years, off and on."

"Wikipedia said she was once rumored to be engaged to a hedge fund analyst. Was that you?"

"Yes. But we were never actually engaged." I paused. "We went into a jewelry store once and someone saw us and turned it into a story."

Her jaw dropped. "You went ring shopping?"

"Actually we were just walking by the windows at Tiffany one day, and she saw something she liked. She dragged me in there so she could try it on. That was it."

"Oh."

"I never considered buying her a ring. I never considered proposing. I never even considered living with her."

Maddie nodded slowly. "Did you love her?"

I exhaled, putting the second hand behind my head. "Honestly, I don't know. Love has never been an easy thing for me to understand. I certainly never *told* her I loved her."

"No?"

"I've never said those words to anyone."

She thought about that for a moment, then snuggled up next to me again. "I saw a bunch of pictures of you guys together at various galas and balls around Manhattan."

I groaned. "I fucking hated those things."

"I have to admit, you didn't look too happy in the photos."

I wrapped my arms around her. "I am much happier right here, right now."

"Good." She kissed my chest. "Sorry for being silly. I know it shouldn't matter to me who you spent your time with in New York, or even if you were madly in love with her."

"I wasn't. So you can stop the cyber-stalking."

Her laugh was sheepish. "Okay. Thanks for talking about this with me."

"You're welcome."

She lay down again. Brushed her fingertips over my chest. "I only have three more nights here."

I swallowed, hearing Moretti's voice in my head. "I think you'll be back, don't you?"

"For visits, you mean?"

"Or you could move back."

She went completely still. "I suppose I could. If I had a really good reason."

My heart was hammering fast. I felt as if I'd run too fast toward the edge of a cliff and had to catch my balance and back up. "What about the chocolate shakes at the diner?"

"Those are definitely good, but I'm not sure they're worth an interstate move."

"Blair's apple pie?"

"Also amazing," she said with a sigh, "but probably not a good enough reason to quit my job and uproot my kid."

I thought for a moment, desperate for another joke to avoid the truth. "I've got it! Old man baseball."

"Um . . ."

"You mean you're not going to be awake all night because you're so excited to see your first Bellamy Creek Bulldogs game tomorrow night?"

She patted my chest. "I will definitely struggle to sleep. I can't wait."

"But it's not a reason to move back, huh?"

"Not really." She laughed softly. "But I bet you could think of something that would tempt me. An offer I couldn't refuse."

I exhaled. "You're a tough cookie, Maddie Blake. But I'll try."

In the back of my mind, I heard Moretti clucking like a goddamn hen.

CHAPTER 16
MADDIE

THURSDAY NIGHT, we all went to the first Bellamy Creek Bulldogs game of the season.

It was a gorgeous summer evening, about seventy degrees with a cool breeze, and we piled into Beckett's truck right after an early dinner.

"Nervous?" I leaned forward to rub his shoulder on the ride over to the high school field. Whenever his dad was in the car, I rode in the back seat.

"Heck no," he said. "We're gonna crush those turkeys, right Elliott?"

"Right." Next to me, Elliott grinned happily. He was wearing his favorite pink T-shirt with his jeans and boots, but instead of the unicorn barrette tonight, he was wearing a Bulldogs cap Beckett had given him. It was a little loose, but he didn't care.

It had been such a joy to watch the friendship grow between them. Beckett was so sweet with Elliott, so kind and generous. Whether he was teaching him how to sit on a horse or muck out a stall or swing a baseball bat, he never criticized or grew impatient. He never said no when Elliott asked him to play catch or drive the four-wheeler.

He never asked why Elliott insisted on wearing a pink dress one day and torn blue jeans the next. He made Elliott feel confident, accepted, and worth his time. And Elliott idolized him.

When we arrived at the field, we wished Beckett luck, and he took off for the dugout. Watching him walk away in his Bulldogs uniform—the team shirt tight on his back and biceps—did swirly things to my insides.

Mr. Weaver, Elliott, and I headed for the stands where Blair, Cheyenne, and Bianca, Mrs. Dempsey, Mrs. Mitchell, and both Morettis were already sitting. Cheyenne hopped down and introduced Elliott to Cole's daughter Mariah. She was a few years older than he was, but asked if he'd like to hang out with her and some other kids at the concession stand.

"Is it okay?" he asked me.

"Sure." I pulled some money from my wallet and gave it to him. "Here. In case you guys want a snack. But stick it in your pocket so you don't lose it, okay?"

"Okay." He did as I asked, and they turned around and walked toward the concession stand side by side.

"I love your boots," I heard Mariah say, which made me smile.

"She's sweet," I said. "And so pretty. She's got those blue eyes of Cole's, doesn't she?"

"She sure does." Cheyenne looked after them. "And you don't have to worry about them. Mariah is very responsible, and she's been coming to these old man baseball games all her life, so she knows her way around." She took me by the arm. "Come sit with us."

"Gosh, I haven't been to a baseball game in years," I said as we settled in on the bleachers. I looked around at the high school, the track and football field, the wide expanse of lawn where soccer games were played, and the graduation stage had been set up. "I feel like I'm a teenager again."

Cheyenne laughed. "Hometowns will do that to you. Have you enjoyed being back?"

"Oh my goodness, so much." I touched my chest. "Much more than I anticipated. I don't think I appreciated Bellamy Creek when I was younger. I just couldn't wait to escape."

"I was like that too," Cheyenne said. "Just desperate to get out of here. But by the time I had to choose a place to settle down and find a job, I couldn't get over feeling like this was where I belonged. Anywhere else I lived had always felt like a stop along the way."

"Yeah. I know what you mean," I said, watching the Bulldogs take the field. Beckett's catcher's equipment made him look even bigger and brawnier behind the plate.

The game was a nail-biter, with the Bulldogs getting ahead by two runs almost right away, but the Mason City Mavericks tying it up in the third inning and pulling ahead in the fourth. They stayed tied through the seventh, when the Mavericks' biggest hitter sent a ball sailing over the right field fence. Thankfully, no one was on base, so only the one run was scored. My throat was hoarse from shouting.

Cheyenne was biting her nails. "Shoot. I can tell Cole's shoulder is bothering him. He should go out and let the other pitcher take over."

Behind us, Blair leaned over and patted Cheyenne's shoulder. "He's good, Chey. Have faith."

She was right. Cole managed to strike out the next batter, and the Bulldogs headed in from the field to bat.

"I wish I could play," said Mr. Weaver on my left. He'd been grouchy today, insisting that he had his own game tonight and arguing with Beckett, who was 'holding him hostage' in his own home. "I could get a hit off this pitcher."

I patted his arm. "They'd be lucky to have you."

The eighth inning passed with no more runs scored, but during the Mavericks' last at-bat, they managed to score another two runs, putting them up by three.

The Bulldogs only had one more chance to win their first game. Griffin was up first, and after two balls and a called strike sent a line drive rocketing between the third baseman and shortstop, deep into left field—a double.

Next up was Enzo, who got a single and sent Griffin to third. Then Cole was up, and Cheyenne grabbed my hands. "Why does he have to bat?" she whined. "He's going to hurt himself."

"Because they all think they're still eighteen," said Bianca behind me.

I laughed, squeezing Cheyenne's hands. "He'll be okay."

But he had a full count on him before a wild pitch sent him jumping out of the way, allowing Enzo to steal second.

"Dang, he's fast." I watched him churn up dust as he slid into the bag.

"He is, but he'll be icing that hip tonight," said Bianca, but I heard the pride in her voice.

"I can't watch," Cheyenne said, putting her face in my shoulder.

I held my breath, watching the next pitch—ball four. "He walked," I told her as Cole tossed the bat aside and jogged to first base.

"Oh, good." She clapped and stamped her feet. "That means bases are loaded and Beckett's up."

Now it was my turn to be nervous.

But Beckett exuded confidence as he walked to the plate. My heart beat faster as my eyes swept over his tall, muscular frame, his strong hands, the determined expression on his face. He looked sure of himself, but he clearly knew the pressure was on.

I held my breath as the pitcher wound up—ball one.

I chewed the tip of my thumb as the second pitch crossed the plate, and Beckett didn't swing—strike.

He fouled off the third pitch and took a few practice

swings as the pitcher wandered off the mound for a second. Rolled his neck and shoulders.

The next two pitches were high and outside. Full count.

At this point, Cheyenne and I were holding onto each other for dear life, and Bianca and Blair each had a hand on my shoulders. Next to me, Mr. Weaver was fidgety. Griffin looked tense on third base. Enzo appeared antsy at second. Cole took a few steps off the bag at first, ready to run. In front of the bleachers, Elliott and Mariah had their noses to the fence.

"Come on, Beckett," I whispered.

The pitcher wound up, cocked his arm, and released the ball—a bullet that I thought looked slightly low and inside, but Beckett's bat met it with a loud *crack*! The ball soared so high I lost it in the light of the setting sun. The centerfielder ran hard, but it cleared the back fence by at least ten feet—a grand slam, delivering a victory for the team.

The Bulldogs fans stood up and cheered. Mariah and Elliott shouted and jumped up and down. Cheyenne stuck her fingers in her mouth and whistled loudly, and Mr. Weaver slow-clapped. "Well done," he said. "Well done."

Smiling, I watched Griffin, Enzo, and Cole cross the plate and wait for Beckett to make it around the bases. He jogged at an easy pace, his expression satisfied but not smug. When he scored, the ump called the game and his teammates hollered, slapped him on the back, and offered high-fives.

"Wow," I said, clapping heartily, "I had no idea how *exciting* old man baseball could be."

Cheyenne laughed and whistled again. "Some games more than others, but it's always fun to watch these guys win."

"Yes," I agreed, watching them grin and congratulate each other, happy for them. "Their friendship is really amazing, don't you think?"

"Totally."

"Maddie, can you come to the pub?" Blair asked. "We always go after games."

"I'd like to, but I have Elliott."

"Bring him!" Cheyenne said. "Mariah can come too."

I turned to Mr. Weaver. "Would you like to go to the pub for a little bit, Mr. Weaver? You feel up to it?"

"Of course I feel up to it," he answered. "I'm no old man, remember?"

Laughing, I took his arm, and we made our way off the stands and down to the dugout, where we met up with the guys, who strutted like peacocks all the way to the parking lot.

The pub, which sponsored the team, had reserved several outdoor tables for us, and we crowded around them. Next to me, Beckett draped his arm over the back of my chair, and I felt like a teenager with a crush.

We ordered beers and hot wings and French fries for the kids, and sat around rehashing the game. Everyone congratulated Cole on getting the win, Griffin and Moretti for their hits and base-running, but the most praise was reserved for Beckett's game-winning grand slam.

"You should have seen the pitcher's face when you hit that ball," said Blair. "I think his jaw hit the mound."

"Pretty sure that's the farthest I've ever seen a ball go on that field," said Cole, shaking his head.

"That's because you weren't there in 1958 when I hit a grand slam to win the state tournament," said Mr. Weaver, sticking his chest out a little.

"I wish I could have seen it," Cole told him.

"I was a big hitter too," the old-timer said. "I know it was a while ago, but it doesn't feel like it. I wish I could still play." He perked up. "You guys ever need a pinch hitter, you let me know."

"We will, Pop," said Beckett.

Later, while he waited for his dad to get ready for bed and

I was listening for Elliott's shower to go off upstairs, Beckett went into the kitchen and opened the fridge. I followed him, putting my arms around him from behind.

"I'm so proud of you," I told him. "That was incredible. And so fun to watch."

He laughed as he patted my wrist and pulled out a bottle of water. "Thanks. Are you thirsty?"

"Only for you."

He glanced down at me over his shoulder as he shut the fridge. "Good. But you have to let me shower first. I don't even want to know what I smell like right now."

"Like a man," I said, sniffing dramatically. "Like hard work. Like victory."

He grinned, leaning back against the counter as he took off the cap. "I'll take it."

I hopped up on the counter opposite him. "You know, I was thinking. You should let your dad play in one of those games."

He looked at me like I was nuts and took a long drink. "He'd get hurt."

"No, he wouldn't. It wouldn't be for real—just one time at bat or playing whatever position he likes to play. It would make him feel so good."

He studied me, his lips tipping up. "You're so good to him."

I shrugged. "We're friends."

"You're going to break his heart when you leave, you know."

My heartbeat quickened, but I laughed it off. "He'll forget all about me once I'm gone."

Beckett shook his head. "Never. Take it from me, Maddie Blake. There's no forgetting about you."

I couldn't breathe. Our eyes were locked, and a thousand words were stuck in my throat.

Come here. Take me in your arms.

I don't want to leave. Tell me not to go.

Even though it seems impossible, just say you want me in your life.

Say I make you believe in the possibility of forever.

But he said nothing, just lifted the bottle of water to his mouth again.

I hopped off the counter. "I should check on Elliott. Make sure he's out of the shower so you at least have some hot water left."

"Yeah, I should check on Dad too." He finished the water and opened the garage door to toss the bottle in the bin. "Will I see you upstairs?"

I smiled at him, but it felt oddly forced. "Of course."

That night, I went to his room as usual, tiptoeing across the hall in the dark, closing his door behind me, slipping into his warm, soft sheets.

He wrapped me in his arms and made me feel beautiful and desired—even needed. He put his mouth all over my body. He clung to me like he'd never let go. He moved his body over mine in ways that were both tender and savage, fluid and jagged, generous and greedy. And when we came together, I took as much pleasure in his orgasm as I did in my own.

But as we lay there afterward, our breath still quick, our limbs still tangled, I felt something new beneath the unadulterated joy.

The cool edge of fear.

What did you expect? This is what happens when you play house like a little girl. You forget it's imaginary. You start to believe it's real.

I tried to shake it off by staying in the moment and focusing on what was right here—the beat of Beckett's heart, the smell of his skin, the warmth of his body on mine.

But the unease continued to ripple outward inside me, like a stone had been tossed into still waters.

Go ahead and live in the moment. It doesn't matter—because even in this moment, you're falling for him. Every time you come to him this way, you're giving him another little piece of your heart to break, and soon there won't be anything left to salvage.

I squeezed my eyes shut, as if total darkness could block the voice from my head.

You can pretend this is all in fun. You can act like you'll be fine when you leave. You can even tell lies—to him and to yourself—about not wanting any promises. But mark my words . . . that's all they are. Lies.

A couple minutes later, I squirmed a little, and Beckett moved off me. "You okay?"

"Yeah."

Lie.

"You sure?"

"I just don't want to fall asleep."

Lie.

He rolled onto his back and opened his arms. "Stay with me a little while longer," he coaxed. "We won't fall asleep."

God, I wanted to. But something in my gut was telling me to go. "I better not. I'm really tired tonight."

Lie.

"Oh." He paused. "Okay."

Quickly I leaned over and kissed his lips. "Night."

"Night."

Ignoring the tightness in my throat, I slid out of his bed, put my pajamas back on, and snuck out, leaving his door ajar.

Back in my room, I allowed myself to give in and cry, muffling my sobs in my pillow. I told myself I was acting like a child, weeping for no reason, but after a couple minutes, I felt better.

Wiping my eyes, I curled up and stared into the dark, too restless to sleep. For what felt like half the night, I tossed and turned, worried that the voice was right, that I'd only been fooling myself about being able to walk away from this thing with Beckett unscathed.

And it wasn't his fault at all. I was the one who'd allowed my feelings to stray into dangerous territory. Allowing myself to *feel* again was so thrilling, I hadn't resisted the rush of the tide. Was I now going to drown?

No—wait a minute.

I flipped onto my back. This wasn't really fair to Beckett. I wasn't even giving him a chance to admit there was hope for us, because I wasn't being honest about my feelings. I was doing exactly what I'd done way back when—pretending I didn't care as deeply as I did because I didn't feel worthy of him.

But I wasn't that girl anymore.

It's not that I wasn't afraid, because I was.

He'd told me he didn't believe in forever. And I might not be enough to change his mind. That was a risk I'd have to take.

But I couldn't leave here without giving us a chance to breathe. To grow. To be even better than we might have been.

Taking a deep, shaky breath, I made up my mind.

I'd tell him how I felt. That I didn't want this to end. That I knew it wouldn't be easy, but I was willing to try.

Then I would know for sure if this was only a little girl's fantasy, or we were always meant to be.

CHAPTER 17
BECKETT

FRIDAY AFTERNOON, I had to attend a ceremony rehearsal over at Cole's house. Their yard was deep, running all the way to the creek, which bordered the back of the property. The wide green lawn held a huge white tent over to one side, under which tables were being set up. On the other side, rows of chairs were set up on either side of an aisle.

As I stood surveying everything, Moretti came up and thumped me on the back. "You ready for this?"

"I have a few lines about love and commitment, et cetera, et cetera, that I found on the internet printed on a note card. Is that ready?"

He laughed. "Sounds good to me."

The rehearsal was pretty quick and easy. I was escorting Cole's daughter Mariah back down the aisle after the ceremony. She giggled incessantly as we practiced walking arm in arm from the floral arch between the rows of chairs on either side of the grass path serving as the aisle. When we reached the patio, I turned to her and held up my palms. She grinned and gave me two high-fives.

"We nailed it," I told her.

"We did," she agreed.

Everyone told me to go get Maddie and meet them downtown for dinner and drinks, but I declined. We couldn't leave my dad and Elliott, and besides, we only had two nights left together. Tomorrow night would be spent in a crowd.

Tonight, I wanted her to myself.

After dinner, my dad and I turned on the Tigers game and settled on the couch. Elliott was on the floor with DiMaggio as usual, and a warm breeze floated in through the screens.

Maddie came into the great room with a plastic bag from the drugstore. "Beck, I put the things you asked me to get on your dresser."

"Thank you," I said, watching her drop to the floor and start pulling things out of the bag. She was fresh from a shower and wore her denim shorts and a clean white T-shirt. Her hair was combed and damp, her feet bare. When the bag was empty, she spread it out and placed her feet on it.

"Okay, Elliott. You want to try painting my toes?" She picked up a bottle of nail polish and shook it, making it click. The sound took me back to childhood, when I'd observed my sisters doing each other's nails at the kitchen table.

"Yes!" Elliott jumped up and came over to sit at Maddie's feet.

"Be careful, remember? You have to hold your hand really steady and go slow."

"I will." Hunching down on his knees, he concentrated hard on the task, slowly applying the bright pink color with Maddie looking on.

"Not bad," she said when one foot was complete. "Now the other one."

Elliott got to work on her second foot. "Oops." He looked up at her. "I messed up and got some on your toe."

"That's okay." She smiled and picked up a little packet that almost reminded me of a condom. Tearing it open, she took out a little wipe and touched up her foot. "All better. Try again. Then we'll let it dry a bit and you can do a second coat."

"Then can I do your fingers?" he asked excitedly.

"Well, I wasn't really planning to wear polish on my hands," she said apologetically, "but you could do it just for practice."

He looked happy about that. "Okay."

"But maybe we should move over to the kitchen table for that." She carefully rose to her feet.

"You can do it here," I said, gesturing to the coffee table between the couches.

Maddie thought for a second. "Elliott, go get some paper towels. I don't want to get polish on the table."

He went into the kitchen and returned a moment later, and together they spread out some paper towels. Maddie sat near my feet, her back leaning against my right leg, her hands flat on the table. Elliott knelt next to her and painted the nails on both hands. It took him a while—my dad was snoring by the time he was finished.

"Good job, bud," Maddie said softly. She held up both hands so I could see her nails. "Look, Beckett. Didn't he do a nice job?"

Actually, it was pretty messy, but I smiled. "Better than I could do, that's for sure."

Elliott beamed. "I could do yours too, if you want."

Maddie chuckled. "That's sweet of you to offer, Elliott, but I don't think Beckett wants his nails painted."

"Well, hold on," I said, hating to disappoint him. Of course I didn't want my nails painted pink by a six-year-old. But I could take it off, right?

Maddie looked at me over her shoulder. "You don't have to. Elliott knows most men don't paint their nails."

"My dad says it's only for girls," Elliott said with a forlorn expression. "And he gets mad when I paint mine. But I've seen some boys with it before."

I made up my mind. "You can paint mine."

Maddie flashed me a grateful smile. "I think it takes a really strong man to feel confident enough to let his nails be painted pink."

"I agree," I said, moving to the edge of the couch and flattening my hand on a paper towel. Maddie scooted over so she was sitting between my feet. "Although I have to say I have never had my nails painted before."

Elliott knelt down again and took the brush from the bottle. "This will be easier. Your fingers are fatter than my mom's."

I gave him a menacing stare. "I'm gonna get you back for that next time we have batting practice."

Elliott giggled and got to work. Between my legs, Maddie glanced up at me and mouthed *thank you*, placing a hand over her heart.

I wanted to take that hand and put it over my heart, so she could feel what she did to me, so that each quick, hard beat could tell her what I couldn't with words.

That I needed her.

That I wanted her in my life.

That I should have made her mine when I'd had the chance.

That I wanted her clothes next to mine in the closet, her toothbrush in the cup by the sink, and Elliott's pink boots in the mudroom alongside my brown ones.

That I wanted to share things with her I'd never shared with anyone—not just my bed or my body or my house, but my fears and my dreams and maybe even my name.

A family. We could be a family.

When Elliott was done, he sat back on his heels. "What do you think?"

I held up my hand—it looked fucking ridiculous. "I love it," I told him.

"Can I do the other one?" he asked gleefully.

"Sure." I put the second hand down.

Maddie hooked a hand around my leg on the opposite side of Elliott and rubbed gently, tipping her head onto my knee for just a second, letting me know what it meant to her.

My heart answered back.

After my dad and Elliott were in bed, Maddie sat next to me on the couch. "Here. Give me your hand so I can take off the pink."

"Will Elliott be upset?" I asked.

"No," she said. "He will be fine, especially since I painted *his* nails. It was very sweet of you to let him do this in the first place."

"I didn't mind."

She met my eyes. "I know. That's what gets me."

I laughed. "Gets you where?"

Her eyebrows rose as she focused on my fingers again. "You name it. You get to me pretty much everywhere."

"Same here."

She laughed, rubbing hard at the stubborn color on my thumbnail. "Spoken like a true man of few words."

"Sorry." I fumbled for something better. "I'm not good at this."

Her eyes flicked up to mine. "At what?"

"At—you know—saying what needs to be said."

She nodded, moving onto the next fingernail. "What about just saying what you feel?"

"That's even harder for me." My heart was pounding. Beneath my shirt, I was hot and sweaty. "But actually, there is something I want to say."

"There is?"

"Yes." I took a breath. "An offer I want to make. Or maybe it's a suggestion."

Maddie glanced up at me, laughing gently. "I'm listening."

I swallowed. My throat was dry. The room was spinning. "I was thinking, you know, about—about the caretaker job. For my dad."

Her hands paused over mine. "Oh?"

"Yes," I said, latching on to a safer way to get at what I wanted to ask her, a way that would not be lying exactly, but didn't involve *quite* the level of honesty and vulnerability Moretti had mentioned. "None of the candidates that replied to my ad were really right for the job, so I was wondering if maybe you wanted it. I could make it a full-time position with good hourly pay."

She kept her eyes on our hands and started rubbing the polish off one of my nails again.

"I've been thinking about it ever since we had that conversation about you moving back to Bellamy Creek. I was supposed to think up a reason, remember?"

"And . . . that's what you came up with? That's why I should move up here?"

My pulse skittered sideways. "Yes."

She was silent for a moment. "Would that—would that be the *only* reason for me to move here? The job?"

"Would you need another reason?"

She glanced up at me. "Yes. I have a job already. And I like it."

"I know that."

She said nothing, and the longer she stayed silent, the more I panicked.

"No pressure, obviously." I tried to sound casual, like it didn't matter to me if she moved back or not. "I was just thinking that the job would offer you some, you know, *security* if you decided to make the move."

"Give me your other hand."

I did as she asked.

She rubbed the polish off my other thumbnail without saying a word for a minute. "I guess I was just hoping you'd give me a reason that had more to do with *you*, or with *us*, than job security."

"What do you mean?" I asked, even though I knew exactly what she meant.

"I don't know, I just—maybe I misread the situation." She dropped my hand and met my eyes. The joy and hope had gone out of hers. "Do you see this relationship going somewhere, Beckett? Or are you just guaranteeing me gainful employment if I want to move to Bellamy Creek?"

"That's—that's the only guarantee I can offer you."

She nodded slowly. "I see."

"You could live somewhere close by, maybe in a neighborhood that has some kids for Elliott to play with." Every word out of my stupid fucking mouth got worse. "He could go to our old schools."

"Right. Well . . ." She looked toward the kitchen, a tear slipping down her cheek. "You've certainly given me something to think about."

"Maddie, I—" I tried to swallow the golf ball in my throat and couldn't. "I've never made you any promises I couldn't keep. And I don't want to start now."

"I wouldn't ask you to." Another tear fell. "I've *never* asked you to."

"You're upset," I said. "I warned you I'm bad at this."

"I'm okay. Really." She brushed the tear aside and tried to

smile. "I appreciate your honesty. I'd rather know now how you feel."

None of the shit I was saying reflected how I actually felt, but I didn't know how to turn this ship around and stay afloat. "Look, you know I care about you. But I can't ask you to change your life just for *me*."

"Why not?"

Agitated, I got to my feet. "Because I don't have the right. It wouldn't be fair to ask you to take such a huge leap when the odds are not in our favor. I've thought this through."

She shook her head like she didn't get it. "What odds?"

"The odds that two people can make each other happy forever. The numbers just aren't there. It's a bad investment."

"A bad investment," she repeated.

"Yes." I ran a hand through my hair and continued deflecting. "If a client had come to me and said they were going to sink their life savings into an investment with this amount of risk, I'd say don't do it."

She rested her forehead on her fingertips.

"If—if I knew that a herd of cattle needed a certain type of grass to stay alive, I wouldn't put them in a pasture where that grass wouldn't grow." Even I knew how ridiculous I sounded.

She stood up, dropping her arms. "I understand the statistics, Beckett. I'm good at math. But what about feelings? Don't they matter?"

"Feelings change." I stood up taller, puffing up my chest. "*People* change. And people get *hurt*. It's not worth it."

She nodded, looking at me for a long moment, her face registering new understanding. "I see your point. And I'm grateful for your honesty. All my life, I've had a tendency to look for love in the wrong places, and I can see I've been doing that here."

"Maddie—" I started toward her.

"No, don't." She held out one hand and moved away from

me. "This isn't your fault. I haven't been entirely honest with you, maybe not even with myself. The truth is, I thought I could just be with you for fun and not want more than you could give. But I was deluding myself."

Her words were like knives to my heart, but I left them there.

"I'm going to go upstairs to bed now, because I think over the last couple years I've developed one good instinct—knowing when to cut my losses and leave."

"Wait." Quickly I moved toward the stairs, blocking them. "Don't go."

"Tell me the truth, right here and now," she demanded, tears spilling over. "You're not doing me any favors by pretending. Did I pin my hopes on the impossible? Did I mistake your feelings for something they're not?"

With panic wrapped around my throat like a snake, I looked her right in the eye and lied. "Yes."

She closed her eyes. "Then let me go."

Feeling as if I had no choice, I stepped aside and let her run up the stairs and disappear into her bedroom, closing the door behind her.

Then I sank onto the steps and dropped my head into my hands, wondering how I'd fucked that up so spectacularly. So quickly. So painfully.

Why couldn't I ever get it right with her?

A second later, I heard my dad's bedroom door open. "Beckett?" he called out.

I got to my feet and walked into the great room where he could see me. "I'm here."

He stood in his pajamas, hair sticking out as usual. "I thought I heard Maddie's voice."

"She just went to bed."

"Oh. Was she upset about something?"

Exhaling, I pinched the bridge of my nose. Of course he had to pick tonight to be sharp. "I don't know, Dad."

"Are *you* upset about something?"

"Yes," I snapped.

"What?"

"It's a long story."

He held out his arms. "I'm not going anywhere."

"It's complicated."

"I bet it's not as complicated as you're making it."

I dropped my hand. "What do you do when you've managed to screw something up really badly and you're not sure you'll get a chance to turn things around or even *how* to do it?"

He nodded as if he understood. "Well, you can't let your team down. You have to get back out there."

Baseball. Of course.

"I don't know, Dad. I feel like I'm at the plate and I've got two strikes already and no clue what to do with the fastball that's coming at me."

"You swing, dummy! You've already got two strikes on you, you swing!"

I glared at him. "Thanks."

"You're welcome." He sniffed. "Now keep it down out here."

He went into his bedroom and shut the door.

I turned off the lights downstairs, locked the doors, and went upstairs with slow, heavy steps. In the second floor hall, I looked at Maddie's closed door. Then I went to it, lifted my hand to knock.

That's when I heard her crying.

Dropping my arm, I leaned forward, silently pressing my forehead against the door.

Leave her be, said a voice inside me. *You can't give her what she wants, and you'll only do more damage.*

Feeling like I'd let down my team, I went into my own room and got into bed alone.

CHAPTER 18
MADDIE

WHEN I LOOKED at myself in the bathroom mirror the next morning, I winced.

Puffy, bloodshot eyes. Pale, blotchy face. Downturned mouth. Pink nose. Matted hair from tossing and turning all night.

Normally, I got dressed and went down to the kitchen right away to get the coffee going, but today I turned on the shower. Maybe it would put some life back in my face and some energy into my bones. Perhaps I could wash that man right out of my hair.

But it didn't work.

Even when my hair was smooth, my complexion had some color, and my eyedrops had gotten most of the red out, I still looked sad and hopeless. Taking a deep breath, I went into Elliott's room to wake him, only to find his bed was empty. Since it was nearly seven, I assumed he'd gone out to help Beckett with the chores on his own, probably without eating anything.

Downstairs, I found Mr. Weaver spooning up Cap'n Crunch at the kitchen table.

"There you are," he said. "I was beginning to wonder if you'd left without saying goodbye."

I managed a smile. "I'm still here. Sorry I'm down so late today."

"That's okay. I made some breakfast by myself."

I noticed Beckett had made coffee and poured myself a cup. "Is Elliott outside already?"

"Yeah. He went out with Beckett."

"Did he eat anything?" I glanced out the kitchen window but didn't see anyone.

"I think Beckett made him some toast."

I brought my cup of coffee to the table and sat down across from Mr. Weaver. Tried to be cheerful. "Looks like a beautiful day, doesn't it? Perfect for a wedding."

He tilted his head. "Are you getting married today?"

"No. Not me." Smiling gently, I shook my head. "Cole and Cheyenne are getting married today."

"Oh, that's right." He picked up his coffee cup. "For a second, I thought I missed the part where Beckett came to his senses."

"You didn't miss anything," I said bitterly, a lump forming in my throat.

It was *me* who'd missed something—the giant sign on the side of the road that said WRONG WAY, sending myself down the path to heartbreak and disappointment. I'd made it possible for Beckett to hurt me. I'd given in to the timeless lure of him, the irresistible pull of *us*, without stopping to consider that I might actually end up in pieces.

While I was sitting there, I got a text from Bianca.

Hey! We're at the salon this morning starting at 10! Can you sneak away and join us for a mimosa?

I want to, I replied. **Let me check with Beckett.**

A moment later, he came into the kitchen. Across the room, our eyes locked, and he stopped moving. Elliott bumped into him from behind.

"Sorry," Beckett mumbled, stepping aside as Elliott went scurrying around him.

"Mommy! Daisy is coming today!"

"Yes." I focused on his happy face. "Are you excited?"

He clapped his hands. "I can't wait! How many hours until three o'clock? That's when Beckett says she's coming."

"Almost seven."

His face fell. "Oh. That's a lot."

"We can play some gin rummy to pass the time," offered Mr. Weaver.

"Okay." Elliott looked back at Beckett. "But are we going to check the fences now? In the four-wheeler?"

"That's the plan." Beckett answered without taking his eyes off me. "But I thought you had to go to the bathroom."

"I do," Elliott said, scampering from the room. "Be right back."

"I'll go out with you too," Mr. Weaver said, pushing his chair back. "I could use some fresh air."

"I agree. Go get dressed," Beckett told his father.

When we were alone, Beckett came over to the table and picked up his dad's empty cereal bowl. I dropped my eyes to my phone. "Morning," he said quietly.

"Morning."

"How'd you sleep?"

"Fine," I lied. "You?"

"Okay." He stood there with the bowl in his hands. "Listen, I want to apologize for—"

"No apology necessary." I rose to my feet and forced myself to look at him, speak brightly. "Really. Everything is good."

His expression told me he saw through my act. "Doesn't feel that way."

"Well, it is. Hey do you mind if I run downtown and have a quick mimosa with the girls at the salon? They're all getting ready for the wedding together."

"Not at all."

"Great. I'll be back shortly." I took my cup to the sink, rinsed it and put it in the dishwasher, then side-stepped past him on my way out of the kitchen, keeping a careful distance.

"You made it!" From her salon chair, Cheyenne met my eyes in the mirror and lifted her mimosa. "Cheers!"

A receptionist handed me a cocktail from a silver tray on the front desk. "Here you go."

I thanked her and went over to Cheyenne, tapping my glass to hers with a delicate clink. "Cheers!"

Bianca and Blair, seated to her left, held mimosas too, and Mariah, on her right, had what looked like sparkling water in a champagne flute. I touched my glass to all three of theirs and we sipped.

Mariah giggled. "The fizz makes my eyes water."

I grinned at her. "Are you excited?"

"Yes. My dress is so pretty. And my shoes have high heels on them," she said dreamily.

"I can't wait to see them. What are you doing with your hair?"

She looked at Cheyenne. "Some kind of braid on the top, right?"

Cheyenne nodded. "Anything you want. This is your day too."

The smile on Mariah's face lit up the room.

Cheyenne closed her eyes. "God, you guys. I can't believe I'm getting married today."

"Believe it," said the stylist, pinning the top of her gorgeous wavy hair into a loose knot at the back of her head.

"How are you feeling?" I asked.

Her eyes opened, and her smile was radiant. "Fantastic. Like the luckiest girl in the world. A fairy tale princess."

Blair laughed. "Good. That's how a bride should feel."

"Even the weather is perfect!" Bianca enthused.

"It is," I agreed.

We chatted about the wedding as the stylists did their hair, and I finished my drink. "Well, I suppose I should get back. I want to get Elliott some lunch before I have to get ready."

"Okay. Come over to the house early with Beckett, and we'll steal another quick glass of bubbly while the guys drink whiskey and thump each other on the back." Cheyenne wiggled her eyebrows suggestively. "How are things going, by the way?"

"Um. Okay," I said, dropping my eyes to my sneakers.

"Uh oh. What happened?" Bianca asked.

"Nothing, really." I took a breath. "We just had a conversation that didn't go the way I'd hoped."

Cheyenne frowned at me in the mirror. "What do you mean?"

"A conversation about what?" asked Blair.

"About what happens after I leave. The other night he brought up my moving back to Bellamy Creek, and I told him I'd need a really good reason to take that leap. He sort of made a joke out of it, but I honestly thought he was eventually going to give me the reason I was hoping for. Instead, he gave me a job offer."

Bianca made a face. "A job offer!"

"Yes. He offered me the position of caretaker for his father if I wanted to move back to Bellamy Creek."

"*That* was his reason?" Cheyenne's jaw fell open.

"Yes. And when I asked him if he saw this relationship going somewhere or he was just guaranteeing me gainful employment if I wanted to move back, his answer was, 'That's the only guarantee I can offer you.'"

"What?" Bianca shrieked, shaking her head. "Why would he say that?"

"Because he doesn't believe two people can stay together forever, and he doesn't want to make any promises he can't keep."

Blair's brow furrowed. "How do you not believe in forever?"

"He doesn't believe love lasts," I clarified. "He doesn't believe people stay to the end."

Bianca nodded, her eyes sad. "His childhood taught him that. You have to feel bad for him, even though he's being stubborn."

"I'm sorry, Maddie," said Cheyenne. "That had to be a really hard conversation."

"It was pretty bad," I admitted, my eyes tearing up. "There I was, basically prepared to tell him I'm falling in love with him and ready to hand over my heart, and there he was, saying he didn't want it."

"No. I don't believe that." Bianca shook her head. "I think he does want it, but he's scared."

"I asked him if I'd mistaken his feelings for something they're not, and he looked me right in the eye and said *yes*." The memory of it was like a punch in the stomach.

"Do you believe him?" Blair asked softly.

"What choice do I have?" I struggled to talk because my throat was so tight. "It's over. I can't be with him knowing that he doesn't think there's hope for us. After all this time, if I'm not enough to make him believe in forever, there's nothing I can do. I have to let him go. But listen." I forced myself to smile through tears. "I'm strong. I've been through some bad stuff and come out okay. And I look at you guys and see that the fairy tale is possible. Real love does exist."

"It does," Cheyenne said with misty eyes. "Don't give up."

Back at home, I made lunch for Mr. Weaver and Elliott and retreated to my bedroom for a nap. I assumed Beckett was still working outside since his bedroom door was open. I couldn't even look inside since the sight of his bed would make me sad.

In my room, I lay on my bed and closed my eyes but couldn't fall asleep. Finally, I gave up and decided to start packing. My plan was to leave first thing in the morning. If Elliott hadn't had his heart set on an evening with Daisy, I might have even left tonight, although I did want to see Cole and Cheyenne get married.

It would be good to see two people promise each other forever and mean it.

Eventually, I opened the closet and took out my new blue dress. Holding it up by the hanger, I looked at it for a moment and remembered trying it on, the way I'd imagined dancing in Beckett's arms. Now I couldn't even imagine the conversation in the car on the way to the wedding, let alone dancing with him.

God, how had we managed to fuck up our friendship so badly in such a short amount of time? It had been the *one thing* I was afraid of—crossing the line and realizing too late it was a mistake. And now we had to spend the entire evening together.

Beckett would be silent and stoic as usual, I'd be fighting tears all night . . . For a moment, I considered feigning illness and backing out. Maybe I could just stay home with Elliott and Daisy. They could play with my makeup and—

Someone knocked on my door.

Laying the dress across the bed, I took a deep breath and pulled it open. It was Mallory.

"Oh, hi," I said, surprised to see her. "You're here already."

"Daisy was chomping at the bit to get over here and see Elliott, so we came early." Her expression was concerned. "Is everything okay, Maddie?"

"Yes," I lied. "Why do you ask?"

"Because Beckett is downstairs stomping around like an angry bear, and when I asked what time you guys were leaving, he said he wasn't sure you were still going."

"Oh." My eyes dropped to my bare toes on the carpet. Elliott's attempt at a pedicure nearly made me smile—good thing my dress was long. "Yes, I'm still going."

"Can I ask what happened? Did you two have an argument or something?" She folded her arms over her chest. "When I left on Sunday night, things looked pretty cozy between you."

"They were." Another deep breath.

"Then what's going on? I know my brother, and he can be a big grump sometimes, but this is something else."

"We, um . . ." I struggled with what to say. "We had a discussion last night about what happens when I leave. Let's just say it didn't go well."

She inhaled and exhaled, nodding as if she'd expected that answer. "Can I come in?"

"Of course." I stood back and she entered the room, turning to face me, hands on her hips.

"Let me guess. Beckett said he doesn't have time for a long-distance relationship."

"It wasn't so much that," I said, closing the door. "Although I can plainly see that such a thing would be really hard for him. He really can't get away from here."

"True," she admitted. "It would be tough."

"Our conversation was actually more about the possibility of me moving back to Bellamy Creek."

Her mouth fell open in surprise. "Really? You're considering that?"

"I was certainly *willing* to consider it. It would be complicated—I'd have to get permission from Elliott's dad—quit my job, find a new one . . . but even those things wouldn't have deterred me if Beckett had asked me to move up here to be with him. If he saw a future for us. But that's not what he suggested."

"I don't understand. What did he suggest?"

"That I move here to take the job as caretaker for your dad."

She stared at me, completely agog. "*That's* what he said? Move back so you can be my dad's full-time nurse and babysitter?"

"Yes." I wiped a tear that had snuck out of the corner of one eye.

"That asshole!" She shook her head and thumped the heel of her hand on her forehead. "I don't get it. The guy's crazy about you. He's always been crazy about you. And now here you both are, finally at the point in your lives where you could be together, and he offers you a *job*? This is messed up."

"Listen, I don't want to blame Beckett for being unable to say what I needed to hear. I had unrealistic expectations, you know? I saw something that wasn't there."

"No, you didn't," she insisted. "I saw it. Even Daisy saw it. She asked if you guys were going to get married. She's hoping Elliott can be her cousin."

I smiled through tears. "What you saw might have just been closeness. We've always had a great connection. But that doesn't mean that he wants to be with me forever. He doesn't even believe that's possible. He thinks people don't stay."

"Did he say that?"

"Yes. Multiple times, multiple ways."

She closed her eyes and sighed. "Can I tell you something?"

"Sure." I went to the bed and sat down.

Mallory strolled toward one window, turned around, and leaned back against the sill with both hands. "You know my mom left when Beck was really tiny."

"Yes."

"He doesn't remember her at all."

"That's what he said. He's only seen pictures. He said that no one ever really talked about her growing up."

She nodded. "That's the truth. We didn't. My dad dealt with his pain by working, and Beckett bore witness to that. I've always thought that's why he was so obsessed with work. As he got older, he saw how our dad used work to cope with feelings of loss and abandonment. Amy and I were devastated too—we were only six and nine at the time—but at least we had each other to talk to. And we cried a lot. Beckett grew up thinking that men should be strong and suffer silently. They work. They provide. They protect."

"He does all of those things," I said softly.

"I think he ended up learning that it was better to just work off your feelings than talk about them. Or keep them bottled up. When he got older, sometimes he would ask questions, but Amy and I didn't really have answers. And we probably made it worse by just trying to distract him or change the subject. I wish we'd known better back then. We all could have used some therapy."

I smiled sadly.

"I've gone since then, and it's helped me a lot."

"Me too."

"Our dad tried hard," Mallory went on, her eyes filling. "He was the best dad he knew how to be, and he made sure we had food and shelter and clothing and never had to miss out on things because of money. And he never yelled or hit us or even got mad very often—he was like Beckett. Even-tempered and strong-willed. Kept those feelings locked up."

I nodded. "They're a lot alike."

"Anyway, when I look back I can see how Beckett's over-achieving tendencies made sense. He wanted approval and validation, and he learned not to seek it emotionally. His rewards were things like good grades, home runs, scholar-ships, an MBA, a high-paying job. But none of that filled the hole left in his heart, you know?"

I nodded, wiping a tear. "I don't think he wants to fill it. I think he guards it with an iron cover."

She came over and sat next to me. Took my hand. "Don't give up. It might take some time, but I cannot believe he's going to watch you walk away."

"I don't know, Mallory. He's pretty stubborn. And I know from psychology class that the fear of losing is more powerful than the pleasure of gaining. Losses always loom larger." I took a breath. "And who knows? Maybe he realized he was waiting all this time for nothing. Maybe I wasn't worth it. Sometimes reality is a shitty replacement to fantasy—maybe I was better as the dream girl."

"I don't believe that for one second," she said firmly.

"But it's hard not to think that way," I admitted. "I've made some really bad choices in my life because I clung to fantasy—what could be rather than what was right in front of me. Maybe Beckett is doing me a favor by telling me now that he can't give me what I want."

"But he's throwing away a chance to be happy," she said angrily.

"That's his choice. And if he chooses to be alone, there's nothing anyone can do about it."

She nodded sadly, and my last hope dwindled to nothing.

CHAPTER 19

BECKETT

STANDING in front of the mirror above my dresser, I frowned, undid my tie, and re-knotted it for the fifth time. Tightened it. Smoothed it. Adjusted it once again.

But it wasn't my tie making me scowl at my reflection.

It wasn't the suit either. Or the crisp white shirt or the matching pocket square or my haircut or my cufflinks or my watch. It wasn't even the note card in my pocket with words on it that felt like complete bullshit.

It was me. It was what I'd done.

I'd lied. I'd hurt someone I cared about. I'd made her feel like she didn't matter enough to me. I'd been unable to make her understand the truth.

But was that my fault? Did I need to punish myself for it?

This was why it was better to focus on things you could control, like work. Personal relationships were too unstable, too volatile. Feelings were irrational and unpredictable.

Boundaries were better. Keeping people at arm's length. Sticking to the things you were good at, so you didn't wind up feeling like a failure.

A knock on my bedroom door made me jump. "Yeah?"

"It's me." My sister poked her head into the room. "Can I

come in?"

"Go ahead."

She shut the door and sat behind me on the foot of the bed. "You look nice."

"I can't get the fucking knot in my tie right."

"Want help?"

"No." Angrily I yanked the tie loose again and started over.

"Beautiful day for a wedding."

"I guess."

"You don't sound too excited about it."

"Why should I be excited?"

"I don't know, you grouchy old man, maybe because one of your lifelong best friends is marrying the love of his life?"

I didn't answer.

She folded her arms over her chest. "I know you had an argument with Maddie."

"It wasn't an argument," I snapped.

"Oh? What was it?"

"It was a *discussion* during which I saved us both a lot of heartbreak down the road."

"How do you know there would have been heartbreak? Maybe things would have worked out."

"I was honest about my feelings." The knot was still crooked. I jerked it loose.

"No, you weren't. You were stubborn."

I spun to face her. "You don't know anything about it."

Sighing, she rose to her feet and came toward me and unraveled the knot all the way, patiently starting over. "Can I say something?"

Even though I wanted to push her away, kick her out of my room, and slam the door behind her, I took a deep breath and let her speak.

"I know what it was like to grow up in this house. Learning your mother abandoned you. Thinking that you weren't good enough to make her stay. Wondering what you did wrong. Believing that your feelings must not matter. Being scared to love someone because they could choose to leave you too."

"That's not what—"

Her eyes flicked up sharply. "I'm not done."

I pressed my lips together and exhaled through my nose.

"Not everyone leaves, Beckett. I'm not saying it's easy, but some people make a different choice."

"Love isn't a choice," I said angrily. "I fucking wish it were."

"That's true. Love isn't a choice. But sticking with someone you love is. Staying to the end. It takes grit and grace and a whole lotta patience and compromise, but it's worth it. There." She adjusted the knot one last time and smoothed the front of my tie. "Perfect."

I turned and looked in the mirror. "Not bad."

"Thank you. Now do you promise to think about what I said?"

"It's no use, Mallory," I said stubbornly. "She has to leave. I can't stop her."

My sister sighed. "Then I guess you'll deserve the way it feels to watch her go."

When I said nothing, she left the room and pulled the door shut behind her.

Alone again, I stared myself down in the mirror, knowing my sister was right. I *would* deserve the way it felt to watch her walk away. But I didn't have a choice.

The set of my jaw grew even tighter, the furrow between my brows even deeper as I yanked my tie loose and started over again.

Fifteen minutes later, I knocked on my dad's bedroom door. "Dad, you ready? I need to go. I'm running a little behind."

"I'm ready." He opened the door, looking dapper in dress pants and a sport coat, his white hair neatly combed.

I sniffed, the inside of my nostrils burning. "Wow. You put on some cologne, huh?"

"This is a fancy occasion," he said, adjusting his coat by the lapels. "And there could be some single women there. I need to look my best."

Any other day, I'd have smiled. "You look good. I'm going to back the car out of the garage, okay? Maddie should be down in a minute."

"I'm ready," said a voice behind me.

I turned and felt the wind knocked out of me. She stood in the great room, lit by the sun pouring in through the massive windows. She wore a long blue dress that bared her shoulders, and her dark hair was piled on top of her head with just a few strands escaping to frame her face. From across the room her jade green eyes looked large and luminous, her lashes thick and black. Her sensuous mouth was painted a soft shade of pink, and I had a crazy urge to vault over the back of the couch between us and drop to my knees at her feet. Tell her I was an idiot. Beg her to forgive me. To love me. To stay.

But I couldn't move. I couldn't speak. Frankly, I wasn't even sure I could breathe.

She tore her eyes from mine and looked at my dad, giving him the smile she hadn't offered me. "Well, look at you. Aren't you handsome?"

"Thank you," he said, strutting into the great room. "Bought this coat in ninety-one and it still fits."

Maddie laughed. "Some things were made to last."

"I was just about to back the car out," I said stupidly.

She looked at me again. "Okay. You look nice too."

"Thanks. So do you." It was not nearly the compliment

she deserved, but my head was a fucking mess. "I'll meet you out front."

She nodded. "I'll say goodbye to Elliott. He's on the back patio with Daisy and your sister."

When she turned toward the sliding patio doors, I saw the back of her dress—what there was of it. Two straps crossed between her shoulder blades, revealing enough skin to make my mouth water.

Unable to stop staring, I stumbled at the edge of the rug on my way to the kitchen.

This was going to be a long night.

When we arrived at Cole's, a valet attendant took my keys, and we made our way up the front walk. My dad had taken Maddie's arm before I could, and I walked behind them like a chastised toddler or a pissed-off third wheel. Hot and aggravated, I wiped my forehead, which felt sticky.

Cole's mom opened the front door and welcomed us inside the house, which was blessedly cool from the air-conditioning. "The ladies are upstairs," she told Maddie, "and I have instructions to send you right up. The gentlemen are having a drink on the patio."

"That sounds good," said my father, offering Mrs. Mitchell his arm. "Shall we?"

Laughing, she tucked her hand in his elbow. "We shall."

Annoyed that my cantankerous old man was more charming than me, I watched Maddie go up the stairs without a glance back at me and followed my father and Mrs. Mitchell to the patio.

The yard looked incredible—the tables were covered with white linen, fancy place settings, and centerpieces; a wooden dance floor and DJ table had been set up at one end of the tent; flowers decorated the rows of chairs on either side of the aisle. On the flagstone patio, a bar had been set up, and my friends were standing around one of several high-top tables nearby. Griffin was pouring shots from a bottle of whiskey.

Moretti looked up as I approached. "Good, we're all here."

"Sorry I'm late," I said. "I couldn't get my fucking tie right."

"Everything okay?" Cole asked.

"Fine," I said shortly.

"Okay then, here we go." Griffin pushed a full shot glass toward each of us.

Moretti grabbed his and raised it up. "To Cole and Cheyenne. May they have a long and happy life together."

Cole laughed. "What, no Italian for me?"

"You guys told me that was selfish last time," Moretti said defensively. "I was trying to show my growth as a human being."

"I like the Italian toast," Cole said. "Let's hear it."

Moretti raised his glass again. "*Beviamo alla nostra.* To us."

"To us," Griffin repeated. "And fuck the Mavs."

We all lifted our glasses and tossed back the whiskey. I grimaced as it burned its way down my throat, then pushed my glass toward Griffin. "I think I need another."

He poured without asking why.

"What's going on?" Moretti was eyeballing me shrewdly.

"Nothing."

"Is it the toast thing?"

"No."

"So what's with the mad face?"

I tried to replace my scowl with a blank expression. "Better?"

"Not really," he said. "Is your dad okay?"

Everyone glanced over to where my dad and Cole's mom stood chatting. "He looks okay," Cole said.

"My dad is fine, I'm fine, everything's fine," I said in a tone that clearly communicated *nothing* was fine. I tossed back the second shot. My eyes watered.

My friends watched me plunk the shot glass back on the table.

"Uh, Beckett?" Cole rubbed the back of his neck. "I'm not judging you, and it's totally cool with me if this is your choice for today, but do you realize one of your fingernails is painted pink?"

"What?" I held out my right hand, and sure enough, hot pink polish still covered my pinkie nail. "Fuck. Maddie must have missed that one."

"Maddie painted your nails?" Griffin asked, tilting his head in confusion.

"No. Elliott did. Maddie took the polish off last night after Elliott went to bed, but I guess she missed one. We sort of got distracted while she was doing it."

Griffin laughed. "I'll bet you did."

"Not like that." I took a deep breath and let it out. "We had a fight. Or not a fight. I don't even know what to call it, but it did not end well."

"Oh, shit," Moretti said.

Griffin poured everyone a little more whiskey, and they threw back their second shots. But I didn't touch my glass.

"It's fine," I said again, trying to brush it off. "It was going to end sooner or later. Might as well be now, before she did something rash like move back to Bellamy Creek."

Cole's eyes widened. "She was going to move back here?"

"She was thinking about it." I dropped my eyes to my empty glass. "We . . . discussed it."

"So what's the problem? Elliott's dad?" Cole asked.

I shook my head. "We didn't even get that far. I fucked it up too fast."

"Why?" Griffin asked. "Don't you want her to move back?"

"I don't know."

"Bullshit," muttered Moretti.

"Okay, fine," I said defensively. "Maybe I *do* want her to move back, but I don't want her to do it for me."

"Why not?" Cole asked.

"I don't understand why I have to fucking explain this to everyone," I said heatedly. "Especially to you guys. Why can't you just respect my decision without asking me to defend it?"

"Uh, maybe because we're your best friends, and we can see that you're fucking up a great thing?" Moretti said with a shrug.

"If she wants to be with you, and you want to be with her, why not encourage her to move back?" Cole asked. "Wouldn't that be so much easier for you than dating long-distance?"

"Yeah. But that's not the point," I argued.

"So what's the point?" Griffin asked. "I thought it was pretty obvious Thursday night when I saw you guys together that she'd move here. Why put it off?"

"Unless you're not sure of your feelings for her," Cole said. "If you've got doubts, I could totally see why you wouldn't want her to take that kind of leap."

"I have no doubts about my feelings for her," I said. "I have other kinds of doubts."

"Such as?" Griffin asked.

I closed my eyes a second, then opened them and threw back my third shot. "I don't want to talk about it."

My friends were silent, and I felt like the world's biggest dick for ruining the moment.

"Look," Cole said, "I don't know exactly what your doubts are, but if they're anything like mine were when Cheyenne and I started dating, it might help to say them out loud."

"Fuck that," I said irritably. Then I sighed, pinching the

bridge of my nose. "Sorry, you guys. I hardly slept last night. I know I'm being a total asshole."

"You are," agreed Griffin, "but I think we all were when we were in the place you're in right now. In fact, I distinctly remember Cole calling me an asshole when I broke up with Blair and told her to leave town."

"That's right, I did." Cole looked happy about it.

"Another thing he said was that given how long we'd been friends, he'd expect me to tell him if he was fucking something up in a big way." Griffin paused. "So I did."

"He did," Cole confirmed. "But I needed to hear it."

"I think it was Blair who called me an asshole when I messed things up with Bianca," Moretti chimed in.

"She definitely said it to me," Griffin informed him with a laugh. "Even if she didn't say it to your face."

"The point is, Beck, we've all been there," Cole said. "We've all fucked up a good thing because it seemed like the safer way to go."

I stared at the empty shot glass. "For fifteen years, every time I've had the chance to tell her how I feel about her, I can't get the words out. I either say nothing at all, or I say the wrong thing."

"Been there," Moretti said.

"Done that." Griffin nodded.

"So how do you get over feeling like you might actually have a heart attack and die if you say the words you're thinking?" I asked them. "How do you force yourself to get outside your head?"

"You finally realize that the alternative is worse," Cole said. "Living without her—and it's your own damn fault."

I frowned. "I just wish I had more time."

"Did you not just say you've waited fifteen fucking years?" Griffin asked.

"Dude." Moretti clapped me on the back. "Admit it— we're right."

I opened my mouth to argue, then closed it again. "I can't think about this right now. I need to get this pink polish off my finger."

"Cheyenne could probably help," Cole suggested. "I can't see her, but you can go upstairs."

"I'll be back," I said, leaving them at the table.

Guests were starting to arrive, and I had to swim upstream through dozens of them making their way through the house to the yard. After taking the stairs up two at a time, I knocked on the only bedroom door that was closed, behind which I heard feminine laughter.

Mariah pulled it open. "Uncle Beckett! You're not supposed to be up here."

"I know, sorry."

She ducked down and peeked around my side. "Is Daddy with you?"

"No, I'm alone." I had to smile. "You look beautiful."

"Thank you." She stood tall again, her grin joyful and proud. Her dress was long, floaty, and peach-colored, and her dark hair was tied back in a braid on the top, the rest loose around her shoulders. She wore lip gloss, a tiny diamond necklace, and some kind of glittery lotion that made her skin shimmer a little. "It's not time for us to come down yet, is it?"

"I don't think so." Over her shoulder, I heard Maddie's voice, and I looked into the room. She sat on a bench at the foot of the king-sized bed, looking at Cheyenne, who stood in front of a full-length mirror on the back of the closet door. Bianca and Blair were on either side of her, fussing the way women did over brides—fluffing her dress, adjusting her veil, arranging her hair just so.

Cheyenne caught my eyes in the mirror. "Beckett! What are you doing up here? Is it time?"

I shook my head. "Not quite yet."

She looked slightly relieved. "Good. I still feel like I need to catch my breath a minute. You can come in if you'd like."

Hesitantly, I stepped into the room, barely flicking my eyes toward Maddie. I was afraid if I really looked at her like I had at home, I'd fall to my knees and beg her to let me try again. And I couldn't be weak. I had to stay strong.

"What can I do for you?" Cheyenne asked, turning to face me. "You look very handsome, by the way."

"Thank you. You look beautiful. Between you and Mariah, we're going to have to mop Cole off the ground."

She smiled. "Thank you. So what's up?"

"Uh, I have a little problem." I held up my hand.

Her eyes widened, and she laughed. "Oh my. That's quite the manicure."

Maddie jumped up off the bench and came to look. "Oh no! Did I miss one?"

"Just one," I said. "It's okay. I didn't even notice until the guys told me a minute ago."

Mariah, Blair, and Bianca came over to peek at my hand too, and they all began to laugh.

"I kind of like it," Bianca said. "I think it's cool when a man is so secure he can paint his nails pink."

"I do too," agreed Blair.

"There's a kid at my school who paints his nails," offered Mariah. "Usually it's colors like black or blue, but nobody even makes fun of him for it."

"Well, that's good, and normally I might not care, but I think for today I'd better get it off."

"Cheyenne, do you have any remover?" Maddie asked.

"In the bathroom." Cheyenne gestured toward the master bath. "Under the sink. I have a whole crate of nail stuff."

"I'll grab it," Maddie said.

"I can get it." I followed her to the bathroom, but she made it there first and bent down at the sink. Pulling out the crate, she set it on the vanity and took out a plastic bottle of yellow liquid. Unscrewing the black cap, she set it aside and reached for a cotton ball from a jar full of them. She wet it and said, "Give me your hand."

I held it out, and she went to work removing the pink. The chemical acetone scent stung my nostrils. "Thanks."

"No problem." She kept her eyes on her work and when she was done, she nodded. "There. No more pink."

I looked at my bare fingernail and nodded, then let my hand drop. "I appreciate it."

She busied herself tossing out the soiled cotton, screwing the cap back on the bottle, tucking the crate back beneath the sink. But she never once looked me in the eye.

It tore my heart in two that we'd been reduced to this painful, awkward silence when all I wanted to do was hold her. "You look really beautiful," I said quietly. "I'm sorry I didn't say so before."

"Thank you." She lifted her head, but her expression was carefully blank. Her green eyes were dull as the creek on a cloudy day.

"Maddie, I hate this."

"Hate what?"

"This silence between us."

Her eyebrows rose. "Do you have something new to say?"

I fought for the words trapped inside me. "I—I missed you last night."

Her lower lip trembled, but she said nothing.

"You didn't miss me?"

"Does it matter?"

"Yes, it matters."

"For what it's worth, yes. I did miss you." Her eyes filled with tears. "I'll probably miss you for the rest of my life."

Unable to stop myself, I cradled her face in my hands just like I had at eighteen, rubbed my thumb over her quivering lips. "I don't want to lose you."

She pushed my hands down and took a step back. "I can't do this, Beckett. I need to be more careful with my heart. I give it away too easily—I give everything away too easily."

With that, she swept past me, leaving me to agonize over the lingering scent of her perfume and the memories it evoked of her skin next to mine. Was that memory all I had left?

A moment later, Bianca poked her head in. "The girls are heading downstairs now. I think you should probably go find the guys."

"Okay." I exhaled heavily. "I should check on my dad first."

"Maddie said to tell you she would find your dad and sit down with him."

Of course she did. My chest caved a little more.

"Hey." Bianca came all the way into the bathroom and faced me, smoothing my lapels, straightening my tie, brushing dust off one shoulder. "You okay, pal?"

"No." It felt like the first honest word I'd spoken all day, and it loosened something inside me.

"I can tell." She met my eyes. "I'm here if you'd like to talk. I'm a good listener. And it's not easy to figure out how to be with someone. I get that."

"Thanks."

She tucked her hand in my elbow. "Shall we go down?"

"Sure." We walked through the bedroom into the hall. Halfway down the steps, I stopped. "It's not that I don't want to be with her."

"I know."

"Because I do."

"I believe you. But *she* needs to hear that."

"I think I'm in love with her," I blurted. My heart was pounding hard enough to make me wonder if I might be in cardiac arrest. "I think I've always been in love with her."

She squeezed my arm.

"But I think about the future, you know? What if I end up

like my dad, eighty-one and wandering around trying to catch a train that's never going to come? Will she still want me then? Will she look at me the same way? Will she think it's what she signed up for?" It was like the dam had burst and all my thoughts were gushing over the spillway.

"Oh, Beckett," she said. "Of course she will. That's what love is."

"But how do you know it lasts?" I asked. "Love isn't always enough to make someone stay. Where's the proof that people stick around? That they'll be there for you forever?"

"Hey! There you are!" At the foot of the steps, Moretti stood looking up at us a little frantically. "Come on, Weaver, we have to get moving."

"I'm coming." I finished escorting Bianca down the stairs, and when we reached the bottom, I kissed her cheek. "Thanks for listening. Sorry I just unloaded all that on you."

"I didn't mind. Did it help?" she asked hopefully.

"Maybe." I wanted to say yes, but something in me refused to give in. Maybe it worked for other people because they were wired differently, or they had different experiences. Maybe I was defective.

Or maybe I was smarter than all of them.

"Come on." Moretti grabbed my sleeve and pulled me out the front door. I followed him around to one side of the house where Cole and Griffin were standing in the shade.

"Oh good, you found him." Cole looked relieved.

"Sorry." Feeling guilty for wallowing in my own bullshit on Cole's wedding day, I clapped him on the back. After what he'd been through, no one deserved this day more than he did. "I'll stop being an asshole now. I'm here for you."

"Good." Cole looked at us all. "I wouldn't be able to do this if a single one of you wasn't here."

"Sure you would." Griffin threw an arm over his shoulders. "But we wouldn't have let you."

"Seriously, you guys. At the risk of getting sappy, I need to say thanks for being there for me. After I lost Trisha, I wasn't sure how I was going to survive as a single dad. And I certainly never thought I'd be in a place where I'd be this happy again. But knowing you always had my back made a huge difference. You never let me get so down I couldn't see my way out."

I felt a tug in the back of my throat.

"What are friends for?" asked Moretti.

"Yeah, but there's friends, and then there's you guys." Cole laughed. "I'd say we're more than friends, but that sounds weird."

"We're brothers by choice," Griffin said, throwing his other arm around Moretti.

Moretti slung an arm around my neck, and I finished out the circle with an arm around him and the other around Cole. For a moment we just stood there, heads together. It made me feel better. Stronger. We'd seen each other through a lot of stuff—good and bad—but we'd been there for each other. We called each other out on our bullshit, but we also lifted each other up. And I had no doubt in my mind that's how it would always be with us.

"Awww, you guys are so cute!"

We separated and looked behind us to find Bianca standing there with a hand over her heart.

"Is it time?" Cole asked.

"Yes. But you're so adorable with your group hug, I don't even want to break it up."

"It wasn't a group hug," scoffed Griffin, adjusting his lapels.

"It was a *team huddle*." Moretti fussed with his cuffs. "A very manly team huddle."

"I see." Bianca looked amused. "Well, if you're done cuddling—"

"I said huddle, not cuddle!"

"—then it's about time you headed out there." She

laughed again. "I really wish I'd had a camera just now."

"I'm actually kind of glad you didn't," said Cole. He smoothed his jacket over his stomach and took a breath. "Okay, are we ready?"

I nodded and put a hand on his shoulder. "Let's go."

We started to walk around the house toward the yard, and Bianca tugged my hand. "Hey," she said, nodding at Cole, Griffin, and Moretti as they walked ahead of me. "There's your answer, by the way."

"Huh?" I wasn't sure what she meant.

"The question you asked me on the stairs." Her eyes lit up as she pointed at my friends, and her voice softened. "Right there, Beckett. *That's* your proof."

I wanted to ask her what the question had been—my brain was such a mess today—but she'd already disappeared into the house. Griffin gave Cole a fist bump and headed toward the patio where his mom stood, waiting for him to formally seat her. Afterward, he'd go into the house to collect his sister, whom he'd walk down the aisle.

With my head still in a fog, I followed Moretti and Cole up the right side of all the chairs, which I was surprised to see were full. I spotted my dad and Maddie in the second row, along with the Morettis. At the sight of her bare shoulders, my stomach muscles tightened.

We stood over to one side while the harpist began to play, and I couldn't take my eyes off Maddie. The way the sunlight made her hair glint with copper. The way her sunburn had faded to a beautiful warm gold. The way the breeze ruffled the dress around her legs. I inhaled deeply, as if I might catch the scent of her if I concentrated hard enough.

She turned her head and looked at me over one shoulder, like she'd felt my eyes on her. But she didn't smile or wave, and her expression was one of sadness, maybe even regret.

As the music began, she looked straight ahead again, and my heart sank deeper.

FIGHTING TEARS, I tore my eyes from Beckett's and stared straight ahead.

I'd been on the verge of a full-on sobfest since I'd left him in the upstairs bathroom. After coming downstairs, I'd ducked into the first floor lavatory and leaned against the vanity, taking a few deep breaths.

I missed you so much last night.

Well, tough!

He deserved to miss me. I hoped he'd miss me for the rest of his lonely hermit-crab cowboy days. He could have had more, but he was choosing to lose me. He was closing off his heart and sending me away.

A tear or two leaked from my eyes, making my eyeliner and mascara run. Before heading back out, I grabbed a tissue and my cosmetics pouch and performed a quick touch-up.

But my heart was not so easily repaired. I felt like pieces of it were littered like scraps all over this town, and stitching them together would be impossible. My best bet was to leave before any further damage could be done. Go on with my life. Dedicate myself to being the best mom I could be. Maybe someday, someone would come along that would make me feel the way Beckett did, but if that never happened, I'd be fine on my own. I was never going to be careless with my heart again.

Holding my head high, I'd walked outside and found Mr. Weaver chatting with a handsome couple I thought might be the Morettis. With a smile on my face, I approached them and introduced myself.

"Oh, hello," the woman said. "I remember you from way back when. We're Enzo's parents, Carlo and Marisol Moretti."

"Nice to see you," I said, shaking both their hands.

"Maddie lives across the street from us," Mr. Weaver said. "But she's at our house all the time. If my son had any brains at all, he'd marry her."

The Morettis laughed politely while I turned beet red. "Actually I'm heading back to Cincinnati right after the wedding. But it's been a lovely visit."

"Returning to your hometown is always lovely, isn't it?" Mrs. Moretti sighed. "No matter how far away you go, whenever you feel lost, you can always find yourself at home. You'll always belong there."

My throat grew tight. I wasn't sure I had a place like that anymore. "Yes. Should we find somewhere to sit, Mr. Weaver?"

"Sure," he said. "Let's go up front. My eyes aren't the best."

"Okay."

"But not because I'm old," he said, taking me by the arm. "Just because they're a little worn out."

I hid a smile. "I understand."

We moved up the aisle to the second row and took two chairs on the right. Once we were seated, Mr. Weaver looked around. "This is a nice yard."

"Yes, it is."

"You could play some good ball games back here. Elliott would like it."

I was surprised he recalled Elliott's name. "He would, you're right. But I don't think we'll have time."

Mr. Weaver looked at me. "You're not really leaving, are you?"

"I'm afraid I have to."

"But why? You live here. This is your home."

"It's not," I said, shaking my head. "Not anymore."

He was quiet a moment. "Cynthia Mae left too."

"I'm—I'm sorry."

"She said it wasn't her home either. She said she'd made a mistake." His gray-blue eyes studied me, remarkably clear. "Is that what you think too?"

I thought carefully before I responded. "I'm trying to stop myself before I make a mistake."

"She said she loved us, but she had to go. I never understood that. If you love someone, you stay. Right?"

So much for the repair job. I grabbed a tissue from my purse and dabbed at my eyes. "Right."

"She said it was more complicated than that, and maybe it was." He sighed heavily. "I don't know."

I smiled through my tears.

"But I thought I knew my son. And I don't get why he'd want to spend the rest of his life looking for you when you're right here."

My throat hurt, it was so tight. "Maybe he won't even look for me."

Mr. Weaver laughed. "Of course he will. He's been looking for you for *years*."

I wasn't sure if the clarity was slipping from his mind or not, so I simply changed the subject. "The weather is beautiful, isn't it?"

"It sure is. Perfect temperature."

The chairs began to fill up, and the Morettis smiled at us as they took the seats to our right.

The harpist, who was seated on one side of the floral arch

at the head of the aisle, began to play a classical tune, signaling the guests to quiet themselves. A warm breeze ruffled my dress, and I closed my eyes for a moment, willing my tears to stay at bay during the next twenty minutes or so, or if they wouldn't, at least let them be for Cole and Cheyenne.

The skin across the back of my neck prickled with the heat of awareness, and I glanced over my shoulder. My breath caught when I saw Beckett standing over to the side of the yard with Cole and Enzo, his eyes on me, his expression serious but unyielding. For several seconds, I couldn't breathe. My pulse raced, and my vision clouded slightly. I looked to the front again, taking in several deep lungfuls of warm summer air.

However, my heart beat erratically again just seconds later as I watched Cole, Enzo, and Beckett appear to the right of the floral arch and take their places. As if drawn by magnetic force, our eyes locked, and I was dizzy again. I had to force myself to look away.

A moment later, Mrs. Mitchell came up the aisle on the arm of a guy who might have been Cole's older brother. They both sat down in the row right ahead of us, which was already occupied by a woman and a couple kids.

Next came Mrs. Dempsey on Griffin's arm, and he kissed his mother on the cheek before seating her and heading back down the aisle with long-legged strides.

The harpist transitioned into a different song, a tune I recognized as "A Thousand Years," and like all the guests, I turned my attention to the foot of the aisle.

Bianca came first, her red hair gleaming like a ruby in the sun. The bridesmaids wore tea-length dresses in deep champagne silk and carried bouquets of roses in cream, navy, and apricot. Bianca was grinning brightly, her steps sure and quick, like she couldn't wait to get to the good part of the show. As she passed our row, she made eye contact with me and winked. I smiled and touched my heart.

Next came Blair, her eyes shining with tears, her smile a little smaller and more sentimental. She walked slower too, looking like the former pageant queen she was, her chin high, her gliding steps careful but confident.

Then the crowd murmured a collective *awww*, and I grinned when I saw Mariah coming up the aisle in her bright peach dress, her dark hair lustrous in the sunlight, her blue eyes wide and bright. Her smile was so huge it revealed nearly every one of her teeth, and when she made eye contact with her dad, he had to wipe away a tear. I pulled a tissue from my purse and did the same.

Then all the guests rose to their feet, and I peered down the aisle to see Cheyenne on the arm of her big brother as they made their way up the aisle. Cheyenne's youthful face was radiant with happiness—you could see the girl with a crush on her brother's best friend, a girl who'd never loved anyone else, a girl whose dreams had finally come true. Griffin's face was more stoic, his jaw set, his shoulders back. But about halfway up the aisle, he looked down at Cheyenne and cracked a smile. She glanced up at him and smiled back, and the love between them was as sweet and clear as the music filling the air.

Cole smiled too as his future wife approached on the arm of his lifelong best friend. I tried to imagine what that would be like—to see your past and your future intertwined. To know for certain you were right where you belonged and surrounded by everyone who loved you. To share your life with people who could look back with you and laugh or cry, then look forward with hope.

I wiped my eyes again as Griffin kissed his sister on the cheek, shook Cole's hand, and took his place between Enzo and Beckett. My eyes traveled over the four friends in their navy suits, their shoulders broad and strong, their foreheads glistening in the heat, their arms at their sides.

At that moment, Beckett looked at me. His lips parted, and he blinked. It was almost like he was seeing me for the first time. My heart began to race.

But then he looked away again, the solemn expression back on his face.

I looked away too, my eyes blurring with tears.

This was ridiculous. Was I going to torture myself staring at him all night? Imagining he saw me differently? Was I so naïve that I thought he was going to suddenly look at me and realize he couldn't live without me? How many times was I going to go looking for an answer he couldn't give? A feeling he didn't feel? A future he didn't want?

Choking back tears, I made up my mind. As soon as I could, I'd slip out of the crowd, order a car to take me back to Beckett's house, pack up and leave Bellamy Creek behind. I'd be sorry not to say goodbye to the girls, but I'd text them— they'd understand.

Cole took Cheyenne's hands, and the ceremony began.

CHAPTER 21
BECKETT

STANDING BEHIND COLE AND MORETTI, I watched Bianca and Blair come up the aisle. The sun was hot on my face, and I was sweaty beneath my suit. The faint breeze was a relief.

But I forgot about my discomfort momentarily as I watched Mariah make her way between the rows of chairs, looking happier than I'd ever seen her. She was like family to me, and seeing her lit up from the inside tugged at my heart. Cole was so lucky to have such a bright, beautiful daughter. And the way she was looking at him, like he was her hero, made my chest tighten. What would that be like?

Would I be as good a dad as Cole? Would I be a different kind of father than my own? Was I a fool to throw away my chance to find out?

As I grappled with those questions, Griffin started walking his sister up the aisle, and I thought about my own sisters, how lucky I was to have them, how much they'd sacrificed for me growing up. We hadn't had an easy time. Yet somehow they'd managed to forge a strong belief in love and commitment, to trust someone enough to build a life with them, to have children together.

I watched Griffin kiss Cheyenne on the cheek, and wondered if he was looking at her and saw—like I did—the little girl in pigtails and overalls who used to follow us around, or the awkward adolescent who used to stare longingly through the fence at baseball practice, or the pretty teenager who came to every game and cheered us on like she had four brothers instead of one.

She felt like family too.

As Griffin shook hands with Cole, I knew that it was more than just a formality. That this wedding wasn't just an exchange of vows between bride and groom. There was a promise being made between Griffin and Cole too. With that handshake, Griffin was telling his friend *I trust you with someone I love*, and Cole was making a promise—*I'll honor and cherish her forever.*

And they believed each other.

Griffin moved past Moretti and I stepped back so he could take his place between us. He looked stoic, but I didn't miss the wipe of his eyes with thumb and forefinger. I gave him a nod and pat on the arm. He laughed and shook his head, as if he felt foolish, but I didn't blame him for being emotional. I was too, and Cheyenne wasn't even my sister by blood.

But how much did blood really matter in the end?

Wasn't it more important, and more meaningful, when what bound you to someone wasn't necessarily DNA but a history of choosing to be in someone's corner? Always having their back? Never letting them feel alone?

The times that Moretti, Griffin, and Cole had been there for me in ways big and small were too numerous to count. The times that their parents had been there for me were too numerous to count. Their entire families had always treated me like their own.

When I was eight, Cole's mom had seen how short my dress pants had gotten one Sunday at church, and she showed up at my house later to collect them. She let the hem down and got them back to me the very next day.

When I was twelve, Moretti's mom sent an extra sandwich and cookie in his lunch bag every single day after he mentioned I sometimes forgot to pack a decent lunch for myself.

When I was sixteen, Mr. Dempsey had sold me a beat-up truck for dirt cheap and let me work off what I couldn't pay with weekend hours at the garage.

And my father had repaid them all in kind—he was always sending eggs or fresh vegetables or steaks to them to say thank you. It was a tradition I'd continued. Food always made people happy. It was a way to show you cared. To show you were grateful for them.

To show up for them.

That's what mattered. More than blood. More than just loving someone. My mother had probably loved us, but she'd still made the choice to leave.

Love mattered, but *loyalty* was just as important.

The choice you made to show up for people, time after time. The promises you kept. The bonds you'd never break. The trust you put in them to be there for you, and the assurance you offered that you'd *always* be there for them.

And it hit me—what I'd asked Bianca on the stairs.

Love isn't always enough to make someone stay. Where's the proof that people stick around?

In my mind I saw her soft, knowing smile as she nodded at my friends, as if she saw the truth so much more clearly than I did.

Right there. That's your proof.

Despite the heat, I felt gooseflesh blanket my back beneath my suit as more than twenty years of friendship—of brotherhood—flashed through my head. They'd been in my corner more than half my life, and I knew without a doubt they'd be there forever.

I looked into the sea of faces watching the ceremony and saw only one person looking at me, her green eyes shining like sea glass in shallow water.

My mouth opened, as if I were about to say something. I couldn't say anything, of course—it was the middle of Cole and Cheyenne's wedding. And frankly, even if we'd been alone, I wasn't sure how I'd explain what was in my head or my heart.

Love still scared me.

But Bianca was right—some people did stay in your life forever.

"Ladies and gentlemen, it is my honor to present to you Mr. and Mrs. Cole Mitchell."

The guests rose to their feet, cheering and applauding as Cole and Cheyenne shared their first kiss as husband and wife. In front of me, Moretti stuck two fingers in his mouth and whistled loudly. I clapped along with everyone, my eyes on the newlyweds, but my heart was racing with anticipation. I needed to talk to Maddie.

As the harpist began to play an upbeat song, Cole and Cheyenne started back down the aisle hand in hand, offering the guests high-fives, huge smiles, and the occasional hug.

They were followed by Moretti and Bianca, then Griffin and Blair, and finally Mariah and me. I offered my arm, and she tucked her small arm inside my elbow. Her eyes were tearful, but her smile was ecstatic.

We made our way down the aisle, and I attempted to catch Maddie's eye when we passed her row, but she was looking down at her phone. Trying not to frown, I escorted Mariah toward the house, where the wedding party was convening in the living room.

"You're going so fast." Mariah giggled. "I can't walk that fast in these shoes with heels. They actually kind of hurt."

"Sorry." I slowed down, glancing over my shoulder. "Want a piggyback ride?"

"Yes!" she cried.

I turned around and she jumped on my back, and we headed into the house, where we were supposed to meet up with the rest of the wedding party while the guests had drinks on the patio or beneath the tent.

The living room was loud and chaotic as everyone rushed to hug Cole and Cheyenne, and Moretti popped open a bottle of champagne. I set Mariah on her feet. "I'll be right back," I told her, moving for the door again.

"Beckett!" boomed Griffin as glasses of bubbly were being poured. "Where do you think you're going? Get over here!"

Reluctantly, I went over and grabbed a glass along with everyone else, raising it high as Moretti shouted, "To the bride and groom!"

"To the bride and groom!" everyone chorused. But I barely took one sip before setting it aside and rushing out of the room.

Out on the patio, I searched the crowd for Maddie's blue dress, but didn't see her. I made my way toward the rows of chairs, where a few people still sat chatting, but she wasn't among them. Turning around, I looked at the dozens of people milling around the yard, waiting in line at the bar, and wandering into the tent, but I saw no sign of her.

Concerned, I scanned the crowd again, this time hunting for my father. I spotted him heading for the tent with Mr. and Mrs. Moretti and took off jogging toward them.

"Hey, Dad," I said, catching his arm. "Where's Maddie?"

He thought for a moment. "She had to go somewhere."

"Did she say where?" I asked impatiently.

He appeared to concentrate hard. "Yes, but I forget."

I took a deep breath. "Maybe the bathroom?"

"Maybe."

Mrs. Moretti turned around. "Oh, hi Beckett. Are you looking for Maddie?"

"Yes."

"She said she just had to make a phone call and she'd be right back," Mrs. Moretti said. "We offered to show Eugene where we're sitting. He's at our table."

"Thanks." I looked at my dad. "You okay out here on your own for a bit? I have to take some pictures."

"Of course I am," he said, as if I'd offended him.

"Okay, but stay in the backyard. Don't wander anyplace."

"Don't worry about a thing," said Mrs. Moretti, catching my eye to let me know she understood.

"Thanks." I flashed her a grateful smile. "And when you see Maddie, could you tell her I'm looking for her?"

"Sure thing." She winked at me. "Beautiful girl."

"Yes." And not just beautiful, I thought, watching for her as I hurried back through the guests on my way to the house. She was smart and caring and funny and generous and sweet, and if I didn't make things right with her, she was never going to let me be her safe place again.

I wanted to be so much more.

When I didn't spot her on the patio, I quickly checked the front porch and the downstairs bathroom. I was about to go upstairs and peek into the bedrooms when Bianca spotted me.

"Here he is!" she called.

"Beck, we're waiting on you!" Cole shouted.

Stopping with one foot on the bottom step, I exhaled and turned around. "Sorry," I said, heading into the living room.

"Okay, let's go out to the front," Cheyenne directed. "I want a photo with the entire wedding party in front of the house."

As the photographer herded us all out the front door, Moretti fell in step with me. "Hey. You okay?"

"Yeah."

"Bianca says you had a come-to-Jesus moment before the ceremony."

I almost laughed. "I don't know about that, but she did help me see something more clearly. I just need to find Maddie so I can try to explain myself."

"You can't find her?"

I shook my head. "She's not with my dad, and he forgot where she went. Mrs. Moretti thinks she went to make a phone call. Who could she be calling?"

"Maybe Elliott?"

"Okay, groomsmen, over here please," the photographer's assistant called.

For the next thirty minutes, I managed to plaster what I hoped was a pleasant expression on my face for photographs. But the entire time, I was thinking of Maddie, working up the nerve to say to her what I'd said to Bianca. By the time the photographer announced she was done, my stomach was in knots.

"Hey, you." Bianca and Moretti fell in step beside me as we all walked around the house into the yard. "Did you think about what I said?"

I nodded. "Yes. And you were right."

"Don't say that to her." Moretti slung an arm around his wife's neck. "She'll get smug."

Bianca smiled with self-satisfaction. "In this case, there was no denying it. And Beckett clearly needed better romantic advice than you guys were giving him."

Moretti was indignant. "Hey, I think I'm pretty good at romantic advice."

His wife laughed. "Says the guy who proposed with a secondhand engagement ring without bothering to have the original inscription removed."

"I made up for that, didn't I?"

"You did," she said as we approached the tent. "But we're not talking about you right now. We're talking about Beckett. So what now?"

"I need to talk to her."

"Do you need me to give you lines?" Moretti asked.

"No," his wife scolded. Then she looked at me. "She doesn't want to hear lines. She wants to hear the truth—how you feel for her, what you want—in your own words. Tell her exactly what you told me."

"Now?" I said, my voice cracking. "I have to say all that here?"

"Why wait? Are you going to let her sit there being sad and miserable all night?"

Standing at the back of the tent, I spotted Maddie sitting with my dad, the Morettis, and a few other wedding guests. She did indeed look miserable. But the thought of having to confess my feelings for her in front of a hundred people was terrifying. "Couldn't I just apologize for being an idiot last night and say all the big scary stuff later?"

Moretti made clucking noises.

"No." Bianca laughed and gave me a push. "Go get her, cowboy. Then meet us up front for the toast."

With my heart knocking hard in my chest and my legs shaking, I walked over to Maddie's table. Servers were handing out glasses of champagne, but while everyone she sat with had drinks in their hands and smiles on their faces, Maddie sat in stiff silence, her face stony and her hands in her lap. The moment she saw me, she rose to her feet.

The look in her eyes—part fear, part determination, as if

she was summoning the bravery to stand up to me—punctured my heart.

"Hey," I said. "I need to talk to you."

"Actually, I don't have time to talk. My ride is almost here."

I shook my head in confusion. "Your ride?"

"Yes. I called for a car. I'm leaving." She glanced at the table and lowered her voice. "I was just waiting for you to be done with pictures, because I didn't want to leave your dad alone."

"But you can't leave *now*."

"I'm sorry, Beckett. I have to." Her eyes filled as she glanced to one side. "Please don't make this more difficult than it already is."

"But—"

Maddie turned to the table. "I'm afraid I have to head out," she said to the group. "I'm not feeling very well. But it was nice seeing you, and I hope you all enjoy the evening." Leaning down, she kissed my father on the cheek, then straightened and rushed past me.

I took off after her, catching her arm at the back of the tent.

"Let me go, Beckett," she begged. "I have to get home."

Her words set off an alarm bell in my head. "Home where?"

"I'm going to drive back to Ohio tonight. I already told Elliott to pack up."

My heart seized up. "No. You can't leave like this."

She looked at her phone. "My ride is already here."

"Cancel it."

"No." Huge tears dripped from her thick black lashes. "I don't belong here."

I was about to argue with her when Bianca's voice came over the sound system asking the wedding party to report to the head table for the toast.

"Fuck," I said quietly.

"Go," she said desperately, tugging her arm from my grasp. "Please."

But I couldn't bear to watch her walk away from me again. I'd watched it happen at eighteen under the maple tree, and again seven years ago in New York. I refused to let it happen again.

"Don't. Move." I squeezed her hand. "Please."

Before she could reply, I turned around and bolted for the head table, where I grabbed the microphone from a stunned Bianca's hand. "I have to say something before I give the toast," I said to everyone at the head table. "Is it okay?"

"Of course it's okay," Cole said, because he was that kind of friend.

Cheyenne met my panicked eyes and smiled. "Do it."

Griffin and Blair and Moretti were there too, their jaws hanging open in shock.

I faced the crowd and spoke into the mic. "Uh, hi everyone."

"Beckett." Cole pulled out a chair and shoved me toward it. "Get up there so she can see you."

Without thinking twice, I climbed on the chair and spotted Maddie exactly where I'd left her, eyes wide with shock.

"Good evening. Can I have your attention please?"

I waited for a moment while the guests grew quieter and my heartbeat louder.

"My name is Beckett Weaver, and I'm honored to be giving the toast tonight for Cole and Cheyenne. Those of you that know me, which is most of you—this is a small town"—I paused when laughter rippled through the crowd—"You know I'm not a big talker. So getting up here like this is pretty scary. But sometimes you have to face your fears, because the reward is worth the risk."

I looked at Maddie again. Her face had gone pale.

"Life can be hard," I said, gaining confidence. "There are setbacks and struggles. Losses and heartache. Sometimes it seems like nothing is within our control, and it's tempting to live in a constant state of fear—always on guard, always looking for the next storm on the horizon, always ready to run back inside and protect yourself from the rain." I paused and took a breath, my eyes still focused on Maddie. "But that's no way to live. And it's no way to love."

Her cheeks were now stained scarlet.

"That's why I owe someone an apology, and Cole and Cheyenne are such good friends, they're letting me pre-empt their wedding toast to do it." I briefly glanced back at the bride and groom, and they smiled in encouragement. "I promise them, and all of you"—my eyes skimmed the crowd —"I'm going to get there in a minute. But before I lose my courage, I need to say something to the girl I've been waiting for my entire life. Because I've blown every single chance I've ever had to tell her what she means to me, and I'm afraid if I let this moment pass me by, I'll lose her forever."

Several people around me gasped. I paused, and fear almost got the better of me, but I forced myself to meet her eyes and say the words in my head.

"Maddie, I'm sorry. You asked me if you'd pinned your hopes on the impossible, and I said yes. You asked me for a reason to stay, and I let pride keep me from giving you one. You said you always look for love in the wrong places, but that isn't true. This time, you looked for love exactly where it's been all along." I put my fist over my heart, and several women seated nearby sighed loudly. "I love you, Maddie Blake, and I'm not going to let you go this time."

Maddie had both hands over her mouth now, and her shoulders were shaking—I wasn't sure if she was laughing or crying, and it might have been both.

But I had to keep going.

"Cole and Cheyenne and Mariah"—I glanced at the newlyweds and their little girl, who beamed at me—"are a perfect example of the courage and commitment it takes to start a life together. They make it look easy because they're such a beautiful family, but I think each of them would tell you they had to fight for this moment."

Cheyenne nodded and wiped her eyes, and Cole put an arm around his wife and his daughter. His eyes were shining too.

"But they never gave up, because they knew the life they'd have together would be worth it." I searched for Maddie again. "No matter the odds, love is always worth the fight."

"Hear, hear!" Moretti shouted from behind me.

Glancing over my shoulder, I grinned at the groom. "I never thought I'd see Cole any happier than the day he pitched a no-hitter during our senior year, but I gotta say—he looks pretty damn happy today."

Cole laughed along with the crowd, and Cheyenne grinned through her tears.

"Cheyenne, you're like a sister to me—and *no one* has sat through as many Bellamy Creek Bulldogs games as you have —so it's a joy seeing you marry a man that truly deserves you."

Laughing, the bride touched her heart and wiped her eyes.

Grabbing a glass of champagne off the table and raising it high, I said, "To Cole and Cheyenne—may you be as happy together forever as you are today, and may we all be lucky enough to share that journey with you. Cheers."

"Cheers!" echoed the crowd, followed by the clink of glasses.

I hadn't even stepped down from the chair when someone started applauding. Completely embarrassed, I glanced around and was stunned to see my father on his feet, clapping slowly but loudly, looking as proud of me as if I'd knocked a game-winner out of the park. One by one, people around him rose to their feet and joined the applause. Pretty soon everyone under the tent was standing and cheering, and I realized Maddie was making her way toward me.

With my heart hammering in my chest, I got down off the chair and handed the mic to Bianca just as Maddie reached me.

"Did you mean it?" she said, tears leaking from her eyes.

"Yes."

"Good, because I canceled my ride." Then she threw her arms around my neck and clung tightly, her face buried in my neck. I wrapped my arms around her and lifted her right off the ground as our friends whistled and shouted.

It was the most exhilarating and mortifying moment of my entire life, but I wouldn't have traded it for anything.

"Does this mean you forgive me?" I asked her.

"Yes," came her muffled reply.

The wedding coordinator began speaking on the mic, telling everyone that dinner would now be served if they would please take their seats.

I set her on her feet and took her by the hand. "Come on."

CHAPTER 22
MADDIE

BECKETT TUGGED me through the crowd, out of the tent, across the lawn, and around the side of the house. Once we were completely out of sight, he spun me around and crushed his mouth to mine. I melted into his arms, and he swept me right off my feet once more.

It wasn't our first kiss, but it felt brand new. It wasn't our last kiss, but it was filled with the deep ache of longing. It wasn't a kiss that accompanied vows, but it was a promise all the same.

I felt forever in that kiss, right down to my toes.

"Beckett," I whispered against his lips. "Did you mean what you said?"

"You already asked me that."

Laughing, I wriggled down so that my heels were on the ground, but kept my arms looped around his neck. "I know, but this feels so unreal. I have to make sure it's not a dream."

"Yes, I meant all of it. I said exactly what I was feeling. I just don't remember what the words were now because the experience was so terrifying, I had to block it from my memory."

"Don't worry. I remember everything. And I'm pretty sure there's a video."

He groaned. "Great."

I pressed my lips to his once more. "We should probably get back to the reception, don't you think?"

"Yes. I should make sure my dad's okay. And I've got some groomsman duties. I think I have to dance with Mariah."

"Aww." I laughed and tugged his earlobe. "I can't wait to see that. Maybe you'll save me a dance too?"

"Sure." He bumped me back against the home's brick wall, his hips pinning mine. "But I can't wait to get home."

I smiled, my eyes closing, my entire body humming. "I can't either. Oh!" My eyes popped open. "I need to let Elliott know he can stop packing—and crying and hating me."

Beckett chuckled. "He wasn't ready to go?"

"Right in the middle of his sleepover with Daisy? Not even a little bit." I sighed. "But we do have to leave tomorrow."

Taking my hand, he began walking back across the lawn toward the tent. "It's okay. I know we have a lot to talk about, but no matter what, it's going to be okay."

"Promise?" I glanced at him, my heart skipping a beat.

He squeezed my hand. "Promise."

As we made our way to the table where his father and the Morettis sat, we felt eyes on us from all sides. Some people smiled, some clapped silently, some whispered and sighed. When she spotted us, Mrs. Moretti jumped to her feet.

"Beckett Weaver! You made me sob!" she scolded, throwing her arms around him.

"Sorry," he muttered, looking at me helplessly over her shoulder.

"No, don't be sorry. That was just beautiful." She hugged me too, then grabbed a tissue from her evening bag. "But this is my last tissue, so I hope I'm done crying for the night."

Mr. Weaver rose to his feet, then shocked me by putting his arms around Beckett. I'd never seen any kind of physical affection between them. From the look on his face, Beckett was just as surprised.

"You found her," he said, thumping his son on his back a few times before letting him go. "And you didn't even need a map."

"Thanks, Dad. I did what you said."

His father looked confused. "What did I say to do?"

"Swing."

Mr. Weaver nodded in satisfaction. "That was good advice."

Beckett motioned to the server setting salad plates on the table. "Looks like it's time for dinner. Do you want us to sit with you here?"

"No, no, you go sit with your friends." Mrs. Moretti waved us toward the head table. "You don't need to sit with the old folks."

"Thanks." Beckett flashed her a grateful smile. "I'll check back in right after dinner."

"Go," she said, smiling wistfully at us. "Enjoy yourselves."

After I gave Elliott the good news, Beckett and I hit the bar and sat down at the head table with Cole and Cheyenne,

Griffin and Blair, and Enzo and Bianca, who couldn't stop talking about the toast.

"I felt like I was watching a movie," Blair said excitedly. "I had no idea what was going to happen next."

"Me neither." Beckett reached for his beer. "I was scared to death."

Beneath the table, I rubbed his leg. "You were perfect."

"When you got up on that chair, I could not even breathe." Bianca fanned her face with both hands, tearing up again. "I knew what I *hoped* would happen, but I wasn't sure you'd really do it."

"Sorry for hijacking your wedding reception," Beckett said to Cole and Cheyenne.

The groom shook his head. "Don't be sorry."

"Are you kidding? You made it unforgettable!" Cheyenne shouted. "I loved absolutely everything about it!"

"Me too," said Bianca. "You made it about more than just 'cheers to the bride and groom,' you know? You made it about something bigger. Something everyone could relate to."

"I liked the part about my no-hitter." Grinning, Cole leaned back in his chair and put an arm around his wife. "Thanks for working that in."

"I gotta ask, Weaver, what the hell gave you the guts to do it?" Griffin asked.

"A combination of things." Beckett took another drink from his beer. "Something my dad said last night. Something my sister said this afternoon. You guys giving me shit on the patio."

"We did give you some shit," Cole said. "I felt bad about it afterward."

"Nah, I needed to hear it. You guys were right. I was being stubborn." He looked at Bianca across the table. "It was actually something Bianca said right before the ceremony that pushed me over the edge."

She smiled knowingly. "It was right there all along."

"What did she say?" Enzo asked, intrigued.

Beckett looked a little embarrassed. "I'd been ranting that there was no proof that people stuck around forever, that people leave when things get tough. And she pointed at you three guys and said, 'There's your proof right there.' And she was right. Suddenly it was so obvious to me. During the ceremony I started to think about all the times we've been there for each other, how our whole families have always been there for each other. And it all just made sense. Feelings might not be a choice, but your actions are." He looked at me. "And when I saw her about to walk away again, I made a choice and got on a chair."

I couldn't speak, I was so choked up, so I just tipped my forehead to his shoulder. He kissed the top of my head.

Blair sighed. "And they lived happily ever after."

"You're welcome," Bianca said, picking up her wine glass. "*Per cent'anni!*"

"*Per cent'anni!*" everyone echoed.

"And fuck the Mavs," added Beckett, Cole, Enzo, and Griffin all at once.

The women at the table exchanged an eye roll and a smile.

"To the *ladies* of old man baseball," Cheyenne said, holding up her wine glass once more. "Because they'd be nothing without fans."

"Yes!" Blair reached forward with her champagne flute and tapped it to Cheyenne's. "And to book club! Just so Maddie knows, old man baseball isn't the only thing we do around here."

"I'll drink to that." Bianca added her martini glass and glanced at me. "How do you feel about teenage vampires, Maddie?"

I raised my glass. "As a matter of fact, I have *always* been Team Edward."

Bianca grinned. "Welcome back to Bellamy Creek."

Later that night, Beckett and I lay in each other's arms as our breathing slowly returned to normal.

"Think we were loud?" I asked nervously, thinking of Mallory trying to sleep in the bunk room with Daisy and Elliott.

"I don't care."

"But your sister is—"

"After the lecture she gave me this afternoon, she deserves to be woken up by the sound of us having sex."

I smiled. "What did she say?"

"She gave me the hard words. Called me some things."

"Like what?"

"Scared and stubborn." He paused. "And she was right."

I kissed his chest. "You came to your senses in the nick of time."

He gathered me closer. "I know you have to leave tomorrow. But when will I see you again?"

"As soon as I can get away." I sighed. "I think Sam is supposed to have Elliott next weekend, but if Elliott hears I'm coming up here to visit, I know he'll want to come with me."

"He's always invited."

"Thanks."

"Should we talk about what comes next?"

I propped my head up on one hand so I could look at him. "*Right now?*"

He laughed. "Yes. I know we won't have all the answers right away, but I can tell you what I hope comes next."

"Tell me."

"I hope you can find a way to move back here."

My heart fluttered. "Really?"

"Yes. I don't want to pressure you, and I know it's complicated with Sam and Elliott and your job, but anything I can do to make it easier on you, say the word."

"You could start by giving me that reason I asked for," I teased.

He chuckled and flipped over, turning me beneath him. "Because I want to be with you all the time. Because you make me happy. Because you belong here with me."

"Here?"

"Right here." He kissed me softly. "When you're ready, I want you to live here with me. I want this to be your home. And Elliott's."

"You don't think that's rushing it?"

"I don't care. I'm done being scared to make a mistake."

My whole body tingled. "That sounds nice. But maybe you should talk to your dad about it first?"

"I will talk to him. But I have no doubt in my mind he'll be happy about it. And even though he'd want you to spend all your time with him, I will hire someone. You could find another pediatric nursing job if you'd like."

"We can worry about that down the road. I probably would find another pediatric nursing job, but there will be licensing issues to take care of first. And even if the move happens, I don't think it will be right away."

"You mean I have to be patient?" He frowned. "Fuck that."

I laughed. "Yes. I need to talk to Elliott first. I have a feeling he'd love to live here, but I need to make sure of that before I even bring it up to Sam."

"I understand." His lips met mine again. "And if he doesn't want to for some reason, we'll deal with it. We're still going to be together."

"Maybe if we said Elliott could name his own goat . . ."

Beckett laughed and rolled onto his back, taking me with him. "He can name them all. I am not above bribing him with goats to have you with me."

"It might take some time," I hedged.

"I've waited years to love you the way I'm supposed to, Maddie. I can be patient." He brushed my hair off my face. "I want forever with you."

"It's yours, Beckett." My heart beat hard against his. "I think it's always been yours."

CHAPTER 23

MADDIE

ONE YEAR LATER

"MADDIE?" Amy opened the guest room door and poked her head in, a huge grin on her face. "It's about that time."

I met her eyes in the full-length mirror I stood in front of. "I'm ready. You can come in."

Her smile grew even brighter as she entered the room. "Oh," she breathed, her eyes tearing up. "You look so beautiful!"

"Doesn't she?" Cheyenne moved one of my curls from behind my shoulder to the front.

"The dress was exactly the right choice," said Blair from where she sat on the bed, leaning back on one arm, the other hand on her hugely pregnant belly. She was due any day now with a little boy, and she and Griffin had just moved into their brand new home, built on the parcel of land Beckett had sold them by the pond. Every time I thought about our kids growing up together, it made me happy.

Glancing in the mirror, I touched my stomach and hid the smile that attempted to give away my secret. I hadn't even told Beckett yet. I'd only confirmed it myself two days earlier.

I looked down at the lace bodice of my dress, with its V neckline and spaghetti straps. The soft chiffon skirt fell in gentle ripples to the floor—a bit much for a tiny backyard wedding, maybe, but I didn't care. Everything about today was perfect.

Beckett and I would tie the knot right beneath the maple tree where he'd first kissed me. Where almost a year ago he'd caught me in his arms and told me he didn't want to let go. Where two months ago, on my thirty-fourth birthday, he'd brought me out to the swing and dropped down on one knee.

"Maddie Blake," he'd said, opening up a ring box to reveal a stunning pink stone surrounded by tiny diamonds and set in rose gold, "I feel like I've been waiting for this moment all my life."

"Oh my God," I whispered, my vision blurring with tears.

"You've made me believe in so many things," he said. "Love and commitment and trust. You've made me want things I never thought I'd want, like a house full of kids. You make my life better every single day—you make *me* better." He took the ring from its velvet and slipped it on my finger.

"Did you do it yet?" a familiar little voice shouted from above.

Confused, I looked up and saw Elliott hanging from a branch high up in the tree.

"Not yet," Beckett called back. "I'm about to!" He met my eyes. "What do you say? Will you marry me?"

"Yes," I said, laughing through tears. "Yes!" I hollered into the tree.

"Yay!" Elliott shouted above us.

Rising to my feet, I threw my arms around Beckett and he lifted me off the ground.

Now it was our wedding day, and I still felt like I was in the clouds.

"The flowers in your hair are perfect," said Bianca from her place next to Cheyenne. "God, I'm going to cry just looking at you."

"You've cried like ten times today already," I said, laughing.

"It's not my fault. It's the babies." She put a hand on her belly, which was also delightfully big and round—her twins, a boy and a girl, who were due in eight weeks. "I cry at everything ten times a day."

"Same," Blair said with a sigh. "Ooh." She shifted positions. "This baby is not happy today. And I swear to God he's sitting *right* on my bladder."

I went over and spoke to their stomachs. "Hey, give your moms a break today, okay? Stop making them cry."

"It's no use," Cheyenne said. "I'm pretty sure we'll all be in tears during those vows."

Blair grimaced. "At this point, I just hope I don't wet my pants."

I laughed. "I remember that feeling. And speaking of my kiddo . . ." I walked over to the bathroom, where Elliott and Daisy were primping, and knocked on the door. "You guys ready?"

"They sure are," called Mallory, who was helping the kids get ready.

A moment later, Elliott and Daisy stepped into the room in matching pink dresses they'd chosen themselves, gigantic grins on their faces. Daisy wore her dress with sandals, but Elliott wore his with a new pair of boots—brown this time, to match Beckett's.

"Wow!" said Blair. "You guys look great."

Elliott came over and wrapped his arms around my waist, hugging me tight. Then he tipped his head back. "You look so pretty."

"Thank you."

I smiled down into his brown eyes, thinking how lucky I was. Elliott had jumped at the idea of moving up to Beckett's ranch. Sam had balked at first, but eventually he agreed to the move. Elliott and I were spending almost every weekend up here anyway. No doubt he was also persuaded by the fact that he and his girlfriend could move into the house once I vacated it. Elliott was able to keep his room there, and he visited his father once every six weeks, with Sam and I meeting at a point halfway between Cincinnati and Bellamy Creek for the handover.

It wasn't exactly the same as having a hands-on dad every single day, but Elliott had "Grandpa Eugene" and Beckett in his life now, and I couldn't have asked for more caring, patient role models. Elliott had asked if he could call Beckett 'Dad,' and Beckett had answered, "Sure." He'd acted like it was no big deal, but I'd noticed him turn away and clear his throat. I'd burst into tears myself.

The weekend we made the move, Mr. Weaver's new part-time caretaker had stayed at the ranch, and Beckett had come down to Cincinnati to help. We'd spent our first Christmas up here snowed in at the ranch and not minding one bit.

Elliott had started at my former elementary school in January, and he loved his first-grade teacher, Mr. O'Brien, almost as much as he loved that the bunk bedroom was now all his. We spent a weekend painting the walls pink and giving it a unicorn theme. Daisy came often to stay over, and the two of them were thick as thieves.

I'd found a part-time job at a pediatrics practice in town, which was perfect because it allowed me to spend some days at home too, helping to keep the house in order and Mr. Weaver safe and occupied. He had a caretaker on the days I worked, but he always told me he liked the days we had together the best.

We'd run errands, have lunch at Blair's bakery, stroll the downtown streets if the weather was nice, and every day, he'd go out and meet Elliott when he got off the bus. Watching them walk back to the house together was adorable.

I had a family, just like I'd always dreamed about.

"Dad's all ready for you downstairs," Amy said. "And everyone's here."

"Are the guys already outside?" Blair asked.

Amy nodded. "Coast is clear."

"Okay." I took a deep breath, and one last glance in the mirror. Suddenly I remembered the bride from the dress shop the day I'd attended Cheyenne's final fitting, the day I'd bought the blue dress I'd worn to their wedding. I recalled looking at that radiantly happy bride wondering if I'd ever feel that excited—that hopeful—about love ever again.

Now I had my answer.

I turned around and smiled. "I'm ready."

Mr. Weaver was sitting on the couch in the great room as I came down the stairs. He wore dress pants and his favorite sport coat from 1991, his white hair was freshly cut and neatly combed, and his white shirt and pink tie matched Beckett's. All the guys were wearing pink ties today, in honor of Elliott —Beckett had let him choose the color. And while our wedding wasn't really formal enough to have official bridesmaids and groomsmen, Beckett's friends had insisted on wearing them too.

When he saw me, Mr. Weaver rose to his feet. "Well, look at you," he said, smiling widely. "All grown up."

I laughed as I reached the bottom of the stairs. His memory still played cruel tricks on him sometimes, but he knew who I was—"You're Beckett's Maddie," he'd sometimes say, as if reminding himself. Occasionally he introduced me to people that way, and I never minded.

"All grown up," I repeated.

"Turn around. Let me look at you."

I obliged him, turning in a slow circle.

"Beautiful," he said.

I smiled. "Thank you."

Elliott and Daisy came bustling down the stairs, followed by Blair and Bianca, who moved slowly and carefully, gripping the handrail. "As much as I'd have loved standing up for you, I'm kind of glad you decided not to do bridesmaids," Bianca said as she reached the bottom and waddled toward me. "I'd have looked like a giant pink blimp in a bridesmaid dress."

"Same," Blair said, pausing at the landing to wince and put a hand under her belly.

"You okay?" I asked.

"Fine. I just need to go sit." She came over and gave me a hug.

"Me too," Bianca said apologetically, embracing me. "My stupid ankles are swollen."

"That's okay." I smiled. "Thank you for everything. I'll see you out there."

Cheyenne hugged me too, and the four of us held hands for a moment. "I'm so happy," Blair said, her eyes tearing up.

"Me too," sniffled Bianca.

"Me three." Cheyenne laughed, misty-eyed. "I keep thinking how our families are going to grow together, and our kids will be so close they'll call each other cousins, and we'll have so many things to celebrate—holidays and birthdays and vacations and old man baseball games."

We laughed, and they headed outside to take their seats.

"You know what to do, Dad?" Amy asked, coming toward me with my flowers in her hand.

"I know what to do," he insisted. "I just did it for your wedding a little bit ago."

Amy, who'd been married for fifteen years, gave me a look as she handed me the small bouquet of roses in various shades of pink.

"We're fine," I assured her. "Honestly, there's really no way to mess this up. We're following Daisy and Elliott out onto the deck, down the steps, and over to the tree."

"Okay," she said, kissing my cheek. "I'll go sit down."

I turned toward Mr. Weaver. "I think I'm ready."

He offered me his arm. "I know you are."

We followed Elliott and Daisy out onto the patio, staying close to the house. Smiling, I looked over the scene with love and pride. It was all so familiar to me now—the faded red barn, the paddock, the goat pen, the chicken coop, the garden, the big old maple tree, the fields beyond. The late summer afternoon sun shone down, bathing everything in glittering, resplendent light.

It was home, and I couldn't have loved it more.

Over to the west side of the house, a tent was set up, and caterers were preparing and setting a casual buffet—pulled pork, maple bourbon chicken, mixed greens with Michigan strawberries and Champagne vinaigrette, gourmet mac and cheese. Blair had insisted on baking our wedding cake, a gorgeous three-tiered confection that looked too good to eat.

About two dozen guests sat in chairs set up in rows facing the tree, under which an officiant stood waiting. Although I could only see them from the back, I knew everyone who mattered to us was here: all of Beckett's family, the parents of his three best friends, and several members of the Bellamy Creek Bulldogs.

The guitarist started playing the song Beckett and I had chosen: "Blackbird" by The Beatles, and a warm breeze caressed my skin. A moment later, Beckett, Enzo, Cole, and Griffin came around from the side of the house and took their places in the shade beneath the maple tree.

My breath caught when I saw him, tall and broad and gorgeous in his blue suit. After all this time, I could hardly believe he was mine. Again I thought of the secret I had, and what his reaction might be when I shared it.

"Okay," I whispered to Daisy and Elliott. "You can go."

Together—just as they'd insisted—they walked side by side down the steps of the patio, across the yard, and down the short aisle between the rows. Each of them scattered flower petals from baskets they clutched in their hands. Guests smiled at them as they made their way to the front.

"Maddie," said Mr. Weaver.

"Yes?"

"I'm proud of you."

Touched, I looked at him in surprise. I wasn't sure anyone had ever said those words to me before. My throat grew tight, and I swallowed hard. "Thank you."

His faded blue eyes regarded me thoughtfully. "You never had a father."

I shook my head. "I never did."

"You do now." He patted my hand.

My heart was too full to answer, but I smiled.

All eyes were on me as I walked toward Beckett, but he was all I could see. Behind him, all three of his buddies were smiling, but his expression was endearingly serious as I approached. He almost looked eighteen again, like he desperately wanted to kiss me but was nervous about what would happen if he did. His blue eyes were bright and full of love.

When we reached him, his father shook his hand and clapped him on the back. "I *told* you you'd marry that girl across the street," he said loudly.

Everyone laughed, including Beckett. "You were right, Dad."

Mr. Weaver hugged me and kissed my cheek before taking his seat next to Amy in the front row.

I turned to face Beckett just as another breeze rustled the leaves above us and blew my hair a little out of place. He reached out and sweetly brushed it behind my shoulder again. His eyes were shining. Looking up at him, I thought my heart might burst right out of my chest.

"I love you so much," I whispered. "Sorry, I know it's not the time where we say that yet."

He shook his head. "You never have to worry about that. I will always want to hear those words. And I love you too."

"Ladies and gentlemen, it is my great privilege to present to you for the first time, Mr. and Mrs. Beckett Weaver."

The crowd cheered as Beckett wrapped his arms around me and kissed me so hard, my back bowed dramatically and I thought he might tip us both right over. But his embrace was strong and solid, and he straightened us up again a moment later.

We headed back down the aisle as our friends and family clapped and whistled, Elliott and Daisy following behind. We made our way toward the house for a moment alone, safe in the knowledge that Amy was shepherding everyone toward the tent.

Once we made it inside the house and out of sight, Beckett wrapped me in his arms again, pressing his lips to mine in a much longer, deeper, and more intense kiss than he'd given me outside. When he finally lifted his head, I was panting.

"Mr. Weaver, you've knocked the breath right out of your wife," I told him.

"Good." He grinned lazily.

"But I'm about to pay you back."

"Oh yeah?" One of his brows cocked, like he didn't believe me.

"Yeah. *Daddy.*"

His brow fell. Then his jaw. He blinked. "What?"

I laughed. "You heard me."

"You mean . . ." He looked between us at my stomach. "No."

"Yes."

"But—" He released me and held me at arm's length, staring at my midsection. "How is it possible?"

"After we got engaged and talked about starting a family, I went off the pill."

"And you're sure?"

I nodded. "I'm sure. I saw the doctor on Thursday."

"Oh my God." He scooped me into his arms again and held me tight, gently swaying me side to side.

"Are you happy?" I asked.

When he finally spoke, his voice was just a whisper. "Yes."

"I have another appointment in a couple weeks for the first ultrasound. Want to go with me?"

"Of course I do." He pulled back and took my face in his hands, his shining eyes suddenly concerned. "How are you feeling? Are you okay? Should you sit down? Can I get you something?"

I laughed. "I'm fine. I feel great. A little tired is all."

He grinned. "A little brother or sister for Elliott. Does he know yet?"

"No. Maybe we can tell him together tomorrow?"

"Yes. And my dad too." He shook his head, as if he was amazed. "I can't believe this. How did I get so lucky?"

Suddenly the patio door was flung open, and Griffin appeared, harried and out of breath. "Sorry," he panted, bolting through the house toward the front door. "But Blair's in labor. We gotta go."

"Oh my God!" I tossed my bouquet onto the couch and picked up the hem of my dress, ready to run. "Where is she?"

"She's outside. I'm parked down the street, so I'm going to pull the car around!"

Beckett and I hurried outside and found Blair sitting on a chair over to one side of the patio, breathing hard and sweating. Bianca held one of her hands and Cole appeared to be checking her pulse on the other.

"Blair!" I squealed. "This is so exciting!"

"I'm so sorry," she said, looking agonized. "I didn't want this to happen during your wedding."

"Are you kidding? You just made this day better!"

Bianca laughed. "None of our weddings were ordinary, that's for sure."

"Let's get her out front," Cole said, helping her to her feet.

"Enzo, can you take this side?" Bianca asked. "I'm not much steadier on my legs than Blair is."

"Of course." Enzo moved to the other side of Blair, and Beckett moved ahead to open doors for them.

Bianca, Cheyenne, and I followed behind, watching as Griffin's truck pulled up in front of the house, tires squealing. Beckett opened the passenger door, and the guys assisted Blair in getting into the front seat and buckled up.

They shut the door and Blair rolled down the window. "I'm so sad to miss the reception, Maddie."

"Don't worry about it! You can see the pictures!"

"Call us!" Cheyenne shouted as Bianca and I blew kisses and waved.

"I will!" Blair waved back, and Griffin drove away much more carefully than he'd pulled up.

The six of us stood there on the front porch for a moment, watching until Griffin's taillights disappeared.

"Griffin is gonna be a *dad*," Enzo said, like he couldn't believe it. "*Griffin.*"

"He'll be great at it," Cheyenne said, sniffing. "Just like our dad was."

Cole took Cheyenne's hand and kissed the back of it. "I agree."

"Life's funny, isn't it?" Glancing down the street toward the house where I'd grown up, I slipped my arm around Beckett's waist, nestling into the boy who'd never forgotten me. "The way things come full circle?"

"But it's good." Enzo put his arms around his wife from behind and kissed her temple. "And I wouldn't trade my circle for anything."

"Think we'll all be here in fifty years watching someone's grandkids get married or something?" Bianca wondered.

"Definitely." Beckett looked down at me and smiled. "Some things never change."

EPILOGUE

BECKETT

"YOU SURE THIS is the right spot?" Cole asked.

"I'm positive." I stuck the shovel into the ground again.

"I think it was a little more toward the barn," Moretti said. "Maybe your memory is faulty in your old age."

I gave him a look. "I'm thirty-eight, same as you, asshole."

He grinned. "Just saying."

"No, Beckett's right. It was more toward the tree." Griffin tipped up his beer. "Got another shovel?"

"Yeah," I said, pausing to grab my beer from the fence post I'd set it on. "In the shed."

Griffin nodded. "Cool. Moretti, go get it and start digging."

"Fuck off." Moretti laughed. "I've got a bad back."

"Well, I've got a bum shoulder."

Our wives, who'd dragged patio chairs out onto the lawn to watch us dig up our time capsule, rolled their eyes. "Watch your mouth, please, Enzo Moretti," Bianca scolded. "There are kids around."

There were kids around—fucking *ten* of them. I glanced across the yard, still amazed to see them all running around, shrieking and sweaty and sticky with popsicles that had melted quickly in the summer evening heat.

There was Mariah, of course. She was fourteen now, a total mother hen, always fussing over the littler ones. Griffin and Blair's son Hank was four, same as Moretti and Bianca's twins—a boy and a girl named Alex and Natalia. Currently Mariah was pushing the three of them on a tire swing I'd hung from a sturdy oak tree.

Elliott was eleven, and he was pulling Cole and Cheyenne's daughter Marabel and our daughter Lily, in a wagon. They were both three years old and already the best of friends. Elliott was an amazing big brother—kind, sensitive, patient, playful—not just to Lily, but to all the kids. He was still a huge help on the ranch but also an excellent student as well. He loved reading and writing, and his teachers always remarked on his artistic abilities. While he didn't wear dresses anymore, and the unicorn barrette was long gone, he still adored the color pink, often painted his nails or wore jewelry, and had his own creative style. Like any kid on the verge of adolescence, he was still figuring out who he was, but I couldn't have been more proud that he called me Dad.

The three youngest kids weren't even walking yet—Cole and Cheyenne's son Roan, Moretti and Bianca's son Rocco, and Griffin and Blair's daughter Charlotte. They were playing on a blanket near the chairs where their mothers sipped glasses of wine and speculated about what their husbands might have put in a time capsule twenty years ago, at eighteen years old.

"It's probably full of baseballs," Blair said.

"Yes!" Cheyenne laughed. "And maybe a stinky old hat or glove."

"A Playboy magazine," Bianca snickered.

"There are *no* lewd materials in there, thank you," Moretti said, as if he was offended. "We took this seriously."

"Do you guys even remember what you put in there?" Maddie asked.

"Vaguely," I said as the tip of my shovel hit something. I dug a little faster. "Hey, I think I found it."

"Pictures," Cole said. "Didn't we put in a bunch of pictures?"

"I seem to recall a giant portrait Moretti put in there of himself," Griffin said.

"Oh brother," said his wife.

When I'd removed enough dirt to grab the tackle box handle, I dropped to my knees and reached for it. It took some muscle, but eventually I worked it loose and pulled it out. Holding it up triumphantly, I jumped to my feet. "Aha!"

Everyone cheered, and I brought it a little closer to where our wives were sitting so they could see. Brushing dirt from the top, I flipped the latch and opened it up.

First thing I pulled out was a baseball, and everyone laughed. "This one says Cole Mitchell," I said, handing it to him. "From your no-hitter, right?"

Cole nodded and smiled, wrapping his fingers around the ball. He peered closer at it and read, "June second, two thousand five." Then he locked eyes with Cheyenne. "Whoa. That's weird."

"Isn't that your birthday, Chey?" Blair asked.

Cheyenne nodded happily. "It is. That's so crazy!"

I took out a second baseball. "Griffin Dempsey."

"My game-winning homer against Mason City," Griffin said as I handed it to him. "Man, that felt good."

I pulled out a few more items and passed them around— my acceptance letter from Harvard, a newspaper clipping about Moretti's record bases stolen, our baseball team roster and stats from senior year, Griffin's letter telling him where and when to report to boot camp, some graduation tassels (although we'd forgotten whose they were).

There was also a takeout menu Moretti had put in. "Look,

it's from DiFiore's!" Bianca exclaimed. "And that's where you proposed to me!"

Moretti laughed. "Yeah. Twice."

"My Mickey Cochrane baseball card," I said, delighted at the discovery. "I'd forgotten I'd put that in here. My dad will be thrilled—he gave it to me when I was a kid."

I stood up and slipped the card into my back pocket, wondering if my dad would recall the exact day he gave it to me. His long-term memory was still incredibly sharp, especially for baseball stats, despite the swift cognitive decline his Alzheimer's had caused over the last few years. He still lived with us, although it was hard, especially once Lily arrived. But Maddie had the most generous heart imaginable, and she never complained. Elliott, too, was incredibly patient and sweet to his Grandpa Eugene, and I thanked my lucky stars for both of them every single day.

Cole peeked into the box and laughed. "There *is* a giant picture of Moretti."

"See? I told you." Griffin reached in and pulled out the five-by-seven.

Bianca laughed. "Why am I not surprised?"

I took out the remaining stack of photos, and everyone gathered around to watch as I shuffled through them.

"Oh look," Cheyenne said. "Griff, it's you and Dad and Grandpa."

Griffin nodded. "We'd just restored that old truck."

"Is that the one you still have?" Blair asked, pointing at the photo. "The red one? We had our first real date in that truck!"

"Yep." Griffin smiled at his wife. "The very one."

The next picture was us after a ball game. "We look happy," Moretti said. "We must have won."

"Did we ever lose?" Cole joked. "I can't remember."

The photo from prom made all the wives laugh. "Aww,

look at you guys," said Blair. "All dressed up in tuxes like proper gentlemen."

"We were," Moretti said. "Except maybe Weaver. He got a little out of control."

I grunted in reply and shuffled to the next photo, which was the four of us after graduation. "I think I put this one in."

Everyone looked at it in silence a moment. "Hard to believe twenty years has gone by, isn't it?" Cole asked.

Moretti shook his head. "I've got three fuckin' kids. How did that happen?"

"Uh, I think you know how it happened, and how many times am I going to have to ask you to watch your mouth?" Bianca gave her husband a menacing look.

"Sorry," he said, tipping up his beer. "It's just so crazy to me. I remember burying this thing like it was yesterday."

"Me too," Griffin said. "Remember how we couldn't imagine what we'd all be like?"

"Yeah. We were scared we might be bald or have big old beer guts." Cole laughed.

"We wondered if we'd still be playing baseball like those old timers on Thursday nights," I said, laughing. "Remember?"

"Oh yeah." Cole took a drink of his beer. "Guess we have our answer. At least we still have our hair."

"You guys still look amazing," Blair said. "Hardly a day over eighteen."

"*Maybe* a day," Cheyenne teased. "Possibly a week. But not a month."

I went to the next photo and heard a gasp. "Maddie!" Blair said. "Is that you?"

Maddie looked closer. "Oh my gosh, it is! I always wondered what happened to that picture!"

"It was here in Beckett's hope chest," Moretti joked. "And look, it worked."

Everyone laughed, and I felt my face get a little warm.

"You must have known even then," Cheyenne said, touching her heart. "That's so sweet."

"I guess I did." I glanced at Maddie, whose eyes were bright and shining. As much as I loved our friends, I suddenly wished we were alone.

But that was nothing new. I never felt like I had enough time alone with my wife. It was hard to balance the demands of the kids and my dad and the ranch with our longing for each other, but we tried. Sometimes we just put everyone to bed and shut our door. Sometimes we snuck out to the barn. Every once in a great while, we begged one of my sisters to come stay for one night while we checked into a bed and breakfast.

Although, truth be told, we never did go to breakfast.

My body and soul craved hers, always.

Later, after we'd said goodbye to our friends, put the kids to bed, and closed up the house, we climbed the steps and slipped into bed.

I wrapped my wife in my arms, and she snuggled into my side the way she liked to at night, with her head on my shoulder and her arm around my waist.

"I still can't believe you put that picture of us in the time capsule," she said softly.

"Why not? You know now I was crazy about you back then."

"I guess, but you just hid it so well. And we were both leaving for college. How did you know we were even going to keep in touch, let alone end up together?"

"I didn't."

"But you must have," she insisted. "Deep down. Don't you think?"

"Maybe. I suppose it could have been fate."

"Or maybe you have magical powers and you made it happen," she whispered dramatically.

I laughed, kissing the top of her head. "If I had magical powers, I'd have brought you back to me way sooner."

"True." After a moment, she picked up her head. "What if I hadn't come back here? Would you have come to find me?"

"Yes." I'd learned how to answer these kinds of questions of hers—with my heart instead of my head.

"How do you know?"

"Because, Maddie Weaver." I rolled her beneath me and looked down into her eyes. It was too dark to see the beautiful bottle green of them, but I'd know the exact shade even with my eyes closed. "You were then, are now, and always will be the only girl I've ever loved. I don't know what I did to deserve coming home to you, but nothing else in the world has ever felt so good, so I'm gonna keep on doing it."

She smiled.

"Was that a good answer?"

"Yes." She took my face in her hands. "I'm gonna keep on coming home to you too."

"Then I guess it's settled. It's you and me forever."

"It's you and me forever."

I pressed my lips to hers and sealed the promise with a kiss.

THE END

I hope you loved the conclusion to the Bellamy Creek Series! For a special peek into the future, use this link to subscribe to my mailing list and the first thing you'll receive is an exclusive Bellamy Creek bonus scene! Cloverleigh Farms fans will not want to miss it either...

Already a subscriber? You can resubscribe for instant access or simply check your last email from me for a link!

Up next is a return to Cloverleigh Farms with IGNITE, book one in an all-new next generation series! If you love single dad romances, you won't want to miss it. Keep reading for a sneak peek...

BELLAMY CREEK SERIES BONUS EPILOGUE

CHEYENNE

I stirred the big pitcher of lemonade and checked the clock on the kitchen wall. Again.

When I saw it was after four, I set the big spoon down and picked up my phone to see if I'd missed a message from Mariah. She was driving up from Chicago and had said she planned to leave around noon, but if she'd gotten on the road by then, she'd have arrived by now.

I didn't want to be an annoying, overprotective mom, but I still worried about her, even though she was 24 years old. Since I'd already texted twice and called once, I decided not to bug her again, but I couldn't shake the feeling that something was up.

"Cole?" I called to my husband through the screen. "Can you come in here?"

"Sure, one second."

After tasting the lemonade, I added a little more sugar and stirred again. Cole entered the kitchen from the patio and slid the door shut behind him.

"What's up?" he asked.

"I'm a little concerned about Mariah. She should be here by now."

"Did you call her?"

"She didn't answer." I bit my lip. "Should I try again?"

He shrugged. "I'm sure she's fine, honey. She said she'd leave around noon, right?"

"Right, but it's only a three-hour drive."

Cole came toward me and wrapped me up in his strong, comforting arms. Even at 48, he was still in great shape, with a solid chest and muscular arms he worked hard to maintain. His hair might have had some gray, but he still had the bluest eyes I'd ever seen, and seeing him walk into a room still gave me butterflies.

"Stop worrying," he said calmly. "She's probably just running late. You know how she likes to sleep in. It's Sunday. Maybe she went out last night."

"I guess." I wrapped my arms around his waist and pressed my cheek to his chest. "But what if she got a flat tire or something?"

"She's a big girl. She'd call for help. Or she'd change it herself—her Uncle Griffin taught her how, remember?"

"What if she ran out of gas? You know how she lets her tank get all the way to E."

"She'd do what anyone does—figure out how to get some gas. She's perfectly capable."

"What if she picked up a hitchhiker and he turned out to be a serial killer?"

"Chey." Cole shook me gently. "Our daughter is smart, careful, and responsible. She does not make bad decisions like picking up hitchhikers. We raised her right, now we have to let go."

"I know. It's just hard."

"It is." He kissed the top of my head.

"For once, it's me fretting about her and not you."

He laughed. "Yeah. What's with that?"

"I don't know. I just have this feeling something is up. When I talked to her yesterday, she sounded weird."

Cole stiffened slightly, as if going on high alert. "Weird?"

"Not *bad* weird. Just . . . different. Evasive, maybe. I can't explain it. Call it a mother's intuition." I might not have given birth to Mariah, but she'd been calling me Mom since she was nine years old, and as far as I was concerned, she was every bit my child as the ones I'd carried in my belly.

Cole's body relaxed, his voice losing its edge. "She's busy these days. It's July, the height of baseball season."

"I know." Mariah worked in media relations for the Chicago White Sox and often traveled with the team. Her job was hectic and unpredictable, but she loved it. And Cole loved that he could go see a game for free whenever he wanted to. "Maybe I just miss her."

"I miss her too." He kissed the top of my head once more and held me a moment longer. A shriek from outside made us both laugh as we looked out the window. We had a whole yard full of people over for a Sunday barbecue—practically everyone we loved.

Out on the lawn where we'd been married, our ten-year-old son Roan was playing volleyball with Griffin and Blair's son, Hank, as well as Enzo and Bianca's son Alex and his twin sister Natalia, who were all fourteen. Also playing the game were Griffin and Blair's ten-year old daughter, Charlotte; Enzo and Bianca's eleven-year-old son, Rocco, and their nine-year old daughter Emilia; and Beckett and Maddie's nine-year-old, Brendan.

Over on some lounge chairs at the far end of the patio, our daughter, Marabel, and Beckett and Maddie's daughter, Lily, were stretched out, giggling at their phones. They were both thirteen and had been best friends practically since they were born.

The youngest kids in the group all belonged to Enzo and

Bianca—seven-year-old Carlo, six-year-old Adam, and four-year-old Becca. They were in their bathing suits, running through the sprinkler.

The adults, including Beckett and Maddie's twenty-one-year-old son Elliott and his boyfriend Joshua, were all sitting around the patio table beneath a huge umbrella, sipping beers or glasses of wine and munching on snacks everyone had brought. We did this fairly often during the summer—sometimes at our house, which had the biggest lawn. Sometimes we gathered at Beckett and Maddie's farm, where the kids loved to visit the barn and play with the animals. Sometimes we met out at the house Griffin and Blair had built by the pond, where the kids could fish or swim or take the rowboat out. Sometimes we went to Enzo and Bianca's—they'd recently put a pool in the yard, complete with slide and waterfall, so their place was always popular.

But mostly we all just loved being together. We were family.

"Come on, let's go outside," Cole said. "I'm sure she'll be here any minute."

Giving him a quick kiss, I grabbed the lemonade pitcher and followed him out on to the patio. After leaving the pitcher on the table in the shade we'd set up as the bar, I poured myself a glass of white wine and joined our friends. Cole took the seat next to me and held my hand in his lap.

About twenty minutes later, the sliding door from the kitchen opened. "Anybody home?"

"Mariah!" Relief washed over me, and I smiled as I rose to my feet. "I was so worried! You said you were leaving at noon, and I—"

I stopped and stared. Mariah wasn't alone. Following her onto the patio was a tall, handsome man with dark hair and an athletic build—and she was holding his hand.

"Yeah, we got a little later start than we planned." Mariah laughed and exchanged a sheepish smile with the guy—the kind of smile that gave me the feeling they'd probably spent the morning in bed together. The blush in Mariah's cheeks added weight to the hunch.

It sort of shocked me, since she hadn't really dated anyone seriously since graduating from college, and she'd *never* brought a guy home to meet her parents, let alone her large, extended Bellamy Creek family—her honorary uncles and aunts and cousins.

I glanced at Cole, who was staring at both of them intently, like he wasn't sure if this was a dream or a nightmare. As Mariah tugged the guy forward, I looked more closely at his face. He looked vaguely familiar, but I couldn't place him. He also looked a bit older than Mariah—I guessed he was at least thirty.

"Mom, Dad, everyone, I want to introduce you to someone." Mariah's smile shone brightly as she glanced at the attractive guy holding her hand. "This is Chip Carswell. My fiancé."

My jaw dropped. I think every jaw at the table dropped.

I blinked at them. "Your . . . your what?"

"My fiancé." Mariah laughed nervously. "God, that sounds so crazy."

"You don't have a fiancé," said Cole, like he was confused.

"I do now. See?" Mariah held out her left hand, where a big fat diamond ring sparkled in the sunshine. Then she looked up at Chip adoringly once more, and he gazed back her her with an equal amount of affection in his eyes. "Chip proposed last night, and I said yes. We're getting married."

I still felt frozen, but also sweaty and my heart was pounding hard.

"Wait a minute. Did you say *Chip Carswell*?" Griffin asked. "As in the pitcher for the White Sox?"

"Yes," Chip answered with a quick nod.

"Holy shit." Enzo grinned. "This is awesome."

"Did you say *married*?" Cole's voice sounded strange. I put a hand on his shoulder.

Mariah laughed. "Yes, Dad. Do you need your ears checked?"

"You can't get married. You're too young!"

Our daughter rolled her eyes, a familiar gesture that made her look even more like the teenager she used to be. "Dad, I'm twenty-four."

Cole shook his head. "Impossible. I just taught you to ride a bike yesterday."

She laughed. "Nope. That was a while back."

I found my voice. "This—this seems so sudden. I'm trying to catch my breath." Smiling at Chip, I laughed a little as I came forward to embrace him. "Forgive us. We're very glad to meet you."

He gave me a slightly awkward hug in return. "I understand. It's nice to meet you too." When he released me, his face relaxed into a smile, revealing a dimple in his cheek. "Mariah is always talking about her family. I've been begging her to introduce me."

"I know it seems out of the blue," Mariah said, slipping her arm around Chip's waist. "But we've been dating ever since spring training—that's where we met. We just couldn't say anything because players are not supposed to date employees of the organization. But we came clean with the management last week, and it's all good. And since he had today and tomorrow off, this seemed like the perfect opportunity to bring him up here." She giggled. "But I didn't realize we'd be engaged already."

"I sort of surprised her with that," Chip said apologetically. "I just couldn't wait any longer." The look he gave her told me everything I needed to know.

"Well, my goodness—congratulations, you guys!" Blair jumped out of her chair and rushed forward, hugging Mariah and then Chip. "This is wonderful news!"

"Thanks," Mariah said breathlessly, hugging her back. Then she went over to Cole and poked his shoulder. "Say something, Dad. You look shocked."

"I am." He looked at her in disbelief, but I saw the twinkle in his eye. "*Married?*"

She nodded and smiled, radiantly happy. "Yes. Married. Can you handle it?"

"Do I have a choice?"

"Nope."

"Didn't think so." Sighing, he got to his feet and scooped her into his embrace. "I'm happy for you, sweetheart."

"Thanks, Dad."

My throat tightened as I watched father and daughter hold onto each other. After releasing her, Cole came over to Chip and shook his hand. "It's nice to meet you."

"You too, sir. I've heard a lot about you."

Mariah laughed and poked her dad's shoulder. "I told him you were a pitcher in your day too."

Cole groaned and gave her the side eye. "In *my day*? What am I, an old man now?"

She shrugged, poking his ribs. "Well, you are the father of the bride."

"Oh my gosh, the first wedding of the next generation!" Bianca jumped out of her seat to embrace Mariah and then Chip. Everyone else followed suit, offering hand shakes or hugs, and we called the kids over to give them the news.

"A toast!" Maddie cried, holding up her glass.

"Good idea." My head was still spinning, and I had a million questions for Mariah—I wanted to know all about their romance and more about Chip and exactly how he'd proposed—but I knew there would be time for all that later. I poured her a glass of wine while Beckett grabbed a beer for Chip. All the kids scrambled to get cups of lemonade or pop, and gathered around the table.

"How about it, father of the bride?" I teased, coming to stand at Cole's side. "Want to say a few words?"

He nodded, even though his expression was a little nervous as everyone got quiet. "Sure. First, I want to welcome Chip to the family. Sorry if it took a minute for the shock to wear off. Mariah has always liked a surprise, but this was a pretty big one."

Mariah smiled at her dad and tucked herself against her fiancé's side. He put his arm around her shoulder.

"I've always known this day would come, it just sort of snuck up on me," Cole went on. "But it is my firm belief that the best guys are all baseball players—especially pitchers."

Chip grinned, making his dimple appear. "My dad would agree with you on that."

"That's right," Enzo interrupted excitedly. "Your dad is Tyler Shaw, right?"

Chip nodded. "He's my biological dad, yes. He and his family live a little north of here, actually."

"Oh, shoot! If I'd known, I could have invited them!" I exclaimed. Tyler Shaw had also been a Major League pitcher, and I vaguely recalled meeting him at Griffin and Blair's wedding. He was married to the wedding coordinator at Cloverleigh Farms, where they'd been married, and one of her sisters had been a bridesmaid. It made me smile at what a small world we lived in, how connected we all are. It also made me happy that Chip's family lived so near.

"We were going to invite them to come down," Mariah said. "But Chip thought it might be too much."

"I've also got a little sister and brother," he explained.

"Next time." I smiled at him. "I can't wait to meet them."

"Second," Cole went on, "I want to say how proud we are of you, Mariah, and how excited we are to see you take the next steps in your life—even if it seems like you just took your first steps yesterday."

My throat closed again. Mariah's eyes grew shiny, and around the table, I heard more than one sniff.

"Finally, I just want to say that even though marriage isn't always easy, I think everyone around this table would tell you it's the best thing they've ever done."

"Definitely," agreed Griffin.

"Without a doubt," said Beckett.

"I mean, if we're not counting the time I stole home to win the—" Enzo cut off when his wife elbowed him in the gut. "I'm only kidding, babe. Of course it's the best thing I've ever done." He slung an arm around Bianca's neck and kissed the top of her head before raising his glass with the other hand. "*Per cent'anni.*"

"*Per cent'anni,*" the rest of us chorused happily as we all lifted our glasses and then took a drink.

"What's that mean?" Chip wondered. "*Per cent'anni.*"

"It means 'for a hundred years,'" Mariah explained. "It's Italian. Not that we're all Italian here, but it's sort of a tradition in our family to say it when someone gets married."

"It brings good luck," said Bianca with misty eyes, "whether you're Italian or not."

"Got it." Chip smiled. "I'll remember that."

Later, after everyone had gone home, Marabel and Roan were in bed, and Mariah and Chip were settling in to her old bedroom for the night, I slipped between the sheets next to a pensive Cole. He was staring up at the ceiling, his hands behind his head.

"Hey," I said, resting my head on his chest. "You okay?"

"I guess. It's crazy, you know? To think she's ready to make that kind of leap."

"I know. But remember what you said to me earlier? We raised her right, and now we have to let go."

"Yeah, but that was when I thought she had a flat tire, not a fiancé."

I laughed, planting a kiss on his shoulder. "I understand. But he seems great. And he adores her."

"He's so much older."

"Only ten years. That's not too crazy."

"He'll be gone all the time."

"She travels with the team."

He was silent. "I like him too. It's just hard to imagine that anyone is actually good enough for her."

"I know." I snuggled closer. "But something tells me he is, and they're going to be deliriously happy together. Just like you and me."

He wrapped me in his arms. "That's all I can ask for."

I sighed, imagining a wedding. "We're going to be the mother and father of the bride."

"I know. It's weird."

"And then grandparents."

"Okay, let's just stop right there." Cole flipped me beneath him and stretched out above me. "I'm not ready to be a fucking grandpa yet. I still want you like *we're* newlyweds."

I laughed softly. "Shh. What if they hear us?"

"Don't care." He pressed his lips to mine. "Life's too short to worry that people will hear you enjoying it."

"True."

"I love you," he said, making my heart race like he always had, like he always would.

"I love you too," I whispered. "Sometimes I still can't believe you're mine, that we have this family and such good friends, and this is our life."

He grinned. "It's a good life, isn't it?"

"It's the best." I wrapped my arms and legs around him and held on tight.

BAKED EGGS WITH DANDELION GREENS AND CARAMELIZED ONIONS

Ingredients

2-3 bunches dandelion greens, loosely chopped (about 4 cups)

1 medium yellow onion, thinly sliced

2 cloves garlic, minced

4 eggs

2 Tbsp. unsalted butter

1 Tbsp. extra virgin olive oil

1/4 cup Grated Parmesan

Harissa or Sriracha

Salt and pepper

Preheat oven to 350 degrees.

1) In 9 or 10" cast iron skillet, melt butter with oil over medium heat. Add sliced onions and 1/2 tsp of salt. Cook down until golden brown, stirring occasionally to prevent burning, about 10-15 minutes.

2) Add minced garlic and cook for another 2-3 minutes. Add

chopped dandelion greens and cook, stirring until the greens have wilted, about 3-4 minutes.

3) Crack eggs over the greens, sprinkle with salt and pepper. Sprinkle Parmesan over eggs and greens. Bake until eggs are set, about 5-8 minutes.

Serve with crusty bread, and a spicy sauce such as harissa or sriracha.

BAKED APPLE RASPBERRY OATMEAL

Ingredients
  2 cups old fashioned oats
  1/2 cup maple syrup, plus more for drizzling
  1/2 cup chopped pecans
  1 tsp. baking powder
  1 tsp. cinnamon
  1 tsp. cardamom
  1/2 tsp. kosher salt
  2 large eggs
  2 cups milk
  1 tsp. vanilla
  3 Tbsp. melted unsalted butter
  2 tart apples, chopped into 1/2" cubes (around 2 cups)
  1/2 cup fresh raspberries

1) Preheat oven to 325 degrees. Grease an 8" baking dish with butter or cooking spray.

2) Mix dry ingredients together in bowl until well combined.

3) In a separate bowl, mix together wet ingredients using a

whisk. Add wet ingredients to dry ingredients and mix until combined. Stir in chopped apples and raspberries just until combined.

4) Pour mixture into prepared baking pan. Bake for around 45 minutes or until the oatmeal is set and golden around the edges.

Serve warm drizzled with more maple syrup.

CHICKEN PAPRIKASH

Ingredients
    1 lb boneless, skinless chicken thighs
    2 Tbsp. canola oil and 2 Tbsp. butter
    1 medium onion, chopped
    2 Roma tomatoes, cored and diced
    1 large banana pepper, seeded and chopped
    2 1/2 Tbsp. sweet paprika
    1 Tbsp. hot paprika
    3 cloves garlic, minced
    1 1/2 cups chicken stock
    3/4 cup sour cream
    Salt and pepper
    Chopped parsley for garnish
    Egg noodles, cooked to package directions

1) On medium high heat, melt oil and butter in deep saucepan. Add chicken and cook on each side until golden brown, about 5 minutes per side.

2) Remove chicken and add onion. Cook for 3 minutes. Add banana pepper and garlic, cook an additional 3 minutes. Add

tomatoes and cook another minute. Add paprika and then salt and pepper to taste. Stir to coat the veggies and cook for 1 minute.

3) Add stock and bring to boil. Add chicken back to pan with accumulated juices. Cover and cook 30 minutes at medium low heat. Remove chicken again, add sour cream and stir. Taste and add more salt and pepper as needed.

Serve over egg noodles with parsley sprinkled on top.

OVERNIGHT YEASTED WAFFLES

Ingredients
- 2 1/4 cups warm whole milk
- 1/2 cup melted butter
- 2 Tbsp. maple syrup
- 1 tsp. vanilla
- 1 tsp. salt
- 2 1/4 tsp. active dry yeast
- 2 3/4 cups all-purpose flour
- 2 large eggs
- 1/4 tsp. baking soda

1) In medium bowl, combine warm milk, melted butter, maple syrup, vanilla and salt.

2) In large bowl, mix together 1/2 cup warm water and yeast. Let sit for 5 minutes.

3) Add milk mixture to yeast mixture. Stir to combine and then whisk in flour. Cover with plastic wrap and let rest in fridge overnight.

4) The following day, mix in the eggs and baking soda. Heat waffle iron, spray with cooking oil spray and cook waffles until golden brown, around 5-6 minutes (or according to manufacturer recommendations). Spray iron with cooking spray in between batches.

Serve immediately while still warm.

ALSO BY MELANIE HARLOW

The Frenched Series

Frenched

Yanked

Forked

Floored

The Happy Crazy Love Series

Some Sort of Happy

Some Sort of Crazy

Some Sort of Love

The After We Fall Series

Man Candy

After We Fall

If You Were Mine

From This Moment

The One and Only Series

Only You

Only Him

Only Love

The Cloverleigh Farms Series

Irresistible

Undeniable

Insatiable

Unbreakable

Unforgettable

The Bellamy Creek Series

Drive Me Wild

Make Me Yours

Call Me Crazy

Tie Me Down

Cloverleigh Farms Next Generation Series

Ignite

Taste

Tease

Tempt

Co-Written Books

Hold You Close (Co-written with Corinne Michaels)

Imperfect Match (Co-written with Corinne Michaels)

Strong Enough (M/M romance co-written with David Romanov)

The Speak Easy Duet

The Tango Lesson (A Standalone Novella)

Want a reading order? Click here!

ACKNOWLEDGMENTS

Once again, I need to thank Dina Cimarusti for all the delicious recipes in this book. I hope you enjoy making them as much as I do!

As always, my appreciation and gratitude go to the following people for their talent, support, wisdom, friendship, and encouragement...

Melissa Gaston, Brandi Zelenka, Jenn Watson, Nancy Smay at Evident Ink, Julia Griffis at The Romance Bibliophile, proofreaders Michele Ficht, Shannon Mummey, and Alison Evans Maxwell, the Shop Talkers, the Sisterhood, the Harlots and the Harlot ARC Team, bloggers and event organizers, my readers all over the world...

And once again, to my family, with all my love.

ABOUT THE AUTHOR

Melanie Harlow grew up attending her dad's "lawyer league" old man baseball games. She writes sweet and sexy contemporary romance from her home outside of Detroit, where she lives with her husband and two daughters. When she's not writing, she's probably got a cocktail in hand. And sometimes when she is.

Find her at www.melanieharlow.com.

9 798987 064184